IMMORTAL AT THE EDGE OF THE WORLD

GENE DOUCETTE

HIC SVNT LEONES

"Here are lions"

— LEGEND ON THE EDGE OF ROMAN WORLD MAPS

*I*t took a lot longer to meet with the physicist than I felt it really should have, possibly because I failed to appreciate how busy a physicist could be.

I'm still under the impression that we've discovered almost everything there is to discover, and from my perspective this is kind of true. I was around back when we thought the stars were pinholes in a solid firmament, and when people thought the universe revolved around us rather than the other way around. I can remember heated arguments regarding whether a comet meant we had to kill the king, and if it was possible to turn base metals into gold. I've seen science explain a lot of things, is my point, to the extent that every advance nowadays seems like an inconsequential bump. That's provided I even understand the advance, which is iffy.

I was never interested in *doing* science, only in the consequences of what had been discovered, especially if the discovery made my life more convenient. This describes basically everything invented in the 20th century that wasn't designed to kill people, and a couple of the things that were.

I had to go to Switzerland to meet with him. There are plenty of physicists hanging out in the United States I probably could have found that were slightly less busy, but this one in particular had written a book. In that book was something that made me think he might be helpful to me, so he was the one I felt I should talk to.

The book was on pocket dimensions and parallel universes. If I was lucky, he was busy looking for them in Switzerland, when he wasn't ramming particles together at high speeds.

This did not turn out to be the case.

"I'm sorry I kept you waiting," he said, upon arriving at his amazingly unkempt office, which he appeared to share with six other people.

I shook his hand. "It's fine. I'm sure you're busy."

"Always, but I can find time to speak to a donor, certainly. How can I help?"

He was an American in his mid-thirties, with the kind of engaging smile one expects to see on a successful author—as he was—more so than on a successful scientist. Scientists, in my experience, are most often looking either down at their feet or at something going on inside their heads, and can make little time for human eye contact. But I knew Newton, and I thought he was a jerk. That has probably colored my opinion on scientists since.

In the eyes of this particular scientist I was a wealthy donor to one of his pet side projects, which might have been why he was inclined to be personable.

"Well, I've read your books," I said.

"Ah! All of them?"

"I think probably, yes. And I wanted to talk to you about other dimensions."

"Of course. You mean, something that didn't get covered in the book?"

"I guess that's true, yes. I was wondering how one might travel between them."

He laughed gently, in a way that managed to not make me feel stupid, which I appreciated. "Well no, you see these are bubble universes. We may live in one, and there may be another one beside ours, but there would be no way to travel between them."

"No way at all?"

"You ... understand that the book we're talking about is largely speculative, yes? I'm putting forward a theory based on some ideas I had about entropy, and while the *ideas* are all supported by what we know, we are talking about, at best, a fanciful hypothesis right now. Proving it would be extremely difficult."

"Because there's no way to travel between the universes, and you can't prove the existence of something you can't find a way to experience."

He nodded, but in a way that looked almost like he was saying I was wrong. "That's more or less it, yes. It's a great deal more complicated only because what we're doing here right now in this building is testing for things we can't directly encounter. What we *can* test for is the predictive consequences of the thing. In principle what you've said is accurate, but in practice we spend a lot of time proving things indirectly. My point here is only that we aren't even at the stage where an indirect proof is possible when it comes to bubble universes."

"I understand," I said, somewhat aggravated either with myself or with him, I couldn't tell for certain. The thing was, his book did say something very much like this but I wasn't convinced I had understood it well enough. I could have sent an e-mail or a letter or placed a phone call to hear what I had just heard from him directly, but when you have a lot of money and a way to get into the same room with someone it's often hard to resist the urge to do so.

"Let me ask you something else," I said. "Let's say I once saw a person disappear."

"A magic trick?"

"No, it wasn't a trick. This person was standing in an open field, and then she wasn't."

His cheerfully helpful expression was starting to deteriorate into something akin to pity.

"I would be entertaining a number of questions before coming to me, if I were in your situation."

"Yes, I appreciate that perspective. Let's say I entertained those questions already and after having done so I arrived in this office and told you, a scientist, that it is legitimately possible for a human being to exit this plane of existence materially and to reappear later. You—instead of telling me that I am hallucinating or suffering from a psychotic break or overdosing on sleep medication—believed me and then told me how such a thing could be possible. Can you do that?"

He smiled genuinely, and said, "Branes, perhaps." Then he spelled it for me so I didn't confuse it with *brains*. For about a half a second I thought I was in for a zombie joke. "Brane is from the word membrane, and it's theoretically possible we live within one."

"Like the pocket universe."

"Different than that. Forget the universe thing for a minute."

"All right, how would this work, then? The disappearing."

"*If* we live in a brane that is bounded by three physical dimensions, it's *possible*, in theory, that this brane is attached to another brane that is *also* bounded by three physical dimensions. And between them is another dimensional space called the bulk. Mind you, that is an extraordinary simplification of a highly complicated idea. I can certainly recommend additional reading for you if you are interested."

"I'm interested, but this sounds roughly as made up as your pocket universes."

"Branes are slightly less speculative. The theory was developed to resolve some experimental problems with elementary forces. If some of the particles that make up matter are allowed to travel outside a theoretical brane, the math works much better. Gravity works much better as well. It's a little like connecting dots on a page by drawing a line that extends off the page. But I can't even imagine what kind of science would be involved to make an actual *journey* off the page. The energy required ..."

"What if a person just did it on her own, with no equipment?"

He laughed again. "Well no. I'm sorry, I can speculate only so much but that just isn't possible."

I nodded, and smiled. I knew he was wrong, because I'd seen it done more than once and there was no machinery involved. But even if the answer to my question was in this brane theory he'd just given me, the rest of what I was looking for would have to be found elsewhere. Knowing it was something within the realm of the possible from a scientific standpoint was comforting, but I needed more than that.

"All right, well, thanks anyway," I said, standing.

He stood as well and took my extended hand.

"I hope you find whatever it is you're looking for," he said pleasantly.

"It's not a what, it's a who. And thank you. I have a couple of ideas I haven't tried yet."

PART I

ALONG THE SILK ROAD

CHAPTER 1

I was surprised he would work with an elf, and told him so.
"It's not that I have anything particular against elves," I said. "It's only that they are pathologically boring."

❲❳

Juergen Heintz was a pale, skinny man of uncertain age. If forced to guess I'd have put him in his fifties, but it was difficult to tell because his hair, while being mostly white, appeared to have begun as a sunny light blond, and also because it was not very bright in the room. He didn't seem to be notably wrinkly, but that could have been as much a consequence of his staying out of the sun coupled with a good moisturizer.

I was meeting Heintz face-to-face for the first time despite a business relationship that went back at least ten years. His relationship with my money went back even further, although not as far as the bank's relationship with it, which spanned about one hundred thirty years. Heintz is my banker because the first time I contacted the bank in more than thirty years he was the one I was transferred to. When I gave him the necessary information to positively identify myself as the account-holder he didn't hang up, call the police or the bank president, or any of the other things one does when confronted by someone who can't possibly be alive. This is the kind of flexibility of thought I look for in people.

The only real drawback was that I was pretty sure Mr. Heintz thought I was a vampire.

"Please do sit," he insisted, gesturing me toward a stuffed leather chair opposite a nearly empty desk, which he then sat behind. The laptop on the desk lit his face and washed out his coloring even more, especially since the only other illumination in the room was a cool yellow floor lamp near the window. And although it was midday the curtains in the room were drawn. They were some impressive curtains—I wouldn't have been able to guess it was a sunny day out, or that it was even day at all.

"I hope your arrival was to your satisfaction?" he asked.

"The limo was great, thank you," I said.

"I'm glad. We employ them only occasionally, but have never gotten any complaints."

"They were very efficient."

The limo ride actually made me feel like something between a visiting head of state and a hostage, but I didn't think this was a good time to bring that up.

Back when I suggested to Heintz that he and I have this meeting all I said was, "the next time you're in New York." It was an offhand thing, coming not long after he'd mentioned that his very private banking organization had offices in the city, and that he sometimes visited those offices when he needed to conduct whatever it is very private bankers do.

Somehow he took this to mean he needed to hop aboard a jet immediately. And that was all fine. I had just gotten back from a trip overseas but I was growing to dislike the solitude my home offered, so any excuse to get away again was a good excuse. And while New York City is not one of my favorite places—this is an understatement—I had a little business to conduct locally. Plus Midtown can be okay when nobody is actively trying to kill me.

Then he insisted on sending a private car, which turned out to be one of those sedans with completely blacked-out rear windows, operated by the least talkative driver in the history of the profession. The driver took me to a private underground entrance and a private elevator that required a key card and possibly a blood sample to operate.

All of this made perfect sense provided I was a vampire, or doing something illegal, or both. In fairness, I *am* a private man, as it's almost never in my best interest to let people know either that I am extremely wealthy or that I'm older than anyone you're ever likely to meet. I'm just not a vampire. I also don't know a whole lot about what my money is doing, so I could very well be doing illegal things with it.

"I am so glad, given our many conversations, that we have a chance to meet in this manner," Heintz said gently. He said most everything gently, but with a firm undercurrent that gave his words a kind of certitude that made him hard to disagree with.

"Me too. It's good to put a face to the voice," I said. And it was, even if it was also a little disconcerting and weird.

I sincerely don't know how most people cope with this, but I will never get used to the idea of knowing someone by voice alone. Up until the telephonic age I never met someone whose face and voice didn't come as a package, and now that happens all the time. I still need for there to be a face, though, so I assign one to the voice. Not once have I been even slightly close to being right.

Heintz tapped out some things on the laptop that caused the screen to change subtly, and then he pulled open a desk drawer and extracted a small stack of papers.

"Now then," he began, "I'm afraid we have a large number of things that require signing in order to fully realize your latest corporate ventures. You will be using the customary surname, I trust?"

"Yes, of course."

The surname in question was Justinian, which was not the name I opened the account under. About a year after conducting business for me on a regular basis, Heintz recommended I create an inheritor for my accounts so that it was less self-evident that I was approximately two hundred years old. We created Francis Justinian, which is who I get to be now when I'm playing around in the world of high finance. Heintz even got me the necessary forged documentation to prove my existence; I now have an ID my usual forger is unfamiliar with. Heintz's man might even be better than mine.

While incredibly convenient, this kind of thing did leave me with some open questions, such as: What sort of client is Juergen Heintz accustomed to dealing with, and will this end up being a problem for me? Possibly, these questions were in the back of my mind when I suggested this rendezvous, although that's hard to say, as I was not sober when I made the suggestion.

He placed the pile of papers at the edge of the desk and put out a pen.

"They are marked as usual," he said.

This meant they had these little sticky arrows all over them indicating where I had to sign. I'd been getting packages full of pages like this in the mail off and on for a while, which was much easier after I got around to establishing a legal address. (On an island. I own an island. Because when you have a chance to own an island, you just do.) Every time I see the removable sticky arrows on the pages I think how incredibly convenient such a thing would have been at just about any point in history.

"If it wouldn't be too much trouble, Mr. Heintz," I said, "could you make it a little brighter in here? I can't really see what I'm signing."

My banker friend stared without expression for long enough to make me uncomfortable before saying, "Yes, yes of course."

He opened a drawer on the desk and extracted a remote control, tapped a button on it, and coaxed to life the lights embedded in the ceiling.

"Is that better?" he asked.

"Much better, thank you."

Vampires can see very well in the dark and are bothered by bright lights. This is not why they avoid the sun—sunlight actually will cause them to burst into flames; I've seen it and it's gross—but it is why when you meet one it's generally in a poorly lit location.

In his assumption that I am a vampire, Heintz was only being courteous, just like he was when he gave me the no-sunlight limo-to-elevator ride. Now that I had proven myself to be possessed of somewhat normal eyesight, he was getting nervous.

Being mistaken as a vampire is one of those things that annoys me. In fairness, from Heintz's perspective it should have been the correct conclusion because I was entirely too old to be anything else. And since the other option is "the only immortal man in existence," I can see how he didn't consider that seriously. But at the same time, nearly all vampires over the age of two hundred are depressed, poorly assimilated, and cranky, and nobody likes being mistaken for one of those.

I probably shouldn't have done the next thing I did, which was to get up and open the curtain.

The good news was that Juergen Heintz was also not a vampire. I didn't consider this until after the sunlight splashed across his face and lit up his eyes. However, there are other things out there that are neither vampire nor human, and he happened to be one of those.

Jumping to his feet, a dagger appeared in his hand more quickly than I could follow. In all likelihood it originated in his sleeve, but someone gifted enough with a blade could have conjured one from a number of other places. It was a narrow bit of steel—we used to call them stilettos before ladies' shoes took over the term—of the sort that was perfect for either stabbing or throwing.

Heintz did neither. Instead, in that calm tone of his, he spoke.

"Who are you, sir?"

This is what I get for cutting corners.

"You know who I am," I said. "We've spoken on the phone so you know my voice, and you've seen photos of me before, so you know my face."

It may go without saying, but the last thing I had expected was having a knife pulled on me by my finance guy. Maybe a very sharp pen.

"My client is of the sort to actively despise sunlight," he said.

"A vampire, you mean."

"I do."

"That would be an erroneous assumption on your part. Did I ever tell you I was?"

He looked confused. "No ..."

"I didn't because I'm not a vampire. Never have been. Don't plan to be."

"But—"

"I think we've both made a few hasty assumptions about one another, Mr. Heintz. You took me for a vampire, and I took you to be human."

The tip of the blade quivered ever-so-slightly. "I'm sorry?"

I laughed. "I know a goblin when I see one."

He inhaled sharply through teeth that were slightly pointed, just enough to catch one's attention if one were checking.

The word I should have used was *elf*, not goblin, so I'd sort of insulted him.

There are northern goblins and southern goblins, and not only do they not much care for one another, most of the time they will insist they aren't even the same species. (The north-south thing is a geographic distinction originally made in a region of the Eurasian continent that has been lost to history. I'm not even sure of where it is myself.) I mostly prefer the southern goblins—an earthy, no-nonsense sort of people overall. The northern versions—and Heintz was clearly a northern goblin—are very pale, they tend to be taller than the southern type, and most of them are kind of stuck up.

Somewhere in the neighborhood of two thousand years ago, the northern goblins started calling themselves elves, and everyone of goblin descent has been pretty happy with that arrangement. It's just not true, which is why I find it annoying.

Another time I might blame a slip of the tongue like that on drink, but I was actually sober. Maybe I just wanted to see what he would do.

What he did was put away the stiletto, which I appreciated. Where he put it I couldn't say for sure. Goblins of all kinds are extremely proficient with sharp things. They make excellent assassins, and *teppanyaki* chefs.

Heintz composed himself and spoke.

"When your account was opened with this institution, paper currency in the country presently beneath us did not even exist. Your first line of credit had an archduke, two duchesses, and the crown prince of Denmark as guarantors. Your signatures—from the first name you gave us to the ones you have since used—are undeniably of the same hand. You appear to be no older than thirty-two, but everything I have indicates you are at least two hundred and seventeen. And you are standing in sunlight right now. At the risk of offending you further than I have already, sir, what *are* you?"

"I don't know," I said, leaving the window to return to the chair. Heintz remained standing in the event I did something weird, like sprouted another limb or whatever he thought I was capable of at this point. "A person."

"A human person?"

"More or less. I stopped aging some time ago, and I don't get sick. But that knife of yours would do me some damage. Where did you put it, incidentally?"

He ignored the question. "How old are you? Truly?"

"I can't answer that," I admitted. "In the neighborhood of sixty millennia."

I get asked this regularly, and it's really not possible to answer. I know nowadays we all understand basic things about the planet, like that it spins around the sun and that one spin equals one year, but this is a modern understanding and there are other metrics available to measure time, like seasonal changes and phases of the moon. But the moon's phases are shorter than a year, and there are some parts of the world where seasonal variation is just not that extreme. On top of that, one needs a civilization that lasts longer than a single human lifespan for there to be a continuous enumeration of years carried down from generation to generation. And there needs to be math, and record-keeping, and symbols for integers.

So really, when I say I don't know how old I am, I'm not being coy. It's not a knowable thing.

Heintz sat back down in his chair as if he'd just gained about fifty pounds.

"The vampires, they have a name for a person, a legendary figure who can walk by day ..."

"Apollo," I said. "I've been called that. They think I'm a vampire too, for some reason."

"But you do not drink blood?"

"I prefer beer. Your kind had its own name for me."

"Leewan Sean," he muttered.

"That's it."

I smiled. That particular name had passed through about five cultural histories and ten or twenty spellings, but it still sounded roughly the same in all tongues, even in Heintz's Scandinavian-colored English pronunciation.

"Keeper of the path," he muttered.

"Yeah, that too." He was referring to one of the culturally specific legends about me that goblins had been repeating for some time. It's a long story.

"I had no idea." If possible, Juergen Heintz had gotten paler since we'd begun this portion of the conversation.

"We should ... maybe get back to business," I suggested. "I have all these papers to sign, a—"

"What should I call you?" he asked. "You have so many names, some I invented for you. None feel right."

"Just call me Adam."

I had tried several times to switch my name over to something else, but in this new age of information I'd found that impossible, so I've basically given up.

"*The* Adam?"

"The ... oh! Biblically? No, no. It's just a name that's stuck with me recently."

"Yes." He rubbed the side of his head like someone trying to forget a bad dream. "Yes, silly of me. My apologies ... Adam. My apologies. Please, sign. And we can discuss new business, if you have any."

I nodded, hoping that putting real world tasks in front of him would get his mind running again. He looked like he was either going to genuflect or faint.

And I actually did have some new business. I pulled out a scrap of paper I'd cut from one of the dozens of magazines I now subscribe to. Being on an island and all, I have to have them special delivered monthly by helicopter.

More than one person has pointed out that this is no longer necessary since most magazines are now online entities. I know this, and I know in another decade or two I'm going to have to get used to the idea of reading without paper in my hands, but I'm going to be making that trip kicking and screaming. Maybe that sounds stubborn, but my relationship with the printed word is the longest one I've ever had and I'm not ready to quit on it yet.

Anyway, the article in question concerned an archeologist who'd been poking around an area of Turkey that held particular interest to me.

"Can you put me in the same room as this man?" I asked, handing over the scrap.

He looked it over. "Just the man?"

"No, actually his being there is really optional. I want to spend some time with one of his recent discoveries. He doesn't have to be there."

"You would like a private viewing?"

"If that sort of thing can be done."

"I'm sure it can. Archeologists always need financial support, and so do the museums that support them. How generous do you want to be?"

This was an impossible question for me to answer because I have almost no understanding of what *a lot of money* is.

"Whatever works," I decided. This would probably end up with a museum wing being named after Francis Justinian, but whatever.

"Just to clarify, are you looking to *purchase* something from him?" Heintz asked.

"No, I just need a few hours alone with what he found. Preferably soon."

"I'll look into it immediately," he said.

~

About two years ago, I realized I needed to learn more about money. I happen to have a great deal of money, and I suppose it's true that, like anything one comes into possession of, I wanted to understand how to use it and what it could be used for. I was the same way the first time I came into possession of a gun, and before that swords, and succubi, and so on. It's just good practice to know the value and utility of what you own before someone who knows that value and utility better than you do tries to take it away from you.

But really, anyone with a decent financial advisor and a *Sharper Image* catalogue can figure out what to do with money. I was more interested in understanding it the way Heintz understood it, or more generally the way someone whose job it is to use money to make *more* money understands it.

I have lived very nearly my entire life with the barter system —I have two things of value and you have two different things of value, and we both agree the things have equivalent value, and so I will give you one of my things for one of your things, and off we go. Money eventually stepped in and became the portable substitute, so now if I want to get one of your things I sell my thing, get cash, and use my cash to buy your thing. It's still the barter system, but with less carrying around of livestock. I eventually learned to accept this, and even appreciated that I no longer had to find someone who not only had what I wanted but wanted what I had.

It was when money stopped standing for real live objects that I got really confused.

One time, after getting a rough balance of funds total from Heintz I asked him if I could visit my money. This led to a two-hour conversation I'm very certain he did not enjoy a second of, in which he explained that while a portion of the total he gave me was in fact "liquid"—and we lost twenty minutes as I tried to figure out why my money was, apparently, a large swimming pool—the bulk of it existed in things like stock, stock options, securities, hedge funds, and on and on.

Some of these were things that represented partial ownership of other things, which I sort of understood. But some were investments in things that were bundled with other things that were actually based on a made-up thing that had value only because everyone agreed it did. I didn't like these things, and when I learned about them I asked him to try and keep my money no more than one step removed from a thing I could theoretically visit and touch. He wasn't happy about this.

That I have money at all is kind of an accident of fate combined with a long lifespan and the fact that I didn't know I had it for a long while. Being wealthy is not something I'm unaccustomed to, only because one doesn't live through the whole of human history without a lucky financial break here and there. At the same time wealth doesn't last forever—it basically ends when the civilization that recognizes it does—so maybe that's why I'm indifferent about it. Basically, I'm good as long as I have access to food, drink, and shelter, and if money gets me better food, more drink and nicer shelter, then that's great.

Lately my education about money has involved setting up companies. Some of these are companies that invest in things that other people make or hope to make, and some are just there to hold money in places where people won't ask too many questions. I'm nearly positive some of it is illegal, although I couldn't tell you which country's laws are being violated and whether that even matters. (I half expect to someday learn that I've been running the Mafia all this time.) My only active contribution to the day-to-day is when I bring something specific to Heintz and ask him to arrange it for me. In this way, having a tremendous lot of money and a private banker is like having a concierge for the entire world.

And like any good concierge, Heintz doesn't know and doesn't ask why I want these things. This is fortunate. Because one of the things I'm trying to figure out is how a person can vanish into thin air, and explaining that would just be awkward.

 he rest of my encounter with Heintz went quickly and nobody was stabbed at any point, which is always the mark of a successful meeting. I signed my fictional financial mogul name several dozen times, we discussed a couple more errands I needed him to deal with, and that was that. It was deeply boring, and there's no point in going over all of it. I nearly fell asleep twice.

My extremely quiet limo driver was waiting for me in the garage. He had undoubtedly been notified of my impending arrival, as he was standing by the rear door of the car and trying very hard to avoid making eye contact. It was impossible to tell if he was doing this because some extra level of obsequiousness was mandatory for this gig or if he didn't want to look at the vampire.

"Back to the hotel, sir?"

"No, actually," I said, "I was thinking of visiting a friend."

"Now, sir?" he asked. Because, again: sunlight.

"If that's not a problem. Also, do you have any alcohol?"

He looked directly at me for the first time. Since the garage was well lit, if he knew anything at all about vampires he'd recognize quickly that I am not one. Aside from the slightly tanned face, my eyes are the wrong color.

"A good meeting?"

"Only in the sense that it ended."

He gestured, and I slid into the back of the car. Reaching inside, the driver unlocked a small bar hidden under one of the seats. "I don't have anything chilled," he lamented.

"It's all right, I'm not celebrating anything," I said. I reached in and found a bottle of whiskey that looked to be of decent quality. "I'm just not expecting to have to think very much for the rest of the day."

"Yes, sir." He closed the back door, then slid into the front seat and lowered the privacy window.

"You're not ..." he began, before stumbling over how to say the word *vampire* to a non-vampire without coming across as a lunatic, "... not like most of our clients."

"Apparently true. I might even crack a window on the ride back, provided they open."

"They do," he said. "So not the hotel?"

"What's your name?"

"Dugan, sir."

"Is that a first name or a last name?"

"Take your pick."

"All right. Dugan, I need to visit a very particular pawnshop in a less than fantastic part of this city. If you'd rather not travel to this part of town in your nice car, I understand, but that's where I'd like to go nonetheless."

I gave him the address, and he tapped it into his onboard trip computer. Not to get all fussy and irritable, but in my day professional drivers knew how to get around without an electronic box of maps shouting at them.

"Pawnshop," he repeated.

"As I said, it's to say hello to a friend, not because I need to pawn anything."

~

The ride to Tchekhy's shop was much more amiable than the trip from the hotel to the bank had been, mainly because Dugan was okay chatting up an ostensible non-vampire.

He had a little soldier-of-fortune in his history, which wasn't a huge surprise given his size, age, and the fact that I was pretty sure he was packing a gun. He kept hinting at various connections he had around the city, and it wasn't until we were nearly to the shop that I realized he was implying he could get me drugs if I wanted them. He seemed to think I was visiting my dealer. It was a nice offer, and would have been even nicer if drugs had any effect on me whatsoever.

Dugan was right in one regard: Tchekhy is much more than the owner of a small pawnshop. He *probably* isn't a drug dealer, but he is the guy I talk to when I want to discuss breaking laws, and avoiding governments, and that sort of thing. He's also the guy who usually handles my passports.

I didn't need any of those things. This was a social call. I don't know very many people in New York City, and almost none of those people would be willing to drink with me in the middle of the day. But Tchekhy, a self-employed criminal expatriate Russian, breaks the law pretty much on his own schedule. He's usually good for a day or two of drinking.

When we got to the shop I thanked Dugan and reached for the door handle.

"Let me get that!" he insisted, slipping out of the car and running around to the sidewalk to open the door.

I'm really not used to being treated like someone with money, and here I was getting out of a very nice car in a very bad neighborhood with a driver holding the door. If I was an easy person to mug I'd be worried about this.

I swung my feet out.

"I'll be happy to wait for you," Dugan said.

"No, no, I can find my own way back," I said, extending my hand with a tip I was pretty sure was generous pressed into the palm. "And you don't want to park the car in this neighborhood for longer than ..."

And that's when the bullets hit the door.

I didn't even know it had happened, nor did almost anyone else since the shots were from a silenced gun from somewhere above the storefront. The only person who knew right away was Dugan, and only because his hand was on the door when the rounds struck.

So, halfway out of the car, I was suddenly shoved back into it again.

"Stay down!" he shouted, slamming the door.

A second later he threw himself back into the driver's seat.

"Are you hit?" he asked.

"Only by you. What are you talking about?" My initial impression was this was a really bad time for my limo driver to be suffering a combat flashback.

"Two shots hit the door," he said. "Clustered, not strays. Bang-bang, double tap. The shooter has skills."

"You think they were aiming for me?" I asked, not entirely believing I was having this conversation.

"Door's jacketed or those bullets would've hit you in the chest," he said.

"Assuming a high-powered rifle."

"I'm assuming."

He threw it into drive and started looking up the street with an effective balance of calm and urgency you don't see in a lot of people. He was trying to get into traffic to get us the hell out of there.

"Who knew you were coming here?" he asked.

"Nobody. It was a surprise."

I cracked the window on the street side to get a look at Tchekhy's shop. It was, I realized, closed. In the middle of the day.

Something didn't feel right at all. Other than the gunshots, I mean.

Dugan saw an opening in the traffic and started to pull out.

"Hang on a minute," I said.

"Okay, but raise that window. The glass will deflect most anything, but it kinda has to be between you and the bullet."

"Fine, but your windows aren't see-through and the shooter is on the other side of the car."

"I'd rather not wait for him to reposition himself."

"Just one second."

The shop wasn't just closed. It was without power. None of the neon signs were lit, and none of the inside lights were up.

And then I saw light inside. But it wasn't electrical, it was incendiary.

"Okay, drive," I said.

Dugan stepped on the gas and jerked the car forward just as the front of Tchekhy's pawnshop exploded outward, showering glass everywhere. Dugan skidded in surprise but kept straight enough to negotiate the limo away from the scene before traffic locked down around us.

"I hope your friend wasn't in there," he shouted over his shoulder.

"So do I."

CHAPTER 2

The succubus Indira once asked me how I had managed to live for so long. At first I thought she was talking about my longevity, as if that was a thing I could explain. But that wasn't what she meant. What she meant was, how had nothing killed me yet, accidentally or otherwise? I told her I was just lucky. She said she was more prepared to believe just about any answer I gave her, from a friendly god staying the hand of death to a magic charm protecting my body, but not luck. Nobody, she insisted, could possibly be that lucky.

I was always pretty sure that on the day I finally left this world it would be because of a gun or an arrow, or whatever the next long-distance lethal weapon someone thinks of inventing will be.

I have adopted a fine set of survival skills that come very much in handy when I'm within range to evade or otherwise counter an assault, but there isn't a lot I can do about a high-powered rifle from fifty paces, especially if I don't know the sniper is even there.

By the way, and without going too far off on a tangent, this world got a whole lot crazier the easier violence became for everyone involved. For most of my life, to kill someone meant getting close enough to get blood on your clothes. Most times one was using something sharp at close range, and most times the consequence was seeing the insides of another person and hearing them die in pain, and basically being okay with that. Now there are triggers and buttons and switches, and killing another person doesn't necessarily involve even being in the same room with them. Guns may seem less barbaric than swords and knives, but the only difference I can see is in ease of use.

Anyway. I am just as capable of dying from a gunshot as I am from a well-swung sword, the difference being I might have a chance of defending myself against a swordsman. With a gun, my best chance is to be someone nobody would want to shoot.

I am asked on occasion why I don't take a more public stance, why I tend to stick to the shadows and keep private and let other people be the kings and conquerors and CEOs and senators. This is one of the reasons. The less important I am, the less likelihood there is that someone would want to blow my head off from a distance.

So the shots at the limo were a surprise. Almost as big a surprise as Tchekhy's shop exploding.

Dugan the driver was puzzling over the same sort of questions, albeit from a much smaller base of knowledge. His first act after getting us away from the scene before fire trucks and police arrived was to duck us into an underground public garage. It was the kind of place one went to complete drug deals and talk to government informants off the record, but it was also exceptionally difficult to shoot into from the street.

"You aren't hit?" he asked for the fourth or fifth time.

"I'm not," I said. "You?"

"No, no. My car door's fucked up ... excuse me ... shot up, but I'm okay."

"I'll cover the door," I said. I know next to nothing about insurance, but I was pretty sure if he wanted his to foot the cost of the door he'd have to file a police report first, and nobody wanted that.

He nodded. "Can I ask you what just happened back there?"

"Don't know. Like I said, nobody was expecting me."

"Fine, but that wasn't random either," he said. "Neither was your friend's store blowing up."

"You're right, it wasn't. Can you get me back to the hotel?"

"Sure. But not in this car. I'm gonna put in a call, get us another ride."

"It drives okay."

"A black stretch limo with tinted rear windows and two bullet holes in the right rear passenger side door was just at a scene where a crime took place," Dugan said. "And don't tell me that wasn't arson we just saw. Now I don't know what your friend was into, but I'll bet my right ... I'll bet anything that there's at least one body in that fire, whether it's him or not. So in the interest of protecting my client, I'd rather there isn't an obvious trail leading from that scene to the hotel."

"I like the way you think, Dugan."

He shrugged. "This is why people like me drive people like you around, and as long as you don't get into trouble while you're in one of my cars, people like you will continue to pay me to do that. Can I ask you one question?"

"Sure."

"Did you have anything to do with that fire?"

"Would it matter to you if I did?"

"No, sir. Just want to know is all."

"I didn't. And if I did, I wouldn't have been stupid enough to go watch it happen. I would have hired someone like you to go watch for me."

He smiled. "Let me make that call."

~

I made it back to the hotel a couple of hours later without any further assassination attempts. Dugan was compensated amply for everything, and I was back in my large top-floor suite and all was right in the world again—except that basically nothing that had happened after I left the bank made any sense at all.

There was one thing I was pretty sure of: Despite being on the other side of a door that had been perforated by a marksman's bullets, I didn't think I was being targeted. Not because it was particularly difficult to fathom someone wanting to kill me but because a hired assassin would have to be possessed of psychic powers to have set up a nest in that exact spot. And oracles notwithstanding, there is no such thing as psychic powers.

I wasn't kidding when I told Dugan nobody was expecting me. I had only decided to stop by Tchekhy's while I was on the elevator to the basement from Heintz's office. Further, an assassin with that degree of foresight probably wouldn't have missed the shot. Twice.

I made my way past the room's vast picture window and to the wet bar. The view was the sort that took one's breath away, especially the breath belonging to someone who never imagined mankind would be able to build anything so tall, but I had spent most of the previous day gawking at the city and now the bar was of far greater importance.

As I tossed some ice into a highball glass a familiar buzzing caught my ear.

"Hello, Iza," I greeted.

"H'lo," she answered as she flew past my line of vision.

Iza is a pixie. She's only a few inches tall, but if she were human-sized she'd probably be the most beautiful human I had ever seen, and not just because pixies don't wear clothing.

Usually, Iza lives in my island home, but before I left for New York she more or less demanded I take her along. Not sure why.

Pixies aren't very bright, but they are loyal, and are almost always a better option than talking to oneself in the mirror.

I poured some scotch over the ice in the glass, found a jar of olives and set a few out on the bar, and then sat down in one of the chairs in the lounge portion of the suite. Said chair was facing the window; the previous evening, after a large amount of alcohol, I began mentally tossing thunderbolts from that same chair. The view has this effect on a person. Or possibly just me.

Iza landed on the bar and began eating one of the olives. I could hear her munching. Pixies are loud eaters.

"Someone took a shot at me today," I said.

"Shot?" Iza asked. "A picture?"

"No, with a gun. Like on television." We watched television for a year, she and I, before she realized there weren't any small people hiding in the wall on the other side of the big screen TV's glass. "Bullets."

"Bullets bad."

"Missed me, though."

"I know. You here."

"I don't think they were aiming for me,"

"Okay."

"I think they were aiming for the car door."

"Door bad?"

"Well I don't know. I don't think the door was bad. It seemed like a regular car door." It really helps enormously to already have a drink in your hand when talking to a pixie.

"Door good, people bad."

"People bad?" I asked.

"Doors good, people shoot doors, people bad."

"I understand."

"Iza try small words."

"Yes, I appreciate that. But I don't think the person with the gun had anything against the door. He shot at it because it was in front of me."

"Try to shoot you, then," she reiterated.

"I don't think so."

"You confused."

One of us was. It might have been me. "I'm still trying to work it out."

"Okay." Iza flew around the room a couple of times, which was her version of thinking. When she was done she landed back on the bar.

"Door not bad, people not bad, maybe you bad."

"I'm not bad."

"*Somebody* bad."

Pixies ascribe to a fairly Manichaean worldview, I've learned.

"Actually that makes sense," I said, because all at once everything did.

"You bad?" she repeated.

"Not that I'm bad, that I'm in a bad place. That I'm not supposed to be there. Shoot the door, because it's the fastest way to get me to leave. The shooter knew what was going to happen next and didn't think I should be there when it did."

"What happen next?"

"There was a fire."

"Fire bad."

"Yes, fire is mostly bad nowadays. So are explosions. Whoever shot the gun knew the fire was coming because they'd set it."

I held up my glass to my tiny companion. She was still eating olives. "And so I know who fired the gun now."

"Good," she said. "All done thinking?"

"Yes. All done."

"Now we go see Clara."

I nearly choked on an ice cube.

"Clara?"

"We go see Clara."

To emphasize the importance of this, Iza flew into my eyeline and stared at me. I was genuinely dumbstruck.

When I first moved to the private island with Iza, Clara had also been with us, and it's fair to say Iza liked her a great deal more than she liked me. The problem was, Clara left me more than seven years ago, and while I knew exactly where she went, I wasn't going there. And New York was not that place.

"Clara isn't here, Iza, I'm sorry."

"New York! Iza not stupid, Iza remember."

The first time I met Clara was in New York City, and Iza was there then, too.

"Not stupid," I agreed. "I'm really sorry, Iza. I should have understood better when you asked to come. Clara isn't in New York anymore. She's in Europe. I wasn't coming here to see her."

"Open window, I find her."

"I actually can't," I said. "These windows don't open."

This was probably the saddest conversation I'd had in about a century, in case you were wondering. Once it was over I fully intended to polish off the entire wet bar.

"Windows made to open!" Iza insisted. "Windows stupid!"

"People can't fly. The windows don't open to keep anybody from trying to."

"If people know people can't fly—"

"It's difficult to explain," I interrupted. Explaining suicide to a pixie would take several days, after which I would end up killing myself.

Blessedly, we were interrupted by a knock at the door.

"Clara!" Iza said.

"I really don't think so."

I went to the door and checked. It was a woman, certainly, but not Clara. A very good-looking woman. My arm took over and opened the door before I had a chance to tell it to wait.

Common sense dictates if someone has just fired a gun at you —even if it was just at your car door—the next time a stranger approaches, you'd best engage them in conversation from a safe remove. On the other hand, she was very pretty. And so I opened the door.

"Hello. Can I help you?" I managed to say. Then there was a blade at my neck.

"I'm here to help *you*," said my guest with a slight smile.

CHAPTER 3

Hsu wondered how I was able to recognize him immediately for what he was.

"There are only three rules when it comes to goblins," I said. "Know how to recognize them, try not to anger them when they are armed, and assume that they are always armed."

There are a few circumstances under which having the sharp portion of a knife or sword against your neck can be considered a valid threat. You could be sitting down in a tall-backed chair. You could be pressed up against a wall. Your assailant could be behind you and pulling you against them. And really any other situation you can dream up in which you can't for one reason or another go backward.

At the threshold of my suite, this was not the case. I had one hand on the door, so had I wanted to, I could have fallen backward while at the same time slamming the door. Even if the woman on the dull end of the sword succeeded in blocking this I'd have still been left with plenty of time to find my feet and maybe the nearest heavy projectile available. I was pretty sure she knew all of this, too.

The woman in question was roughly my height thanks to an impressive pair of leather boots that looked to have at least three and a half inches of heel to them. Tucked into the boots were a pair of black denim pants, and going up from there I could make out what appeared to be a halter top beneath a calfskin jacket. Her skin was copper colored, her hair was jet black, and her eyes were slate gray.

She was probably a goblin. I was in love with her anyway.

"Would you be Francis Justinian?" she asked.

Her accent was a creative mixture of Southern Italy and Lower East Side.

"Today? Yes. And you might be?"

"I might be Mirella. And I might be here to help you."

"As you've said. And the sword?"

It was a narrow, straight-edged sword that fell somewhere between a katana and a medieval half-sword. Probably a custom job.

"It's here to help you, too. This is my resume," she said.

"It's very impressive. Could you lower it now, please?"

She hesitated long enough to make me reconsider the not-falling-backward-and-slamming-the-door decision I'd just made, and then lowered it. "Earlier today a person fired a gun at you, and now you open your hotel room door to a stranger without hesitation."

"I was just beating myself up about that, yes," I said. "But in my defense I didn't know you had a sword."

"Was it because I'm a woman? You didn't see me as a threat?"

"No, it was because you're a really attractive woman," I said.

I'm usually more tongue-tied around women I find attractive, so this was actually sort of impressive for me to come right out and say. Either there was something about her that made me comfortable, or the liquor I'd been drinking all morning was having a larger impact than I appreciated. There was also the possibility that I could see no way to screw this up given she was already *at* my hotel room.

She was nonplussed by my response, and tried again. "And so because I am a really attractive—"

"Oh for goodness sake," I interrupted.

I was in no mood to get a speech on not underestimating her because she was pretty.

"Why don't you come in?" I stepped back and opened the door wider.

Mirella shrugged, sheathed her sword—the sheath was strapped to her thigh—and more or less glided in. I could tell already that having her around would be difficult because just seeing her walk was a singularly captivating experience.

"So why *did* you open the door?" she asked. As she spoke her eyes darted around the room. She was examining angles and obstructions, and possible exits. Definitely a pro.

"I opened the door because this is a private suite. The hotel wouldn't have allowed you up unless you had permission." This was a *post facto* rationalization, but it sounded pretty good.

"And so how did I get here?" she asked.

"You had permission, naturally. Did Mr. Heintz hire you directly, or do you work for a service?"

She smiled. "Both. My employer was contacted by your man, and I was requested. Your Mr. Heintz knows enough to ask for the best."

That was a distinct possibility. It was also possible Heintz was aware of just exactly how difficult it would be to decline Mirella's services once I got a decent look at her. It was further possible that my banker knew me a bit too well.

"I'm sure that's true. I'm also sure you're difficult to turn down. Would you like a drink?"

Mirella treated me to a raised eyebrow. "It's much too early for either of us to be drinking. Also, I *am* the best. And why would you even consider turning down my service, which incidentally is only of the bodyguard variety?"

"Of course it is," I said. I retreated to the bar to refresh my own beverage. "And it's past noon. Since when is that too early?"

"Fine. I'll have a scotch."

"Really?" I was surprised. I was just being polite.

"The room is secure, and you don't look like you're going anywhere, so why not? Although I don't know if you realize this, but there's a tiny naked woman flying around this room."

Clearly a goblin. Nobody else has eyes that good. "That's Iza. And she's unhappy with me right now because you're not someone else."

"*How* unhappy?"

"Only a little bit. She's not a threat."

"Yes, I was worried about an aerial assault from a Barbie. This is a creature I've never encountered before, and I find recognizing the moods of new things as soon as possible is an advantage."

She lifted the scotch I'd set down for her on the end of the bar and took a decent-sized gulp. I honestly couldn't recall if goblins were good drinkers or not. "What is her kind called?"

"She's a pixie. And when she's upset she just ... flies around faster, I think. Anyway, as I was getting around to saying, I don't need a bodyguard."

Mirella took her eyes off Iza for long enough to finish her drink and place the glass on the edge of the bar. "Most of the people I work for, Mr. Justinian? If someone took a shot at them and then they saw me at their door, they wouldn't be asking why I was there, they'd be asking where the rest of my team was."

"You have a team?"

"No, I don't like teams."

"Right. Anyway. This situation is different."

"Different because you're bulletproof?"

Being bulletproof would have been fantastic. I got universal immunity instead, which was probably better, but still.

"Unfortunately no. But the door was, and that's what the bullets were meant for. Those shots weren't to hurt me, they were to warn me to get out of there."

Mirella gave me a look that implied she was hearing this particular excuse for the first time. I wondered if she often found herself trying to convince someone that they needed protection.

"And why is that?" she asked.

"Because the pawnshop was about to explode."

And that was definitely something new for her. "Maybe I should get a refill before you explain."

~

My assumption was that Dugan the limo driver submitted some manner of report to his bosses and the report had been forwarded to Heintz, and this was how I ended up sharing scotch with a goblin bodyguard. But that report clearly did not include the words "exploding pawnshop" so I had to back up and present the entire case to Mirella.

Well no, I didn't *have* to. Technically, she was there at my whim, since someone I was paying, paid someone who pays her to be there, but as long as I had her I saw nothing wrong with telling the long version of my theory. Possibly just to show how clever I thought I was.

"So this Russian is the one who shot at the door," she said. "This is what you're suggesting."

"I am. And Tchekhy likes me." I'm pretty sure this is true, since he takes my calls even when I'm not paying him to. Sometimes when you have a lot of money this is the only way to identify friends. Also, his dad made him promise to do right by me, on his deathbed. That carries some weight.

I continued. "As I see it, he had already cleared out the shop and knew what was going to happen next. When he saw me getting out of the car he did what he could to get me to leave quickly. Best way to do that was plant a couple of rounds in the door."

"I see gaping holes in this theory," Mirella said. She was nursing her third scotch and didn't appear to be feeling any of the effects. I considered this more impressive than the sword, to be honest.

"Well, a couple of holes. They aren't gaping."

"*Gaping.* Why was your friend destroying his own shop?"

"That I don't know."

Tchekhy had lined the walls of his basement—which was where all of his computer equipment was—with aluminum foil. The idea was to turn the entire room into an oven that would destroy all of the equipment completely before anyone with a fire hose was aware of the fire. I knew this because he had peeled back the wallpaper down there once to show it to me. And since I knew he had his share of both real and imagined enemies I never really got around to asking him what kind of circumstance would be required before he did this.

"And there is the coincidence," she added. "You tell me you haven't visited this man for a long time, then decide to drop by on a surprise visit at the exact moment he's busy immolating his own shop."

"I agree that does seem like an impressive coincidence."

"Unless it isn't a coincidence, and the reason he did this has something in common with you being in town."

"But almost nobody knew I was going to be in New York, aside from the man who hired you and the people he hired."

"Yes. And it's the people who know what they shouldn't that ought to concern you. Wouldn't you agree?" She gave me a remarkably winning smile and for a moment I forgot what we were talking about.

"I suppose I would, yes," I said.

Truthfully, I've found that most of the time coincidences are just the result of a poor understanding of what actually happened. I probably would have gotten around to realizing this on my own once I'd separated myself from the bar for a long enough period.

"But, you don't need a bodyguard."

"What I need is someone around who is thinking faster than I am, and in that regard you appear to be ideally suited."

She smiled again. "Excellent. Let me fetch my go-bag from the concierge."

"Is there a passport in this bag?" I asked.

"Will I need one?"

"I expect so. Unless you think the dangers I'm facing are confined to this city."

"I have a passport, and I'm fluent in four languages. It shouldn't be a problem."

I'm fluent in more or less all of them, but this didn't seem like the time to brag about that.

"And incidentally," she added, "not that I have any desire to talk you out of your decision, but I suspect your mind will work much faster without so much alcohol running through it."

"Thanks. Now you sound just like a woman I used to date."

CHAPTER 4

My encounters with goblins and elves are too numerous to recount, as their species has always been plentiful, if not particularly well identified, through history. Unlike demons and pixies, and even vampires, they look enough like humans that it's entirely possible to spend your life around them without knowing they're there at all.

This would not be the first time I traveled with a goblin, nor the first time I employed one as a bodyguard, mercenary, or warrior. They're very good creatures to have on your side in a fight, provided you are fortunate enough to be at least as clever as they are. I happen to be, but I'm something of an exception in a lot of ways and that's one of them.

The first goblin I called friend was named Hsu, and I made his acquaintance sometime following what you would probably call the fall of the Roman Empire.

I have a lot of problems with historians. I think they spend too much time looking at the past as if the entire point of history was to lead up to the present. But people one and two and three thousand years ago weren't any dumber or less evolved than they are now. They had their own prosaic understandings of how the world worked, certainly, and while a lot of those understandings were—when analyzed from a historical distance— somewhat facile, the same could be said about a lot of what people believe today.

Ask a scientist why a tornado happened and you might get a complicated weather-related response that underlies the random destructiveness of nature. Ask someone else and they might tell you God did it, and surely He had His reasons. The second answer implies an ordered universe, which is nice, even if it's an ordered universe run by an angry god who appears to have overreacted somewhat.

I personally find the second answer a good deal less comforting than the first, but that's just me. The point I'm trying to make, though, is that this is the same answer you might have gotten to the same question if it were asked ten centuries earlier. The only difference, possibly, would have been the name of the god.

One thing I can agree with historians about is that the Early Middle Ages—you might call it the Dark Ages—was a complete mess. I lived through it, but if you want me to explain everything that happened back then I might have to turn to the nearest historian and ask them because they probably have a better shot at putting it all together than I ever will.

This is a thing that's true about history, whether you lived through it yourself or not: If there was no major unifying force in existence during the era in question, it's basically impossible to figure out what went on.

For a very long time the Roman Empire was that unifying

force. Now, I'm on record as hating the Romans, but my reasons are fairly petty. Basically, they were boring as hell, and when you've lived as long as I have you find yourself judging dullness much more harshly than dullness itself might deserve. Especially in this instance, because being boring did have its advantages.

The Romans were literate, culturally advanced, and had established an enormous boring kingdom that made it possible for one to know what happened in every part of that kingdom as it was full of people who were documenting it and marking it on a calendar everyone agreed to use, and communicating what they had learned. Granted, *what happened* was usually *not much, thanks*, but history was recorded nonetheless.

The reason it was so boring was that taxation will never, ever be interesting, and taxes were the key to the entire Empire. Sure there was military might and political savvy, and they had the highways and the aqueducts and the literacy and the public education. All of that was good. But Rome was built by taxes.

Never in history has a government been as effective at taxation as the Romans. Nowadays we see *taxes* and think in terms of monetary income, but this was more about goods: spices, grains, wine, wood, stone, and so on. Really, one of the biggest advantages of such a vast empire was that nobody starved, because if there was a lack of food in one part of the world, the Romans owned a part of the world where food was in abundance. So they would collect grains as tax and use it to feed the people who didn't have food. This was also how cities managed to exist, given that was where the most people and the fewest farms coincided.

And then the Roman Empire collapsed. Or so I've read.

It was a thousand years before someone suggested to me that the Empire collapsed, as if this was a thing that took place overnight. Like the barbarians turned up, Rome fell, and the entire government apparatus just disintegrated. And then, I guess, we were all left stumbling in the dark. Because: Dark Ages. I will grant that when Alaric and the Goths seized the city of

Rome it had a not insignificant psychological impact on the European sphere, but there were still plenty of Romans around and half an empire left—in the East—that went on for another twelve hundred-odd years. (For reasons that I will never understand, the Eastern Roman Empire is called the Byzantine Empire in the books. I never met a Byzantine, and nobody called them that. They were called Romans because they were Romans.)

Taxes were a big reason Rome fell, too, in a way. All it took for the Romans to lose the power they relied on to maintain their vast holdings was for one or two key territories to go south. If you lose the land that produces the crops that feed another region, you may end up losing both regions. I mean, sure there were the barbarians and all that, but one of the other things the Romans did well was bring "barbarian" cultures into the empire, until the people from that culture started to act like Romans. So there were always barbarians hanging around, and the truth was, they were basically like everyone else, especially after a generation or two.

Anyway, what *did* happen was that the localities that had been part of a unified top-down structure all tried to create their own smaller governments based loosely on the political structure the Romans had perfected. With only one exception—the Catholic Church—nobody got this right. Literacy went to hell, as did a tremendous amount of common sense, and it became a lot more likely that political disputes were resolved violently.

Most importantly, if you were in the middle of all of this, you pretty much had no idea what the hell was going on. This is an excellent way to get killed.

~

I tried to lay low for the majority of Roman rule. As I've explained before, it's not always a good idea to become a prominent citizen in the local community when you don't get old. For a while it's okay, because you can amass a decent-sized fortune if you do a couple of things well, and having a fortune makes it easier to convince people—monetarily—not to notice that you're the same guy you were four generations ago. But that's impossible to maintain, especially in cultures that have a strong belief system involving some sort of personified evil force. And most of them do.

So when the empire unstrung itself, I was not exactly left destitute because I had nothing substantial in the way of wealth— or at least land—to lose. I had already been traveling from town-to-town for years by then, peddling various wares that people might find useful enough to barter for.

Usefulness changed from area to area, as did quality of product. In good times, I'd have some silver bowls, rare spices—like pepper—or silks. In bad times, maybe nothing more than a few clay pots.

The way it worked was not dissimilar to how the Romans distributed taxes, only on a smaller scale. I'd get stuff from one region and cart it to another region to trade it for things a third region might want. It was extremely time-consuming and the profit margin was always verging on zero, but I had so much free time to work with there was really no way not to succeed. Plus, I got to see a lot of different places and meet a lot of different people, learn all the local languages right when they were born, and most nights I could sleep comfortably in the back of my wagon and under the stars.

It was a good deal, right up until it wasn't anymore.

I was visiting a region I'm pretty sure is now taken up by either Germany or Austria. I *think* it was part of the Rhine valley, but I'm not positive and I'm not positive partly because I didn't return to it for a very long time after the fact. This would have put it in the hands of the Franks ... I'm pretty sure. Again, I have to apologize, but people stopped writing and following calendars and place names changed and it was a mess, so I barely know where this happened, and *when* is just as difficult.

One of the good things about being a peddler was that I didn't have to care all that much whose territory I was in because most days I was dealing with the peasantry, and peasants didn't really much care who was who as long as nobody took their land or set fire to their houses. Any king—or emperor or bishop—who successfully kept that from happening was okay with them. Granted, they had to know who to give taxes to and which armies to feed and which to hide from, but a lot of that was pretty easy to pick up quickly. Taxes tended to go to whoever had the biggest house in the area, and armies were usually okay if they had the same colors as the guy who lived in the biggest house. And neither army nor lord had much impact on their daily lives.

Village hierarchies did have an impact, though. On the ground, most of the little villages and hamlets and whatnot had local politics to settle local issues. It was different in every place: he could be the tax collector; the nearest priest or religious equivalent; the guy who lived in the *second* biggest house; or the only literate layperson in town. It was almost always a man, and the village was almost always exactly as sane as he was.

So I was traveling with my wagon and my ass, and I came to this particular nameless town. The center of the town was a modest crossroad, which was also pretty common. Towns tended to pop up any place two main roads intersected, because I guess lots of people decide they'd rather stop and build a house than make a left turn. Or something.

At the time I had a wagon full of some pretty classy porcelain I was going to claim came from China if anyone with a decent coin purse asked, and some crude brass jewelry that was common about a thousand miles east of the village but likely to be seen as exotic locally. I also had a lot of stoneware that was superior to anything they had on hand, and a few other trinkets.

The porcelain was going to be too costly for most of the locals, so my goal was to find the biggest house and start from there, but I reached the crossroad toward the tail end of a long day of travel and decided to stop and set up on the spot. I thought I could maybe make a few deals before sundown, get some directions to whatever castle might be nearby, and start the next day off heading for it.

Stopping turned out to be a massive error.

"What sort of man are you?" was the first question anyone thought to ask. I had just unhitched my wagon, fed my ass, and was in the process of unloading a few of my goods when this question was posed by a simple-looking fellow on the opposite side of the street.

"Only a man, friend," I offered. This seemed an obvious enough answer, and more or less true.

"You are here to sell those things?" he asked.

My inquisitor was short and hairy, with a pretty common farmer's build and with teeth of the quality one might expect for an area that had little fruit. He also had a large wooden cross around his neck, which was very useful to me as it wasn't always obvious which god I should be invoking from location to location. He was the only one out on the street, which was a little surprising as it was a lovely day and the farmland I'd passed up the road led me to believe I was dealing with at least a modest-sized population. Generally a crossroad such as this would have plenty of peddlers, and locals would be accustomed to seeing them. But this fellow seemed to be shocked by my profession.

I turned to pull a clay pot from the back of the wagon in an effort to visually elaborate on what I was there to do, but the guy with all the questions had already decided the conversation was over. He scurried off down the road, leaving me to wonder if every customer in town was going to be a hard sell.

A few minutes later another man happened by and we went through the same questions: *What sort of man am I* and *am I here to sell things* and then he ran off, too. Nobody, it seems, had seen a private merchant around here before.

Then came the crowd.

All right, it was a small crowd, but while they appeared to be unarmed there were enough of them to separate me from my body parts by hand if they felt like it. Especially since, when it came to farmers, upper body strength was something they excelled at.

Leading this crowd was the local chieftain or whatever it was he went by. He was cleaner and better dressed than the people who followed, and the wooden cross around his neck was a touch larger, which could have indicated he was a priest. There was really no way to be sure; village priests didn't often dress like the way we expect priests nowadays to dress. Sometimes the only way to tell was if they emerged from a building that looked like a church. Not that churches looked much like churches back then either.

He stopped across the road from me, as the others before him had. This was actually very close given it was a small road with no real traffic to speak of.

"What sort of man are you?" he asked.

With yet another chance to answer this same question, I decided not to. "What sort are *you*?" I asked.

"I am a humble man," he answered immediately, and I guess that was what I was supposed to have responded with.

"I, too, am a humble man," I said, hoping nobody minded I cribbed the answer.

"And you are here to peddle your wares?"

It was an innocuous question, but the way he said it was in roughly the same tone someone might use to say, *you're here to rape my daughter?*

The people with him had begun to spread out. The intent was to surround me, and by all rights I should have been the one who was worried, but there was a lot more fear in their eyes than I imagine there was in mine. It was me they were afraid of, but until I understood why I couldn't really use that to my advantage. There are times when being fearsome is useful, but it always helps to know the reason for and limit of that fear.

It was obvious that my way out of this situation was through the man with the largest cross.

"If I could speak with honesty, friend," I said, "the concern you and your cohort express on the matter of my profession appears to have little to do with what I sell."

"My name is Garivald, and I am no friend!" he shouted. "And you are no man."

"You have me at a disadvantage, Garivald," I said, as calmly as I could manage. "What do you imagine me to be if not a man?"

Religious fanatics are the *worst*. They're basically impossible to bargain with, they accept no outside opinion about anything, and they departed from reality well before you met them. The best thing to do when encountering one is either hit them before they get a chance to hit you, or run.

I couldn't run. I had a sword and a knife, neither of particularly high quality but both decently sharp and pointy. But they were in the wagon under my bedding and I was standing several feet away from them. If you think it was foolish of me, in this time and this place, to be so far away from a blade of any kind, you aren't wrong. In fairness, I didn't know how dangerous the time had become until it became dangerous for me at that crossroad.

"Your coming was foreseen," Garivald said. "That you would appear at the corner of these roads with cursed goods from far-off lands and a forked tongue with nothing but poison on it. Your face would be new to all men."

"You don't see a lot of strangers around here, I take it. This is a pretty old face, I have to be honest."

He actually spat on the ground, which is just a disgusting habit. "A devil is what you are," he barked.

"But my tongue is perfectly normal, see?"

I stuck out my tongue. This was probably a bad idea, but the whole thing sounded so stupid I couldn't really take it seriously.

Garivald was not impressed by the normalness of my tongue, but the guy next to him at least had the decency to recoil.

"What exactly do you intend to do with this devil once you've found him?" I asked.

"Send him back from whence he came."

"Oh all right. I came from over there." I pointed up the road.

Garivald didn't laugh or anything. This is because almost nobody had a sense of humor in the Early Middle Ages. It's true, look it up.

The people he brought with him had more or less surrounded me by then. Just so we're clear, I am very good in hand-to-hand combat. And if I was incredibly lucky, and these lunatic yahoos charged me one at a time like in a karate movie, I would probably be okay. But that seemed really unlikely. Still, if I was going to have a chance, what I needed to do was identify who would be attacking first—there is always a first, even if he is then joined by many—which was what I was working on when a man on a horse rode up to the crossroad.

Actually—and this was really the height of irony—he wasn't a man at all.

When you're about to be lynched because someone thinks you're not human and an actual goblin rides up, I'll be honest, it's hard not to point that out to somebody. I didn't, but I sure thought about it.

When he stopped at the scene everyone there took a half step back and relaxed, like kids who were about to fight until Mom walked by. Given how this lot felt about strangers, I had to think they knew him.

The goblin took a long look at me, and I at him. He had thin black hair and a tiny wisp of a mustache. His riding gear was an expensive combination of leathers of a unique design for this area. No sword that I could see, so he probably only had one or two. He was from the Orient, quite clearly, and yet of the two of us I was the one who everyone seemed to think did not belong.

"Ho, Garivald," the goblin said. "What goes on here?"

Garivald looked annoyed and spoke tersely. "Nothing to concern you, Hsu. Travel on peaceably and leave us to the Lord's work."

The goblin named Hsu did not, thankfully, do this. Instead he dismounted and led his horse off the road, handing me the reins. I took them without comment. I also took the small dagger he slipped into my palm without comment.

I was going to like this Hsu fellow, I decided.

"Is this he?" Hsu asked. "The legendary crossroad devil you have been anticipating?"

"As I said, it's not your concern," Garivald repeated.

"*Into town he rides, on a great steed with promises of wealth untold, and on his head there would be horns and on his feet hooves. And the steed would carry him on six legs and breathe fire. His eyes would glow in the night with the souls of the damned.* I will be honest, Garivald, I do not see the resemblance."

"He works magicks to appear as a man to us," Garivald said, as if this was the most obvious thing ever.

"That seems like a waste of a good description, then."

Hsu reached into my wagon and pulled out a ceramic bowl. To me he asked, "Is this cursed cupwear forged in hellfire?"

"No, it's a bowl made in China," I said. He gave me an arch look. "Fine, Persia."

"Persian ceramics, Garivald. I suppose having touched this I am now cursed?"

"You trifle with the wrath of the Lord," Garivald spat.

Hsu sighed and rolled his eyes. "This simple merchant is not the devil you seek."

"Simple?" I asked.

"Simply human."

"Yes, that."

Garivald was still having none of this. "One final warning, Hsu, this is not your concern."

Hsu paced around my wagon, poking at the stuff and generally looking like someone who didn't much care how many people threatened him and told him he had to leave. I was glad for this, even though I was a little annoyed by the visible disdain he showed for my goods. Some of it was pretty decent.

"How goes your church?" Hsu asked Garivald, while holding up a trinket in the waning light. "Have you set your foundation?"

"You know well we have not," Garivald said. He was turning red from the exertion of being civil.

"Oh yes, that's right. You require a relic first." He put the trinket back. It was a crappy piece of brass hammered to a chain by someone with not a lot of skill at hammering, but on a good day I could talk it up into being the rarest necklace in the kingdom.

"A relic?" I asked Hsu. "What sort of relic?" I was mentally conducting an inventory.

"A holy relic," Hsu said. "As a God-fearing man you know this, I'm sure. And perhaps you can help?"

"How might I do that?"

Hsu laughed. "I have looked over your wares, peddler, and there is little to see. But *I* know you have a treasure. A holy treasure. A treasure that only a God-fearing and definitely entirely human man such as yourself could carry without bringing down the wrath of the heavens. Tell me! Where have you hidden it?"

Garivald was nearly as confused as I was. "Hsu, what are you talking dobout?"

"Oh, he knows!" Hsu said with a laugh. "Many miles have I traveled looking for the very man that stands before you now, for word of him has spread all through this valley and many lands beyond!"

"But why did you seek him?" one of the townsmen asked. At least the rabble was buying into this.

"Yes," I agreed. This was turning into quite a performance and I still wasn't sure where it was going. "Why *did* you seek me?"

"Humble Garivald," Hsu said grandly, "you have sought a relic on which to base your humble church to honor our Lord."

"Humbly," I added helpfully.

"While I have gone far and wide looking for the peddler the people spoke of, the man who carried with him just such a thing!"

Garivald looked nonplussed. He still had lynching in his eyes. "And this is such a man?"

"Imagine my surprise, to follow his path right to the very spot I'd hoped to lead him! It is truly the work of the Lord!"

In a grand gesture, Hsu wrapped his arm around me as if to lift me, or possibly embrace me. He didn't fully commit to either option, but when he was done my pocket felt heavier than it had a moment earlier.

"You would have us believe that the foundation of our church is delivered in the hands of a devil?"

Hsu sighed. Garivald required some patience, as the smartest person in the village was still not all that smart, clearly.

"This is what I have been trying to tell you, my humble friend. This is no devil." To me he asked again, "Where is your treasure? If you reveal it I swear you will be given a fair audience."

"I always keep it on my person," I said. "It is the only safe place. But I do not trust these men, Lord Hsu. I don't think they are ready to see it."

The question of why Hsu was doing any of this was one that would have to be answered as soon as I was no longer at risk of being torn apart by fanatics, but I had finally caught on to what he was doing.

"No, these are only humble, god-fearing men!" Hsu declaimed. "They don't truly mean you any harm! Tell him, Garivald. Tell him you are humble."

"I have said so," he said.

"And that you will not harm him," Hsu added.

"I would see what he hides."

"The burden I carry is great," I said, trying to very hard to sound extremely serious and powerfully burdened. And humorless, because again: no sense of humor around these parts. "For years I have carried it, and wished only to pass it on to he who was worthy, he that the Lord Himself spoke of when I first came into possession of this relic."

"The Lord spoke to *you?*" Garivald said in disbelief.

"In a dream, yes."

I pulled the thing Hsu had given me from my pocket. It was a partial leg bone from a pig, as near as I could tell. "The night after I discovered this ... bone ... He came to me. I knew it was special, for truly when you touch it you can feel its ..."

"... Holiness?" Hsu suggested.

"Sure, yes. Holiness and grace and God things and such. All that. And the Lord said to me, he said, 'Take this ... finger bone? ... to the place where it is most needed.' So I have looked for that place."

"And here you are!" Hsu said.

"Here I am! With this finger bone, which belonged to ... a saint. I'm pretty sure."

"Not just a saint!"

"No, not just a saint!"

Okay, I knew there were saints, but coming up with the name of one was going to be difficult. This would probably have been easier if I'd actually met Jesus back when I worked in Galilee.

"Whose bone is it?" Garivald said breathlessly. I realized we finally had him.

Hsu looked at me, but I wasn't nearly confident enough in my Christian lore to pull out an impressive name. At that time Christianity was still an upstart little doomsday cult to me.

"None other than John the Baptist!" Hsu said. Everyone there gasped and took a step back, which was really, really funny.

And thankfully, he picked someone I had heard of. "It's true! This bone is from the hand that baptized Christ!" I said.

It was hard to believe they were taking this seriously, especially since if anyone was capable of positively identifying a pig bone it had to be a gathering of farmers. But it was working.

"It appears," Garivald said, "we have been mistaken, kind sir. That you would travel all this way to deliver so great a relic to so humble a setting ... you truly do the Lord's work. But what can we give you as trade for such a great thing? We have so little."

He had gone from pompous to obsequious so suddenly it took a lot of effort not to be a little obnoxious, but Hsu had already described it as a gift and while I could have probably gotten a decent meal or something out of it, I pretty much just wanted to get the hell out of town before someone introduced a new crazy.

"Just take it," I said. "Found your church on it, and I promise no devils will darken this road."

I walked it over to Garivald, and honestly when he fell to one knee to accept it I nearly cracked up. I was *that* close.

And that bone must have come from one remarkable pig, because the second Garivald touched it he started to tremble with the kind of ecstatic joy you only really see in full-blown fanatics and very expensive prostitutes.

"It is truly a holy relic," he declared.

And just like that I was free to go. The lynch mob was no longer lynch-inclined, and instead wanted to take turns holding the exhumed finger bone of John the Baptist.

"You should pack your wagon now," Hsu said under his breath.

"I believe you are correct," I said.

"Up the road, on the other side of a crest, there is a dirt path that leads to nowhere in particular. Meet me at the end of this path."

So I guess we were dating. "I thank you for your help here, lord Hsu, but why should I agree to meet an armed goblin alone in a deserted wood?"

He smiled, just widely enough for the sharp points of his teeth to reveal themselves. "Because this goblin has been looking for you for a very long time," he said.

~

The dirt path was as Hsu described, although it didn't actually lead to nowhere. It led to a very old tree on a low hill. The grass around the tree was trampled down, and the markings on the lowest bough suggested this had been a hanging tree not so long ago. I wondered if this was where I'd have ended up had Hsu not come along, and decided probably not—hanging is something people tend to do to other people, not to devils.

There is no such thing as a devil. Or suppose I should say there is no species I'm aware of that uses that word to self-identify. I feel like I need to make this clear given what I've already said about demons and iffrits and so on. *Devil* is a word generally reserved for Judeo-Christian hell-spawn. They're often described in a way reminiscent of satyrs—hooved feet, for instance—and satyrs are also real. Likewise, devils can prey on the living and are associated with the night, much like vampires, who are real as well. Basically, if you took the worst aspects of demons, satyrs, and vampires, and threw in the personality of an iffrit, you'd have yourself something pretty close to a devil.

But again, devils aren't real. As far as I know.

It was nightfall by the time Hsu reached the clearing. I'd started a small fire by then, in anticipation of spending the night under the hanging tree and thinking about all the food I wished I could be cooking on said fire.

"Good thinking," was what he said by way of a greeting. "It

will get chill around here soon enough." He tossed a pair of dead rabbits at my feet. "And now we can cook these."

He'd arrived by leading his horse up the path rather than riding to me, which made his approach quieter. I still heard him, but I was expecting someone so I was listening. It was a more polite entry, certainly. If I had heard someone riding hard toward me I might have braced for a less pleasant guest.

Rabbit was definitely one of the things I had been thinking of maybe cooking over my fire. I held them up.

"Fresh."

Hsu sat down on the opposite side of the fire, cross-legged. It was a pose I associated with the Hindus of the Far East.

"It's a gift. Not from me, from Garivald and his people. I told them it seemed a shame, you going away hungry."

"Hungry, but with all my parts attached," I said.

"If that is your bottom line, you must be a terrible peddler."

I laughed.

"On certain days, continuing to breathe comfortably is sufficient payment. On other days, a good meal and perhaps some wine."

"Then wine we shall have," Hsu said. Reaching into a saddlebag he pulled out a leather pouch and handed it to me over the fire.

"This village had wine to spare? I should have stayed longer."

"No, this is mine."

I took a sip, and handed it back, and then got to work skinning the rabbits.

"You passed through Constantinople," I said. "Your wine gives you away."

"The wine wasn't made in Constantinople."

"Nothing is made in Constantinople. It is from a particularly fertile valley in the northeastern corner of the Mediterranean— whatever that territory is called this season—but the marketplace for this wine is Constantinople."

It should not be an enormous surprise to anybody that I am an expert in the field of alcoholic beverages.

"You could just say you like the wine."

"It's wine. I like it for being wine. I don't expect that opinion to change."

Hsu laughed and took a sip while I finished skinning the first rabbit, which is messy business. These days, when everyone washes their hands every time they touch a public surface, the idea of tearing the skin off an animal with a knife and your bare hands seems a lot nastier. Back then I wiped the blood off on a cloth, shoved the carcass on a stick, and moved on to the next rabbit, and thought back to a time when I would have just eaten the them raw, fur and all. It was not a fond recollection.

"So I have a lot of questions for you," I said. "For starters, I wonder if you could tell me why I nearly lost my life back there? And maybe if there are any other towns around here that don't take kindly to strangers?"

"To the last question, yes," Hsu said. "There are several such places around here. You may wish to keep apace with the local realities. I can help."

"Do you mean to ride into each town to talk the area priest into accepting a holy pig bone in exchange for my head?"

He grinned. "There is a merchant guild in this area that wards off competition by fueling local fears of devils and demons and such. The legend you just ran into was invented by a professional fabulist that rode through this valley a few months back. He dresses like a holy man and delivers inspired performances, convincing most who witness that God is speaking through him."

"And you have to be in this guild to pass the non-devil test?"

"Yes, because only guild members know the answers to those questions you failed to answer correctly."

"What are the correct answers?"

"Let me worry about that."

I finished the other rabbit and put it on a second stick,

extended both of them over the fire, and then set about cleaning the knife. It was Hsu's knife, and it was a really excellent one. I was hoping he wasn't planning to ask for it back.

"That's the second time you've invited yourself along with me," I said. "Perhaps I should be blushing."

"As I said, I have been looking for you for some time."

"Yes, that was another one of my questions. Who do you suppose I am?"

"I *suppose* you are Li-Yuan, the eldest of the eight."

I stared at him for a good long time.

"I think you need to hand me back that wine," I said eventually. "Either you have had too much of it or I have had too little."

～

There are a *lot* of immortals in mythology. Every god is a *de facto* immortal already, and I've been confused with several different gods over the course of my long history. I actually *was* one of them, in the sense that the name I went by became one of the names of one of the regional gods. And then the old stories became stories *about* me, and suddenly I was Dionysos, god of wine and theater and insanity.

That was a little unusual, though. Most times what happens is I get directly associated with a regional immortality legend by virtue of being the only person who comes close to the correct description.

Li-Yuan is one of those names. I don't even know how that one in particular got pinned to me, since the legend involves a Chinese immortal named "Iron Crutch Li" and I don't walk with a crutch or anything. Likewise, I have nothing in common with this immortal's life story. Frankly, it's not the most flattering comparison in the world, but whatever.

It had been a while since anyone called me by this name, though. I'd traveled the Silk Road a few times and ended up close enough to China to pick up the title, but while I'm not great at keeping track of time, I was very certain this happened long before Hsu had been born. So either someone was keeping a description of the legendary Li-Yuan alive somewhere—and it was accurate enough that it was possible for Hsu to find me—or something else was going on. I was banking on it being something else.

~

"You are too young to associate that name with my face," I said.

"And you look too young to be the owner of that name."

"I am also not a Chinaman with a crutch, if you'll notice."

"I know. You are not truly the legendary Iron Crutch Li, but I know you to be an immortal man, and right now that is the kind of man I seek."

I was possibly even less fond of revealing my age in Hsu's day than I am now, but by the time he'd said this I didn't see any point in disputing it. If things got out of hand there was a decent chance I could beat him in combat. Maybe fifty-fifty, depending on how many swords he had hidden on him.

"What could I do for you?" I asked. "And why would I?"

"These are both very good questions."

"Thank you. I put a lot of thought into them."

"I need you to help me find something I have lost. And in exchange for helping me, I will help you navigate your way through a world that is changing far more quickly than you are prepared for, as today proved. And your rabbits are burning."

"So they are," I said, pulling them quickly from the flames before they legitimately caught fire, which they were moments away from doing. I handed one rabbit to him. "But you're going to have to make me a better offer than that."

"Better than making sure your head isn't removed by religious fanatics? And keeping you from burning dinner?"

"I'm a quick study," I said. "These are strange times, but I've seen plenty stranger. I'd like to know what it is you've lost, and why I am the one who can help you find it."

"I feel as if telling you now would be premature."

"How am I to help you find something when I don't know what it is I'm finding?"

"It is in the possession of a Jew merchant who does not know what he truly has. I need to find him and get it back before he figures this out."

"Again, I ask why I am the one who is meant to help you do this?"

"I need a man who can work miracles."

I laughed. "I may be old, but you are mistaken if you think I have miracles in me."

"Ah! That's where you are wrong, Li-Yuan. For I know you performed at least one."

"You have me at a loss, Hsu," I said. "What are you talking about?"

"Tell me, when did you last hear the name Li-Yuan?"

"In truth, I don't know. I'm not very good with the passage of time. I would say nearly a century, perhaps a little longer."

"Yes, that's about right. And you were called Li-Yuan by an elder on the day you saved his village from an angry god."

This was only a little bit correct. The angry god was a dragon, and while that may still sound pretty impressive, that's only because humankind never really got dragons right. They weren't all that much of a big deal back when they actually existed, although it helped to know this in advance of encountering one.

The village Hsu was talking about had a problem with its livestock getting picked off by a particularly annoying water dragon, and I happened to be around, so I took a big stick and hit the dragon on the nose with it until he went away. Then I told the elder not to let the animals go near the water at night anymore, and that was that.

It wasn't really a thing, to be entirely honest, and I wouldn't have even remembered it had it not come with a godhood. Granted, you have to know that water dragons—these are more serpentine than the land-based ones, and smaller—don't like to be hit on the nose, but *most* creatures don't like to be hit on the nose, so it's not like it's a big secret.

"Honestly, Hsu, I couldn't find that little village again if I wanted to. I haven't set foot in China since, and I was only there in the first place because that elder owed me money. Are you telling me this story is still known a century later?"

"It may be. I don't know. I did not receive this information secondhand, though. I was a young boy in that village."

The oldest goblin I ever met was eighty-two, and he didn't look nearly as healthy as Hsu. Some species have longer-than-normal lifespans, like imps and succubi. Some have shorter-than-normal, like pixies. One or two— vampires, for instance, and some species of moss—could in theory live forever. But goblins and elves have very human life spans.

"I don't believe you," I said.

"Said the immortal man to the goblin."

"You make a fair point. But you are a goblin in your twenties."

"I am indeed."

"Possibly math is something you have not excelled at?"

"You asked why you are the man I need to help with this quest. The answer is, you knew how to defeat a dragon, and that is the kind of knowledge I can't find elsewhere."

"You're expecting dragons?"

"No, but the man I seek is surpassing clever, and there are rumors he employs monsters. I need a clever merchant and a monster expert."

"What sort of monsters?"

"I do not know. The stories may be exaggerations to make this man sound more impressive, and the truth is I believe that to be the case. However, I would rather be over-prepared for an imaginary monster than underprepared for a real one."

"That depends. If I'm what you consider preparation you should expect to be disappointed. I've found the best recourse when facing something monstrous is to run faster than it can. And I still haven't heard a good reason to agree to any of this."

"Hmm. Can I appeal to your sense of adventure?"

He could, because I actually was intrigued. Hsu was turning out to be the most interesting person I'd met in a long time. But he wasn't telling me anything close to the entire story yet.

"I have no sense of adventure," I lied. "That sort of thing can get a man killed, and you may have noticed I excel at not getting killed."

He sighed, although it felt like he was expecting to reach this point in our conversation anyway.

"Very well, but I warn you now that you will likely not believe me. You may even send me on my way for fear that I'm mad, and the only way I can prove to you that I am *not* mad is by catching up with the Jew."

"I can believe a wider range of things than most men."

"I hope so. Because the reason I am in my twenties while a century has passed since my childhood is that I didn't spend all of my life in this world."

I blinked. About five or six times, I think. "Are there other options I'm unaware of?"

"I walked the shadow world for a time."

"I'm afraid I still don't follow. Do you mean death?"

"No. No, no. Not the land of the dead. I met a man when I was younger. A special man, who was in truth no man at all, much as I am in truth no man."

"Another goblin?"

"Something different. He had many names for himself and his people, but the one used most often was *faery*. The realm I speak of is the faery kingdom. And the thing I need your help to reacquire is a way to return to that kingdom and to the faery that first brought me to that place."

"Well," I said. "You're correct. I don't believe you."

"You understand my reluctance, then."

"But it's a good story, and I have chased plenty of imaginary objects based on far worse stories. So why not?"

CHAPTER 5

*I was with Hsu one time when I saw her. We were in a busy market-
place near Angora and having a heated discussion regarding the value
of a number of furs we wished to obtain to keep us from freezing to
death while en route to India and China.*

*The merchant was a gifted haggler, and we were impatient, which was a
terrible combination. With patience we could have reached a number we
were all happy with after an hour. Our impatience would get us a
number that was more beneficial to the seller, but take less time.*

*I saw her red hair from half a market away, and only because the road
was uneven and we were standing on a slight rise. I couldn't tell what
she was shopping for, but she was standing still and I was seeing the
back of her head. This was a fortuitous thing, because most other times
when I saw her, she also saw me, and when that happened she tended to
disappear on me. I didn't know why.*

*Hsu was a little shocked when I shoved the fur I was holding into his
hands and ran off, unkindly forcing my way through an already tight
knot of people. I soon lost sight of the red hair, but since the market was
essentially one long corridor I felt confident that so long as she didn't
move I would catch up to her.*

I was wrong, as always. I managed to reach the space where I swore

*she'd last stood, and then past it and around it and behind it, looking
quite mad to a large number of people. She was gone.
Hsu found me after a while, sitting at the edge of the market and no
doubt looking forlorn.
"I have our furs," he said. "It became easier to negotiate once it was clear
I was partnered with a madman. Do you wish to tell me why you went
mad, or was that merely a show to get us a better price?"
"We all have our own faeries to chase," I said. "I spotted mine."*

*T*he events taking place on the television screen were as
follows: a man stood near the edge of a fence next to a
redheaded woman and a blonde woman. The blonde—Clara,
although the name is not apparent from the video—wore army
fatigues, while the redhead and the man both had on the sort of
one-piece jumpsuits issued to prisoners.

I'm the man in the jumpsuit. The redhead is someone who has
no doubt had hundreds of names, but for convenience sake I've
been calling her Eve. In the video I can be seen speaking to Eve as
Clara runs up, carrying a rifle. Just before that, a man named
Robert Grindel was shot—by Clara— and carried off under a hail
of gunfire by his bulletproof demon bodyguard.

When Clara arrives she draws my focus, and for a few
seconds neither of us is looking at Eve.

Eve then turns and walks away.

I hit pause at that point, a moment before everything on the
video stopped making sense altogether. I knew this because I'd
looked at the footage a thousand times, and a thousand times
through it I still couldn't understand what was happening.

"What are you watching?" Mirella asked. She was staring out
the window, probably wondering if I'd brought a movie and if it
was any good.

"It's difficult to explain," I said.

We were 35,000 feet in the air on board a private jet I own, and let me just say if you have a lot of places to go and the money to spare you should definitely get one of these for yourself.

"I've been looking at cloud formations for half an hour. Why don't you show me and not bother with the explanation? Maybe I can figure it out?"

"Sure. It's more interesting than clouds."

This is something I probably wouldn't have said not so long ago, when flying was new to me. Then, the idea of looking from the sky down was astonishing.

She walked over and sat next to me on the couch.

Of course I have a couch on my plane. I also have a big TV and a wet bar, and the couch opens into a bed. This is a great time to be obscenely wealthy, I'm telling you.

I backed up the video and explained to Mirella who everyone was, in broad terms, then let it play.

"Okay, now watch right here," I said, once we reached the point where I had previously hit pause. On the screen, Eve has turned away from me and Clara once more, and as happened every other time I watched this video, she simply vanishes.

Mirella blinked a couple of times then said, "It's a special effect."

"If I wasn't one of the people in the scene, I'd agree with you."

"Wait, so this is real?"

"It's real. She really did vanish, and I really don't know how she did it."

"Play it again."

I did, and I slowed it down for her.

In the video, Eve notes that nobody is looking, turns around, takes three steps toward the fence, and then she just isn't there anymore.

"I still don't believe it," Mirella said. "It doesn't even look like a *good* special effect."

"What do you mean?"

"Give me the remote."

I handed it over. She played with it for a few minutes before figuring out how to get it to move in super-slow motion. This was something I never tried because I didn't know there was such a thing as super-slow motion.

We watched the events play out once again, only now it took a tremendously long time. Finally, Mirella saw what she was looking for and paused it.

"There," she said.

She'd frozen the image at the very instant Eve disappeared from the camera.

"She's ... bigger," I said.

"Yes, that's what I mean. It's a terrible effect."

"Except it isn't an effect."

"As you say."

She started it up again and we watched as Eve expanded until she was no longer visible. It was like watching a balloon stretch so thin it becomes transparent, as if the parts that made up the person of Eve decided they wanted to be further apart from each other, until there was nothing left. I might have considered the possibility I was actually seeing a person being destroyed by some sort of invisible weapon, except I had seen Eve since the day this happened.

More to the point, I had been looking for Eve off and on for a solid ten thousand years. She was the only person I knew who was at least as old as I am, and according to her she's actually older. But she has a trick I don't have, which is why every time I thought I had finally found her she ended up eluding me. It was the trick I was watching her perform on video now, and since I knew she had been doing this for a very long time, I also knew there was no mechanism involved. It was just her, somehow vanishing into the wind.

Mirella backed up the video and we watched it a few more times.

"If I could observe, you are clearly some sort of prisoner in this video. As is this vanishing woman."

"That's true. This was filmed the night we both escaped. My escape wasn't as classy as hers, though. I had to use the front gates."

I also had to orchestrate the murder of a whole lot of people, but I don't really feel all that bad about that because I didn't much like any of them, except for one or two of the scientists. Plus the vampire who did the actual killing was an old friend, and it was really good to see her.

"Would you like to explain how a wealthy man such as your-self ended up in a situation such as this?"

"I think maybe another time," I said. "It's a long story and you're unlikely to believe a significant portion of it."

She rolled her eyes. "You have too many secrets, Mr. Justinian."

"That's not true. I have two or three secrets, but they are really good ones."

We watched it over again. Super-slow motion is strangely hypnotic. I resolved to watch more movies in this mode in the future.

"Where is this shot from?" Mirella asked.

"A security camera on a building nearby."

I didn't know footage of what happened that night existed until the disc showed up in my mail about eight months ago. It had no return address and no note, but I have a friend in the FBI who is in the habit of sending me copies of things the govern-ment might have on me, and this certainly looked like one of those things. This was, hopefully, the only camera angle in which I could be identified because an awful lot of awful things happened that evening that I would rather not be connected to. I could ask the sender, but since he works for a government I don't want to notice me, we try to keep out of touch except in emer-gencies.

Mirella handed back the remote. "You are going to be a difficult man to guard. I can tell this already."

"Why is that?"

"Secrets will either get you killed, or they will get me killed, and I am not happy with either possibility."

~

The jet was heading for Istanbul, which is not exactly a quick pond-skip from New York, so I was glad to have the couch and the bar, and the privacy of my own plane in general. It also obviated any need I would have had to worry about the blades hidden on my bodyguard's person, as we didn't have to pass through any metal detectors first, and nobody's suitcase had to get X-rayed. Likewise, Customs is much less of a problem when you own your own jet.

I even have a phone on the plane. I know, you're thinking *yes, of course I do,* but that's because you're used to having a phone everywhere. But for most of my life communication was defined by the speed with which it could be delivered. If a war was over, say, we had to rely on someone going from wherever the war ended to wherever we were to tell us it was over. Now if I need to talk to someone I can summon their voice on a little square. That I can do it while also traveling at ridiculous speeds on the wrong side of the clouds is the sort of thing that makes an immortal man stop and wonder how all this happened so quickly.

Anyway, I mention the phone because about a half an hour after my knife-wielding bodyguard dozed off in her reclining chair it started to ring. I stumbled across the room—stumbled because of the bourbon I'd been drinking, not because the plane was unsteady—and sat down at the desk and answered it.

It took a few seconds to register what the man on the other end of the line was saying. He worked for the company that monitors the electronic security for my house, but I barely remembered even having a security system. It came with the place, and most of the time I left it off when I wasn't there, just because Iza had a tendency to trigger it. But she was sleeping in a pressurized box under the desk—the pressure change from the plane ride hurts her ears—so I'd activated the system on my way out.

"Are you saying there's been a break-in?" I asked for I think the second or third time.

"No sir," said the man whose name was either Randolph or possibly Joseph. Something with a *–ph* in it, I was pretty sure. "That is, we don't believe your home has been breached physically."

"Then I'm afraid I don't understand."

"What I'm saying is, someone ... communicated with your security software."

"Communicated?"

"Transmitted into, I guess."

"No, that isn't any better."

Randolph/Joseph sighed. "Maybe I can just send it to you?"

"Send me what?"

"It's a still image. We don't know what it means."

"I've been hacked. Someone hacked my security cameras and inserted a photo."

"Yes, now you're understanding."

"I refilled my drink, I think that helped. Why don't you send me the image?"

"Yes, I can do that."

I dictated an e-mail address and opened the laptop next to the phone. I barely knew how to use the laptop, but I knew how to turn it on and how to check my e-mail from it, and that was all I needed most of the time. Tchekhy had given it to me, so it could probably hack the Pentagon. I'm sure I was underutilizing it terribly.

In a few minutes I managed to open the e-mail from the security person—according to his address his name was actually Larry, so I was pretty far off, it turns out—and download the picture.

I got back on the line. "You're saying this photo was ... where again?"

"It was buried in the online memory for one of the security cameras. We think it was just inserted recently. Every ten seconds this image replaced the camera's footage, for only about an eighth of a second. I've asked around and truthfully none of us has ever seen anything like this. We're not even sure how it could have been done remotely, if it was done remotely at all."

"But there's no video evidence of anyone in the house."

"No sir."

"Which camera?"

"The study. Why?"

"No reason, just curious."

The picture being displayed for an eighth of a second every ten seconds on the camera in my study was a picture of me, bald and wearing a red parka. It was likely the only verifiable photograph of my face to ever make it onto the Internet, which meant that in theory anybody could have pulled it down from there at one time or another. It was my own fault, really, since I was the one who put it online.

"Sir, do you want us to send someone around to check out the property?"

The property is on an island off the coast of Seattle. It was tremendously unlikely anybody had made it all the way out there to breach one camera and insert a prank photo, only to not be detected by any other security measure. Sending someone out to check on the integrity of the island seemed like overkill.

"No, I'm sure it's fine," I said. "Let me know if any other images pop up, though, huh?"

"Yes sir."

He hung up and left me with my mystery photo. I stared at it for a few minutes before deciding I had no idea what was going on and clicked the e-mail box to close it. That was when things really went wacky.

The mail messenger asked if I wanted to save the image before closing, and I said yes because that seemed like what the machine wanted me to say. It even highlighted *yes* to be helpful. But as soon as I did that the laptop jumped to life.

Saving the photo caused something else in the computer to activate, or ... whatever goes on in these devices, and suddenly the picture took up the whole screen. Then just as suddenly the photo began to melt away and when it did this it left behind a message.

You are being watched.
Move your loved ones to safety and then meet me. I am with father.
Trust nobody.
---T

Tchekhy, it seemed, was alive and well.

CHAPTER 6

"Understand that if the day comes where I have to flee to survive or fight by your side in the face of certain death, I cannot guarantee the latter?" I said.
"You must not keep many friends," Hsu said, accepting my extended hand. "And yes, I accept this condition. I don't believe in certain death."

I don't really have loved ones.

I guess that's not entirely true. I mean, I do have people I care about, whose lives I would feel badly about shortening whether through some direct action of mine or indirectly because of me. It's bound to happen from time to time, because I have to interact with people or I go crazy—I tried the hermit thing once, it wasn't for me—and interaction can have consequences. Every hundred years or so I become involved in circumstances that could end with me dead, and that also tends to put the people around me at risk.

But *loved ones* is really a term reserved for family, and it's fair to say I don't have a family of my own, or even people I could readily identify as relatives. Tchekhy sort of knows this, but he also knows I have in the past gone out of my way to avenge someone whose death I felt responsible for, and to put myself in harm's way to prevent other people from being hurt, and he knows this because I put myself at risk *for* him on one occasion.

Anyway, it took me about ten minutes to understand what happened on my laptop. Since Tchekhy was the one who'd given it to me, I had to think there was something installed on it that could decode a specific encrypted message, and that this message was attached to the photograph somehow, so when I moved it from wherever it lives when it's sitting in an e-mail box to wherever it goes when I agreed to save it, the code was recognized and unlocked.

Incidentally, while I know next to nothing about computers I know a great deal about encryption, because people have been trying to send coded messages for as long as there has been written language. Actually, secret communication was why written language was invented in the first place.

The question was what to do with the message. The clear implication was that somebody planned to use the people I cared about against me in some way, but the effectiveness of such a plan required that they know who those people are, and that those people might be important enough to get me to do something I wouldn't otherwise be willing to do.

I didn't feel like notifying every last person I could think of that they needed to go hide in a panic room until further notice, not when I didn't even know why I was telling them to do that yet. Really, about the only person who came to mind as soon as I read *loved ones* was Clara, and she was probably the safest one on my mental list who wasn't a three hundred-year-old vampire.

Clara was currently living somewhere in the Northern Italian countryside—I didn't have the exact address but I could get it with a phone call—on a large private estate. She had her own security detail, in part because she already knows how dangerous it can be to know me, and in part because she happens to be immortal. There are some people in this world who would care about that last part very much if they ever found out.

Despite Iza's repeated insistence that we go see her, I had been keeping my distance since Clara left, which was something like seven years ago. I knew about the security and the estate because I wanted to make sure she was okay, and because maybe I didn't want to lose track of the only other immortal around who can't vanish on command.

That said, because she is like me, she also can't be poisoned and she can't get sick. So if you throw that in with the security detail and the private estate and her personal wealth, she was easily the safest person on any list I might wish to make—safer, certainly, than the Russian computer hacker who told me to warn everyone.

Other than Clara, there was Eloise, the aforementioned vampire who can really take care of herself just fine. There was Mike Lycos, the FBI agent who sent me the disc, and who is also a werewolf and thus probably not at great risk. There was Ariadne, who last I checked was working for the Greek government and was high enough up the political ladder to have her own security. There was another vampire in Boston I was pretty sure nobody could connect me to at this point, an oracle in California who likewise had hardly any connection to me, an iffrit I wouldn't mind seeing dead, a satyr or two that nobody in their right minds would mess with, Heintz, and Iza.

Oh, and Eve. Good luck to them if they want to try and catch her.

I wanted to call Clara and warn her. She knew Tchekhy, so there was a decent chance she'd recognize that my call was due to the gravity of the situation and not for some other silly reason like I missed her and needed an excuse to get her on the phone. But I was nearly positive that's how it would look if I tried. So instead, I made arrangements to visit Tchekhy's father.

The only good thing about getting the message when I did was that I was already crossing the Atlantic. It would have been even better if Tchekhy's father had been buried in Istanbul, but the gravesite was in Tbilisi, Georgia, which was a much less convenient location.

Tchekhy's father passed back when you had to make plans to avoid involving yourself in the Soviet Union whenever you could. But since one side of the family was from Georgia—which was only ever barely a part of the USSR as a whole—getting him a plot in an old Armenian burial place there was feasible, and actually preferable, as I believe the kind of Christianity his family practices is Greek Orthodox.

I didn't ask why it mattered where he was buried—for most of the time I knew him he lived in the US and that seemed like a perfectly good final resting place—but I assume there was some sort of familial/sentimental thing going on.

I am not super-understanding about death, I'm afraid. I've seen more of it than anybody, and am so used to it I have to be careful not to say something insensitive.

It took most of the morning to alter our flight plans from Istanbul to Tbilisi, and another half day to make the necessary arrangements on the ground. I also had to get Heintz to contact the museum in Istanbul to ask them to postpone for me. He would probably have to agree to donate more money to put the collection on hold until I got there, but it was worth it if what I was looking for was there. If it wasn't, well, I'd thrown a lot of money away already and I still had plenty left.

I have a long history with Tbilisi and with Georgia, enough that I have to remind myself not to call them Tiflis and Iberia. Tbilisi is right in the middle of a major trade route or two, so nearly every time I traveled east I stopped there. Sometimes I even liked it better than Constantinople, which still had a certain Roman arrogance to it that was wearisome.

When we left our very modern airplane and took a hired car to Kala, the oldest part of the city, it was like time traveling.

"You can afford the nicest hotel, and you pick the oldest one instead," Mirella said, watching the buildings become older and less dependent on sound architecture and suffering more obviously from the consequences of gravity.

"Modern hotels are all modern in the same way," I said. "Old hotels are unique."

"What if they are unique in a way that doesn't include hot water?"

"There's always that risk, yes."

It was going to be hard to travel with someone who didn't know how old I was. I just wasn't sure yet how she was going to take that information. But the more questions she asked the harder it was going to be to satisfy her curiosity. Not that I wasn't enjoying her curiosity.

There was almost nothing left in Tbilisi to remind me of the city I used to market my goods in—even in Kala the buildings are only about two hundred years old—so it wasn't all that depressing, really. Traditionally I visit a place again after a while away and I'm just devastated by what's changed, but I already went through that when I was in Tbilisi for the funeral. Between that trip and my previous visit the entire city had been burned to the ground by the Turks, and it had been a beautiful place that was burned to the ground. It's beautiful now, mind you, but a slightly more modern (to me) beautiful. It's not as bad for me as a place like Athens, say, which still has pieces of things standing that I remember being built.

Anyway we checked into a room large enough so it didn't feel weird sharing it with my attractive female bodyguard, and after waking up a very hungry pixie the three of us went out and found some more appropriate clothing for Mirella.

It goes without saying that Tchekhy was not actually sitting at his father's grave waiting for me. He'd likely not even gone near the grave himself since arriving in Tbilisi, and instead had sent someone he could trust. He *might* have had somebody watching it, but it was much more likely he left something there for me to find. I wasn't about to walk to the gravesite myself either, not without having a better idea of what was going on. I could send Iza, as pixies make for excellent recon solutions under most circumstances, but I wasn't sure if she was clever enough to recognize a dead drop when she saw one.

Mirella was, but she looked too much like an American tourist and/or a ninja assassin depending on the outfit, so we picked up some local clothes for her.

"I look awful in this," she said grumpily, emerging from the bathroom dressed in a colorful skirt and loose cotton blouse, with sandals. She didn't look awful in it—I sincerely doubted there was anything she could look awful in—but she did look a little bit more like a resident.

"You look fine," I insisted. "Iza?"

"Look fine," she agreed between bites of mushroom. Iza was still getting over the fact that Clara was not actually located in New York, and was probably still a little angry with me even though I had no control over this.

"I am going to burn these as soon as this is over," Mirella said.

"If you want. Just don't do it on the airplane."

She grumped back into the bathroom and I thought again about what I was asking her to do and why it was that I trusted her enough to involve her at all.

Tchekhy's message—which I had not shared with her—said to trust nobody, and that presumably included Heintz, and by extension the person he hired to keep an eye on my back. But while I had known Heintz for a while, I didn't have any trouble with the idea that I shouldn't trust him. Mirella I had known for less than a week and I was already getting her involved in a game of espionage.

"Hey, who pays you?" I asked her through the door. Possibly because the question was so peculiar, she opened the door again. She had unbuttoned the blouse already, intending to try on another set of clothes. We'd bought four outfits, as I was under the mistaken impression that the shopping was something she was enjoying. She still had on a bra underneath so this wasn't nearly as exciting as it could have been.

"I'm paid by the security firm. You know that."

"Yes, but how does it work exactly?"

"Your Mr. Heintz pays my firm, and my firm pays me. I'm well compensated, if that's your concern. The clothing isn't so bad that I'm going to file for hazard pay."

"You *do* like the clothes."

"I didn't say that."

She closed the door again.

"All right, but let's say I wanted to hire you directly, how would I do that?" I asked through the door.

"I thought you weren't in any real danger."

"I'm not."

"Good, because if I have this correctly you're sending me to meet with the man who shot at you, and I'm going to have nothing to protect me but itchy cotton."

"You'll have knives on you, don't even pretend you won't."

She opened the door again and emerged looking better than she had in the last outfit by a wide margin. The blouse was bright yellow and the skirt was a mix of light blue and green. Summer colors. She had her hair pulled back, which made her European ancestry pop out through her cheekbones.

"This isn't so bad," she decided. "I'm going to take the difficulty you're having forming words right now to mean you agree with me. Now, why do you ask?"

"I'd be more comfortable paying you directly, that's all."

"That's not all. You're keeping secrets again. But all right. Do you mean pay the security firm directly rather than through your banker friend?"

"No, just pay you directly myself."

"This arrangement isn't unheard of. But let me repeat myself. I'm very well compensated."

"I understand. How about after this is over you make a couple of phone calls, and I'll put a few million into an account for you, and we'll go from there?"

"A few ..." She fixed me with a look that was both devastating and a little scary. I decided to be turned on by it, even though I probably should have been thinking about defending myself. "You understand my services don't include *that,* no matter what you want to pay me."

"It's not like that."

"You take me off to this nice city and dress me up, pretend you have an important job for me to do ..."

"I swear."

"Because if it turns out you're some kind of insane kinky lunatic ..."

"Really. Ask Iza."

"The naked pixie would know from kink."

"Oh, just make the calls."

She huffed back into the bathroom and closed the door.

"You're going to explain yourself one day," she said after a minute or two.

"What do you want explained?"

"Today? Today I want to know why you're the only wealthy man on Earth who legitimately doesn't care about money."

"I have enough not to care all that much about it. Isn't that normal?"

She emerged wearing pieces of the second outfit mixed with elements of a third outfit. The combination made her look positively dowdy.

"I liked it better a minute ago," I said.

"You want me to not be memorable, so this will do. And no. It's not normal. Rich people care more about money than poor people do. You spend money like a man with no heirs and six months to live."

"Well, you're half right."

~

Mirella visited the grave the following morning, armed with a smartphone, a pixie, and for all I know two-dozen blades. It didn't take long before I received news from her in the form of a total lack of news.

"There's nothing here," she said over the aforementioned smartphone. I'd given her the precise location of the headstone from memory, and so long as there had been no significant geographic upheaval in the interim, I expected the directions to be accurate. And of course she knew what name to look for, even though the writing was in Cyrillic.

I had also started to tell her not to go directly to the grave, but to wander around and not spend too much time examining the headstone, and all of the other things you tell someone committing espionage in your stead. But it was quickly apparent that in offering such instruction I was insulting her gravely, so I stopped.

"No markings or notes or packages?" I asked.

"No. I'm not stupid. I looked for those things. There's nothing chalked on the stone either, and the only newly upturned dirt was upturned to plant flowers. I had your pixie helping and she was also unable to find anything."

"Yes, but Iza thinks you're talking to your hand right now," I said. "Go back to the grave and take a picture of it for me."

"There's nothing there."

"I believe you. Take a picture and send it to me anyway."

Ten minutes later I had three pictures from different angles around the grave. I was able to confirm that she was in fact looking at the correct stone, and beyond that I saw exactly the same nothing she did.

The flowers looked fresh, though.

"Are there flowers on the other grave sites?" I asked.

"Some, yes. They all look like they were put in at around the same time."

I looked at the flowers again. They didn't look like anything special: orange lilies, a white flower I think was called a Siberian something, and a yellow flower that looked sort of familiar.

I was about to tell Mirella to get a close-up of the yellow flowers when I remembered I could zoom in on the photo on the phone. I'm surprised the modern age hasn't caused my head to explode yet.

"It's the yellow flower," I said after looking at them more closely.

"What is the yellow flower?"

"The message."

"That's a terrible message."

"It's probably attached to the stem or the root."

"And you know this how?"

"It's not a local flower," I said, which was true but it wasn't why. The name of the yellow flower was Immortelle. I wasn't prepared to explain to Mirella why that was significant.

"So now you'd like me to go to the gravesite of the father of a man who we know has a high-powered rifle and dig up the flowers planted there in memory of the deceased, in the middle of a sunny day in a crowded public cemetery?"

"Yes, please. You can plant the flower again after you've found whatever's attached to it."

"I'm going to hell for this."

"We can keep each other company there."

Another few minutes passed before I heard from her again.

"You're doing this yourself next time," she complained. "I'm covered in dirt and an old man shouted at me in a language I'm unfamiliar with. I nearly slit his throat just to shut him up. And your pixie won't stop buzzing around my head like she's on fire."

"But you have something."

"I have something. There was a small waterproof packet tied to a string on the stem of one of the flowers. Would you like me to open it?"

"Please."

A short pause. "Honestly, you boys with your games."

"What is it?"

"It's a cell phone. He couldn't just call you?"

"No," I said. "And I don't think that's an ordinary phone."

"Enh, all right. I'll bring you your toy."

"Thank you. But don't come directly."

"Why not?"

"If Iza is buzzing around like that it means you're being followed."

~

It was three hours before Mirella made it back to the hotel room, with Iza circling around behind her.

"We are no longer being followed," Mirella said. This caused Iza to buzz about faster. "The pixie disagrees."

I had been sitting at the window with the drapes drawn, peeking through the thin curtain at the buildings around us to see who was looking back at me. I didn't identify any kind of pattern in the window occupants, but absence of evidence isn't evidence of absence. I wasn't sure what to think.

Because we were in a terribly old building we were dealing with thick old walls that were not soundproof in any technologically modern sense, but which were heavy-duty enough to make it unlikely anybody in one of the rooms next to us could press up a glass on the wall—or whatever today's equivalent would be—and listen in effectively. We had no adjoining doors either.

But again, that didn't mean nobody was listening. It just meant I didn't know how they were doing it.

"What did you see, Iza?"

"Men," she said.

"How many?"

"Lots."

Talking to a pixie is an unnerving experience sometimes. I'm mostly used to it, but I imagine it looked a lot like I was talking to a spirit or something because one only ever addresses the air formerly occupied by the being one is addressing. And her words tended to come from every direction at once.

"This is absurd," Mirella said. "I know how to shake a tail."

"I'm sure you do. Iza, are they here in the hotel?"

"Uh-huh. Waited."

"They waited for you to come back?"

"Waited."

"Well, that's your explanation," I said to my increasingly aggravated bodyguard.

"That's no explanation."

"You may very well have successfully lost whoever was following you at the cemetery, but they weren't tracking you because of Tchekhy, they were tracking you because of me. They must have been here at the hotel already."

She shook her head and took a turn at the window. It's one of those things people do when they find out they're being followed, as if a sneak peek through a curtain will be miraculously illuminating. "I'm very good at what I do, Mr. Justinian. If we were being followed from the airport I'd have known it from the airport." She closed the curtain. "Paranoia is something new for you. Everything you've done to this point has been loud and attention getting. You don't act like someone who cares about any of this."

"I didn't, but now I do. Did you bring the phone?"

"Of course I did." She pulled the device from her pocket and handed it to me. "Provided it's actually a phone at all."

"It is."

"It has no key pad."

The device in question was a flip phone with a single button and a small screen. It looked like the sort of futuristic device someone in the 1960s would make in anticipation of what this kind of technology would eventually look like.

"If you want to know why I'm suddenly acting paranoid, this is why," I sort of half-explained. "If he's using this, we have a serious problem."

Mirella stared at me levelly with a cold expression I was growing used to and starting to like a bit more than I probably should have. "You are not going to explain this in a way that will make sense, are you?"

"Not right now, no."

"Fine. I'm going to go wash this city off of me."

She marched to the shower, which was actually perfect because I needed all the background noise I could get before using the phone.

I flipped it open.

A little while ago, a man named Robert Grindel put a bounty on me. The men—and other creatures—he hired all received a phone like the one in my hand. According to Tchekhy, the phones used an advanced form of encryption that was essentially unbreakable. So in a way it actually *was* a futuristic device, in the sense that it was the only truly secure electronic communication method in the world. That I was aware of.

They were also supposedly one-use-only devices, and one of the two I'd given to my Russian friend had already been used. But he'd had a long time to fiddle with them.

I hit the button and waited. It didn't ring. Instead I heard a series of clicks, and then a familiar voice.

"Who is the girl?" Tchekhy asked without preamble.

"It's good to hear from you, too."

"Yes, yes. Who is the girl?"

"My personal bodyguard."

"I told you to trust no one, and you send this girl and your insect to the drop site. I should hang up and leave you to your fate."

"Oh come on, that's not fair. You know better than anyone that was the safest play. Now what's the problem?"

"Right now my problem is that you are not listening to my advice."

I never heard him so agitated before. Historically, I'm the one upset about something and he's the person I call if I need to calm down and figure out what the hell just happened. He once spent a very patient hour on the phone with me to explain how a DVR worked.

"I trust her," I said. "She's okay."

He laughed. "Yes, because you putting your trust in a pretty girl is something we have learned to rely upon as sound practice."

"That is so unfair I don't even know where to begin."

"Very well, we will put it aside for now. Tell me how many are watching you?"

"I don't know. Iza seems to think a lot are, but she still thinks cars are a kind of animal. She might have been noticing people whose interest doesn't extend beyond the fact that we look like Westerners."

"But you do not think so."

"I don't. I think she's probably right."

"We are going to assume they are listening to you right now."

"But they can't hear us on these phones, right?"

"They can't hear me, but assuming there are devices in the room, they can hear your responses perfectly well."

I'd thought of this already, actually, which was why I hadn't said his name aloud.

"We need to speak face-to-face," he said, "in a location I can control."

"Where?"

"I'm in the city. Can you follow instructions without repeating them or writing them down?"

Now he was just being mean. "Go ahead," I said.

"All right. Here is what you do. Step one, don't bring the girl."

CHAPTER 7

"I don't understand how he can know so much about language and philosophy and still manage to be so stupid," Hsu said after a particularly frustrating evening, in reference to our friend Xuangang.
"He never looked up from his books," I said. "It's hard to see what's happening around you if you aren't looking."

When I first heard of it, the fortress was called Shuris-Tsihe. It's called Narikala now, and it's no longer much of a fortress. It's more like a series of walls and a couple of towers staring down at Tbilisi from atop a distant hill.

Shuris-Tsihe occasionally defended the city when such a thing was necessary, but more often housed the soldiers who could exit the fortress and defend the city, as that was a much more practical function. (Fixed battlements have their uses, but are limited by a total lack of mobility. Armies can go around them, in other words. Like the French Maginot Line, they are only as useful as the enemy is uncreative.)

Tbilisi rested along a couple of profitable trade routes: By land it connected the Southern silk roads with everything north of the Caucasus, and by sea everything coming through Constantinople across the Black Sea and headed eastward. This meant it had to be defended somewhat often because there was money to be made there, and influence to be applied, and power to be used.

Tbilisi's problem, historically, was a microcosm of everything wrong with the middle of the European/Asian theater for about the last two thousand years. Geographic access meant profitability, but profit led to envy. Access also meant vulnerability, so anyone with a half-decent army and the element of surprise stood a chance of taking a city or two here and there. Constantinople was a rare exception because its location was uniquely accessible and also nearly impregnable thanks to some very impressively high walls and an extremely defendable port. And it was still sacked two or three times.

This is really why the United States and Japan are so economically strong. I'm not even kidding. The only way Japan is getting taken by an invading army is if that army is also Godzilla, and the United States is never going to see a serious threat from Mexico or Canada. Whereas a country like Turkey or Uzbekistan or Poland can wake up one day and find one of its neighbors has gotten all warlike and suddenly they're getting occupied or renamed. And this used to happen every week in the Middle Ages, for about a thousand years.

I'd never been in the fortress before, which is sort of amazing considering it's the oldest thing in the region that isn't me. But most of the time when I was in Tbilisi I was down in the city either stopping to trade or passing through with goods, and if doing that ever landed me in the fortress it would have meant I had done something terribly wrong. So I was glad the first time I saw it up close was when Tchekhy directed me to the top of one of the towers.

There were some nice public walking paths that led from the city to the historic sites like Narikala, and I didn't take any of them, which was really too bad because finding a decent pair of hiking boots had proven impossible, and that was what I needed.

Buying new clothes had been the first step. Just like Mirella, I had to try and go native, and that meant changing all of my clothing from head to toe, including my shoes. Anything less than that would have been unacceptable, not just because the possibility existed that I might be recognized because of my footwear, but because electronic tracking devices are real things that exist somewhere. This being true, Tchekhy assumed they were definitely attached to my person and had to be shed before I could do anything else.

Getting out of the hotel room without anybody knowing I'd left was challenging, too, because even if I dressed in different clothing it wasn't going to be hard figuring out who I was if I was the only guy entering or leaving the room. We were also several floors up with no fire escape, so there was really only one way in or out.

But it turns out if you order enough food from room service —and I always stay in hotels with room service because people bringing food to your bedroom is really the best thing about hotels, and don't let anyone tell you otherwise—they send a big rolling cart, and you can ask them to leave it if you're nice enough about it. And if you order all that food right when the kitchen closes you can keep the cart all night.

So at around six the next morning, Mirella pushed the cart to the elevator, took it down a couple of flights, and left it in a hallway. She then returned to the room and complained loudly to me about having to do that. She had to yell because that was the only way she could be heard over the shower that I was surely standing in at the time. Then she closed the hotel room door.

An hour later a staff member found the strangely heavy cart in the hallway and wheeled it down to the kitchen, and that's when I got out and left the building through the staff entrance.

For the next three hours I wandered the streets of Tbilisi,

picking up different bits of clothing along the way while speaking half-decent Georgian—spending lari instead of US dollars—and doing everything I could to shake anybody who might still be following. Then I took to the hillside and climbed up to the fortress the hard way: through the woods. It was easily the most unpleasant way to get there, but I'm used to walking through forests so it wasn't as awful as it could have been. And it was a decent way to guarantee nobody was following on foot.

The section I'd been directed to find was one that was closed off due to safety concerns. I was inclined to trust the warning signs, since even the parts of the place that were considered safe looked like they were a loud sneeze away from collapsing. As I stepped over the low barricade and climbed the narrow steps to a particularly alarming tower, I could only hope my friend knew more about the stability of the place than whoever owned the signs did.

The view was really nice. I was alone for more than an hour, looking at the city and wondering what it must have been like for one of the caliph's soldiers to stand in that spot waiting for an attack that probably never came. The fortress was impregnable for the time, but you didn't have to attack the fortress to win the city so it didn't matter much. In the end, it was an earthquake that took down Narikala, not an army.

"You were not followed," Tchekhy said, stepping beside me. I'd heard him coming, and felt confident that he was not in a mood to push me off the edge. Otherwise I might have stepped away before he got that close.

"That's not a question."

"No, it is a statement. I watched you climb, and nobody climbed after you."

"I could have told you that."

"Yes, well." He clapped me on the shoulder. "Perhaps on another day we will rely upon *your* instinctual risk assessment skills. Come."

I followed him down a flight of steps and up a second flight until we were in a small space that would have been for archers if we were under siege and people still used arrows for defensive purposes. I kind of miss those days, if only because an arrow in flight is both beautiful and fairly easy to get out of the way of if you're looking for it. A hail of gunfire is much harder to evade and not nearly as picturesque. Noisier, too.

Tchekhy had two chairs set up for us next to a cooler. He sat himself down slowly in one of the chairs, which was alarming to witness, honestly. He had never been a small man, but he always had a certain nimbleness to his movements. That agility was largely absent now, and I didn't know if that was due to age or infirmity or some combination of the two. But this was a man I'd known since he was a child, so no matter what, he was going to appear much older than he should be, to me.

He opened the cooler and pulled out two beers, extending one to me, which I took while taking the other chair.

"Here we have privacy," he said.

"We had a view before."

"We did, yes. But if we can see, so we can be seen. And I do not want to be seen."

"Are we worrying about satellites right now?"

"We are worrying about everything. Satellites, missiles directed by satellites, eavesdropping equipment deployed by drones. All is on the table right now."

"So we're going full-on paranoid. Good to know. I thought you were dead, by the way."

He laughed. "No you did not."

"I did, for like an hour."

"Then you had started drinking earlier in the day than usual, my friend. I was concerned I was being too obvious."

I had already finished my first beer and was reaching for a second. I find myself drinking more heavily around Tchekhy than just about any other human, because almost without fail he has something to say that makes me want to get very drunk very quickly. I've often wondered if he had this effect on everyone, or just me.

"So what happened?" I asked.

"With the shop?"

"Yes, start there."

"Actually, it begins earlier."

"Super. Begin wherever it begins. We have some time, right? Unless this place is about to collapse around us."

"No, the *Do Not Enter* signs are mine. This room might outlive you. And we have all the time we need unless one of my compatriots below alerts me otherwise."

"Or until the beer runs out."

"Yes," he said, taking a long sip of his own. "I am embarrassed to say this story begins with my getting hacked."

I blinked emphatically. "I'm sorry, *you* got hacked?"

I don't know very much about computers, and I probably never will, but what I do know is that my Russian friend is one of those people everyone thinks probably exists out there in the world, but nobody expects to actually meet because what they do is too fantastic.

It's true that most everything nowadays runs on computers, and it's also true that there are people out there living off this fact, and it's further true that Tchekhy is one such person. It's likely he hasn't earned an honest income his entire life, paid a bill for anything, or put down a single penny for taxes in any country. I don't believe that legally he even exists.

He doesn't get hacked, because he's the guy you hire to do that job.

"*Da.* I was as surprised as you."

"Who was it?"

He shrugged. "I thought I knew all the people who were potentially capable of doing such a thing, but over the last few weeks I have concluded only that it was none of them."

"The last few weeks?"

"This was some time ago. I noticed a modest energy spike in a subroutine on one of my servers and decided to figure out what was causing it. It was so small it could have been a broken code or a shorted wire, so I was surprised to discover it was neither of those things—someone had snuck a self-propagating program into my hard drive."

"You know I don't understand any of this, right?" I said, grabbing beer number three.

"I will put it more simply. A Trojan horse was inserted into my computer, and the Trojans inside were searching for information in my files, bundling what they found, and transmitting it in small packets."

"I'm sorry if you think that was simpler."

I knew the Trojans and actually fought in that war, so while he might have imagined this was an analogy that would work for me, all I could picture were tiny men poking a circuit board with a sharp stick. It was not a useful image.

"I isolated them as soon as they were discovered, so they could still collect data but not transmit. I had to find out what they were looking for before I destroyed them. What I learned was that they were looking for you."

"The tiny Trojans were."

"In this scenario, yes."

This didn't seem like a huge deal to me. "I'm not that hard to find right now."

"Yes, you are living a very noisy existence of late, I have noticed. We will talk about this presently, but first you should know that this rogue program did not find anything important— some of your past IDs, but not much else. I would say this is because I have purged records on you, but truthfully I had very little to purge. You have no parentage or national origin that anybody would recognize, so anyone looking into my files to figure out who you really are would be stymied most thoroughly. You are not in any real legal sense a person."

"So this isn't why you torched the shop?"

"It is the beginning of the why."

Tchekhy took a deep breath and another beer and fidgeted in his seat as if he was suddenly uncomfortable, and maybe that was exactly correct.

"I had to destroy the shop because of the dead man inside," he said finally.

"Oh. Well, that's a good reason."

"I thought so, yes."

"Who was this man?"

"I do not truly know. It was the second time he had appeared. The first time he presented an above-average counterfeit of a government identification badge that claimed he was FBI."

"FBI? Yeah, it probably was a counterfeit."

"I know it was because I examined it, but why do you say this?"

"I have a guy in the Bureau I can trust. I know you're about to remind me not to trust anybody, but I have good reason. If the Feds were looking for me again he'd have tipped me off."

"Well this man, whoever he was, knew a good deal more about *me* than I was fully comfortable with, but he attempted to use that information primarily as leverage to obtain details about you that were not readily evident from any of my files."

"What sort of things?"

"The usual. What is your real name, where do you come from, where does your money come from? Who is your family? He wanted to know not only who you are, but how to get at you. I, of course, did not answer."

"Why didn't you tell me this was happening?" I asked. "When it was happening, I mean?"

"I did not know who he was or what he represented, and I further did not know what he already knew about you. It seemed likely the entire point of his showing up and saying these things was to inspire me to contact you. So I did not do this."

"There are less direct ways to reach me. I think you already proved that."

"*Da,* but I thought I could unearth who he truly was first. I imagined if it were knowable, I had the tools to know it. I was mistaken. I knew nothing more about him when he returned a second time than I had when he first visited. This was the same morning you came to see me, and he turned up because you were in New York."

"He knew? Nobody knew. It was a last minute trip."

"But as you say, you are not difficult to find right now. You are an elephant in the tall grass, Efgeniy. You understand I knew you were in town within hours of your arrival, yes?"

"But you have people."

"I have one or two, but I was not camping out at the airport in anticipation. You say nobody knew you were in New York, but you have a flight crew on that plane of yours, and you landed at an airport with staff, and you were driven in cars steered by other people, and you checked into a hotel staffed by dozens upon dozens more. Everything you are doing right now creates a ripple. Why is this?"

"I'm working on a project."

"Does this project involve being taken hostage for a ransom? Or attracting the attention of some local dictator?"

"No, it involves being obviously rich and using those riches to gain access to places I might not otherwise be able to gain access to."

"Can I ask why?"

"Sure. I'm looking for the faery kingdom."

"If you do not wish to answer you can simply say so."

"Anyway, so the guy turned up again the same morning I was in town."

"He said they were expecting you to make a visit and had

some demands of me along the lines of placing a tracking device on your person and obtaining travel information and a great many other details I was no more interested in providing at that time than I had been on the previous occasion."

"I appreciate that."

"You are welcome, although I believe I acted with both our interests in mind. This time his threats were more specific and while I did not for a moment believe this man had the full force of the US government behind him, he had a dangerous level of knowledge regarding both of us. I decided the only reasonable solution was to invite him into my sound-proofed basement and shoot him in the face."

"That's ... very decisive of you," I said.

There have been conversations between us in the past where the topic of murder came up, but I was usually the one playing the role of murderer, for one reason or another. I always knew if it came to it, Tchekhy would pull the necessary triggers, but it was still a little surprising to hear him speak so frankly.

"It was obvious then that the shop had to go, but I was uncertain if the dead man on my floor was alone or not, so I rigged my incendiaries to a remote and left him there."

"You weren't seen leaving?"

"No. Anyone watching would have assumed that both myself and my visitor had perished in the same explosion. But I left through the tunnel."

"You tunneled your way out?"

"It was already there. Many parts of that city have underground tunnels, my friend. This is one reason I never left that location. I had an escape route, which led from my basement chamber to the basement of the building across the street. I rented a room on the top story that overlooked my storefront. There I kept an emergency bag and a few other things."

"Like a sniper rifle."

"Yes. I had it out not in anticipation of your arrival, however. I imagined if I waited long enough whoever was with my visitor would reveal themselves. I know I was told to expect you to visit, but I did not know whether I could trust anything I was told. And the rest I suspect you know."

"I showed up and you shot at me."

"I shot at your car door to get you out of there before anyone saw you. And as soon as I did that I knew it was time to start the fire and then leave."

"So you never saw anyone else?"

"If the man was with a second person, that person was patient beyond all reason. I think he came alone."

My own memory of that scene was something of a blur. Between the explosion and the gunfire and—maybe—the alcohol, there was no way I was going to remember someone out of place on the street. A mature yeti could have been standing next to me and I probably wouldn't have noticed.

"I can find out if the guy was a Fed," I told him. "I'll make a call."

"That will not be necessary."

"It's okay, I owe him a call anyway. Have you followed up on the fire?"

"*Da,* in the official reports there were no persons in the building so no deaths were registered. The private files in the police computers have identified the partial remains of a human but there is not enough to determine whose. The detective closed the case positing that *I* was the dead man, except, of course, he does not know who I am either, as none of the legal property documents record my actual name, or truly the name of any real person. This detective sounded very aggravated in his write-up."

"I'll make sure there aren't any other investigations going on."

Tchekhy sighed the way he always did when I didn't understand something he was telling me. "Perhaps I have undersold the gravity of this situation," he said. "Somebody is after you."

"That's been happening a lot lately. I can deal with it."

"No. This is not as it was before. This is not some bounty, or a group of religious fanatics. This is larger."

"Like what?"

"I truthfully do not know, and that is the problem. The man I killed worked for someone capable of hiding from *me*. Not only that, they hacked my computer, and that is something I did not think anyone was capable of doing. These are not the people you stand up to, Efgeniy. I think it is time for you to disappear."

"You're scared."

"I am worried."

There have been many times in my life where the solution to a problem was to outlive that problem. It made a lot of sense for the bulk of human history, because sometimes a long walk or a boat ride would be enough to completely exit the sphere of influence of whomever I might have pissed off. It worked fine when I fled Egypt and just hung out on the Greek side of the Mediterranean for a few hundred years. It worked when I left England for America, and about ten or eleven times in the Middle Ages, when every roving band was its own autonomous culture.

Ten years ago I would have thought I could do the same thing: lock up my money for the next time I needed it, take enough to travel with, and disappear for a hundred years or so. But I was pretty sure there weren't any places left to hide anymore, not unless the moon has developed nomadic tribes since the last time I checked.

"I don't know if I can," I said. "Not without getting rid of a whole lot of money and staging my own death, and those things take time to do right."

What I didn't say was that I would also have to suspend the quest I was currently on, and I wasn't fully prepared to do that just yet.

He nodded, and stood. "Well, it is my advice to you. Disappear, and make this the last conversation we have together. If you will not take my advice, then speak to me only on the phone I gave to you, and only after you have secured privacy on your end of the call. We are using technology that could make me very wealthy if I had the time to exploit it, so please put it to good use."

He extended his hand and we shook, like men concluding a business meeting rather than friends who were probably never seeing one another face-to-face again.

"What will you do now?" I asked.

"I have places I can disappear into. I will be in a Baltic state, but please don't ask me to tell you more than that."

"I'm sorry it was my association that caused this problem for you."

"It's nothing. You are family."

I turned to leave, but another thought occurred to me. "Hey, do you still have what you need to hack your way into stuff? Or whatever you call it?"

"I do. Whom did you want me to hack?"

"A bank."

"I do this often. Which bank? I may have inroads already established."

"Probably not *this* bank," I said. "But I do have a way for you to get in."

CHAPTER 8

I used to talk a lot about wealth with Aurus. As a Roman he had trouble grasping some of the basic concepts behind acquired merchant wealth because he grew up in Constantinople, and the mentality of the old Empire was still embedded in that culture. Wealth in his reckoning meant political power and influence, and while that held true for the people lucky enough to be born into the right kind of families, it tacitly excluded people like us, trying to earn our own wealth.

It's a problem that doesn't really make sense to a modern person, because now wealth is more directly equated with money, and money is a fungible substitute for birthright. So I spent hours—Aurus was not stupid but he was also less than brilliant—going over what it meant to be a wealthy merchant, and what he could do with that kind of wealth. We used to use a hundi broker to send funds back to the Middle East when we were traveling in the Far East. Aurus had a sister and brother-in-law who owned a tiny fragment of farmland in the countryside beyond the walls of Constantinople. As soon as he had earnings, he began sending them to her. It was an act of faith on his part because he didn't understand the idea behind what he was sending, and if he had understood it he would then not understand how it got to her.

To the latter point, a hundi is really simple. If I give a broker in India three hundred pieces of gold and tell him I want someone in Constantinople to have it, he will keep the gold and record my having given it to him. He will then forward a ledger that includes my transaction to his brother, who lives in Constantinople. Meanwhile, I've sent a letter of my own to my friend in Constantinople telling him to go to the brother to get the gold. My friend goes to the brother and gets gold from him, and the ledger transaction is completed.

And that's it. Very simple, really. The brokers keep a fee, and they always have gold on hand to pay out because people send money in both directions. But Aurus could not get the idea down. It wasn't until we returned to Constantinople after two years of travel, and he got to visit his sister on her now-much-larger farm, that he realized this money was real.

The most surprising part of the conversation with Tchekhy might have been that he didn't just come right out and say a government was after me. That was the sort of speculation I'd come to expect from my friend, who is either the only sane man on the planet or a high-functioning paranoid. But aside from making sure we weren't visible to satellites, which certainly indicated he had a government on his mind, he never came right out and said so.

And it probably *was* a government, or someone with those kinds of resources. I'd changed our destination from Istanbul to Tbilisi while in flight, so if they picked up our trail from the airport they had to have had operatives in both cities. That meant a pretty large operation, the kind that was only possible if you were a government or a major corporation.

What was also interesting was that I was being followed, but not hunted. Being hunted is something I'm used to, as that's a thing that sometimes happens to me. It's one of the consequences of being the only immortal man on the planet, because people for some reason think I have some sort of wisdom or magical significance or, depending on the era, scientific value. I remember a tribe a very long time ago that convinced themselves my urine would heal the sick, and I could not take a piss without someone throwing a bowl under me for about seventy years. It sucked, and it only got worse when someone decided my blood must be even more important.

Being followed was an entirely different thing. The last time it happened was because someone thought I was possibly financing terrorism, because that's what we immortals do with our money or something. I would say it was a harmless presumption since I wasn't doing anything of the sort, except proof isn't necessarily a prerequisite for getting oneself imprisoned, either historically or right now. And long-term incarceration for me is just not a good thing.

What I was currently doing with my time and money—still nothing to do with terrorism—also didn't really deserve anyone else's attention. If I was feeling romantic about it I'd call it a quest, but all I was really doing was trying to answer a question I'd been ignoring for a thousand years. It was a project that could at best be considered frivolous, and at worst ridiculous and silly, as would be obvious to anybody I bothered to explain it to if I ever got around to doing that. It was important to *me*, but I couldn't see how anyone else would care. It certainly didn't deserve full-time surveillance.

I tried to tell myself it was probably a corporation. They're the size of governments nowadays and sometimes have more clout, and they're nice and predictable because at the end of the day their motivation is to make money. I can work with that.

Governments have all kinds of different motivations, and only one of them is monetary. A government can be run by a fanatic, which can make them just about the most dangerous organized entity there is, because fanatics don't listen to reason and don't act logically. (Corporations can be run by fanatics, too, but fanatics aren't big money earners in the business world, historically. So they don't last long.) I will go to the other side of the planet to avoid a fanatical government apparatus if I have to.

By the time I got back to the hotel room I had decided it didn't much matter, because both options were terrible.

Mirella greeted me at the door in a bathrobe, which was a simply fantastic way to be greeted.

"That's a good look for you," I said.

"Shut up. It's in case anyone came to the door wondering why you had not left. What are you doing here?"

"I don't understand the question."

"If we're being watched, the people watching us think you've been in the room this whole time. Now they know you weren't."

This was a good point.

"I hadn't actually thought about how I was going to sneak back in."

"Well, now they'll spend the day reconstructing your morning. I hope your friend took the appropriate precautions."

"He'll be fine. But we have to get out of here."

"To where?"

"At least as far as the plane. After that I haven't decided yet."

~

I still hadn't decided by the time we were in the air, which was a decision in its own right, since we were bound for Istanbul next and I didn't tell anyone on the flight crew not to bring us there. I was torn between radically altering my schedule and maybe tipping off the people following me that I knew they were following, and keeping to the itinerary and acting ignorant until I decided what to do.

I don't much like going to Istanbul. I haven't been there very often since the name change, and I only went a handful of times when it was Constantinople. It isn't that I don't appreciate the place. I saw Constantinople when it was the most beautiful city on the planet, and I don't honestly know if I have ever seen any man-made thing as magnificent since. I would compare it to seeing a woman's beauty fade with old age, except I have seen that thousands of times and what happened to this city was far worse.

Well all right, not *that* bad. Not as bad as, say, Dresden. But until you know what the Hagia Sofia looked like after it was finished—and you can't know, because there are no pictures— you just can't understand.

There were a couple of other good reasons for not spending a lot of time there back then. First, as beautiful as it was, it was still full of Romans. Second, my business dealings always left me one step removed from the center of the merchant class in the city, and that was partly by design. I didn't want to become settled, and I didn't want my wealth tied to land, because—and I think I've said this before—land is only useful if the empire (or country or tribe) that recognizes it as yours continues to exist. A deed isn't going to do you much good if the government that gave it to you has been burned to the ground. So when I dealt with the marketplace in Constantinople it was as a supplier of goods to a taxpayer. I barely made a profit, but it was worth it for the hassle I avoided.

Istanbul was where the collection I wanted to see was located, though. I imagine it would have been less of a psychic burden had it been in London or Irkutsk or Cairo instead, but I don't get to decide these things. And by the time we were halfway there I decided I wasn't going to be changing my mind about going there. If I disappeared as advised, it was going to have to happen after my trip to the museum.

Then I remembered I promised Tchekhy I would place a call

to Mike Lycos, my FBI contact. If I had attracted the official attention of the United States government, Mike was the best person to talk to about it.

He was not pleased to hear from me.

"Are you on fire right now?" he asked.

"No."

"Is there someone holding a gun to your head?"

"Not in any literal sense."

"It is three in the morning, Adam. Please tell me you're bleeding from somewhere."

"Oh, sorry. I'm calling from a different time zone."

"Let me clear this up for you: The world is round."

I laughed. "I've noticed. I'm sorry I woke you, but stop whining for a minute. I need to know if you've sniffed anything about me around the office lately."

"About you? No. Not since your file got accidentally deleted five or six times and then thrown into a fireplace. But it's a big office. Why, should I have? What'd you do?"

"Someone was asking questions about me, said he was FBI. We figured he was lying. I just wanted to make sure."

"What's the guy's name? I can check tomorrow. Like when the sun is up and shit."

"No name. And he died in an explosion."

Mike sighed. "Was that explosion in *any* way related to the questions he was asking about you?"

"Might have been, yeah."

"Hang on."

I heard grunting and the sound of a door opening and closing, and then I heard cicadas. He'd stepped outside. A *fwoosh* sound indicated he was also lighting a cigarette.

"This explosion," he said. "Was it in New York City by any chance whatsoever?"

"It might have been."

"In a pawnshop that looks like a front for a terrorist cell?"

"A what again?"

"Adam, remember when I told you not to go financing terrorism or it'd make me look bad?"

"No, no, there wasn't ... just a hacker, that's all."

"Maybe you'd be surprised to learn that nowadays we at the Bureau consider cybercrime a potential terrorist act."

"Wait, why did you even think to bring up New York? Aren't explosions a little more common than that?"

"Lucky guess. So okay, that's great, is there anything connecting you to the explosion other than this stupid phone call you just made?"

"No, but the dead body inside the pawnshop belonged to the guy who was looking for info on me."

"The supposed FBI agent."

"Yeah."

"Well he wasn't. We don't know who he was. Thought maybe he was the guy who owned the place since he's in the wind."

There was a pause. If we were face-to-face he'd be giving me the kind of stare you give when you think if you do it right the other person's head will explode. I could almost hear it. "That's your friend, isn't it? The owner?"

"Yeah."

"Adam ..."

"He isn't *anybody*. He just knows a lot about me."

"And you aren't going to tell me who he is, are you?"

"Of course not. But look, I'm being followed. And if the dead guy wasn't with the FBI, I don't know who's behind it. I'm pretty sure everyone I know is in some danger right now."

"So you're calling me to confess to knowledge of a crime that is currently being investigated as an act of terrorism *and* to notify me that knowing you might put me at risk? I already knew that."

"Just don't send me any more stuff or anything, I guess. For a while. Just in case."

"Send you any more what again?"

"Like the tape."

"What tape?"

"Or ... sorry, the DVD, disc, whatever we're calling this kind of thing now. I swear the technology changes every week. It's really hard to keep up."

"Yeah, buddy, I still don't know what you're talking about."

It felt like something bounced through the bottom of my stomach.

"A little while ago a package was sent to me. Had a security camera recording of ... you know what? Never mind. I thought you sent it to me—my mistake."

"Of what? Don't stop there. I'm already going to jail if anyone on my side of the law is listening to this."

"You remember Robert Grindel?"

"I remember investigating Grindel after the fact, yeah. He died along with a lot of other folks on a private compound out in the desert, but I don't know much more than that because it's classified."

"But you're the FBI."

"Yeah, genius, it's classified above my grade. I figured you knew more but since I don't actually care about a rich dead guy I never much bothered to ask."

"Let's say there was security camera footage of what happened the night Robert Grindel died. If the whole thing was classified, who do you imagine might have access to that footage? Like, the kind of access that would allow them to make a copy of some of it and mail it to somebody?"

There was another long pause on Mike's end. I heard a second cigarette getting lit, and wished I had one of my own.

"You are in some serious fucking shit, bud," he said after some consideration.

"I'm getting that same impression, yes."

Mirella, who had been ignoring my phone call as much as that was possible—the cabin wasn't terribly huge—waved her hands in front of my face to get my attention.

"The captain said we're about to descend," she said, pointing to the intercom.

I wasn't supposed to be on the phone during takeoff or landing. I didn't know why this was so, but I was willing to accept the opinions of people who understood this technology better than I did.

"Mike, I have to go. Keep your head down for the next few weeks, okay?"

"You do the same. And maybe stop associating with criminals so much. I'd like that."

I hung up.

"You look like you've gotten some bad news," Mirella noted as I moved to a proper seat and belted myself in.

"I did."

"Would you like to talk about it?"

Getting that tape motivated me to do a lot of things, like visit with scientists and research museum collections. I thought I was acting in my own interest, but now there was the idea that someone other than Mike sent it, and that someone might be connected to whoever was following me, and I couldn't shake the idea that I'd been manipulated all along. That included the trip I was about to embark upon.

"We shouldn't go to Istanbul," I said. "This is a mistake."

"I don't think we have a choice about landing, but we can always leave again as soon as we refuel."

"Yeah, we could do that." I looked her in the eye. "How good are you at your job, really?"

It was an offensive question, but she took it. "I'm the best."

"Good. I think tonight you're going to have to be. I'm going to do the stupid thing and stick with the plan."

"It's stupid why, exactly?"

"I just learned I'm not the only one who cares about what I'm doing here."

"You already know you're being followed."

"Yeah. And they'll probably keep doing that. But just in case, bring your sharp things. I don't like walking into traps without a weapon, and you're the only weapon I have."

CHAPTER 9

"Running away is always a valid option," I told Hsu. "You will care surprisingly little about how many songs are written about your bravery when you are not alive to hear them."

~

I am apparently a tremendously generous contributor to the Istanbul Archeology Museum, because despite having postponed my meeting at least twice with the associate curator, he was not only incredibly polite to the point of embarrassment, he opened the entire museum to me—should I wish to view the entire museum—two hours after the building had been locked down.

You can add museums to the list of things I'm not all that fond of. I don't mind popping by one from time to time to view artwork, but I find unsettling the notion of putting old stuff on display just because it's old.

For one thing, the title cards on the pieces are almost always inaccurate. I don't blame anybody for this, because you figure out what you can with what you have, and if all you have left of an entire civilization is a few statues and a clay pot fragment or two, you're going to screw up some details. I get it. But when what I remember as a mighty warrior tribe is reduced to half a carved stone face misidentified as belonging to a culture that didn't exist for another two hundred years, it can make me bitter. I imagine if I could convince enough museums to believe me, I could do some correcting for them.

Another thing I don't like is that some of the stuff on display is mine. I can't usually prove it, but I know my stuff when I see it.

The Istanbul Archeology Museum was set up in what I remember as being a palace for the Ottoman sultans, sometime after Mehmed II finally ended the Roman Empire. I'd never been inside it before and I didn't really care for what the Ottomans did to the city in general, so I wasn't feeling particularly wistful as I walked the cavernous, darkened halls.

The associate curator introduced himself as Mr. Acar and he was, as I said, phenomenally good-natured. He greeted us at the great hall entrance, did a lot of handshaking and bowing, and had many nice things to say about the emperor Justinian I, whose name I had stolen on a whim back when I was picking a name for myself. Had I known I was going to be traveling to the city Justinian helped build, I'd have gone with something less pretentious.

Of course he had to give us a tour. I didn't want a tour, because again, me and museums and old things. But he was the kind of polite that was really hard to say no to without being rude. I was getting very close to being rude.

"Is Alexander the Great buried in this?" Mirella asked Mr. Acar. We were staring at an enormous stone rectangle with carvings all around it depicting—with the usual hagiographic exaggeration of the time—the great life of Alexander. Mirella was thoroughly enjoying the entire tour—genuinely, it seemed—and also doing her best to pretend to be the girl-on-my-arm rather than my bodyguard. It was a decent disguise, and I kind of liked having her on my arm. She even called me *dear* without grimacing. It was sweet.

"No, no miss," Mr. Acar said. "It's not clear *whose* sarcophagus it was, but certainly not Alexander himself. He was long dead before this great thing was carved."

Alexander was a dick, by the way.

"Then why ..." she asked, pointing to a scene where Alexander routs Persians all by his lonesome.

"It's for the ego of the person who *did* commission it," I said. "Comparing oneself to Alexander or Constantine was a popular pastime."

"Eh, yes, I suppose that can be said," Mr. Acar decided.

"Maybe we can move on?" I asked.

"Yes, of course! If you would follow me!"

Mirella sidled up next to me and took my arm. "Be nice. I can't be polite for both of us, I don't have the energy."

"This is me being polite."

"You're terrible at it. All the trouble you went through to get here, I imagined you loved museums. Where is your pixie?"

"Not sure. She's flying around here somewhere. I'm sure she's fine."

"I'm sure she's fine, too, but I ask because I was hoping she could tell me who else has entered the building. I don't believe we're entirely alone."

I turned to look over my shoulder, which is what one does when someone says there's somebody following. I know I'm not supposed to, but even sixty thousand years later I still haven't been able to condition myself to stop. Mirella hissed at me, and I turned back and continued to act interested in what Mr. Acar was saying.

"And here is a bust of Alexander. This is *also* a very important piece for our museum."

"Ooh," Mirella cooed, "is that what he really looked like?" She had this way of leaning forward and shaking her breasts that made her cleavage practically blind whoever she was facing. In someone else I'd have suggested it was how she got what she wanted. In her I think it was meant as a weapon.

I took a look at the bust Mr. Acar was standing next to and before he had a chance to respond—due to the weaponized cleavage in front of him—I was answering. "Yes, pretty much."

This was met with confusion on our host's part. "It's ... very possible, yes," he agreed. He looked askance at me for a moment or two, and I really wanted to tell him how I knew what Alexander looked like. "Continuing! Up ahead is the Kadesh Peace Treaty, one of the most important ..."

"I'm sorry, Mr. Acar, but would it be possible for us to skip ahead?" I asked. I had really had enough of this.

He looked gravely wounded, as if I was saying this because of some personal fault of his.

Mirella tried to soften up my rudeness. "What he means to say is we are under a terrible time constraint. We would *love* to come back and put ourselves at your disposal on another occasion, but tonight we have a thing."

"Yes, a thing," I agreed.

"Of course!" he said loudly, and I wondered if he was going to bow again. "I am so sorry. But really, the Kadesh Peace Treaty ..."

"We will have to come back for it," I said.

"Because of your thing."

"It's an important thing."

"Of course! Please follow me."

He led us through two more halls it probably just killed him not to tell us all about the contents of, and to a *Staff Only* side door, which he unlocked. This led to a stone stairwell and down to the basement.

Mr. Acar threw a switch, which turned on some unpleasant fluorescent ceiling lights. The place looked a lot like an office building sublevel, except that here and there were pieces of very old things sitting on tables or in boxes or crates, and then it felt more like history's attic.

He led us quickly down the hall past all of the random bits of archeology. Mirella, holding onto my arm and—I think—watching our backs, whispered, "Why exactly are we here?"

"I'll explain when we get there," I said. "Are we alone?"

"Yes. I don't believe whoever is sharing the museum with us left the main hall entrance."

"That's good."

"Yes, except that means there is only one other exit should we need to leave without crossing their path. Now would be a good time to tell me if you believe this is going to be a violent encounter."

"They haven't been violent so far."

"This is not an answer."

"I realize that."

At the end of the hallway we turned a corner and came upon a white door with a square window in the center of it. I was reminded of those doors they always use when they're showing insane asylum holding cells on television shows.

"You understand this is a highly irregular request," Mr. Acar said in a library-quiet voice. He looked very uncomfortable, and when he spoke it was actually to his necktie rather than us.

"I do," I said.

I would have apologized, but I didn't want him to take that as a hint that we weren't going through with this.

He hesitated, and I got the impression that the fulfillment of this request was something he was very specifically against.

"Very well," he said finally, turning on the light in the room on the other side of the door. "To the left of the door you will find gloves, which I implore you to use before touching anything else in the room. You are aware that the oils from your hand will be very damaging to the contents."

"It hasn't been opened?" I asked, surprised.

"Oh, no, it has. And the documents catalogued and under glass."

"Then why do we need the gloves?"

"Please humor me, Mr. Justinian. This find is public, but we haven't catalogued and shared the details of its contents with anyone as yet. It's extremely important we not make any mistakes tonight. I hope you understand, and do not take my precautions as an affront. It's only ... again, this is a very unusual request."

He opened the door for both of us and stepped aside. "I will be just down the hall."

Mirella looked surprised that he wasn't joining us but didn't offer a comment of any sort until the door was closed.

"What the hell is going on?" she asked.

"Don't forget to put on your gloves."

There was, as described, a large box of polyurethane gloves on a table next to the door. I took two out and put them on, and then turned on the rest of the lights in the room.

It was not a particularly large space, and it was very, very clean. It almost had the feel of a scientific laboratory, except that the labs I've seen had a lot more chemicals lying around. At the far corner of the room was a large crate resting on a wooden pallet, and in the center of the room was a long glass table.

Mirella glared at me as I handed her a set of gloves. "You said you would explain once we got here. We're here."

"All right. An archeologist working on funding from this museum recently uncovered something I'm interested in looking more closely at."

"I will bury a knife in your thigh if you don't start answering straightforward questions."

"I'm a complicated fellow."

"Nobody is ever as complicated as they think they are. Where did this archeologist find this thing?"

"In the ruins of an old synagogue in southern Iraq."

"And what did he find?"

"I'll show you."

I led her to the crate in the far corner, which as I suspected held a big square of dirt, at the center of which was something that looked like a brick chimney.

"An old oven?"

"It's not an oven. It's a geniza. And I only actually care about what's inside of it."

"Dirt? More bricks?"

I went over to the glass table and felt around the underside until I found the switch. The table was backlit, and when the faintly bluish light was turned on we could see what was under the glass countertop.

Mirella circled around the table, looking at the scraps.

"These look like letters."

"They are." But there weren't very many. I was expecting more.

Against one wall was a case with what looked like very thin drawers. That was, I imagined, where the rest of them were stored.

"What language is this?" she asked.

"That one's in Hebrew."

"And do you read Hebrew?"

"I do. I also read Judeo-Arabic, Yiddish, Judeo-Persian ..."

"Fine, I understand. Now why are we opening old mail?"

"I'm looking for a particular piece of correspondence from a particular Jewish merchant."

"And you believe that correspondence is in this room."

"I sincerely hope so. This is the third geniza I've checked and the closest one to the right region."

I bent down at the table and started skimming the headers of each letter. Formal correspondences back then were very conveniently rote, the best part about them being that they always included something along the lines of *may God bless you,* and it was because of that salutation that these letters even existed.

According to Jewish law at the time, it was a sin to destroy anything that had the name of God on it. This created a few problems, because every correspondence began or ended with an invocation of His blessing to the recipient. To not do so was to invite His displeasure, or something. I'm not really clear on why they kept writing that when it created such a hassle, but everyone did so I'm sure they had a reason.

The consequence was that no letters could be destroyed. But they couldn't be kept around, either, because the Jewish merchant class had a lot to lose. These letters held shipping manifests, and business plans, and the names of suppliers, and all other manner of confidential business information. It wasn't safe to have those documents lying around, but there was that pesky problem of God's name on all of them.

The solution was to build a geniza. This was a brick compartment that was completely sealed except for one missing brick, built against an outside wall of a synagogue. Whenever anyone was done with a letter—or a book, or anything else with the Lord's name on it—they'd drop the item through the opening. Once the geniza was full, the last brick would be put in place and they'd build a new one.

It was the kind of genius solution only religion could come up with. And it resulted in hundreds of dead letter drops buried throughout the Asia and Europe.

"What's so important about this one correspondence?" Mirella asked. "And how do you know that it exists, if the people who found this haven't even finished reading everything yet?"

"These are in a dozen different hands and employ at least four language variants I can see. It would take years to translate all of them properly. All they're going to do is post a summarization of sample contents and invite scholars to interpret the more interesting ones. I could wait for that, but they might not even find the letter I'm looking for as interesting as I do."

"And you can read these all right now."

"I can, yes."

She sighed. I was sort of falling in love with her sighs. There was an outside chance I was exasperating her on purpose just to hear it.

"Would you please just explain this in a way that doesn't raise more questions than it answers?"

"I probably can't."

She stepped between the table and me and lifted my chin until I was looking her in the eyes. "Try."

"All right. The letters I'm looking for were written by a Jew named Abraham bin Yasser. They were written to his uncle Menachem and concerned the spice business Menachem owned and Abraham managed. The letters were written over a thousand years ago and sent from different parts of India, Africa, and Eastern Europe, depending on where Abraham's travels took him. And I know these letters exist because I studied Abraham's business practices carefully and eventually did business with him directly, and I learned that he documented absolutely everything."

She stared at me for a solid ten seconds before saying anything.

"Yes, all right, that makes sense," she said finally, stepping aside.

"You don't have any more questions?"

"Not right now."

"Then I'm going to keep looking."

"Yes, do that. I'm going to stand by the door and see if your pixie shows up."

"All right."

I gave up on the table and opened one of the drawers. More letters under glass, as I'd hoped. The drawers were removable, so I pulled the first of them out and placed it on the table.

"Oh yes, I do have one more question," Mirella said after a time. "What are you looking for in the letters?"

"That's an even longer story," I said.

"Ah. Save it for when we get out of here."

~

I looked for an hour before finding a promising sign that I was in the right place, in the form of an actual letter from Abraham. It was only a list of spices and some nominal accounting information but the year was about right, and it gave me a sample of his handwriting.

"Did you find what you wanted?" Mirella asked. She had been standing at the door for most of the hour, trying to get a good read on what was going on in the hallway from the vantage point of the tiny window. When she didn't do that she paced, which made me as anxious as she clearly was.

"No, but it's a good sign," I said, moving on to the next tray of letters.

"He was a spice merchant. Are you looking for spices? I think we passed a supermarket on our way here."

"Not spices. A treasure of a different sort."

"Yes, of course," she said, shaking her head. She had a few unkind things to add under her breath and then went back to staring out the window.

It was not spices. It was the thing Hsu never quite got his hands on, and since Hsu was not with me and I had never seen the object in question, I didn't really know what I was looking for. All I did know was that Abraham parted with it, and when he did so he wrote about it in a letter.

It was very likely that the thing no longer existed. History is unkind to man-made stuff, and the proof of that was in every corner of the museum over our heads. Even if it did still exist, after a thousand years I had no reason to think there was any sort of trail I could possibly follow that would lead me to it. But again,

I could be wrong, and until I found Abraham's letter I wouldn't know for sure.

My money was what made it possible for me to fly around the world looking for this letter, and until I succeeded I wasn't ready to disappear. Another chance might never come along. I was aware that this was a stupid reason to put myself at great personal risk—according to Tchekhy—and maybe that was why I didn't want to tell Mirella what was going on. Or maybe I just didn't want anybody to talk me out of it.

I was running through all of that in my head when I realized I no longer had to worry about anybody talking me out of anything, because I was looking right at the letter.

"Here it is," I said.

"At last. Can we leave now?"

"No, I kind of need to read it first."

"Fine, what does it say?"

"*Dearest sir, I am forwarding a most unusual item. It is to understand the sky. Please if you find no need for it yourself to give it to Isaac to inspire his studies.*"

Mirella looked unimpressed. "He's describing your treasure?"

"I think so."

"You were looking for something to *understand the sky?*"

"Apparently? I know Isaac was his son, and that's good news because Isaac lived not far from where this was found. But Abraham thought it was a child's toy, and I really don't know what the understanding-the-sky part means. So I still don't know what I'm actually looking for."

"You can think about it later. Now I think we very much have to go. I don't like being trapped in this room."

"I realize that. But hang on a minute. He didn't sign this."

"Perhaps he was in as great a hurry as we are."

"No, he signed the other ones. So did everyone else. Oh. I understand."

Carefully, I lifted the plexiglass cover that was protecting the letters from the harmful effects of fresh air and oily skin.

"What are you doing?" Mirella asked, aghast.

"The letter is two-sided."

I picked out his letter and flipped it over.

Abraham, Yahweh bless him, had drawn a diagram of the toy he sent back for Isaac so his son could use it properly. I knew what I was looking for now, and I knew what the face of it looked like. I also knew I was going to have to keep the letter.

"If this helps add some urgency to your process, your pixie is on the other side of this window and she is extremely agitated," Mirella said. She actually sounded happy about this, as if she now had someone else there insisting I was in grave danger and that made it okay to rush me.

"I'm nearly ready."

I had in my jacket pocket an empty envelope for this exact occasion. I carefully folded Abraham's letter and put it in the envelope, then arranged the remaining letters under the glass until it looked like there was no space where the letter had been. It was very likely someone was going to eventually notice it missing, but hopefully not for a while.

"Put the case back," Mirella said. "I'm going to open the door before she tries to break the window."

A second later Iza was flying around my head while I was still trying to load the letters back into the cabinet.

"Iza, calm down," I said. "Tell me what's wrong. Someone's following us, yes?"

"Yes, follow," she said. "Someone."

"All right, well they've been following us for a while. We knew about this. We'll be okay, just tell us where—"

"No. Not okay."

"Not okay? Why? Who's following us? Are there a lot of them?"

I know it's better to ask a pixie only one question at a time, but now that I had what I wanted I was ready to sign up for all of Mirella's nervous energy and add some of my own.

"Man," Iza said. "Big man."

"A big man."

"Big man. Big D man."

Mirella's head snapped around. "What did she say?"

"Demon," I translated. "She said demon."

CHAPTER 10

*"Anyone can be seduced," Indira was fond of saying. I spent only a few
years with her, but in that time she more or less proved that point,
almost as a dare. Human, non-human, male or female, it didn't much
matter to her.*
When it came time for us to part she asked if I now believed her.
"Nearly," I said. "I never saw you try to seduce a demon."
She grimaced and spat into the dirt. "Don't be disgusting," she said.

irella reached over her head and pulled a sword
out from a sheath on her back. It was lined up
with her spine, as far as I could tell, and it was a remarkable thing
to watch because I could swear the blade was longer than her
back. She swung the sword around a little bit either to loosen up
or to keep Iza's attention.

"Well go on, put your papers away. I'd like to get as close to
the exit as possible before engaging anybody, and we are a long
way from an exit."

"Demons are things you run away from, not fight," I said. "That sword won't even go through their skin."

"I told you I was the best and I wasn't exaggerating. I know demons, Mr. Justinian. The surprise is that *you* do, although perhaps I shouldn't be surprised by anything from you going forward. Can we dispense with your obviously fake name as well?"

"You can call me Adam if you want."

"Mr. Adam?"

"Just Adam. We can be on a first name basis."

She pointed the tip of her sword at me.

"Maybe you're older than the thousand years you claim to be and never had a last name. Is that what I should think?"

"That's actually true, but Adam is just what I've been calling myself recently. So no last name, no first name really either. Or lots of them, depending."

"Demons, pixies, and the oldest man in the world. If I survive remind me to ask for more than three million."

I slid the last drawer back into place and pulled off the gloves. "There's supposed to be an associate curator out in the hall. That sword might alarm him a tiny bit."

"He's probably dead."

"Cheery."

"She said demon. She knows what they look like, I take it?"

"She does."

"Then if he came across one, he's either dead or working for the same person who sent the demon. Either way, demons don't much care who they're killing on the way to who they are there to kill. And killing is almost the only reason to send one."

I knew all of that already, but it was kind of fantastic hearing it from someone else for a change. I joined her at the door. "Maybe you'll tell me how you know so much about demons after this is over."

"It's my job to know," she said. "Now, we're going to open this door and go straight. At the end of the hall is a door leading to a stairwell that should get us back to the ground floor. We'll be three rooms away from an exit to the compound. That's provided all of the maps I examined on our tour are accurate. If the car is no longer there we'll have to take to the streets. Are you a good runner?"

This was becoming insulting. "I can keep up."

"I know you can," she said with a brilliant smile. "Old man." She pulled open the door and out we ran.

Iza buzzed ahead of us and up the stairwell. If she came to a closed door at the top she'd probably take to the vents and meet us on the other side. This was how she navigated buildings. She would hopefully double back and warn us before we walked into a trap, provided she recognized a trap when she saw one. That was always iffy when it came to pixies. Sometimes I wished she had some of the intelligence I'd come to expect from other small creatures, like iffrits. Of course, they're obnoxious little assholes, mostly, but that also sometimes comes with intelligence.

The floor plan for the Archeology Museum was simple enough that it was pretty impossible to get lost in, but also so simple that it was difficult to avoid running into someone who might be looking for you inside.

It was basically one long chain of rooms with two right angles in it, so that it looked—based on the bird's-eye view maps at every junction—like a bisected square. There were two main entrances that could be reached from two of the middle rooms, which is an annoying design decision if you want to see the place without ever doubling back on yourself, because that's impossible to do. I imagine it made a lot more sense as a palace than as a museum.

The stairwell we ran to led to the back of a corner room, which put us five very large rooms away from the nearest main exit. There was a lot to be said for finding a side door somewhere and sneaking out, except the fire doors I'd seen were all alarmed, and since we weren't sure yet whether our car was even outside anymore—I had hired a car to take us from the airport and back again—it didn't seem like a super idea to call law enforcement to the scene on top of whoever else was already with us in the building. Add to that the fact that we didn't know for sure whether Mr. Acar was still in one location or scattered across several, and we didn't want to be around to explain anything to anybody.

I'm being glib, but only kind of. Demons are nasty creatures. They're large and violent and indiscriminate when it comes to who they kill and why, as Mirella had already noted. Thus if the associate curator encountered one he was probably no longer alive, and he was also probably no longer recognizable as Mr. Acar or possibly as something that was once a human being.

Demons are also nearly indestructible, all except for truly awful immune systems. This makes them germophobes, which is great for everyone that isn't me. I can't get sick, and if they know me well they know this, too, and know I'm not going to be infecting them with anything.

The only time I ever successfully dispatched a demon it was because I had a concentrated bacterium on hand. If I were smart, I'd carry a vial of it with me everywhere.

There was no sign of Mr. Acar or any of his body parts in the stairwell or in the main exhibit area. There was also no sign of anyone else.

Mirella, ahead of me, came to a stop when we reached the first room off the stairs and signaled that I do the same. We stood still and listened. I couldn't hear anything, but her hearing was better than mine so I wasn't expecting to pick up much other than Iza's buzzing.

"We are alone here," she whispered after about five seconds.

"They could be downstairs."

We'd been taken to the basement, from a stairwell on the other side of the building and down the corridor. If they were been following our scent that would have been the path they took, which could mean we had a clear path to the front if we moved fast enough.

She was thinking the same thing.

"Quickly," she said. And then we were running again.

The exhibit design of the museum was cleverly varied so that no one room looked even remotely like another. This was incredibly annoying when attempting to exit the building quickly, as there were no straight lines from door to door. And the floor was slick stone and I hadn't brought running shoes, so there were a few tragicomic moments when I or Mirella—in heeled boots also not meant for running—nearly skittered into a display holding something ancient and delicate. We probably made a lot of noise too, but speed was what we were aiming for and not stealth. And it worked. We reached the exit without incident, and a second later we were outside and in the courtyard.

The Istanbul Archeology Museum was technically three museums in a single compound. We were in the main building. Across the yard was the Tiled Kiosk, where the sultan had kept his girls and was now an art gallery. I didn't know much about the third building other than that Mr. Acar called it the Museum of the Orient. The three buildings surrounded a grassy garden area, which was encircled by a cobblestone road.

Our car was supposed to be waiting on this road, in front of the Kiosk where we had left it.

It wasn't there.

Mirella stopped us again, at the top of the stairs.

"This seems emptier than it should be, doesn't it?" she asked.

I nodded. Museum grounds or no, we were in the middle of a city. It was close to three in the morning locally, but when we entered a few hours earlier there had been plenty of people about, and now there wasn't a soul.

"Iza, tell me about the demon," I said.

"Deeman big."

"Yes I know. Where did you see him?"

"Over there," she said.

"*Outside?*" Mirella asked.

"Maybe we should have asked that earlier."

Mirella quite suddenly whipped her sword through the air in front of her face. The sword slapped aside something metal, and then there was a dagger skittering along the steps a few feet away.

"That wasn't from a demon," she said. "And it wasn't aimed at you."

She grabbed my arm and pulled me behind her in a sprint for the grassy area between the buildings. It was just the shortest way out of the courtyard, and with the most cover, even if that was only from a few trees. Anything was better than standing at the top of the steps in front of a lit entrance.

If we were going to make it any farther it would have to be by running into the middle of the city to the nearest cabstand or whatever the Turkish equivalent of that was. We were too far from Ataturk airport to make it back to the plane without a vehicle, and I hadn't bothered with a hotel because I didn't expect to stay any longer than necessary.

Tactically, then, the grass was a smart move. The only other real option was to try and reenter the museum, but the door had locked behind us; even if it hadn't, it would have just meant allowing ourselves to remain cornered.

Of course, the best strategy when planning an ambush is to expect the ambushed to act rationally, and so the grassy space was exactly where they were waiting for us. If we had been given a little bit more time to think about it, we probably would have worked out another solution, but there were knives being thrown and that kind of impacted our decision-making skills. And perhaps that was the point of the knife, no pun intended.

Thankfully—and oddly, really—there were only two of them: one demon and one goblin. A human would have been nice because, frankly, I can take a human no problem. But goblins are tough, and demons are entirely out of my weight class.

Mirella stepped in front of me protectively. "Can you fight?"

"You mean do I know how?"

"Yes, that's what I mean."

"I can, but I need a weapon."

She grimaced and handed over her sword. Almost immediately, two shorter blades were in her hands.

"When we get back to the plane we're going to talk about arming you properly," she said. "I'll take the demon. Try to keep alive until I'm finished with it."

This was undoubtedly bravado. If she knew anything about them at all she knew she stood little chance with the sword and almost none with those little knives of hers. But I didn't get a chance to suggest another option, both because she had already launched herself at the demon and because there weren't any other options. I had tried everything on demons from swords and pikes to firearms, and the only things that work are the flu or enough water to drown them.

I still appreciated watching her try.

The first thing that happened when she got into range was that the demon attempted to punch her in the head, which is what demons do. They're really good at it, and they can be pretty fast despite their size. But she ducked below the attack and cut him in the side, then somersaulted far enough away to get her feet under her again safely. She adopted a defensive posture and waited for him to charge. As they also do.

I nearly forgot I had a goblin to deal with, but fortunately he was a very polite goblin, as it happens.

"Excuse me," he said. He was standing next to a tree a few feet away, his own sword drawn. He was dressed in black clothing and his sword was matte black, and it felt an awful lot like I was facing a movie ninja. I was dressed in a sports coat and jeans, but nobody told me to dress for combat.

"Hi," I said.

"Hello." He stepped closer and raised his sword in a formal fencing gesture indicating the combat was about to commence.

"Hey, hang on a sec," I said. Sticking the tip of the sword in the ground next to me, I took off my jacket. "You don't mind?"

"No, please. Prepare yourself."

I took my time folding the jacket and trying to study my opponent, although the truth was I was more interested in how Mirella was doing. The demon had yet to touch her and had been sliced a half-dozen times. None of the cuts were in any way serious, but maybe he would die from infection in a week or two. There was no reason for her to look half as confident as she did.

The ninja goblin decided he was tired of waiting and charged while I was still putting down the jacket, which was downright unsportsmanlike.

Goblins are in almost every way superior hand-to-hand fighters, but I'm not exactly bad at it either, and while I was enjoying the fight at the other end of the compound I had kept him in the corner of my eye, so he didn't really take me by surprise. What *was* surprising was that he hadn't stayed where he was and just buried knives in me from a safe distance until I stopped moving, since I'm not nearly good enough to knock a knife out of the air with a sword.

Anyway, he charged and I saw him coming and had the sword out of the ground and up to block a straightforward overhand attack. He was strong and put a lot of weight into the blow, but he was also a little off-balance as a consequence. I deflected the attack and shunted him to one side, and he nearly fell over.

But only nearly. As he stumbled I tried to get in a shot at his side, but he regained his balance and caught my sword with his, and held it there.

"I commend your teachers," he said with a slight smile. "Not her, surely. Your style is very different."

"Not her, no. I'm used to a heavier sword."

He stepped back and attacked again.

He wasn't really trying to hit me, exactly. He *was*, in the sense that his blade was being swung at my body repeatedly and being met each time by the one in my hands. But he'd seen enough of my technique already to expect me to be capable of blocking these attacks. He was looking for a weakness in my defensive approach that he could exploit. I was doing the same thing, but since he was stronger I was looking for the times he over-reached and left himself exposed. And I was wishing I had more than one short sword, because it was going to be difficult to exploit what I might find with just the one weapon. Surely he had more than one. I couldn't imagine why he hadn't tried using it.

After thirty or forty seconds of this—it felt like much longer —I had found only one weakness. He had probably found five. My technique was rusty and probably susceptible to anyone using a longer sword than I had in my hands, as he did. So I was probably in some trouble. But his one weakness was a good one. He didn't know about Iza.

Mirella spotted Iza the first time they met, but that was in a well-lit hotel room while nobody was fighting anybody. My goblin foe, while likely having the same heightened senses, was outdoors in semidarkness— there were street lamps—and moving about rapidly. I could hear Iza, and maybe he could, too, but he might not have known what he was hearing. Spotting her under these conditions, given she flew faster when she was nervous, was probably impossible.

He let up and stepped back and we both caught our breath. This gave me a chance to see how my bodyguard was doing.

I glanced over just in time to see a particularly impressive maneuver. The demon, looking sort of exhausted and appearing covered in a hundred paper cuts, took a clumsy swing at Mirella. She avoided it cleanly as she had all of the others, but instead of slicing at his skin again—their skin is incredibly thick—she got underneath him and managed to bury one of the knives hilt-deep into the back of his knee.

He roared and rattled off an impressive string of expletives, and then fell down. She had damaged muscle, enough of it to render the leg useless. She also lost the knife, but that didn't appear to matter, as by the time she got to her feet and he had gotten up on his one good leg there were two blades in her hands again.

"Let me ask you something, while we have a minute," I said.

"Go on."

"Why are you even here?"

"We're here to kill you. I thought that was self-evident."

"Fine, be difficult."

I went on the attack, and drove him back a little with a series of overhand and underhand cuts. I was as cautious as I could manage to be in case he decided to go on the attack again or saw an opening where I overextended. But he seemed happy to just counter and wait for me to exhaust myself. Every now and then I caught him watching Mirella and the demon. I nearly suggested we just stop fighting each other to watch them.

Instead, I backed off and waited for him to counter. He didn't, or at least not right away.

I caught him favoring his right shoulder a tiny bit. It was probably a little thing, a sore muscle or a recent bruise, but it was useful to know.

"Iza, be ready," I said.

"What?" the goblin asked.

"I said I'm ready. Whenever you are, I mean."

The demon on the other side of the field wasn't doing well at all with only one good leg. The wounded leg still held him up, sort of, in the sense that he wasn't hopping about. But he was in a lot of pain, and his swings were less emphatic because the more force he applied the more off-balance he ended up being. It wasn't a huge surprise when the arm he preferred to swing with was also taken from him when Mirella buried another of her daggers into the beast's elbow.

Both the goblin and I witnessed this, and I think it was the first time either of us thought Mirella could possibly emerge alive from the fight. For the goblin this meant he was going to have to figure out how to deal with both of us soon, so he had less time to toy with me than he thought. His renewed assault was thus less playful and much more difficult to defend.

The maneuver that nearly ended my life was one that I didn't see coming at all, which is how these things usually work. He had been right-handed all the way down to his footwork for the entire fight. Usually you can tell when someone is either fully ambidextrous or left-handed and pretending not to be. There are indications, and I know what they are, so I'm customarily prepared when someone shows a sudden talent for opposite handedness. But he didn't have a single tell. So when he switched his sword to his left hand, changed his stance, and went on a mirror image attack, I nearly fell to him.

And then I did fall, because after all of that toying around he decided to use more than one blade. While I was busy trying to regain command of my defenses against a suddenly left-handed attacker, a knife appeared in his right hand.

It slashed across my stomach before I had a chance to get entirely out of the way of it. The wound wasn't mortally deep, but it wasn't exactly shallow either. It was the kind of wound that came just ahead of a killing blow, mainly because the victim has a tendency to stop paying attention to the person who inflicted it and more attention to the cut itself.

I didn't make this mistake, but only because I backpedaled so quickly that I actually tripped and landed on my back. There was no immediate follow-up blow from the goblin, because then he was in no hurry.

I stole a glance across the compound to see if I could expect any help, but Mirella was still busy bullfighting the demon to a slow ending. He was waving his one good arm at her, staggering around and being a handful. And she was starting to look tired.

The goblin stood over me with his sword and prepared to lower it in a swing meant to remove my head.

And then he hesitated.

I didn't know why. There was no reason for it, but it was there and it was enough for me.

"Now, Iza."

Iza and I have a long history together. Sure, we don't talk a lot, and sometimes she can be a pain, and every now and then something would happen like her not bothering to mention that we were running in the direction of the demon she warned us about. These things happen. But she was very good to have around in a fight, especially if you needed someone blinded temporarily.

That was what happened to the goblin when she flew as fast as she could into his right eyeball. He screamed and clutched his head and didn't finish his swing, and a second later he was out of luck entirely because I had shoved my short sword up through his belly, under his ribcage, and into his heart.

He stopped screaming about the pain in his eye after that. Then he fell over onto his back and had the courtesy to only get a little blood on me before dying.

I rolled over onto my side and felt my stomach. My hand came away wet, and I didn't think it was goblin blood.

Fortunately, Mirella was nearly finished doing something I would have said only an hour earlier was impossible: She was killing a demon with knives.

The monster was almost entirely incapacitated, as she'd taken out his second leg, which left him only his left arm. It was an incredibly powerful arm, though, so whenever she got near she risked getting crushed. I was about ready to suggest loudly that we just leave since he was unlikely to be following, but then she finished him in a move that was frankly breathtaking to watch.

At first it looked like he'd finally caught her, because his huge hand managed to get a hold of her left arm, but before he could do anything with it—a tight squeeze and a twist and he could have snapped the bone—she was turning until her back was to him and using the force from this spin move to help propel her right arm around until the knife in the hand met the demon's eye. Then it was obvious she'd allowed her arm to be grabbed because it was the only way she'd ever get close enough to finish him off.

The knife went in deep. I was never entirely positive demons *had* brains, or if they did that they were located in the head, but she certainly acted like someone who knew the answer to that question. She held the blade there while the beast underneath her bucked and contorted, and then she twisted and dug it deeper and higher up into the skull until the demon let go of her arm and stopped moving.

She pulled the knife out and ran over to me.

"I see you *can* fight," she said, pulling her sword from the goblin's chest.

"No, but I know a pixie who can."

She used the goblin's clothing to clean off the sword and slid it back into the sheath. "Good. Now let's get out of here before ... you're hurt."

It wasn't easy to tell I had been wounded with all the blood everywhere, not until I tried to stand and found out that caused more blood to show up.

"He got me pretty good, yeah," I admitted.

"Lie down."

I was only up on one knee so this was really no problem. She raised my shirt and got a good look, and then I got to hear the name of the god she usually prayed to. I heard some cloth being torn— pieces of ninja pajamas. Then she was wrapping me up, which hurt enormously.

"We need to get you sewn up," she said.

"Hospitals are inconvenient. Let's get back to the airplane."

"Do you have a doctor on the airplane?"

"I have a needle and thread on the airplane. I'm sure you can do stitches."

"Don't be absurd."

"I'm being practical. The only anesthetic that will work on me is bourbon, and most doctors don't prescribe that, so just get me back to the airport and we can worry about it then."

She growled. "You are impossible. I'm going to ask for five million."

"Fine. But only after we get to the plane."

CHAPTER 11

When I first met Hsu he made it clear that he'd sought me out mainly for my experience and knowledge. While this was undoubtedly true, there were times when it was clear he took my godhood seriously, even though I just as obviously did not.

We sparred often, to keep our battle skills sharp. One time he nicked me with one of his blades. It was on the arm, and it wasn't deep, just enough to draw blood. I only thought about it as long as it took to bandage up, but he looked legitimately confused by the whole thing.

"I forgot," he said afterward, "that you can be harmed."

"I've told you as much, many times over."

"I know. But ... never mind. For the great Li-Yuan, for Bres, it doesn't correspond."

"Who is Bres?"

"What?"

"You called me Bres."

"It is one of the names I have heard for you. I thought you knew it."

"I don't. Where did you hear this name?"

He stared for several seconds before responding.

"I will tell you another time," he decided. "Can you continue?"

I could, and so we resumed our sparring match. And Hsu never told me the story behind the name he gave me that night.

~

I've been wounded before, plenty of times. I imagine if the scars didn't fade after a century or so my body would be covered in them, because it's not easy to go through life in any era and not end up with some skin damage here and there, even if it's only the consequence of a bad paper cut. I've been cut by swords and knives, taken a few arrows, and been bitten by large beasts that didn't appreciate the spear I was stabbing them with. I've also been shot, and burned, and beaten. I've broken one of my legs five or six times, one of my arms ten or eleven times, my shoulder blade twice, and my nose more times than I can really recall. And I have been incredibly lucky, because nothing I have had damaged has been something that wouldn't heal over time. I've never lost a finger, or an eye, or had to deal with a spinal injury.

I wasn't thinking about how lucky I was as the car took us back to the airport, though. I was thinking my stomach was about to spill out on the floor. I trusted Mirella's opinion that the wound wasn't deep enough for this to happen, but only a little bit. Once the adrenaline left and the shock hit I was in significant pain, and it's hard to be reasonable when you reach that point.

The car we were in was the car we had hired to bring us from the airport to the museum in the first place. The driver hadn't disappeared entirely, but only relocated to another street after being told by "a man with an American accent" that he couldn't park where he was. There was a story behind this that I made Mirella promise to get from him after I was safely aboard the plane.

"We should go to the hospital," she said quietly. It was the third time she'd said it, possibly because she had nothing else to say. Her arm was around my shoulders while I had my hands on my stomach to try and keep the bleeding from being too obvious. I would have balled up my sports jacket to help with this—it was sitting on the seat next to me—but I wasn't going to risk damaging the letter still in the pocket of the jacket. It would have been a terrible irony to go through all this trouble only to bleed on the letter and render it unreadable. Then I thought of Mr. Acar's clean room and the gloves he made us wear and I nearly laughed out loud.

"I told you," I said, "drugs don't work on me, so we can sew this up ourselves or you can put me in the position of answering a ton of questions from somebody in the medical profession. Neither of us wants that."

"It will hurt."

"It already does. And it won't hurt less if a doctor does it. You've stitched a wound before."

"How do you know?"

"Lucky guess."

She looked out the window. I couldn't really see much of the city from my position, crouched in the back and leaning on her, but I couldn't imagine I would much like what I saw.

"Tell me why drugs don't work on you?" she asked.

"I don't know. I can't get sick, and I can't be poisoned, and I think those things are related to drugs not having an effect."

"And you're over a thousand years old, you say."

"Yes."

"How much more?"

"Why?"

"If you bleed to death I want to know what to carve on your gravestone."

"I don't know how old I am."

"Ah. That's all right. I don't know what name to put on it." She poked her head up and looked around as the car came to a stop. "We're here."

~

*G*etting your stomach stitched up with nothing to dull the pain but hard liquor is exactly as fun as it sounds. And since I have an obscenely high tolerance for alcohol—Clara called me a high-functioning alcoholic and she was probably right—it was a little while before I even felt drunk enough to let Mirella tie me down and start stitching. The only good thing about the alcohol was that it made it easier for me to pass out when the pain got to be too bad.

I was down for about ten hours. Since I'd left no instructions regarding where the plane was supposed to go next we stayed at the airport. When I came to, I found Mirella at the desk on my computer, the video of Eve's disappearing act paused on the television, and the skyline of Istanbul out the window.

"You need to restock your commissary," she said when she saw me staring at her. "There is only a few more days' worth of food in there. If you were thinking about living on this plane for a while we may need to plan for pizza delivery at wherever we end up."

"How's the alcohol?" I asked.

"There's still plenty of that. But if you want some you'll have to get up yourself to retrieve it."

I tried to do just that and realized my belly was sewn to my thighs. Or that's how it felt.

"Maybe I should stay here instead."

"That's a good idea. I can get you some water if you're thirsty."

"Water would be lovely."

She got up and handed me a bottle of water, and I noticed she was wearing a light dress instead of her usual ready-for-action tight-fitting clothing. It was like seeing a police officer off-duty.

I also noticed her wince when she stood.

"Don't worry, I can still protect you while wearing a dress," she said, noting my observation. "I didn't expect us to be going anywhere for some time."

"I saw you kill a demon yesterday. I'm not worried. And you're injured."

"You say it like killing one is difficult. I'm just bruised. He caught me with a backhand."

"Last time I saw someone kill a demon in single combat the winner was a six-hundred-year-old vampire. That was also the only time."

She shook her head as if this was the silliest thing she'd ever heard. "The mistake is trying to match their force with your own force. Demons are slow and angry, and rely on their presumption of invincibility too much. Stick them in the right places and they'll fall, just like anybody else."

She sat back down at the computer and continued doing whatever it was she was doing, while I fought the urge to fall in love with her.

"So are you playing solitaire on that or what?" I asked.

"I thought that while you were out I might use the time to figure out who you actually are."

"On my password-protected computer?"

She laughed. "You picked a very good password, but you shouldn't have written it down."

"I was told to change it monthly by some people who know more about those things than I do. I didn't want to forget it. And it was written down on a piece of paper in my wallet."

"So it was. And your wallet is on the desk here. I had to take it out of your pants to pay the driver. Then the flight crew asked for some walking-around money so I gave them some cash, too. I didn't think you'd mind."

"No, that sounds like about what I'd do."

"I know. It's what you did in Tbilisi."

"And then you happened upon my password."

"Yes. Unfortunately you have the least interesting personal computer I have ever seen."

I imagine I should have been upset that she was looking through my computer, but I'm still not used to the idea of electronic contents of a computer—or a phone—being something that belongs to me, in the same sense that the things in my wallet or my pockets belong to me. I say this even though with that computer she could probably steal a ton of my money if she wanted to.

"What were you looking for?"

She shrugged. "I don't know. Something that would help some of this make sense."

"You could have waited for me to wake up and then asked."

"I'm impatient."

"I see that. I'm mostly interested in why I'm still alive."

"Because I should have taken you to a hospital?"

"No, not that. I mean taking on the goblin."

"You fight very well for a human," she said. "Especially for one as old as you seem to think you are. That goblin was surprised, I'm sure."

"He hesitated. It was only for a second or two but when I run through it in my mind ... if Iza hadn't popped him in the eye just then I'm not sure he would have finished off that blow. I don't think he was there to kill me."

"You have stitches that say otherwise."

"That's another thing. I'm wondering if the severity of this wound was intentional. I think he short-armed it on purpose."

Mirella smiled and leaned back in the chair. "Actually, I agree, and I've been wondering the same thing. If the goblin wanted to kill you he could have done it without engaging you directly at all. And whoever was responsible for those two being there could have done one better and just planted a man with a rifle in the woods to shoot you when we walked outside."

I thought about the scene again, because she was right.

Assuming the people who sent the demon and the goblin were the same bunch that visited Tchekhy—this seemed like a good assumption—they had been following me for a while. Changing up suddenly and jumping me on an Istanbul street didn't really make a lot of sense.

But then I didn't know why they were bothering to follow me at all. I was starting to get a notion of who was doing the following, though.

"You talked to the driver about who asked him to move the car?" I asked. We had possibly already had this conversation prior to my getting stitched up, but I couldn't remember, for pretty obvious reasons.

"He gave a description that fit nearly every white American male in the world. He could have been describing you."

"I'm not technically American."

"I realize that, but the point is the same. We're looking for a white man with dark hair, thin, and your height, who speaks Turkish but with an American accent. That's a largely useless description."

"That might be intentional."

"You mean this was an intentionally bland person? I don't think you can decide to be bland."

"I often strive to be bland and forgettable. It's a lot easier to disappear into the background that way."

"Then you're failing miserably."

"I'm not sure how to take that."

"Take it however you like. But what's your point?"

"You were watching the tape," I said, pointing to the television.

"I was. You have no movies and I can't seem to get a decent television program to come through, so I watched this instead. Stop changing the subject."

"I'm not. This video was sent by someone with access to the footage and an awareness of who I was *and* what this footage would mean to me. I know only one person who fits all that criteria, and he swears he knows nothing about it. So now I think it was sent by the same people following me. And I think those people might be the CIA."

"You think the US government is secretly following you around the world?" Mirella asked, in a tone that suggested something less drastic than full-on disbelief.

"All the pieces fit, yeah."

This was only sort-of true. The pieces fit, but the pieces could have fit to form a picture of another large secret government apparatus belonging to a different country. I never learned who Bob Grindel was in bed with financially, so it was entirely possible the owners of that footage were Mossad or whatever took the place of the KGB, or some group I never heard of. That was always the problem with secret organizations—they tended to be secret.

But CIA seemed right. That was clearly what Mike thought, even if he wasn't prepared to say so explicitly over the phone.

"This sounds paranoid," she said. "And I would have said as much a week ago. But between your Russian friend not trying to kill you with a rifle and the CIA not trying to kill you with a goblin, I'm ready to accept just about anything. But why would they? Who are you to them?"

"I don't know."

She got up, grumbling something I couldn't quite catch that might have been about me. "You have this video of a woman vanishing, you have the government chasing you but not interested in catching you, there is a damned tame pixie flying around this room, you killed a goblin in single combat with a sword, and you are over a thousand years old."

"That's about right."

"No more secrets."

She tossed the envelope holding the letter I'd stolen from the Istanbul museum onto the bed next to me.

"Tell me everything, starting with what this is a drawing of and why it's so important to you. And if you think you need to hold back a detail because it's something I might not believe, don't bother. I'm already standing on the other side of the looking glass."

I opened the envelope and unfolded the letter. It felt wrong to touch it without gloves on, but I wasn't ever returning it to the museum so it didn't really matter.

Briefly, I wondered if Mr. Acar was still alive, and whether this was something I should check on. If they killed him, the prime suspect was the billionaire who was last seen with him. I've found that it's always useful to know in what part of the world one is wanted by the authorities so I can avoid that part of the world, so it was something worth knowing.

The drawing on the back of Abraham's letter was crude, and full of notations that would probably make very little sense to most people. For me, it was something of a *eureka* moment because I'd heard this object described a long time ago by someone—Hsu—with a flair for the poetic. It was possible he just had no word for it, so he described it as well as he could. Or he was being a pain in the ass on purpose.

That was probably it. He liked being a pain in the ass.

"I was told that if I held this against the sky and walked toward the star that wasn't there I would step off the edge of the world."

"That makes no sense."

"It made no sense when I first heard it. With this drawing it makes a little bit of sense. This is called an astrolabe. Now sit down, and I'll tell you the whole story."

CHAPTER 12

*I*f I had more than one lifetime to work with I could have built sufficient equity and standing to get the attention of the person Hsu needed to get the attention of. But I only had one lifetime, and even though it was the lifetime of a goblin who was already much older than he was supposed to be, it was still a limited one.

We were further limited by the expected lifespan of the person we were trying to attract, one Abraham bin Yasser, a Jewish merchant who, while still young, was nonetheless only likely to be approachable for another decade or so.

Let me back up.

Hsu lost an object to Abraham and wanted it back. He seemed to think for whatever reason that Abraham still had the item, and hadn't sold it because the nature of said item was unusual enough to warrant keeping. Hsu wouldn't tell me what the object was, only dropping hints and wondering, I guess, if I was going to figure it out on my own. All I did know was it was small enough to be worn around a neck.

There were a large number of different ways to get the object back from Abraham, but all of those ways involved finding him and getting into the same room with him, and this was where we were running into a problem because unless you were doing business with Abraham bin Yasser, you weren't going to be sitting down with him. He was the son-in-law of one of the most successful merchants in the Middle East, and undoubtedly the most successful unconverted one.

Converting to Islam was a very popular business decision during this period. If you asked me at the time which religion would survive into the twenty-first century, I would have picked Islam before Christianity, and probably Hinduism, too. Back then the Christian faith was a hot mess built on top of a Roman architecture that had already shown itself to not be all that tolerant to change, whereas in Islam nobody forcefully converted anybody, they just made it economically advantageous to do so. Converted Muslims paid lower taxes on bought and sold goods, so if you happened to be a merchant in a region that had fallen under the influence of Allah, it was in your best interest to bow to Mecca. I converted myself. It was like having coupons.

Anyway, Abraham's family had not converted, but they didn't have to because he and his father-in-law controlled the market on a number of rare East Indies spices, so if their taxes went up they just raised their prices to offset the loss. Since the people liked their spices, they rarely had a problem with taxation.

Abraham's family—this was before the concept of companies, really—had a trade route that went from Indonesia by sea to India, over land to the other side of the Indian peninsula, by sea again to North Africa, and from there north to various parts of the Middle East. Their miniature commercial empire was seemingly impervious to political changes, religious disputes, or wars. If a region got too dangerous for one reason or another, Abraham just negotiated a different route.

In a lot of ways, then, he was one of the more impressive people nobody has ever heard of. For that period, he and his family were something like geniuses.

Abraham bin Yasser was not an easy man to meet, however. He was constantly on the move, and his business dealings were intensely private matters. This made perfect sense to me. When I was a successful merchant in Carthage I guarded my list of suppliers very closely, too. It was just smart business.

Because of how successful he was, there were people in the world whose entire job consisted of trying to figure out where the man was going to be, and who he was going to be sitting down with, and when. None of them were having much luck with this.

Hsu and I, with almost nothing in the way of resources aside from our wits, had no chance of locating him at all. So the only obvious solution was to make Abraham want to come to us. This meant remaking myself into a merchant important enough to attract his notice, which was, as I said, something I could do if I had a couple of lifetimes to spare. Since I didn't, I did the next best thing—I stole someone else's reputation.

～

Traveling along the Silk Road was not an incredibly safe thing to do, because the trade routes—there were several and they were all called the Silk Road—went through some pretty unkind territories full of raiding Mongol hordes and self-important warlords, people who thought of themselves as kings, and crusaders and bandits and the occasional dragon.

Since by nature travelers along the trade routes had their valuables *with* them, it was in their best interest to surround themselves with for-hire freelancers, family, and anyone else who fit the description of someone they could trust with their lives. It was also in their best interest to know where the nearest Buddhist monastery was.

In the first regard, after Hsu and I agreed to work together— he because it was his idea, I because he had piqued my curiosity—

the first thing on our agenda was to put together a band of trust-worthy people.

We both had some people we could turn to, although techni-cally very few of them were actual people. Hsu had two goblin friends—one male, one female—that owed him their lives for something that was never explained to me. The female was by her own definition an elf, but we didn't hold that against her. I had a few humans who owed me favors, a friendly but suicidal vampire named Sven, and a succubus who called herself Indira.

I don't recall exactly how I became an acquaintance of Sven, only that I remember spending a lot more time than it was really worth trying to talk him out of staying up to watch the sunrise. Indira I remember very well. Not only was she fantastic to have around—for the sex, obviously—but she was the best recruiter I could have asked for when it came time to build the small army I would need just to get around.

But first I had to come up with a reason to have a small army, which was where the monasteries came in. Almost half the Silk Road—the part that came after what's now Turkey if you're heading east—was dotted by Buddhist monasteries. They were like the Denny's of the ancient world. For a small donation, a traveler could get a meal and a place to stay, and a near-absolute guarantee of personal safety, because nobody shed blood in a holy place. Even if you weren't a Buddhist, it just wasn't done.

It was also a really fantastic place to get information.

Hsu and I spent several months loitering around three key monasteries that lay on cross routes between China, India, and the Turks. It wasn't ideal insofar as we were not going to be learning a lot of useful information about Abraham bin Yasser while among the monks. He wasn't using the overland route for shipping. But it gave us lots of details on what kind of trade was going on in the regions where his influence could be felt.

It was through our mostly gentle questioning of the locals that we met Xuangang.

To say that he looked aggrieved when we first met him would be to undersell the degree of distress that marked his appearance that night in the monastery. We had been sitting with a large group of men, who we were pretty sure were full-time bandits when they weren't enjoying the violence-free hospitality of the Buddhists, when Xuangang walked past and took the most isolated part of the room for himself.

Hsu and I made for a pretty good team. He was much better versed in Eastern languages and customs than I was, which saved me about a hundred years of the practice needed to become fluent. (I am still not fully fluent in Chinese, because I had Hsu to speak for me.) I was more familiar with Western customs and had a lot more business experience to work with, and I knew a more about non-human cultures than just about anyone alive.

Between us we could speak familiarly with nearly anybody. If they were Westerners, I was a wealthy traveler and Hsu was my manservant or slave. If they were from the East, Hsu was a learned scholar and I was his pupil.

Xuangang entering the dining space alone was unusual enough to catch our attention. Most people on these roads traveled with friends, family, vassals, or employees. It just wasn't safe to do otherwise. And inside the walls of the monastery everyone was equal, so it wasn't likely he left the people he was with outside or something. And he was not dressed in a way one might expect a lone traveler to dress, which is to say it didn't look like he was capable of independently defending himself. He had on the finery one would expect of a well-respected man from the emperor's court. It's difficult to describe how one *looked* well-respected, but it was possible. I think it was the combination of gold filigree, carriage, and general cleanliness.

More obvious than his station in life, it was clear he was in the midst of some species of misfortune.

We excused ourselves from the table of brigands—making note of everyone's face as we stood, because it's never a bad idea to keep a mental record of what the local robbers look like—and sat down next to the sullen Chinaman.

"Hello, friend," Hsu greeted him, in his native tongue. I knew basic greetings and a smattering of other words, so this I understood. Essentially, I could talk to someone in Chinese for about twenty seconds before I ran out of things to say.

Xuangang didn't reply, or even look up from his rice. Hsu and I exchanged a glance, and then I tried.

"Everything all right?" I asked in Latin. And then in Hindi, "You appear troubled."

He finally looked up, and studied us one at a time.

"I am no one. Please leave me," he said. Only he said it three times, in the three tongues we'd spoken.

"Clearly, you are a learned man," I said. I stuck with Latin. "Why would such a man be traveling alone on roads such as these, in times such as this?"

"As I said, I am no one. My life was taken from me today. You speak now only to the earthly remains of a man once known as Xuangang."

"You are very lively for a dead man," Hsu said.

"The arrow that will fell me has already been loosed. There is nothing I can do to alter its course, and to step aside would be dishonorable. You speak to the dead."

He was so depressed I felt like I should buy him a drink, except there wasn't really any alcohol to be had in the monastery. Not unless you count rice wine, which I do not.

Hsu said, "We, too, are learned men, scholars such as yourself, and well versed in the ways of this route. Can we offer you any assistance?"

"I am a scholar, yes," he said. He spoke it in Greek, though, which Hsu didn't speak. "And you cannot help me."

"These roads are not safe for one as studied as yourself," I said, also in Greek. This caused him to raise an eyebrow, which was a tame expression of surprise.

Xuangang was young and gaunt, sporting a tiny mustache and the beginnings of a beard. His eyes flickered with intelligence but not necessarily wisdom, which comes more with age. He struck me in much the same way most recent college graduates do. He was full of information but had no applied knowledge.

"I know the roads are unsafe," he said, switching back to Latin. "I have seen this for myself. But unless you two have an army lying in wait beneath your stools you have as much hope of aiding me as an ant in repelling a rainstorm."

"We may well have an army, and insufficient room beneath our stools for them all. Why don't you tell us what has befallen you?"

He looked us up and down a few times before deciding he had nothing left to lose. And based on the story he told, he actually didn't.

"I am the official representative of the great Fa Xi Han, of whom I am sure you have heard."

We nodded heartily and looked impressed and silently agreed we had never heard of this person.

"Of course," Hsu said. "What a great honor. Please continue."

"It is the greatest honor."

"Yes," I said, hoping we didn't have to discuss how great the honor was for very long.

"It was my greatest honor to take letters of introduction and a number of valuables to the court of the great Abbasid, and to negotiate matters of terrific import."

This sentence raised many questions. First, the *valuables* in question could have been just about anything, but it was clear from looking at him that if there were a great many such valuables he no longer had them. A large quantity would take up a lot of space regardless of what those valuables happened to be.

Metal—gold or tin—was the most portable wealth around,

and it tended to be heavy enough to be noticeable if he had it on him. If he was coming from a Chinese court, the odds were decent the wealth in question was in the form of either silk or spices, both of which could travel great distances and not lose value, but which were also very bulky.

Foodstuff such as grain held less value, took up even more space, and didn't do well in long bouts of inclement weather.

The valuables, then, were no longer with him.

The second was the letters of introduction, which he may or may not have had. Depending on what they said they *could* have been extremely valuable, because they served as a form of identification for the carrier of said letters. If you had one, and it was from an important person, and it declared that you were someone who spoke for that important person, you could travel quite a long way in style. Yet our new friend was alone in a roadside monastery, not dining with princes and great men of power. This either meant that Fa Xi Han wasn't nearly as important as he thought— which was what I suspected—or Xuangang didn't know how to properly exploit letters of introduction. Provided he still had them at all.

Third, there was no such thing as the court of the great Abbasid. The Abbasid Caliphate was the Islamic dynasty of the time—and for some time after—but it was not a singular economic force in the same way the dynastic emperor of China was. Really, outside the Chinese court there was no monolithic economic force left. The Abbasid dynastic courts were economically and militarily independent in most respects, and the Eastern Roman Empire of Constantinople either owned its resources or taxed its resources. It didn't deal with merchants and exporters directly; it only taxed them.

"You will forgive my impertinence, I hope," Hsu said. "But this wealth of which you speak does not seem apparent just now."

"It was stolen from me. I traveled with silks of the highest quality, and I hired the finest men to help me transport it, but not a half-day's ride from here I lost it all. And so now, once my belly has been filled, I will return to my dray and ride back to the court of Fa Xi Han and admit my failure, and he will take my life in exchange. And I will be glad to give it to him."

"What of the men you hired?" I asked.

"Slain, or fled. We were ambushed by skilled highwaymen, and vastly outnumbered. I barely escaped with my life. Temporarily, as is clear."

Hsu coughed, and shot me a knowing look. I had the same thought. Something about this smelled rotten.

"Xuangang, my friend," I said, "as you expect to be traveling to your honorable death soon, would you share with us the intent of your journey to the court of the great Abbasid?"

"Very well. I was to negotiate an open trade arrangement for a medicinal spice known as amomum."

"Black cardamom," Hsu said.

"Locally, yes. But not of the sort grown by the Hindus. This is from the Javanese and the Malays. It is much better, and Fa Xi Han controls it."

"You were negotiating a spice trade arrangement, then?" Hsu asked.

"Yes, exactly."

"With the Caliphate directly?"

"That was the intention."

"Honorable Xuangang, it is possible we may be able to aid you," I said, trying very hard not to smile. "But first I need to ask you about these letters of introduction. Do you still have them?"

~

He did still have them. They were five identical *to whom it may concern* letters to be used at the discretion of the holder. Each letter was written in three languages, and each said the same thing—the holder, Xuangang, speaks for Fa Xi

Han on all matters, and Fa Xi Han serves at the behest of the emperor himself.

The letters were probably more valuable than the silks he had lost. But if those silks were of as high quality as he said, they would help negotiations greatly because they served as proof of the wealth behind the letters. Hsu and I assumed that nobody outside the Malaysian peninsula, Java, and parts of China had ever heard of Fa Xi Han, so showing that he had some nice silks would be important.

After talking to Xuangang, Hsu and I convened privately, promising the broken and somewhat foolish man to help but not yet knowing exactly the best way to go about it.

"We should probably just kill him," Hsu said after considering it carefully for approximately the time it took to get some privacy. "As long as he doesn't bleed on any of the letters we will be fine without him."

"I agree that he's entirely prepared to die already, and if we do it here it will be no less honorable than if it happened to him in the court of Fa Xi Han, or back on the highway. But if we want to find those robbers and the silks we're going to need his help. We also know next to nothing about selling cardamom."

"Do you suppose he does? The idiot took the Road with *local* help to guard a small fortune. He would have needed twenty men just to get through the Khyber Pass, and probably fifty, and he would have had to be related to three-quarters of them to have had a chance. I don't think he has any wisdom whatsoever to share with us."

From where we were talking we could see him. He still looked like a man who was about to drown himself in his rice bowl. "I don't think we need to kill him. But clearly he cannot continue to be Xuangang of the court of Fa Xi Han."

"How do you suppose he will react to this information?"

"I don't think he needs to know that right *now*, do you?"

We returned to Xuangang and spent the rest of the evening

convincing him not to leave at sunrise to ride home to his certain death.

"You are only two men," he said. "You can't expect me to believe you alone are capable of finding and overcoming the same brigands that slew the best men I could hire?"

"We have additional resources at our disposal," Hsu said.

"But why would you help me? You would be risking your lives."

"As it turns out, we are looking for a way to involve ourselves in the spice trade, and you have provided us with just the kind of association we require."

"I'm not really ... authorized to discuss a partnership," he stammered.

I had to put my hand on Hsu's sword arm to keep him in check.

I said, "Honorable Xuangang, please believe me when I tell you that an association with us will be more profitable to you and your patron than anything you were prepared to negotiate for individually. And we will find your silk."

~

One thing that goes underappreciated in today's world is how much nothing there used to be. These days you can't turn around without hitting something, be it man-made or mankind itself. But in the days when the Silk Road trade routes were lively and active it wasn't like an actual road populated by people walking and riding in one direction or another. It was a lot of nothing separated by even more nothing with occasional dots of something here and there. It wasn't unusual to be able to go for multiple days without coming across anything or anybody in either direction.

This was why the monasteries were so useful. They were the first effort by anybody to consolidate and coordinate hospitality for travelers. Not that they were really consolidated—the monastic orders didn't really talk to one another and some were in competition philosophically—but they were all put in place with the same intent.

Appropriately, then, when Xuangang crossed the border of China he went to a monastery to hire the best men he could find. What he found instead were the first men he could find.

"They are all dead," he told Hsu when Hsu tried, quite patiently, to get more information about these men out of him. Hsu still preferred killing Xuangang, forgetting the silks, and seeing what we could do with the letters. Nearly everyone in our party agreed with him, especially after having spent a little time with the Chinaman. It turned out he was just exactly learned enough to be insufferable, but not enough to *know* that he was.

They took turns offering to kill him. Indira offered to do it in such a way that Xuangang might quite enjoy it. I was still pretty sure he had some use, though.

"Let me see if I can explain this to you in a way that you will understand," Hsu said. "You hired a number of men that you had only just met, took their word for it that they were trustworthy, and showed them a fortune in silk. You *then* asked them to take you down a secluded path at night."

Xuangang looked aghast. "These were honorable men!"

"You see a band of brave men who died defending you. I see a small band of performers who became rich without having to shed a drop of blood."

"Impossible! You have mistaken me for a fool. Why would you think such a thing?"

"I think this is so because in the same position as the men you hired, it is what I would have done. As would any one of us."

The elf woman—her name was Lassa—added, "Except we would have killed you."

Once we'd gotten Xuangang to grasp this basic notion, we started taking him from monastery to monastery, looking for familiar faces from the band of brave men who all died defending him. It was nearly a week before he saw one of them, which was nearly a week of listening to him tell us over and over again how wrong we were. He appeared to have no instinct for self-preservation whatsoever.

The hardest part after that was trying to seem like an easy mark without being too obvious about it. Ideally we would have sent Xuangang back in, because he was the only one who could really pull off the naïve traveler routine. But that was obviously not an option, so we had one of the men in our band—a Roman named Aurus—play the role. Aurus wasn't stupid but he was incredibly dull and that often came off as stupid, so we figured he'd be okay. He didn't even particularly mind the characterization.

We didn't need Aurus to do a whole lot anyway. We already knew the *modus operandi* of our target audience, we just had to play along with it. To that end, our Roman cohort claimed to be a wayward traveler trying to get to China with a lot of gold to trade for spice. There was a risk that the robbers would ask to see the gold before agreeing—Aurus carried a few coins with him to sell the story, but we had no fortune otherwise—but the men who approached him were so eager to jump into an agreement that it was never an issue. I guess after they had made a killing off Xuangang they were ready to perform the same act. If I were one of them I'd wonder how it was possible to come across two once-in-a-lifetime opportunities within a few days, but I'm not a highway robber. Maybe this happens all the time.

It had been our intention to lay an ambush, but we didn't have to bother, because after two of the men Xuangang recognized spoke with Aurus they left the monastery and headed up into the hillside—we were in an unkind mountainous region that I believe is now part of Afghanistan—to an encampment at the mouth of a cave. We knew this because we had a vampire and it was night, and vampires are very good at tracking people at night. They are not so good at it during the day, when it's sort of a pain to have one around because they basically have to be bundled up and carried, but worth keeping when you need someone who is fast, has heightened senses, and can follow a man across an open rocky hillside without being detected.

We didn't bother with the ambush. Instead, we surrounded the cave and shouted until they came out, which was much more efficient.

"Who are you?" came the response from a man I presumed was the leader of their band. He stood at the mouth of the cave before a low fire that served as the only illumination on a moonless night. He was large and looked capable, but he was only a man and we had things in our group that were a lot more than just men.

"We're here for the silks," I said.

Xuangang was standing beside me, and when we stepped into the firelight and the robber saw him he doubled over in laughter.

"The silks," he repeated.

"Do you still have them?" I asked.

"Yes, they're in the cave. We haven't had a chance to do much with them yet."

To Xuangang he said, "You make new friends fast."

"You are a dishonor to your family," the Chinaman said.

"You're not the first person to say so. You realize they're going to kill you, right? After they've gotten the silk."

Xuangang looked at me, a little flicker of fear in his eyes.

"I trust these men," he said.

"Well," the robber said, "you are a fool for your trust. And we are fools for having let you live. But if you survive *this* night you are the luckiest fool I have ever met." He returned his attention to me, and drew his sword. "Shall we have at it, then?"

In a fight like this it's always a good idea to be on the side of the team with a vampire, two goblins, and an elf, if at all possible. I was, and so it really wasn't much of a fight. Maybe ten or fifteen minutes of heavy skirmishing and then another half hour of cleanup. There were only twelve of them, and we killed them all, as one does. Not killing them would have been downright disrespectful, and would have resulted in us watching our backs for the rest of our lives.

The only person for whom all this was unexpected was Xuangang, who didn't fully appreciate the sort of beings he had fallen in with until then. He was a little rattled.

I lost track of him during the fight, busy as I was with people who could actually kill me. After it was done I was busy making sure we found the silks—we did, in the back of the cave, in an ornately carved box that was also worth quite a bit—and making sure we hadn't lost anyone.

Evidently, sometime after witnessing Sven the depressed vampire rip someone's head off, Xuangang decided it was in his best interest to escape into the hills. He made it about twenty feet before Aurus caught up with him. When Hsu and I reached them the Chinaman was busy throwing up the rice he'd had at the monastery.

"Will you kill me now?" he asked. "As that man said?"

"It would be no less an honorable death than the one you expected to face in the court of Fa Xi Han," I said.

"Less honorable for knowing now what a fool I have been."

"A shame that would not go any further than this valley."

"As you say."

He remained on his knees and lowered his head for my sword.

"Hand me your letters," I said.

Without speaking he reached inside his coat and held them out. I took them, and handed them to Hsu.

"I'm not going to kill you. But you are no longer Xuangang of the Malays. *He* is."

CHAPTER 13

It took a few years to turn Xuangang's silks, letters, name, and connection to a cardamom exporter into a profitable enterprise for all concerned. It was fortunate that Hsu and I had spent all those months beforehand talking to people in monasteries along the Road and trying to understand how to get close to Abraham bin Yasser, because we ended up absorbing a great deal about how trade went through the Indies. It wasn't at all long before we managed to connect a stable distribution of black cardamom from Javaland and Malay to India by sea, and then overland to the markets of Constantinople, Tbilisi, and especially Baghdad and Samarra.

The real Xuangang proved worthy of being kept alive, because even though it was Hsu pretending to be him whenever it came time to discuss business with regional merchants or ship captains, we needed the real person when dealing with Fa Xi Han. This was especially true one or two times a year when we had to travel to Han's court to run through the numbers. Fa Xi Han was a big fan of numbers. To make it easier on Xuangang we let him do the books.

Hsu and I were traveling more or less constantly those years, trying to keep the modest one-product shipping business afloat. It was actually an enormous pain, and since neither of us were necessarily out for the money—I was more interested in it than he was, which was an curious reversal—we found it difficult at times to pass on the most convenient deal in favor of the one that made the most business sense. We both recognized that looking like anything less than shrewd businessmen would not be in our interests, either in the eyes of our supplier or our competition.

To that end we kept small residences throughout India, as well as in Baghdad and a couple of other places. These residences were for our use or for the use of anyone remaining from our original band of trusted associates, depending on where the business winds took them.

That list of associates did not include the vampire, who eventually got bored again and went to the beach one morning, and that was the last we heard of him. Indira the succubus likewise found work as a spice merchant not to her liking. She took her cut and set up a bordello in Chennai. I stopped by on her whenever I was in town, which was often since our ships usually landed on the same coast.

Everyone else stuck around. I didn't have the heart to tell any of them we were only doing this to attract the attention of another merchant, but then we were pretty sure if we got his attention it would end up being profitable enough for people to start thinking about retiring.

As to *why* we were trying to get the attention of Abraham bin Yasser, I had nothing more to go on than what I originally heard from Hsu years earlier under the hanging tree. He managed to describe the sought-after object obliquely at best, saying if I used it properly I would be able to "step off the edge of the world". I took this to mean by doing so I would visit his faery kingdom.

I didn't want to visit the faery kingdom, but I knew he did, and while I was entirely unconvinced that anything he told me about the place was more than legend, exaggerations, and outright lies—either told to him or by him—I was interested in seeing if he could prove me wrong.

I had heard of the faery folk before. Versions of them came out of a lot of different traditions stretching from the Britons to the Hindus. But I had never seen one, much as I had never seen an angel or a devil. I know it seems like history is rife with creatures most people would stack in the same pile—goblins, elves, satyrs, dragons, demons, pixies, vampires, and on and on—but there were real versions of these things in the world at one time or another, and in just about every case the real version was not at all as fearsome as the legendary kind. (Nymphs would be the exception. They are much worse in real life, and I don't want to talk about it.) My point is faeries were always mythological. I based that on my having never seen one, which is usually all the proof I need. And the one or two times someone told me about one, it turned out to be an ordinary person with a few magic tricks and better-than-average PR.

Despite all that, Hsu persisted in claiming he had lived in the actual faery kingdom, and that it was a real place that was possible to visit. He had no proof of this, other than the fact that he was apparently much older than he looked.

Admittedly, that was the kind of evidence I took to heart, since I was also much older than I looked. But I needed more. Clean living and a decent moisturizer seemed like a more plausible explanation than an entire secret world.

Hsu's age was actually starting to show. His hair was graying, and the laugh lines around his mouth were starting to become wrinkles.

I am routinely startled by the changes made by time on the people around me, because from my perspective it's extraordinarily sudden. Hsu was only exhibiting tiny differences so far, but I was studying him more closely to see if he aged. So I noticed.

Other than describing a kingdom that couldn't possibly be

real in florid language that sounded straight out of every other faery myth, Hsu spent a lot of time describing the faery who took him there. His name was Byha, a literally radiant figure my friend was clearly in love with. They were only together a short while before Hsu realized that time was passing differently where they were, and he had missed almost the entire lifespan of his family. So he asked to be returned home. Byha agreed, and gave him the object now in Abraham's possession. He told Hsu if he wished to return he needed only to hold it up to the sky and walk in the direction of the star that wasn't there, and when he arrived to speak the word *Byrgddun*.

It was no word in any language I knew, and Hsu couldn't tell me what it meant, but insisted he was speaking it correctly. And it was impossible for me to forget because I heard him recite it to himself every evening, just in case saying so evoked a visit from his faery.

Upon being returned to the world, Hsu went back to his village to find his family was all dead, and in his mourning he ended up getting very drunk. Then came a drunken wager and the loss of the one thing he needed to return to Byha.

It took him months to track down the man who'd won it, only to learn that he had used it to pay off a debt to one Abraham bin Yasser.

And that was when Hsu sought me out.

~

It was during our fourth year in the spice trade business that a correspondence reached us from an associate representing the interests of one Abraham bin Yasser.

I say it *reached us* because that's the way letters had to work back then. They were sent out into the world with the hope that one of them would reach its destination. This was a likely prospect when the recipient was not mobile, as for instance the letters Abraham sent home to his father-in-law. Those were sent in sealed envelopes with ship captains along with goods being sent to the same area, then passed from person-to-person until they got to the right person, or until they didn't.

In our case the one that reached us had been dated six months earlier and was noted as being one of three identical such letters, each sent along different routes. It stated an interest in a joint business venture and asked us to meet with the sender, giving a date that was, to the time and place we received it, three months and two mountain ranges away.

Hsu was ready to pack up and go immediately.

"It's not Abraham," I said. "It's a guy speaking for Abraham."

"But he can get us to him."

"No, I don't think so. I think if we agree to meet with him he's the only one we'll ever meet with."

"How about if we *force* him to get us to Abraham?"

Hsu was, shall we say, growing impatient.

"You have to trust me on this."

Hsu stormed off muttering some swear words in Chinese he never bothered to translate for me, but which I believe defamed my parentage in some way.

My response to the letter was to tell this representative—his name was Moshe—that Xuangang had no interest in sitting down with any man who was not Abraham bin Yasser. I then notified him of ways in which the great Xuangang might be reached in the future.

I only sent one letter, because I knew where Moshe was going to be in three months.

～

As I hoped, a second letter arrived from Moshe six months after I'd sent my reply. In it, Moshe described at enormous lengths the incredible importance of Abraham bin

Yasser as a person, how very impressively busy he was at all times, and how it was hardly necessary to bother the great man since Moshe's word was as good as his boss's.

And also, if we could be in Mangalore in six months, it *might* be possible for us to say hello to Abraham as he would be in town at that time.

Hsu had been impossible for the entire six months, which I guess was not unexpected. I think of this whenever someone complains to me about having to wait a while for an e-mail or a phone call, incidentally. You have no idea.

"*Now* can we go?" he asked after I showed him the letter.

"Yes, now we can go. Let me draft a reply first and send it ahead so we don't appear too eager."

"Perhaps we can appear too eager by showing up at all."

"Go pack before someone asks why the great Xuangang is acting like an infant."

~

*M*angalore was a port town in southwestern India, and it wasn't a huge surprise that Abraham was going to be there at some point during the year, since all of the spices he shipped from overland through India left that port. He practically owned it, which was why I never even tried to negotiate the departure of a spice ship from there, even though it would have been a more efficient route—across the Indian Ocean to North Africa and north from there—than the perilous trip we made down the Silk Road every year.

We were three months away if we took our time, which was difficult to do as Hsu seemed to think the faster he got there the sooner six months would pass.

"You appreciate, don't you, that we have no reason to hurry?" I asked after he spent yet another day pushing our group too hard through some particularly unpleasant mountains.

We had a large contingent with us, consisting of the real Xuangang—now older and somewhat wiser, and no longer convinced we intended to eventually murder him—a few goblin associates of Hsu's, two cooks, three local terrain guides, two of the merchants who would be in charge of shipments later in the year, and fifteen men with real soldiering experience to guard all of us. That wasn't counting the wagons, carts, and horses.

"This plan of ours, it's taken too long. I expected to be facing this man before now."

"My concern is that he long ago parted with your bauble."

He grumbled and picked at the food we'd had prepared. We were now doing well enough to expect a decent meal every night, which was nice. It mostly consisted of whatever animals our party managed to kill over the course of the day or, failing that, whatever stored salted meats we had, plus any vegetables and so on we came across. We hired cooks out of two of the poorest areas in a hundred miles, because even though they had next to nothing to work with, they made very edible food. This is how I'd run a restaurant if I ever owned one, by the way. I'd give them some junk that was nearly spoiled and ask them to do something with it. If they made an edible meal, I'd hire them.

Hsu spoke again after a time. "If Abraham no longer has it I'll find out who does and formulate a new plan."

"You know, if this goes well you'll end up modestly wealthy. Maybe your friend Byha will want to relocate here with you instead."

"Yes, but I can't really ask him that, can I?"

"He wasn't called the first time you met him either."

"No. But last time we had no arrangement. He parted the curtain from his world and stepped into ours because he thought I was beautiful. Now I am older and no longer beautiful and he is probably as young as when I left him. And he will not return to me because he is waiting for *me* to return to *him*. And I can't."

"You're still a beautiful man, Hsu. I'm sure he will greet you happily."

"And you speak with the tongue of an imp. But thank you anyway. Would that I aged as slowly as you."

~

We reached Mangalore in plenty of time to arrange for quarters for our contingent, and to get a feel for the city and how things worked there.

The basic homogeneity of the modern city is a new thing. If you're in America it's very easy to stand on a street in a downtown area and have no idea which city you're standing in. European cities have a little more character because they're older, but there are still a lot of similarities between them. But the cities of the Early Middle Ages were miniature fiefdoms. It wasn't just that you had to know what language was spoken and where the bad neighborhoods were, you needed to know how politically strong the ruling class was, what religion people adhered to and exactly how crazy they were about it, what behaviors were taboo, who was the law on the streets, and on and on. This is another reason I tried to stay away from large cities when I could.

Plus, they always smelled.

Mangalore wasn't so bad, smell-wise, because it wasn't tremendously overpopulated like many of the cities became before the plague came along and took care of a lot of that, at least in Europe. We got our bearings, learned which officials to bribe and which to avoid, and everything else we needed to know if we were interested in doing business there. We were not, but we wanted to appear as if we were, so that was what we did.

We also notified Moshe by letter that we were in town and asked for details on when we could expect to meet with Abraham bin Yasser. Moshe pretended we were never going to be meeting with his boss for enough successive correspondences that Hsu had to be held down to prevent him from finding Moshe and putting his head on a stick.

Finally, we got back the information we needed. And that was good news. Less than good news was where the meeting was to take place.

One of the things we learned when doing our reconnaissance was that—as was true quite often back then, and also now—the real power in the city was in the hands of a single family, and by that I mean mafia. It was not, of course, *the* mafia, but an ancient permutation of the same essential dynamic.

We never met anyone representing this family, by design. But we knew the family name was Talus, and we knew where the head of the family Talus could be found, and it was the same place where we were to be meeting with Abraham and Moshe.

Showing, for a change, some degree of restraint and common sense, Hsu suggested we negotiate for a different meeting place, but I didn't see how that was possible at such a late date. Instead we opted to bring a small show of force and hoped Abraham knew what he was doing.

Nothing we had uncovered about the Talus family intersected with anything involving the spice trade—or at least not Abraham's corner of it—so there was no telling what the point of the location choice was.

~

When we arrived at the palace compound we were met at the gate by a man who introduced himself as Bosphor Talus. He was tubby, had a deep shade of coffee for skin, and displayed a multitude of tattoos and piercings.

I wasn't sure he was actually a man. I couldn't tell *what* he was, however.

"Greetings, plentiful salutations, and welcome," he said.

"Beyond these walls there is only peace, so we ask that you leave your weapons here."

The walls he was talking about were gigantic for something attached to a private home. They looked more like the sort of thing one would find encircling the palaces of Kashmir. Possibly they were meant to convey exactly that.

"Friend," I said, "we have no quarrel with the Talus, nor anyone else in these walls, but your battlements are alarming."

"They are meant to protect you!" Bosphor said. "As are the men who will hold your weapons."

There had been two sentries standing beside Bosphor, but now they were joined by five more. All of *them* were armed and wearing battle armor. We could have taken them—we had more people, more weapons, and a few goblins—but for all we could tell there were another hundred inside waiting to come out and play.

"I suppose, then, we ought to hand over our weapons," Hsu said gamely, demonstrating his generosity of spirit by handing over the sword at his hip. It was maybe a tenth of the total number of sharp objects on his person, so the generosity was understandable. It was a little less of a pleasant experience for the rest of us, except maybe the other two goblins.

Xuangang was the only one not inconvenienced, since he didn't have any weapons in the first place. He had books with him, which they let him keep. I might argue that books are also weapons, but only in a philosophical sense, not as a practical way of fending off a broadsword.

Xuangang was playing the role of Lo, household servant to Xuangang, who was being played by Hsu. The name I was using was Blasius, and I was claiming to be a learned merchant from the Crimea. These were the roles the three of us played whenever we were in public outside Fa Xi Han's court, and we had been doing it long enough that hardly anybody knew it was inaccurate. As it was, Xuangang—the real one—didn't know me by any other identity. We were fortunate Hsu hadn't inadvertently called me Li-Yuan around him, since that was a name Xuangang would likely recognize.

We handed over our swords. But given we had hired a decent number of men to accompany us with swords, and given those swords represented the extent of their service to us, taking them away—peacefully or otherwise—didn't make a lot of sense. So I selected two captains to enter the building with us and left the rest at the gate. Bosphor gamely agreed to let them remain armed if they stayed there and guarded all the sharp things we were leaving behind.

This was all a bad idea, and if it weren't for the fact we were doing this to take a business meeting we'd been anticipating for more than half a decade, we would have walked away from it long before crossing into the Talus inner compound. Even Xuangang thought so, and he had no instinct for these sorts of things whatsoever.

"Should we not reconsider this meeting?" he asked Hsu quietly, in a language only we were familiar with, in case anyone was listening. We had learned over the years what languages we all had in common, and what languages nobody around us had ever heard, and this was one of the better ones. It was, I believe, an early German progenitor.

"It will be fine," Hsu insisted. He was lying, but it was too late to turn around.

Bosphor Talus led us to a large common room with a vast central table, at the head of which was an older version of Bosphor Talus. This was, I quickly realized, Gorrgon Talus, the great patriarch of the Talus family, and someone I had never hoped to meet.

To his right sat two Jews. I took the younger to be Moshe, and the older Abraham. The only other people in the room were guards.

It was frankly amazing to me that Abraham sat alone in this

room with nobody but Moshe to protect him. He surely knew exactly who Gorrgon Talus was. If they were that trusting of one another this was not likely to be a very good meeting.

The elder Talus was quite heavyset, but this did not impede his ability to leap to his feet with alacrity, and rush over to greet each of us one-by-one with a handshake. Four of the seven of us weren't even important to this meeting, but we didn't want to interrupt him.

"SO very GLAD you could make it here, ALL of you!" he said.

To Hsu, "And you are without a doubt the GREAT Xuan-gang!" He clapped my friend on the shoulder and gestured for all of us to take a seat.

Soon, we were opposite Abraham and Moshe, and Gorrgon was at the head again. It felt like a treaty negotiation instead of a business meeting.

"Honored guests," Gorrgon said as he sat, "the Talus are MOST pleased to host you under our roof. We would like to thank honored friend Moshe for making such a thing possible."

Moshe nodded and smiled. Abraham nodded as well. He didn't seem all that engaged. Other than acknowledging his own name, Moshe didn't look alert either. I wondered if there had been drinking prior to our arrival and, if so, where it was. I am never one to pass on a drink.

"And I would like to thank the GREAT Xuangang for taking the time to come and visit our humble home!"

Hsu nodded as well, and smiled graciously. I was glad he had not yet jumped over the table and pulled open Abraham's shirt, as he was still convinced that Abraham had the trinket on him.

"Now then, on to business! And then when we are DONE we shall have a GREAT feast!"

I was seriously confused, and decided to say so.

"Honored Talus," I said. "I am Blasius, and I speak for Xuan-gang's interests in many things. Do I have your permission to speak in these walls?"

I have found, over the years, that when one is talking to royalty or people who like to think they are, and when you are in a disadvantageous situation strategically, the very best possible recourse is to flatter the hell out of them.

"Of COURSE, great Blasius, indeed much has been said about your GREATNESS as well!"

I was glad we were all great. "Gorrgon Talus, if I may ask, why are we meeting here? When I awoke this morning it was to engage in a discussion of business matters with bin Yasser. I am doubly honored to sit in the presence of one such as yourself, but I fear these are the most mundane of details that could scarcely interest you. Abraham bin Yasser, if I may ask, you wished to speak with us and I believe the matter concerns our spices and your trade route. Is this not so?"

"Yes," Abraham said. And then he looked at Gorrgon and didn't say anything else. He was either the dumbest negotiator in the world or something very odd was happening.

"We speak here today because bin Yasser's business interests coincide with my business interests, as do the interests of Xuangang," Gorrgon said, without using his dramatic voice. "We are here because I am interested, and that is all that is important to you."

He smiled again, and returned his attentions to the rest of the table. "I am so VERY pleased Moshe decided to bring us all together. It seems—and please, correct me if I misspeak, Moshe— it seems the market has been unkind to Abraham bin Yasser of late. Black cardamom, a spice YOU specialize in, great Xuangang, has been pricing out the cardamom arriving to market on bin Yasser's ships, and while it is clearly an INFERIOR product it is doing well because it is cheaper. Is that accurate, Moshe?"

"It is," Moshe said.

"And so a solution was arrived at whereby bin Yasser intended to BUY the supply line for black cardamom from Xuangang and add it to his extant inventory, and make Xuangang and his associates wealthy men."

Gorrgon rose from his seat and stood behind Abraham, placing his hands on the older man's shoulders. "Now, when Gorrgon Talus HEARD of this he thought to himself, SURELY there is another way to go about this that will make both parties VERY HAPPY. Surely it would be best for EVERYONE if both Abraham bin Yasser and the GREAT Xuangang handed over their businesses to ME."

I nearly laughed aloud, until I realized I was going to be the only one laughing. I looked at Hsu and saw that he had the same blissed-out expression on his face as Abraham and Moshe. And so did everyone else at the table.

"You mean, you would take over the black cardamom trade, *and* all of the business passing through here on Abraham's ships?" I asked.

Gorrgon looked extremely annoyed that I was speaking again. "You will REFRAIN from speaking, for I am only interested in what the great Xuangang has to say."

"Well, no, I won't refrain from speaking," I said.

Gorrgon Talus stared at me for a long time, then said, "Does everyone else here agree that this is a fantastic plan?"

Everyone did, in a variety of nods and grins and muttering noises. They all looked extremely happy about it, too.

"Excellent," he said. Then he took his seat again and returned his attention to me. "The only question remaining, Blasius of Crimea, is what sort of being you happen to be."

"I was going to ask you the same question, Gorrgon Talus. Except I think I know. You're a djinn, aren't you?"

"Indeed."

This was the second or third time I had ever encountered a djinn, but the first time I'd met a family of them. It was also the first time I'd seen them as anything other than an odd sideshow, because I never really got what the big deal was.

The book on djinn was they granted people wishes, but nobody believed that, even back when they were actually around. Up until the day I met the Talus family I thought djinn were just drug dealers, to be honest.

All charm had left the demeanor of Gorrgon Talus, whom I had clearly displeased for not swooning in time with everyone else at the table.

"It was the handshakes, wasn't it?" I asked.

"Yes. The hands of a djinn issue the stuff of pleasant dreams. These men are going to be happier in signing over their fortunes than any man before them or since, and I can make it so they remain exactly that happy for the rest of their lives if I am feeling generous. But you are a problem."

"My apologies to the great Gorrgon Talus for being a problem."

"You may stop that now. I'm going to have to have you killed, but before I do that I need to know what you are so that in the future, when I encounter one such as you, I can be more adequately prepared."

I could have gone any number of ways with this. The truth was, there aren't any men like me, and only one woman who *might* be like me. The odds of him encountering her were incredibly small, especially since I had been trying to encounter her regularly for a long time by then and had failed spectacularly.

But telling him this wouldn't have done much good because, assuming he believed me, it would bring to an end our conversation and my life.

I also couldn't *not* answer, because he'd just end up torturing me until I gave him an answer he liked. My best option was to come up with a response that was so impressive he let me go, hopefully along with everyone else in my party. But I knew almost nothing about the djinn as a species, and this particular one had come across as alarmingly pragmatic when he wasn't flattering everyone into submission. I didn't think the odds were exceptional that he had a god I could pretend to be.

My only real chance was that he assumed I had no chance, and also assumed that I had no weapons. I didn't, but I knew where four were found on Hsu. Two were close enough for me to reach, and Hsu was in no condition to either protest or to defend himself.

There were the two guards in the room that I was going to have to contend with, but they looked like they were part of the family, and the family was not blessed with a particularly athletic build. I was pretty sure I could take Gorrgon and the others all alone, in other words. But I had no clue what I was going to do after that unless I could figure out how to wake everybody up.

Then I decided maybe I should just ask.

"I'm something new," I said, and hoped that would tide him over for the moment. "But tell me, how does your spell work? Or whatever this is?"

"It's a drug. Makes them very susceptible to suggestion. Enough of it and they are as docile as a pack mule."

"I'm surprised I didn't know this already," I said. "Have you considered expanding into the drug trade? I imagine you would make a killing. They certainly do look very happy."

"It has to be fresh, or we would be running the world right now. It also fades quickly."

"And can anybody give them a command?"

"I don't feel particularly satisfied with your response. What sort of new thing are you?"

"A faery," I said.

He laughed. "Those aren't real. Try again. And don't say vampire; I know those *are* real but you are in daylight. You are too large to be an imp, and you are clearly no demon. You may be a shaved down yeti, but I think that's unlikely. A dragon, perhaps?"

"Perhaps I am."

"No. You are also no sprite, nor iffrit, pixie, goblin, or elf. You could be a troll, I've never met one of them. Are you a troll?"

"I'm not a troll, no."

"No, I think you are not large enough. And you are no incubus, for when do they care about anything but women? Hmm. Perhaps you *are* a faery."

"I could be a banshee."

"Those are a kind of faery. And you are not a woman."

"Both true. I confess. I am only a man."

"A human man?"

"Yes. But one who cannot be poisoned, which is what you tried to do to me."

"But why? How did it not work?"

"I don't know. I would ask someone else who is like me why this is true but there is nobody to ask."

"Ah. Well then, if you are unique, I have no need to worry about coming across another such as you. Your death will solve my problem and I can go on with these negotiations without any further interruptions."

It almost goes without saying, but nobody else at the table was doing anything while Gorrgon and I spoke. They just sat there looking happy. I was wondering what would happen if I told them to stop that, but it would have to wait.

Gorrgon signaled to the two Talus men in the room. They hadn't been listening to our conversation, which was probably self-preservation on their part considering the sorts of things that probably got discussed at the table.

"Take this man in back and kill him," the patriarch said. Nobody looked surprised by the request, so I gathered it wasn't an unusual one. They flanked me as soon as I stood up.

Having two guards on the portly side wasn't necessarily a good thing for me because their important blood vessels were under an extra layer of fat, and while the two daggers I'd slipped from the sleeves in the small of Hsu's back were unquestionably sharp, they weren't all that large.

Mind you, I wasn't worried about *if* I could dispatch them, I was worried I wouldn't be able to do it *quickly*. I can kill three men pretty fast when they're not expecting it, especially if they're all nearby.

It took about eight seconds. They had armor on but their necks weren't protected, so when they turned to escort me out I stabbed the one in front in the side of the neck, and I was already slicing into the second one with the other knife while the first one fell. I don't think either even got their hands on their swords.

The idea of hitting them in the throat was pretty basic. Aside from the obvious mortal wound aspect, hitting the right spot meant keeping anybody from shouting loud enough to be heard outside the room.

Gorrgon was not prepared to do anything in eight seconds other than stand, and by the time he did that the second man was dead and I was throwing one of the daggers. That's about where my luck ran out. Because of the range I took the surest shot, which was through the eyeball. But sometimes people with undamaged throats can manage a cry or two even after their brains have had a blade shoved into them. They don't usually have anything exciting or coherent to say, but they can still say it loudly.

In this instance, Gorrgon's dying word was "Heyuh-lurggggha!" which I am pretty positive doesn't mean anything. But he was not at all quiet.

I had no clue how long it would take for someone to respond to this noise he made, but the windows to the room were open and the place was big enough to garrison a battalion, so the worst-case scenario was incredibly grim. All I had going for me was that there was only one entrance to the hall, through double doors that opened in and could be barred with something heavy.

What I needed was a bookshelf or a credenza or something,

neither of which was in the room. There was the table and a bunch of chairs, a lot of blissed-out people, and three dead bodies, and that was it.

A few minutes later I'd relieved two swords from the dead guards and stacked all three of the Taluses up against the doors. They were not bookshelves, but they would do. Then I stood at the head of the table.

"Hello, everyone," I said. "I need you to ..." But I didn't know what to say. Telling them to *snap out of it* seemed like a plan that was unlikely to succeed inasmuch as they were not likely aware of how out of it they were.

I cleared my throat and tried again. "We are all in terrible danger. We have been double-crossed by Gorrgon Talus and now all of us are going to die unless you get up right now and defend yourselves."

"Did you say we're going to die?" Abraham said. "That's terrible."

"I agree," Hsu said. "Terrible."

And then neither of them moved. Nor did anybody else. I was beginning to wonder if my best bet was to climb up to one of the windows and find my own way out of the compound. The windows were near the ceiling so reaching them would be difficult, and the drop on the other side was significant as the room was on the second floor, but I thought my odds would still be better. If I lived to the end of the day I'd be short a few friends, but at least I'd survive. I could always find more friends.

There was a loud bang at the door then. I suppose someone on the other side had already tried pushing gently and I simply hadn't noticed, but now it was obvious one or two people were out there and they were hitting the doors hard. The bodies of Gorrgon and his relatives weren't going to hold very long.

I needed Hsu. He was the best warrior there that wasn't me, and he had two or three weapons other than the crummy swords

I was working with, and he knew how to use them. I jumped up on the table and walked to him.

Pointing the sword at his face I said, "Defend yourself," and slapped the flat of the blade against his cheek.

"What?" he asked.

"I said defend yourself." I slapped him again. "Or I will take off your head."

There was another loud thump at the doors, and this time it was joined by the sound of wood splintering. I swung at Hsu's head again and I was about 50/50 on whether or not to actually take his head off at this point because I was in this mess because of him. But this time he put up an arm to block the sword. This might seem like a dumb thing to do with a sharp thing coming at you but his wrists were sleeved in mail as a defensive measure.

"Li-Yuan. What are you doing?" he asked.

"We are a very short time away from being overrun by soldiers because I just recently killed the patriarch of the Talus family and they are upset about that."

He gave this a little thought. "Yes. Of course. Can I have a sword?"

I handed him the one I'd been slapping him with and jumped off the table.

The Talus blockade of bodies was actually holding quite nicely, but the doors were still nearly broken in two from the force being applied from the hallway.

Hsu took a position behind one of the doors and I took the other. "What was he?" he asked. "A sorcerer?"

"A djinn. The whole family is."

"I didn't know they were real."

"I did, but I didn't know they were a big deal before now. That reminds me, when you're fighting, don't let them touch your skin with their hands."

"How about their blood?" he asked.

"I have no idea."

"Well. We will find out."

The first large hole in the door was followed by the head of one of the soldiers and, self-evidently, another Talus relative. Hsu removed the head before it had a chance to report what it saw.

"Evidently the blood is not a problem," he said. "And this sword is terribly dull."

Nobody stuck any other body parts in for a few seconds, and the banging on the doors also stopped while someone on the other side tried to figure out what to do next. And now there were four Talus bodies blocking the door.

Hsu looked over at Abraham. "Did you speak to him?" he asked.

"I haven't had a chance. And he's not really here right now."

"None of them are. But perhaps I awoke sooner because I am goblin-born." He looked me over. "And this magic did not affect you because you do not believe in magic, I suppose."

"It's a drug, not magic."

"So you tell yourself. Man the door alone for a moment, if you would."

A few minutes later Hsu and I were joined by the other two goblins we had with us.

"He doesn't have it on him," Hsu said.

"Abraham."

"Yes. We will need to get him out of this alive so he can take me to it."

"That is going to get more difficult the longer it takes him to wake up and the more bodies we stack up at this entrance," I said. "They're doing a good job of keeping us safe, but this is still the only exit we have, unless we learn to fly."

The soldiers in the hallway decided to attack again at that point, perhaps out of fear that we *could* learn to fly in the time they were giving us. They blew open the doors with the largest battering ram they could find that fit in the hall, and then several of them stumbled into the room, off-balance and slipping on all the Talus parts lying on the floor.

Off-balance is a terrible way to start a fight. Soon we had all the swords we needed.

As more guards charged into the breach, the men seated at the table finally began to stir, possibly because aerosolized blood has that effect on people. Since two of them could be trusted with a weapon, the battle actually started to work out in our favor, at least in the room.

One of the captains stuck his fingers into his mouth and gave two loud staccato whistles. I fought my way to him.

"What was that for?" I asked.

"The men outside will take the yard, lord," he said. "We should drive for the exit now."

"Do you have a whistle that tells them not to touch anybody?"

"I wouldn't know how to signal that, no."

He was right about needing to drive for the exit, though. We formed a wedge around the non-fighters among us—Xuangang, Abraham, and Moshe—and pushed out of the room and into the hall. A few minutes later we'd forced our way outside to the courtyard to what we were hoping was the friendly faces of the ten or so soldiers-of-fortune we had hired to protect us in the event just this sort of thing were to happen.

We did not find this.

The problem with open courtyards is that they are not narrow, enclosed spaces that nullify uneven odds. So while we had been holding our own with a handful of men, goblins and me against a superior force inside the building, once we got outside that force was much more effective, and the additional men running to our aid didn't make all that much of a difference.

～

I've been in a lot of battles. Maybe not as many as I could have been in, since historically I have found the best way to survive a war is to leave the place where the war is going on until everyone is done having their war and people go back to making decent alcohol and cooked meat and all of the other nice things that come out of peacetime. But sometimes that's not possible, and I have to pick up a sword, or whatever people are using to kill other people, and defend myself with it.

One thing I have learned is that it's impossible to understand —from the middle of a battle—exactly how it's being fought. By that I mean in terms of strategy and counterstrategy and more fundamentally who is winning and who is not winning and why. This is why generals who lead from the vanguard, while very inspiring, don't tend to do as well as the ones on the hill or on a horse at the back of the battle. Those are the ones who can see how things are going and can adjust their approach on the fly. It's also why the best accounts of battles rarely come from foot soldiers.

My point is I don't know what happened in this fight, not really. It was an elbow-to-elbow melee that involved lots of blood and severed things and it was exactly as unpleasant as any fight with large sharp objects is bound to end up being.

Hsu and I were separated early on. He and his goblins were drawing the most attention from the Talus guardsmen because they were the most dangerous. The least dangerous—Abraham, Moshe, and Xuangang—were not actively attacked, but weren't allowed to leave either, so I was doing everything I could to clear a path for them to the gates, with some help from the captain with the loud whistle and a few of his men.

This was what I was doing when I saw Hsu fall. My immediate opponent was a particularly annoying human guard whose technique was deeply flawed, but who simply refused to let me kill him. He kept managing to parry my attacks at the last second.

In a minute I was going to bull-rush him to knock him over and maybe step on his face a couple of times so I could get on with killing the guy behind him and maybe progressing in a positive direction.

This man had just blocked a fourth otherwise lethal attack when I heard my friend cry out. I turned in time to see Hsu spin around and remove the head of the guard who had just buried a knife in his back. And then he fell to his knees.

As basically the only person there whose well-being I cared about other than my own, I didn't really hesitate in racing to his aid. It left everyone I had been defending without a flank, but I wasn't thinking of that. I was thinking that Hsu had just disappeared into a crowd of unfriendly men, trying to stave off a killing blow with one good arm, from the ground. The goblins at his side had closed around him, but they'd barely been able to hold off this army as a threesome. They stood little chance as two-and-a-half.

But I couldn't get to him. As soon as I pivoted and charged I was met by two guards, both less flawed than the one I'd been meaning to kill a few seconds earlier.

And that was when the most remarkable thing happened. A new fighter entered the battle. At first all I saw of him was the reactions of the Talus defenders. They ran toward him, and then they backed quickly away because his arms were a blur of bloody motion. He had curved swords in both hands and he swung them with amazing grace and efficiency, and cut down everything that came near him almost without effort.

This man—although he was no man—was taller than I was, thin and deathly pale, with bright blond hair framing a triangular face that ended at a sharp pointed chin. He wore nothing but a leather tunic and the gore of the men he was slicing his way through.

I had never seen such a creature before, but the word for him came to me immediately—faery.

It wasn't long before the soldiers opposing him backed away and gave the room he wanted to reach Hsu.

My friend was on the ground, exhausted, and bleeding badly from the knife that was still stuck into his back. The faery knelt down beside him, and when Hsu saw who was there he sagged into the creature's arms.

I was shouting for Hsu but I still couldn't get close, as the men I was fighting were more eager than ever to face me rather than the faery in the courtyard.

I would love to say I knew for sure what happened next. I know the faery picked up Hsu and cradled him in his arms, and I'm nearly positive Hsu died at that moment. I also know that despite being unable to defend himself, the soldiers thought it best to fight around the faery rather than risk going at him again and discovering that he had a third arm or something, which was a degree of caution I could understand.

But I don't know what happened to either of them. I was looking at them one second, defending myself the next, and when I checked back they weren't there anymore.

~

I'm not sure why, but we didn't have much trouble fighting our way out of the compound after that. Maybe it was because the numbers of the Talus force had been significantly dented by the path the faery cut through them, or maybe they were worried we had another faery at our disposal and didn't want to keep us around long enough to meet him. Probably they were all just tired, as it had been a costly engagement to say the very least, and most of the damage had been incurred on their end.

For whatever reason we made it through the walls and into the street, and then a block away, and then two blocks, and then we decided nobody was chasing us and so we stopped in an alley and rested, and checked for wounds.

Something you don't really realize when in the middle of a heavy melee is that you've taken a cut. The adrenaline takes care of any pain you might feel, right up until the battle is over and you catch your breath and calm down a little, and then suddenly you're sore everywhere, bleeding, light- headed, and sometimes you throw up a little bit. It sucks.

In the midst of all the wound checking and bandaging and vomiting and whatnot, Abraham decided to talk. He had been wearing the same stunned look since we'd left the conference room, but now that he was pretty sure he wasn't about to die he decided it was time to assert himself.

"Could someone please tell me what just happened?" he asked. It was an open question posed to any and all of us, since he couldn't tell who was in charge and what they might be in charge of. He looked like a guy that had sleepwalked into a bordello.

"I have a question for you, Abraham bin Yasser," I said. "Ten years ago a man named Aleph repaid a debt to you with an unusual golden medallion. Do you remember this?"

He looked at Moshe and then at Xuangang, both as confused as he was. "Why would you ask me this odd question?"

"The debt was for a shipment of black pepper, and it cleared Aleph's account. He was a short man with one eye and a drinking problem, and a leaky boat. Do you remember?"

"Yes, but why is this important to you? And what does this have to do with what happened today?"

"I assure you, Abraham, of all the questions you may be asked in your lifetime this is one of the more important, as it is a question that has gone unspoken for a decade. It's only unfortunate that I am the one asking instead of my compatriot, for it was his question and he died unable to pose it. What did you do with the medallion?"

"The gold was, as you said, for the repayment of a debt. It was sent home, as are all goods I receive when there are books to be cleared. I'm sure it has been melted down by now, if it was truly gold."

"It cleared a *large* debt. I can't imagine you were unsure as to the quality of the gold."

He laughed. "Really, sir, you are covered in the blood of a dozen men and perhaps some of your own, and this is what you want to talk about? I cleared the books because Aleph was indeed a drunk with a leaky boat. I had no intention of using his service again and did not doubt that I would see no further payment regardless of whether the medallion was valued sufficiently to offset the pepper or not. I confess that I found it to be eye-catching and clever, and perhaps I let this assessment better my good judgment, but regardless it is doubtful the thing exists as it had ten years ago. Now can you explain to me *why* you are covered in the blood of a dozen men?"

"Yes," I said. "But it would take longer than it is worth to explain. However, in the future I suggest you consider not taking the advice of whomever put us all in the room with the Talus."

～

It was in the best interest of all of us to get out of Mangalore immediately. Once I impressed upon Abraham the fact that the death of Gorrgon Talus was likely to put his own life in danger even if he had not personally performed the murder, he agreed that it was time to find a new port for his business dealings. That was where the businesses intersected, since we had a number of other ports he could use and he had the sea route that made bringing black cardamom to market much easier for us.

Or rather, for Xuangang. The business meeting between us took place in the hold of one of the ships Abraham used—he didn't own any ships but employed trusted vessels—and began with my introducing the true Xuangang. I then took part in helping everyone come to an equitable agreement, and once that was done I named a price for my stake in Xuangang's venture.

Then I walked away. In doing so I left behind a sizable chunk of money that nobody could truly argue belonged to me, but I didn't really mind. I had been rich many times and knew I would be again, but I'd lost all interest in the spice merchant trade, so I took only one pouch of gold and snuck out of Mangalore on a stolen horse in the middle of a moonless night.

I wondered, as I left, what had actually happened to Hsu.

Over the years I convinced myself that he and the faery just escaped through another exit, or had perhaps fallen to an enemy sword. It wasn't until recently that I came to a different conclusion. The faery appeared out of nothing, and when he and Hsu departed they disappeared back into nothing.

If I wanted to find out how the red-haired woman had accomplished this exact trick I needed to know how the faery had done it. I needed to find Hsu's imaginary faery kingdom.

CHAPTER 14

"Men will always make poor business decisions when their children are involved."

"I'm not prepared to wait until bin Yasser's son is a part of the business,"
Hsu said. "That could be two decades, if ever."

"You misunderstand. I mean, we can find the whelp and use him to get
Abraham to come to us."

He looked at me for a time. "That is perhaps more ruthless than I am
capable of."

"I mention it only as an option, if you are desperate."

"Desperate, I am. But I'm no savage."

I could understand why Abraham lied about the outcome of the astrolabe given he forwarded it to his son. That his son was—by the time we spoke—an adult and raising a family of his own didn't mitigate the possible risk he would be putting Isaac in, and on top of that he didn't know me at all. I was also asking him the question while covered in blood, for reasons Abraham only had a dim grasp of. For all he knew I was willing to kill for that little trinket, given everything he had already seen of me.

I wasn't willing to do any such thing. Hsu was, but as far as I was concerned he was dead.

I had already begun to doubt what I'd seen with regards to the faery, and I was certainly not entertaining the idea that what I saw was a grown being vanishing into nothing. I was so very certain that such a thing was impossible that when I saw the red-haired woman perform the same trick it was almost ten years before I even remembered Hsu's story.

Mirella held up Abraham's drawing to get a better look at it in the cabin lighting.

"This is the thing your friend was trying to find?"

"I think it is, yes."

She shook her head, put the paper down on the bed next to me, and walked over to the bar. She was pouring herself a drink, something I only really saw her do when I was also drinking, which I was not. So this was new.

"That's insane," she said.

"Yeah, maybe."

"So ... all right, I want to get this correct." She gestured with her drink— it looked like she was trying my bourbon, which was a very good bourbon. "Your friend Hsu, he has this great love, this faery. And this faery gives him the ..."

"Astrolabe."

"The astrolabe. And tells him this is the thing he can use to return to the ... I'm sorry, do I have to call it a faery kingdom?"

"Not if you don't want to, no."

"He loses the astrolabe in a bet, it ends up in the hands of the one merchant who is kind enough to record every single thing he does on a document that somehow manages to survive until *now*, so you can find a *drawing* of that thing waiting for you in a museum. Now I suppose you'll tell me there's some reason to think that astrolabe might still be around somewhere, instead of buried in an undiscovered pit or melted down for the gold, or just vanished somewhere and lost forever to history. And of course, let's remember how old you are supposed to be. We can't forget that."

"You seem to be doing pretty well with all of this."

"Thank you, I'm not. Look, if you want to go around telling people you're a thousand years old, that's fine as long as you're still paying me."

"It's really much older than that."

"Of course it is."

"Sorry."

"You want to be an eccentric rich man, that's all right. I protected someone once who insisted he was an incarnation of the god Rama, and if that made him feel better about himself I was entirely okay with it. But I had no obligation to believe any such thing."

She downed her drink and refilled it. I was torn between wanting a glass myself and wishing she stopped drinking the expensive stuff. I kept both wishes to myself, since she appeared to be having a moment of some sort.

"But then you come along, and not only do you think you're the world's oldest man, you fight with a warrior style I've never *seen* before, you defeat a goblin in single combat, you seem to know more about this Abraham fellow than anyone should, you *refused* to go to the hospital or even take a damned aspirin, and I am nearly convinced that the woman on that videotape actually did disappear like you said she did. I am running out of explanations for this other than the ones you are giving me, and it's making me very angry."

"I really do think you're handling this very well," I said again. "Also, I wonder if I could have some of that?"

She reached behind the bar and found a second rocks glass, and walked it over with the bottle. "I would tell you this is a bad thing to do while you're healing, but I have no idea if this is true in your case. Maybe it's the alcohol that's been keeping you alive all these centuries."

"It's not," I said, filling the glass. "I just wanted some before you polished off the bottle. So do you believe me?"

"I'm prepared to conclude either that you are performing an incredibly elaborate and dangerous hoax exclusively for my benefit, or all of it is true."

"That would be one impressive hoax."

"I'm leaning toward the other option. I don't think I'm worth the expense of such a hoax."

I smiled at this. And it may have been the bourbon, but she smiled back.

"I think you would be surprised what someone with a lot of money and time might do to capture your attention," I said.

"Thank you, that's very nice. It's also creepy, so please tell me you aren't doing that."

"I'm not."

"I didn't think so." She picked up the page with the drawing on it and walked over to the computer. "So now maybe I'll find your astrolabe and we can have this conversation again."

~

I spent the next two hours finding the bottom of that bottle of bourbon, and then I stared at the wall for a while and asked Mirella roughly fifty times how the search was going. She was using the Internet to find a match to the astrolabe, this much I understood. I didn't know *how* she was using the Internet to do this or what kind of success rate I might expect, or how long that might take.

The truth was I didn't expect this to work at all. As positive as I felt about the idea that Hsu's faery token could still be out there somewhere, I didn't expect to actually find it. Sure, I had just gone through a lot of trouble to find the right geniza and the right letter, and I hadn't really expected that to pan out either. Now that it had, the only next step to take was to find the astrolabe. But it just couldn't have survived.

And if it had? The idea that this object would help me understand what Eve had done was an article of faith at this point, and it wasn't even my faith. It was Hsu's. I spent a decade with him and never really decided if he was crazy or not. The faery showing up to carry him away certainly improved his side of the argument, though.

"So far I have found seven libraries of astrolabes online, and it isn't in any of them," Mirella said.

It was the first time she'd spoken in a while, and the sound of her voice made me jump.

"There are that many?"

"Yes. These things are historical oddities. It improves the odds that the right one will show up."

There was a trembling sound coming from another part of the cabin. It was barely audible, and really sort of annoying because I was pretty sure it wasn't the first time I'd noticed it.

"Do you hear that?" I asked.

She looked up from the screen, annoyed, then caught the sound.

"Oh that? That's been happening off and on for a while. I don't know what it is. It started when you were unconscious. It's coming from that cabinet over there, but I can't open it. I'm sorry. I stopped hearing it after a while."

"Which cabinet?"

She pointed it out for me.

There is a fairly limited amount of storage space on the plane, because as wealthy as I am I wasn't going to throw in for a jumbo jet to carry just me around the planet. That struck me as actively obnoxious. So it's not a huge plane, space-wise, and most of the interior storage was taken up by food, liquor, and one or two changes of clothes. The rest of the space was electronics and the mandatory emergency gear, except for the contents of the one overhead compartment Mirella had just pointed out, which contained a bag.

This bag went with me everywhere and contained everything I needed if I had to walk away quickly: fake passports, cash, extra clothing, and cell phones. There were six different phones, all of them prepaid "burners." The active ones were programmed with one number each, corresponding to a person in my life I might need to contact if I had to disappear, and each of those people had the number for the phone they were programmed into.

I left the phones on, and rotated the charger on them to keep them ready for use. Every time I pulled one out and charged it I told myself this was all silly and unnecessary and dumb and something only Tchekhy would agree with because he was indiscriminately paranoid. But we all have our own outlets for paranoia, and this was mine.

Now one of those phones was ringing. Or rather, vibrating. I didn't even know I'd set them to vibrate.

It was a good ten minutes before I could get to the bag. First, I had to find the key, which was in the pants that were on the other side of the cabin, which mean walking to the pants in my boxers, which Mirella didn't seem to care about but still. I have looked better when in front of attractive women than I did at that moment. It especially didn't help that it was difficult to stand upright due to the battlefield stitches she'd put in my stomach. Those stitches also made it impossible for me to raise my arms over my head, which was something I really had to do in order to get the bag down from the bin. Mirella had to help with that, and then not only did I not feel particularly attractive, I actually felt old for the first time in a while.

Finally I got the bag down onto the table at the foot of my bed and opened it up.

By then the phone had stopped vibrating. I would have had to go from phone to phone to find out which one received an incoming call, but the first one I checked—the one I was most afraid of checking— was the right phone. It was Clara's.

I couldn't breathe for a second so I sat down on the bed and hit the callback button, and waited. It only rang twice.

"Adam?" It was indeed Clara, and she sounded frantic.

"It's me."

"Oh my god, where have you been? I've been calling and ... are you okay?"

"I'm fine, but you obviously aren't. What's wrong?"

"Oh ..." She lost her voice for a second and I realized I was hearing her fight the urge to cry. "They took him," she said, choking out the words. "You have to help me."

"Took him? Took who?"

"They took him and they told me ... they told me to call you about it and I didn't know what else to do but then you didn't *answer* and I ..."

"Clara, who did they take?"

"My son, Adam. They took my son."

PART II

THE GOD OF IMPOSSIBLE THINGS

Clarabelle Wasserman of the Connecticut Wassermans, formerly of New York City and a small island in the Queen Charlottes, lived on a private estate in Southern Italy on a hill that overlooked a valley on one side and the Mediterranean on the other.

It was an unpleasant distance from the nearest decent airport and most of the other traditional indices of modern civilization, such as grocers and coffee shops and bars. It reminded me of about ten different places I'd lived at one time or another and, except for the electricity and the running water, it could have been most of them. I especially liked the proximity to local vineyards.

It was exactly the sort of place I would have loved to spend time in, but I never had because I'd never been invited. This didn't stop me from learning everything about the place when she relocated to it.

I don't think it's considered stalking if I don't actually show up.

Anyway, her estate kind of bothered me. Clara lived with me for about three years, and that was three of the better years I'd had in a long while. But then we started fighting. One of the things we'd fought about was how I never wanted to go anywhere or do anything. My counterpoint had been that she and I had as many centuries to go out and do things as we wanted, but on the island we had everything we needed so why bother? She said she wanted to see the world, though, and decided she wanted to do that without me along.

So after all of that *see the world* nonsense she ended up seeing herself to a walled estate in Italy that was almost exactly as isolated as the island, and she hardly ever left the place.

This made me bitter, and contributed to the conclusion that it wasn't the island she needed to get away from at all.

I said *centuries* because, as I mentioned before, Clara won't be getting any older. It's a long story, but the short version is she received a medical treatment that isn't going to be repeated anytime soon because everyone involved in creating it is dead. This makes her the only other person on the planet that's like me —aside from Eve, the red-haired woman who may not actually be like me at all given she can vanish and I can't. Clara's utter uniqueness is one of the reasons I like to keep tabs on her, even if that comes off kind of creepy.

But I obviously didn't do a fantastic job of keeping track given I managed to not have any idea that she had a child, so I can't have been *that* obsessive about it.

~

*I*t was three days before we made it to her front door. This was partly due to the estate's distance from any meaningful form of civilization, but not entirely.

First we had to extricate ourselves from the Istanbul airport. This took half a day because the airspace above Turkey is somewhat complicated. It could have been worse. It turned out Mr. Acar from the museum had not been damaged in any way, which we discovered after Acar reached out to Mr. Heintz to ascertain why it was that we had left the museum hurriedly without addressing him, and also whether by any chance we had removed anything before departing.

Heintz assured me this inquiry would be the extent of any official issue provided I didn't need to get back into the Archeological Museum again anytime soon. Had Acar been caught in the mess that happened outside the museum he would have been dead, and I expect then we'd have had to deal with the police, which would have been a lot more time-consuming.

Istanbul to Rome is an incredibly short flight. I think if planes had been around when it was still Constantinople, that whole Eastern/Western church split would never have happened, only because those guys would've been an afternoon's flight away from a decent conversation.

Once we got on the ground we had to hire a car and a driver who was willing to log in a solid day on the road. Mirella tried three or four times to convince me she could drive the car herself, but I'd seen cars on the Italian roads and I don't care if she *did* learn to drive in New York City, it still wasn't a good idea. Plus, it was something best done either by a professional or by more than one person in shifts, and there was no way my getting behind the wheel of a car was ever going to be a good idea for me, Mirella, or the nation of Italy as a whole.

We ended up hiring a very expensive man named Rollo, who spoke no English, owned a town car, and had a home five miles from our destination, so he wouldn't require overnight accommodations at Clara's once he got us there. I considered this his best feature.

Speaking of Italian roads, they can be bumpy, especially when you get out into the hills. Given I'd recently had my leg sewn to my stomach, this was a rather awful experience that was only marginally eased by alcoholic beverages.

By the time we got within sight of the estate, about the only one in a good mood about it was Iza, who was pixie-on-meth happy.

"Maybe we should give *her* some of this," Mirella complained, waving a bottle of vodka at Iza, who was flying in concentric circles in the air between us. It was a small miracle Rollo hadn't noticed her. Or if Rollo noticed, he didn't care.

"I don't think alcohol calms them down," I said. "I'm not sure what does. I could feed her some more mushrooms; she might stop for that."

"I have a better idea. That's the place up there, yes?"

"That's it." We were at the base of the last bumpy hill my stitches were going to have to endure for a while. At the top of the hill was a walled-off building that was reminiscent of the Talus estate in old Mangalore.

"Good." Mirella lowered her window. "Shoo, bug."

"Okay thanks," Iza said, obediently shooing. She zipped out the window and hopefully headed in the right direction.

"I guess that works," I said.

"Clara will be happy to see her, and maybe nicer to you for it."

Mirella had heard the entire story of Clara and, really, everything else I could think of that was pertinent to our current circumstance, which was why she had a bottle of vodka in her hands. It was beginning to look like the only way she could handle all of it was if she was at least semi-buzzed. I would have worried that this made her less of an effective bodyguard, but at her most competent she killed a demon. I was pretty sure having her at sixty percent was plenty good enough. Plus, most of the time I can't handle me unless I'm semi-buzzed either, so I understood the problem.

It was another fifteen minutes before we reached the front gate, and a few more seconds to wait for the gate to open electronically to admit us into the compound behind the walls. I was happy to see Clara put so much money into her own security, even if I never fully understood whom she was trying to keep herself secure from.

The gate closed behind us and we got out of the car into an empty compound. Nobody was there to greet us, which was odd because I was pretty sure she had a half-dozen people on staff for just this sort of thing.

"Hello, Adam."

Clara stepped out of a shaded alcove at the front of the main building. She was dressed simply in shorts and a sleeveless shirt, barefoot, with a pixie on her wrist. She was tan and beautiful and exactly as I remembered her, which was appropriate given she wasn't aging.

"Sorry we took so long," I said. I felt like walking over and giving her a hug was appropriate, but I was still figuring out how to stand up straight without wincing.

"I'm a little out of the way over here," she said, petting Iza gently without fully realizing she was doing it. It was like her hands automatically knew how to tend to a pixie in the same way someone might instinctively rock when holding a newborn. Clara and Iza had been very close before Clara had moved out.

I watched her eyes track past me and land on Mirella, and for a half second I saw a flash of something that was probably jealousy.

"Oh, hi," she said.

"This is my bodyguard," I said. "Mirella."

"Bodyguard. Right. Why don't you take care of your driver and come in?"

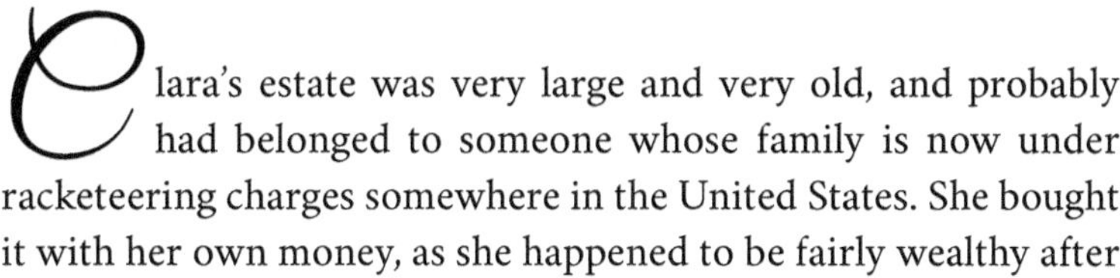

Clara's estate was very large and very old, and probably had belonged to someone whose family is now under racketeering charges somewhere in the United States. She bought it with her own money, as she happened to be fairly wealthy after collecting on a bounty that had been on my head. If she didn't have the money I'd have given it to her, but I'm pretty sure she liked it better this way.

We didn't get much of a tour, stopping at the first common room on the other side of the front door. This could have been because she didn't want us to see the rest of the house, but I think it was mostly that she noticed how uncomfortable I looked standing upright.

"Jesus Christ, Adam, what happened to you? Another demon?"

"No, I have her for demon control," I said. "This was from a goblin's sword."

I lifted my shirt to show off the wound. After it healed it was going to leave a nasty scar, which was okay. Scars made for great stories, especially when picking up women.

Clara looked suitably impressed and a little concerned.

"Maybe you should sit down. For a month or two. Goblins now?"

"Yeah, they're fun. You've already met one."

Clara was stridently ignoring Mirella, who was taking being ignored in stride. She seemed too preoccupied checking the angles in the house for any potential dangers to worry about a social *faux pas*. I was still wondering where the house staff was.

We sat down at a table that had the kind of sturdy, used look one came to expect from handcrafted wood. Mirella chose to remain standing and circle the room suspiciously. Iza perched on Clara's shoulder, making a cute buzzing sound I forgot she used to make all the time back when Clara lived with us.

"So why don't you tell me what you've gotten yourself into this time?" Clara asked. "Now that I've been dragged into it."

"I'm not involved in anything," I said. "Maybe you should start by telling *me* how you have a son I never knew about?"

She sighed grandly, a sound I was deeply familiar with. "I have a son. There, now you know."

"Clara ..."

"No, this isn't about him, this is about what you're into and what you're going to do to get him back for me, and that's all. I am sorry I didn't tell you about him before, but we weren't really talking, were we?"

"Where are your people?" Mirella asked. She had made it to the far end of the room and was standing under a security camera. Every few seconds the light on the camera blinked on for a half second and then off again. "Your staff, I mean?"

Clara looked at her with a touch of menace in her eyes. "You speak."

"Yes, quite a few languages. Where are they? This place looks like a fortress, but you have no soldiers on the walls."

"I sent them all packing when they let someone take my son. I assumed it was done with help on the inside." She looked at me. "You were serious; she's really your bodyguard."

"Yes."

"How'd she let you get cut open like that?"

"I was killing something more dangerous than a goblin," Mirella said. "Has there been a ransom demand?"

"No, I don't think that's what this is about."

"You're a wealthy woman living alone with a young child. Ransom is the most obvious conclusion. But you don't think so. You reached for *his* number first, didn't you?"

"It's *about* him."

"And you know this because the men who took your son told you this."

"Yes."

"Thank you. When will they be arriving?"

"Adam, I don't like her."

"Don't turn to him," Mirella said. "He already figured this out, he just doesn't care to confront you about it yet. It's my job to care, so when are they coming?"

Clara glared at her, but didn't answer.

"Is there actually a child?" I asked.

"Oh my God! How can you even ask me that?"

"I'm just saying I didn't know, and that's a big enough surprise to plant the notion. What's his name?"

She looked like she was going to cry, and I immediately regretted this line of questioning, which was probably why it was a good thing Mirella was there. I'm really terrible when it comes to thinking straight around women I'm involved with, even after that involvement has ended.

"His name is Paul, and you didn't know about him because I didn't want you to. I kept him here because I didn't want anyone else to know about him either, because I was afraid that one day someone who wanted something from *you* would find us. And that's just what happened, isn't it? So what did you do to put us in danger, Adam?"

Mirella leaned on the table, and to make her point abundantly clear she had her sword in her hand.

"When. Are. They coming?"

"They're already here, dammit."

"Thank you." Mirella sheathed her sword. To me, she said, "If we want to get this woman's son back we need to speak to the people who took him, do you agree?"

I didn't answer because I saw Mirella look up suddenly and put her hand back on the hilt of her sword. Someone new had entered the room.

"My goodness but you are a difficult man to motivate," a man said from the doorway behind me. Mirella hadn't killed him, so he probably had no weapon or if he did it wasn't pointed at me.

I could have turned around to see who was there but every time I twisted like that my stitches behaved badly, so instead I waited until he walked around the table and into my view. What I saw was a slight man, shorter than average but strangely graceful. He looked youthful, with slight wrinkling around the eyes suggesting he was in his early thirties. He had a round face, cropped brown hair, and a nice suit. Aside from that suit, which appeared to be tailored, he was extraordinarily ordinary. It was as if he strived to be the person described as *average* in as many metrics as possible.

This extremely average man sat down at the opposite end of the table as if he were joining a business meeting he had called himself.

He began by addressing Mirella. "You can take your hand off that sword. I'm not going to be doing anything violent."

To me, he said, "Your goblin is very impressive. I look at her and honestly, I don't know whether I should be hiring her or trying to fuck her. Do you have this problem?"

"Who are you?" I asked.

His eyes took in everyone else in the room, slowly, settling on Iza, who was still sitting on Clara's shoulder.

"Why, look at you," he said almost to himself. "You must be his goblin-killer."

"H'lo," Iza greeted.

He looked at me. "It speaks."

I was uninterested in explaining the taxonomy of pixies. "I asked you who you are."

"All right, we can start there. I'm Mr. Smith. That's not who I actually am, but that's what you can call me. I could call *you* Mr. Justinian, but I think I'll stick to Adam, if that's all right. Unless you have a different name you feel like going with today."

"Adam is fine. What do you want, Mr. Smith?"

He smiled and held the smile for about two beats longer than was comfortable for anybody. "From you? I want a lot of things."

"You're CIA?"

"I'm Mr. Smith. I think we went through this already."

"All right. Mr. Smith of the Central Intelligence Agency."

"Adam. Who I *am* is not as important as what I *want*. I think you were on the right track a minute ago."

"Then answer the question."

"I'm getting there, but c'mon, let's get to know each other a little bit. Sure, CIA, why not? They're in the mix, but I don't want to talk about them. I've been looking at you for a very long time, so this is really exciting for me. Don't take all the fun out of it."

I really, really didn't like this man. I was about ready to let Mirella kill him.

"I just found out about you, so I'm less enthusiastic," I said. "You understand."

"I do! Actually, you've found out about a lot of new things and people recently, haven't you?" He was looking at Clara when he said this. Clara was not being all that forthcoming, expression-wise.

I hate going into something like this knowing nothing about the person at the other end of the table. Even when I sat down with Gorrgon Talus I knew a little something about him. True, I didn't know he was a djinn and it was a trap, but I did know he was someone from whom such behavior might be expected.

I had nothing on Smith at all, other than that he took Clara's son, a son about whom I also knew nothing. It was actually sort of frustrating because as much as I wanted to figure out Smith, what I *really* wanted to know was who Paul's father was. It turns out I'm the kind of guy who gets jealous when people have intercourse with my exes. I'm surprised, too.

"Exactly how *long* have you been looking at me?" I asked Smith.

"Hard to say. Sometime shortly after the death of Robert Grindel, I think. Him, and fifty-odd other people. That sort of mess sends ripples."

Somehow it always came back to Grindel. "You mean, through the intelligence community."

"I mean through a lot of places. Grindel wasn't what I'd call a visionary, but he had one good idea, and that and the right connections can do a lot for a person. Now to *you* the people backing him financially were nameless, faceless entities too far removed to worry about, so you never dug deeply enough to see them for what they were. I'm talking about governments, Adam. Governments and some of the largest corporate interests in the world. There was a lot of money riding on the notion of medically induced immortality."

He was actually wrong about some of that because I asked Heintz to look into the finances, which led to a venture capital group. The last time I checked I was one of the investors in that group. It was true, though, that I didn't know who the other investors were. Also, the last time my banker and I discussed them, they were chasing something with potential military applications. That was a year ago, and it was probably my fault for not following up and maybe getting some more details.

Smith continued. "Of course, most of those financiers didn't know how Grindel was going to deliver what he promised. Most of them didn't know about *you*, in other words."

"Well, that's good."

"We agree! The fewer people the better, eh?" He winked at me when he said this, and I kind of wanted to kill him myself then.

"I've always felt that way, yes."

"So let me tell you a story. Seems that after that little blood-bath you orchestrated out in the desert, one of the ripples it sent out found me and my people. Unlike you, we were interested almost immediately in who Grindel was in bed with and how much fucking was going on in that bed, and what everybody expected the baby to look like."

I was guessing there was more involved than just sniffing around, since I'd tried that. Perhaps government clearance was the thing Heintz and I had been missing.

"Did that include the person who was bothering my friend in New York?" I asked.

"The pawnshop? Yes, that was Martin, or ... well, I called him Martin. He was legit CIA. Good man, kind of pushy, a bit of an ass. I probably should have sent someone with more finesse to do that, but between you and me somebody was going to end up killing Martin one day anyway. Next time you talk to your Russian phantom, you tell him no hard feelings for me. I might even hire him someday. My tech guy speaks very highly of him."

"I think the less you know about him the happier he will be."

Smith nodded. "Fair. We pay really well, though. Anyhoo, so we wanted to find Grindel's moneymen, and that wasn't easy. Clara here did a *very* good job of dumping the hard drive data at the base, and you bought up everything else Grindel owned and destroyed most of it, so it took a while. But, as I said, these things cause ripples, and sometimes the absence of a thing can cause ripples, too. So when a guy heading a billion-dollar project dies suddenly and all the research that cost those billions is destroyed —or walks away—that void is filled by people in nice suits asking uncomfortable questions and waving large expense accounts in the air to get answers to those questions. We listened to those questions."

I was beginning to think we were never getting to the point, or maybe that Smith had no point to get to at all. I was also wondering if Clara had any alcohol lying around.

"Why don't you skip to the end?" I asked.

"I'll get there, I promise. Let me tell you about the surveillance video you've been spending the last few months looking over. I'm sure it's no surprise by now that I was the one who sent it to you."

"Not anymore."

"I knew if I sent it that way you'd give the credit to your federal friend. If you are concerned, by the way, that he knew anything about me at all, you needn't be."

"I wasn't."

"Good, I'm glad. A man should trust his friends. Agent Lycos actually did know nothing about that footage, nor did the FBI as a whole because those guys, I swear, they need a map to find their own assholes. No offense intended."

"Sure."

"I stopped by that facility a year after all the bodies were picked up and found that footage all by myself in a couple of hours. I still can't believe they missed it."

I made a point of checking in on the compound from time to time. It's out in the middle of nothing in particular so it never had any value as anything aside from a military base or medical facility. I knew nobody was using it, and that after all these years the crime scene tape, though tattered and occasionally replaced, was still across the chained gate at the front. I never thought seriously about going back there to look for left-over evidence because I assumed the FBI had some basic standard of competence, and Mike sent me everything they had found.

Smith continued. "The FBI did find the hard drives in the main building, destroyed, but nobody bothered to check the security equipment, which was on a separate system and housed in another building. That's really too bad, because *everything* that happened that night was recorded there, and it is *gripping*. Speaking as someone who has read the reports of the investigators and seen their utter bafflement over your mess, it pained me to know that everything could have been explained if they'd just checked the right computer. I very nearly sent it to them just so they could sleep at night. But maybe that would have made things worse. Who wants to write in an official report that a vampire did it?"

Something occurred to me. "You wanted me to see it because you wanted me to find out how she did it."

"That's spectacular thinking, Adam, and right on the nose. Actually, it's still a little more complicated than that because the people I'm working with are just as interested as ever in this immortality thing you've got going on. They seem to think if they put you and Clara here under enough microscopes they can work out the details without ever having to borrow anything from your vanishing mystery woman. And who am I to say? I'm no scientist. But I'm not interested in that *right now*. In another year, sure, or whenever they're finally done with Grindel's corpse."

I must have registered surprise when he said this because he reacted with a smile. I had gone through a lot to destroy all the research in that compound, but it lived on in Clara. And I never thought about it before, but of course it was also in the dead body of Bob Grindel. I should have burned the corpse.

"So yes," he said, "I sent you the security footage because I know you're a curious man when properly motivated, and if I was going to find out how she did it, my best method aside from asking her myself was to get you to figure it out."

"How do you know I don't already know how she did it?"

"That's a question, isn't it? I asked myself that many times. But the more I looked into your recent history, the more it looked to me like the actions of someone who is just as stuck on this mortal plane as any of us. You didn't use this skill to escape Grindel, and honestly the expression on your face when she first disappeared right in front of you was really priceless. A few years later you were staring at what sounds like *nearly* certain death in the form of an angry wood nymph, and if you could have vanished then I'm sure you would have."

Clara looked at me. "A nymph?"

"Dryad. Not nearly as awesome as it sounds. Long story."

"But I had my doubts, still," Smith continued. "I sent you off on this little quest, and at first you seemed to be right on point. You saw that physicist, for instance. Then you spent months running around the world checking out things in museums, and for a while I thought you were still on the trail. Now I think you were just collecting old letters from friends and retrieving some things you used to own and consorting with the occasional criminal. And maybe enjoying the company of this little number over here."

He gestured to Mirella. She hadn't moved from her position at the back of the room. It was the only part of the room that enabled her to see anyone entering from the hall and anyone outside through the window. She ignored his obvious attempt to annoy her.

"But I couldn't ignore the possibility that you *had* figured it out, especially after you seemed to disappear from a hotel room in Tbilisi for hours, according to my sources. Admittedly, these were not the best sources I could buy, but they were the ones available at the time. My best were in Istanbul, where you were supposed to have been going."

"The attack at the museum," Mirella said. "It *was* a test."

"Yes," Smith said. "They weren't there to kill you, Adam, but they had to make you think they were." He looked at Mirella. "How'd they do?"

"The demon was very convincing," she said. "The goblin less so."

"Yes, well. They were allowed to kill *you*. It was encouraged. One would think a man bereft of his expensive bodyguard would be more prepared to vanish to save his own life."

"Except I still don't know how she did it," I said. "And unless she turns up again I'll probably never know."

"Well, that's unfortunate," Smith said. "Because not only do I remain convinced that you are the best person available to find this out for me, right now any hope that Clara has of seeing little Paul again hinges upon my being right."

"That seems rather unfair," I said.

"Life is not incredibly fair. I'm sure you've learned by now. Some people are given the gift of immortality. Some people are born sterile. Some live tragically short lives due to the actions or inactions of people they have never met. That's just the way the world works sometimes. As it happens, there are billions of dollars and several government organizations interested in the skill set displayed by this woman and you are the closest thing we have to her, so you had better do everything you can to figure it out."

At that moment I felt a little stupid. Heintz told me the investment group was looking at something with a military application and I should have followed up, but immortality is not a military weapon. Mine isn't, at least, as the wound across my stomach proved. Eve's trick *was* a weapon, though. I had just never seen it that way before.

"All right," I said.

"All right? Does that mean yes?"

"It means I figured out how to do it." I was lying, obviously.

"Good! Then show me."

"I don't have everything I need yet."

"Adam, I saw the redhead wearing nothing but a prison jumpsuit do this, twice. You don't *need* anything, just do it for me, and when you get back we can have you moved to our testing facility so all the very smart people who are waiting for you there can measure you doing it, and *then* we can get Paul back to his mommy."

"Here's the truth, then, Mr. Smith. I have not figured out how, but I have figured out how someone who cannot do what she did can *learn* how to do what she did. But I need something I don't have right now, and to find it I'm going to need more time than an afternoon at a table in Southern Italy."

Smith's eyes lit up, and he leaned forward on the table, clearly excited. What I said was entirely the truth, but it sounded to my ears no more honest than what I'd just said a minute earlier. Smith appeared to have a very good bullshit detector.

"What is this thing you have to find?" he asked.

"I'm not going to tell you. I'm also not going to tell you where it is, or how it works. But when I do find it, you'll be the first to know."

He stared at me for a while, sizing me up, it seemed, which was odd for someone who professed to have followed me for as long as he had been. I would think he'd know by now what to expect. "How much time do you need?"

"Six weeks." This elicited a strangled cry from Clara, but she didn't say anything more linguistically astute.

"You can have two, and then I expect to see you at our lab with the results."

"Your lab?"

"It's a private facility in Scotland, so factor in travel time accordingly. I'll give you the exact coordinates when you're ready. Oh, and the place is surrounded by sun lamps, so don't bring any vampires with you."

He stood and extended his hand, which I ignored until he lowered it. "Ms. Wasserman knows how to reach me. I'll show myself out. You two enjoy your reunion."

CHAPTER 16

"The only thing anybody understands is violence."
This was one of the last things Sven said to me before he killed himself.
As an older vampire he had a touch of the melancholy that was common
to the elders of his kind. I usually attributed it to simply running out of
things to do, but in Sven's case it was more complex than that. We spent
hours discussing the nature of man, long enough to convince me that
what he suffered from was more like a philosophical nihilism.
This may be hard to believe, but I'm pretty optimistic about mankind
overall. I grant that I am comparing myself right now to a vampire who
killed himself after being unable to bear the idea of humanity any
longer, but it seems to me if you wait around long enough, evidence will
come along that proves people aren't all that bad all the time.
I couldn't convince him of this. "You have told me your stories," he said.
"All of them end with you having to either flee or kill everybody. You
have sustained your life with the blood of more people than I have."
He had a point.

r. Smith showed himself all the way out of the building to a car that was waiting on the other side of the gate. Mirella watched through the window in the sitting room as he left.

"Was he the only one here?" she asked Clara. "Or are there more men hidden in the walls?"

"Only him," she said. "But there are probably listening devices in the house, and I think they jacked into the security feed. So if there's something you guys want to talk about, we probably can't do it here."

"I think it's safe to say we have some things to talk about, yes," I said.

Mirella—whom I could already tell wasn't going to be warming up to Clara anytime soon—said, "I'll search the house and find a safe room for us."

Clara looked like she was going to mount a protest but decided it wasn't worth it. Instead she got up and went to a credenza and pulled out a pad of paper, and put it on the table between us. Then she pulled a chair up to the video camera in the corner, stood on that chair, and unplugged the camera.

When she sat down again she had a pen in her hand. On the pad she wrote, *They can still hear us but not see us.*

"Was all that true?" she asked. "Do you know what you're looking for?"

"It was true." On the paper I wrote, *If it still exists. If it doesn't, I may have to bluff.* "Did you ... I didn't ask them for proof of life but ..."

"I did. You don't know what he looks like so it wouldn't have meant anything to you. Adam, I swear, until yesterday I had never even met that man. When I called, I didn't know I was setting some kind of trap."

"But he knew you'd call."

"I wouldn't have. If it was just ransom I would have paid it and kept you out of it. I didn't want you knowing about Paul."

"Why not?"

"Because I didn't. And don't ask me about the father. I know you want to."

"Why did you call, then? If I was the last person you would have called."

She sighed. "Paul disappeared in the middle of the night. When I found his room empty in the morning all I had waiting for me was a note on the bureau that said, *Tell him we took the boy.* I couldn't have imagined *him* being anybody but you. So I called, and I expected you to know something about it already. You always seem to have a handle on what people are about or when someone is after you or at least *why* they are. But you didn't know anything, you just said you'd get here as soon as you could. And then this Smith guy showed up, and said when you got here I was supposed to get you to talk about what you'd been doing. He wouldn't say what that was or what he was hoping to hear. But he had a video feed of my Paulie, so I was going to do whatever he asked."

I nodded, and didn't say the first thing that came to mind, which was that she had a history of betraying me for causes, since at least this particular cause was one I could understand a lot better than the last one.

Clara took the pen from my hand and wrote on the pad, *Not just CIA.*

"Do you still have the video?" I asked, while at the same time with the pen I was writing, *I know but why do you say that?*

"It was a live stream off his phone, not something I could keep."

His men were not Americans, she wrote. *Heard French, German. Tech expert was Korean.*

"Was there anything in the background to help us figure out where he's being held?"

"He was playing with toys in a windowless white room. I think they thought of that. And that's probably why I didn't get to keep anything."

I took the pen from her, and nearly wrote down what I decided to say out loud instead. "I can't believe you kept him from me."

She looked like she was ready to say about ten different things all at the same time. In fairness, she also looked exhausted. Her child had been missing for days, and she was being confronted in her house by a guy she had apparently been trying to put behind her for a long time. So it was not an ideal circumstance. "Do you know how hard it is to move on from you when I know neither of us are ever going to get any older? Do you realize how small the world really is?"

"I do, actually."

"I wanted something for myself. A life, a son, a lot of things that were just mine, but you have the whole world and all I have is this little house on a hill, and I wanted it to stay mine. This was supposed to be an Adam-free zone. But you still got in, didn't you?"

"I didn't get in," I said. "Someone else did."

Mirella appeared in the doorway and nodded to me, a signal I took to mean she found a place where we could exchange information without having to use a pad and a pen. "I wasn't the one who took Paul away from you."

"I know. But he was taken because of you, and that's close enough."

～

A half an hour later, while ensconced in Clara's huge kitchen, we opened up one of the computers she had in the house.

It was clear that since we had last spent time together she'd advanced beyond macaroni and cheese and scrambled eggs. Either that or she had hired people who knew better.

I know surprisingly little about cooking despite having spent every day of my life eating food. I have an eclectic combination of skills—I wouldn't know how to make a pasta sauce from scratch but I could construct a still out of spare parts and make alcohol out of potatoes with it. I am probably the first person to ask if you want to know if a plant is edible, but probably the last person to ask if you want to make it taste good.

Clara's kitchen had spices hanging from the ceiling to dry, which is something I only ever did if I wanted to spend the night unbothered by vampires. She was also either making her own sausage or slowly torturing sacks of meat. Best of all, sitting in an unlabeled jug was a liquid that looked suspiciously like red wine.

"Don't drink it directly from the jug, I reuse that," she said when she saw me eyeing it.

I didn't drink from the jug, and since she was busy trying to make the Wi- Fi signal secure enough for us—I don't know how she did this, so I'm not going to even pretend to explain it—I just used the nearest receptacle I could find, which was a coffee cup.

While Clara was tapping away, Mirella gestured me to the other end of the kitchen for a private conversation.

"I don't think this woman has a child," she said as quietly as she could manage.

"It was a surprise," I said, "but I wouldn't go that far."

"I've searched this entire house. I found a child's bedroom, with child's things in it, and these things belonged to a child whose name appears to be Paul, but ... what is the one thing you have not seen since coming in here?"

"I'm not sure what you mean."

"Pictures. There are no pictures anywhere. Parents have pictures of children, it's what parents do."

"Mine didn't. Maybe a cave painting here and there."

"I'm not joking."

"I know. And I know you're doing your job, and I understand why you wouldn't trust her."

"She's betrayed you before, and she's given me no reason so far to think she's not doing the same right now."

I nodded. She was right, and if it were anybody but Clara I'd have decided this on my own already. "If she says there's a son, there's a son. We can figure out the rest later."

"Guys, if you're done talking about me, I have a secure connection," Clara said from across the room. "Do you want to tell me what you're looking for now?"

I pulled Abraham's letter from my pocket. "It's called an astrolabe."

"Ooh, those are nifty. Any one in particular?"

"Yeah. Looks like this." I held up the diagram. "You know what an astrolabe is?"

"Sure. Never used one, don't really understand them, but they look cool."

She took the page and began typing rapidly. This was something I was accustomed to from her. Other than Tchekhy, she was always the one person I could turn to if I needed the Internet to give me an answer to an exotic question. I had gotten much better at it over the years— certainly more accomplished now than I had been when I first met Clara—but there was no replacing the talent of someone who was born understanding computers.

"They're pretty simple," I said. "The face has stars on it in their proper location. If you point it at the night sky and turn the dials until the face of the astrolabe matches the stars in the sky you can figure out what time it is from where the dials stopped. Or when sunrise is going to be, if that's important to you. Vampires tended to use them for that."

"What's so special about this one?"

"Other than that it's made of gold, I'm not sure. I won't know until I have it."

"Gold? That's rare, right?"

"Most of them were made out of brass or something cheaper. Gold was for tender and jewelry, and the occasional decorative bowl. Astrolabes were for travelers and astrologers, and those weren't the sort of people who had enough gold to spare to make a tool out of it. So yeah, it's probably very rare."

Mirella shot me a look, possibly because it hadn't occurred to her to define her own search by the metal of the astrolabe.

"Okay, we could start with museums, but I still have my university library access so ... oh. Is that it?"

She turned the screen so I could take a look.

"Looks close," I said. I held the drawing up to the picture.

"Description says it's gold," she said. "And the face looks right."

Over my shoulder I could hear Mirella *humph* and walk away. It was hard to fathom, but I could have sworn she was jealous.

"Where was it found?" I asked.

"Doesn't say. Well, it does, but all it says is it was donated from a private collection. The college might have better provenance but they aren't putting that on information online."

"Which college?"

"Harvard University. Is it safe for you to show your face in Boston yet?"

~

I was officially wanted for questioning in Boston, relating to the murders of two college students in which I had no direct role. More or less. The thing that killed them was looking for me at the time, so that does sort of make me indirectly responsible, but only on nights when I'm feeling particularly bad about myself.

Historically I have dodged official interest by getting out of the jurisdiction of the interested officials until such a time as they all died and everyone forgot I existed or assumed I had long since died as well. That wasn't the case here, as not nearly enough time had elapsed. But what was true then is true now—I was identified as a homeless guy, so the best disguise was to not look like a homeless guy, and that was something I was currently very good at, insofar as I dressed well, looked clean, and had multiple homes, one of which was also an airplane.

So I wasn't terribly worried that anybody would be confusing Adam the homeless guy with Francis Justinian, multimillionaire philanthropist. What was worrisome was that the collection we were looking for wasn't public.

I had spent a lot of time with private collections of all sorts in the past several months, but those meetings were brokered by Heintz over long periods of time following a healthy donation to whatever cause was pertinent to the situation. We had less than two weeks to do this and I had no monetary connection to the university that I was aware of. And I was afraid to ask Heintz for anything at the moment.

I probably had no reason not to trust Juergen Heintz. He had been offering me good advice and managing my money phenomenally well, and he had done it all despite my ignorance of all things financial. And it wasn't his fault that the only venture capital group I actively cared about was secretly trying to capture me and/or harm me and my friends for financial gain. I hadn't given him enough information to work with, really. I just figured when they were coming after me again I would recognize the signs, and I hadn't.

At the same time, now that I knew there was a huge secret conglomerate after me, I had a strong reason to distrust anybody directly connected with the financial industry, and that included Heintz. If there were governments and large corporations involved, there were also big banks involved, and as much as any banker is looking after the interests of their clients, they are also looking after the interests of their banks. It wasn't always true that the best thing for the bank was also the best thing for the bank's clients, and if this was one of those times I didn't want to find out too late.

More to the point, the fact that Francis Justinian was an investor in the secret venture capital group that was now applying pressure to an immortal man named Adam was an advantage. But it was only an advantage as long as that secret venture capital group didn't know about it. Talking to Heintz might cost that advantage, because even if the man himself had no intention of acting against me, the phone he spoke on belonged to his bank, and who knew who was listening in on that phone other than the two of us?

It was a quandary, because I couldn't very well leverage my involvement as an investor without asking Heintz to probe, but I couldn't have him probe and risk losing that leverage.

Fortunately, Tchekhy had a secure phone line, and he'd been spending the past couple of weeks hacking into my bank account.

"You are unreasonably wealthy," was the first thing he had to say to me.

"So you got in."

"I did, thanks to the information you provided. I have spent some time roaming through quite a few accounts with this institution. Once behind the firewall I am afraid I could not contain myself."

This is what happens when you hand your account number and password over to an anarchist. Those two items—account and password—only got me as far as access to my balances and a limited ability to move funds within the bank. To do what I did when I set up Mirella's private account required a back-and-forth with Heintz, or whoever deals with his e-mail account. Any significant funds movement had to be touched by a banker, especially if it meant funds exiting the bank. So while it may be fair to argue that Tchekhy didn't truly *hack* my account after I handed him the password, I needed him to figure out how to take Heintz out of the loop if I needed him to be out of the loop.

"I hope you didn't steal too much," I said.

"I didn't steal anything. But I established some clever little programs that will be siphoning off large quantities of small sums in a few months, so I expect to steal very much in the future. I am glad to hear you are still alive."

"I am, thank you. I don't know how much longer that'll last, but so far so good."

"I've thought some about what you asked of me, and I am not sure it will be possible."

"Why not?"

"As I said, you are unreasonably wealthy."

What I asked him to do was see if it was possible to make me poor. As you can imagine, this is something I would have to go around Heintz to accomplish, because bankers are not the sorts of people you go to if you want to deliberately destroy wealth. They are fantastically good at doing it unintentionally, but it was probably too much to hope for that Heintz would accidentally ruin me.

"It's too much to get rid of?"

"It is too much to steal. It is also diversified nicely, so you will not find yourself a pauper due to a depressed investment in a single market. And I believe you are currently impervious to a full market crash. I would need to redirect a large portion of your money toward an investment that would then collapse."

"Can you do that?"

"Only if I could find such an investment."

"Do you know what an Ouroboros is?"

"Yes I think so. This is the snake that eats itself. Ah. What you are describing is a Ponzi scheme."

"Will that work?"

"I don't believe so. That is mainly effective in convincing other people to invest their money. If you are the only investor, there is no point. Likewise, a kiting scheme would involve inflating your funds and then watching the inflated funds disappear. But that is both the creation and destruction of imaginary money, whereas your money is currently actual."

"If you say so. It's all numbers on a page to me."

"They are large numbers on an important page."

"All right, then maybe you can find something worthless for me to invest in, and we can see about moving everything I've got into it."

"I'll see what I can find. It's a very curious problem. I will talk to some people over here and perhaps come up with something clever."

"Thanks. And while you're in my bank account, I need you to check on one of my investments and get back to me with whatever you can dig up."

"Are you looking for something in particular?"

"Yes. I'm looking for a site in Scotland. I'll explain."

~

I had a few more phone calls to make, but we also had to get moving. Getting from Italy to Boston was going to be a travel nightmare, especially since we were starting out half a day's travel from the plane and had no car to take us there.

"How do you not have a car?" I asked Clara.

"I have a moped, and I hire a car if I need to go anywhere."

"Groceries?"

"Delivered. And I garden."

"Since *when?*"

This was an argument that began when Clara insisted she was coming with us, or possibly it began several years ago before she left me and we'd simply taken a long break.

After listening to us for more than an hour, Mirella had about had it.

"Could one of you reach the point where you call someone with a car so we can get out of here?"

"No," Clara snapped.

"No? We'll take your moped then? Or should we walk?"

"I mean no, not a car. I know a guy."

"Can this guy carry us there?" I asked.

"He can, in his helicopter."

~

*H*elicopter was definitely the better way to travel through Southern Italy, especially if you aren't interested in seeing anything. I'd seen Italy plenty of times before, whether I realized I was standing in Italy all of those times or not, so I had no sightseeing to get out of the way that I hadn't already taken care of in the car ride to Clara's. But at the same time this was the first time I'd seen it from a few hundred feet above the ground, and that was pretty cool.

It was approaching evening by the time we made it back to the plane. I should mention that most airports aren't super happy about having people living on planes on their property, even if the plane is in a hangar, and even if that hangar is being paid for with rent fees. I think it's an insurance thing.

Sometimes this works out okay. Istanbul was really nice about it, for instance, which was good since we didn't want anyone knowing I looked like a man in dire need of modern medical treatment. Rome was not as nice. We ended up in something of a bureaucratic catch-22, where we wanted to leave immediately but they couldn't let us, and they didn't want us sitting in the plane for hours while waiting.

We couldn't leave immediately because airports have limited numbers of runways and a finite airspace, so impromptu departures were thoroughly frowned upon. This is why I look for private airfields whenever they're available.

So for a solid two hours I argued with people in Italian at the foot of the staircase leading to the jet's door, while Clara and Mirella were aboard—trying to be quiet enough to pretend they weren't since this would have evidently aggravated the Italian airport Gestapo even more—and doing some very specific web searches. My pilot and his crew were also aboard, but not in secret, since they had to have the plane ready as soon as somebody decided to open a hole in the sky for us.

The pilot and crew, incidentally, changed all the time. It's a service provided by the same company that sold me the plane. I'd worry that one or two of them might be spying on me, but they change crews so often I can't imagine they're learning very much.

It's also possible I have officially become a jaded enough wealthy man that I'm actually ignoring the help as if they weren't there. This was yet another reason it was a good idea someone got around to making me poor again. Not the biggest reason, but one of them. The biggest reason was that as long as I was one of the wealthiest people on the planet I wouldn't be able to disappear properly.

We finally got an official who was okay with letting us stay on the plane while the flight plan was finalized. The trick was to keep asking for superiors until we reached one with decision-making abilities. That same official pushed through the flight arrangements, so within the hour we were airborne and heading for the East Coast of North America.

The two women were in their respective corners in the back of the plane, Mirella on the couch and Clara at the desk next to a sleeping Iza, both of them staring at laptop screens. I doubted they had spoken a word to one another since I'd left them alone. Mirella didn't trust Clara, didn't want Clara to come with us, and promised me twice already that she wouldn't be responsible if something were to happen to Clara. I was trying not to think of that as a threat. Meanwhile, Clara thought Mirella was too pretty. I think. I was afraid to ask.

"I may have figured out where the collection is being held," Clara said, once we were alone in the cabin. "It's a part of their *Collection of Scientific Instruments*, but it's not exactly on public display."

"What is *not exactly*?" I asked.

"It's available on request from visiting scholars, arranged in advance. To see it officially you would need to submit a formal reason."

"I want to steal it. Is that formal enough?"

"You might need to pretty that up. Also, these things are arranged months in advance, and we don't have months."

"I know. We need a thief."

Clara looked at the transparent box next to her. "What about Iza?"

"I don't think she can handle this, there are too many variables. Mirella, have you found me a thief?"

"I've found what you told me to search for," she said. "If you tell me this will lead you to a thief, I believe you. But I don't know how."

"He does that a lot," Clara said. "You get used to it."

"Show me what you found," I said to Mirella. "And where."

CHAPTER 17

I thought it would be a good idea to recruit a pixie for our little merchant adventure.

Hsu had never seen a pixie, and once I explained what they were he was less than enthusiastic about spending our time trying to find one. It made more sense to him to find human-sized assistance.

"I don't see any use in such a being," he insisted.

"Even the tiniest and most annoying creatures have particular talents that make them valuable," I argued.

I never found one, which was a shame. I really wanted to prove him wrong.

Someone had been setting fires in Philadelphia. It wasn't big news because the fires weren't large enough to be big news, and because no lives had been lost. But there was property damage of a very specific sort, and there were details that didn't make a lot of sense to a lot of people.

It was the details that convinced the local arson inspectors the fires were linked. For one thing, they were only taking place at businesses that served alcohol—bars, restaurants, nightclubs. For another, whoever was doing it drank a lot of the alcohol first. This was evident even after the fire damage, because the arsonist set fires in a part of the room that had no alcohol, so the proof of a drinking binge was usually semi-preserved. This also told investigators that whoever was doing this liked alcohol and liked fire, but didn't like those two things together.

The part that had been left out of the news was the lack of evidence that anybody broke into these places. It was implied in the language of the early articles, where employees and owners were considered persons of interest, because that meant they were looking at someone who had a key.

What they should have been looking for was somebody who wasn't human-sized. There is a certain kind of creature that is small, irritable, clever yet extremely one-track minded and predictable, and makes a very useful thief.

It's called an iffrit.

There are two default states for iffrits: drinking and happy, and drinking and unhappy. When they're happy, it's because they found someone to drink with them for a little while. When they're unhappy, it's typically because their drinking buddy finally got sick of them or died from alcohol poisoning.

An unhappy iffrit has a tendency to set fires. Nobody knows why. Even the iffrits don't know why.

I'm sort of fond of them, because I'm always looking for a drinking buddy, too, and a good iffrit can get me into locked places, and they're really entertaining drunks even if they're a pain when you're sober. They're like my spirit animal. But none of the ones I knew could explain the fire thing.

Before the advent of Internet-delivered news it was pretty hard to track down an iffrit, but since one only rarely tried to track them down—you were really better off running into one by chance—it wasn't an issue I ever found myself worrying all that much about.

"I'm not sure I want to meet anything like what you just described," Mirella said after listening to me provide Iza with as detailed a description of an iffrit as I could.

We were sitting in one of the two adjoining suites I'd snapped up in the poshest downtown hotel I could find in Philly. It was ridiculously ostentatious. One might think I was trying to impress one or both of the women I'd checked in with, and I'm sure that's what the hotel thought. Honestly, I just figured the best way to impoverish myself at this point was to spend all of it as rapidly as I could.

"Are you sure she can handle this, Adam?" Clara asked. When she wasn't sleeping, Iza was attached to Clara like some kind of parasite. Someone looking on at a distance would think I'd been talking to her and not the tiny winged person on her shoulder. "Iza's not as young as she used to be."

"She'll be fine," I said. "Just stick to bars for today, Iza. You know what bars are?"

"Stinky drinkies," she said. That's what she called everything I drank, basically.

"Close enough."

Her instructions were to find a bar in town that had a person about twice her height hiding somewhere inside. That little person would be naked, would probably smell bad, and would be curled up asleep somewhere in a ceiling tile or hole in a wall. Someplace where it was unlikely for them to be discovered. I could only hope there wasn't a large rat or small cat that smelled like liquor somewhere in the city, because if there was, that's probably what Iza would send us to find.

I cracked open a window: this time I'd picked a room with windows that would open at least enough for a pixie to get out. Reluctantly, Clara sent her off.

"I don't like this," Clara said.

"You've made that clear, yeah."

~

*I*za returned so soon it was difficult to believe she'd found an actual iffrit. In her absence I had successfully polished off two drinks, talked myself out of asking Clara about the father four times, and watched Mirella sharpen her knives.

It seemed appropriate to at least discuss the child with Clara, since we were doing all of this to get him back for her, but I got the clear sense that she had no intention of giving me any details. If there had been any way to get me to help her without knowing about Paul I'm sure she would have tried it first.

"How many bars did you check?" I asked Iza once she paused long enough in her plate of mushrooms to speak without a full mouth.

"Dunno," she said.

"She can't really count," Clara pointed out.

"Well all right, but roughly. More than this many?" I held up four fingers.

Iza nodded. "Told you, found iffit. Smelled."

"All right, but what did he smell like?"

I should say there was no question that the iffrit was a he. I don't think there is such a thing as a female iffrit, and if there is, even the iffrits don't know where to find one. If you want to know how they reproduce, so do I.

"I would really rather not know what this unbathed little creature smells like," Mirella said. "Let's just go to the bar and find it."

"Smoke," Iza said.

"It smelled like smoke?" Clara asked.

"Smoke and stinky drinkie."

"That does sound like our iffrit," I said.

~

*T*he bars in Philadelphia closed at 2 a.m., and after that basically the whole city shut down, so rather than try and figure out the best way to get the three of us plus a reluctant naked iffrit into the back of a hard-to-find cab at sometime on the wrong side of four in the morning, we went out and bought a car. I could have rented one, but that seemed like more trouble than it was worth.

Mirella had to be the legal purchaser because she was the only one of us who had a US driver's license. I'm pretty sure the guy at the dealership thought we were all insane. He double-checked the card I used four or five times to make sure it was okay, which was the same thing the hotel had done the day before.

I knew even using the card at all was sending up a flashing light to anyone who might be trying to follow us around, such as Mr. Smith and his better-than-Tchekhy computer guy. But it wasn't like landing a jet at Philadelphia International Airport was going to go unnoticed. And as agent Mike Lycos had stressed to me before, using cash wasn't a whole lot better. In other words, there was no way to travel everywhere we needed to travel in the time we had without making a lot of noise. So we may as well enjoy it by buying a nice car, even if we only planned on using it for a day or two. We took the car—it was actually an SUV, and was large enough that if you had told me it was also a small boat I'd have probably believed you— to the bar a few hours before closing just to get a feel for the place we'd be breaking into later. Also, I was in dire need of about twenty drinks and we all needed food because we were fighting some serious jet lag. Philly was six hours behind Italy, so Clara was ready to call it a day before the sun went down, and Mirella and I were even more out of sync.

Unfortunately, the bar in question was a ratty dive bar on an ugly side street, and while I have been on my share of ugly side streets and in a fair number of ratty dive bars, I was glad in this case that I had a bodyguard with me. The front façade was an unwelcoming set of nailed-up wood panels that needed a paint job or some shingles, and the one window was either frosted or smoke-stained, which didn't much matter since to see through it you'd have to look past the large neon beer sign that turned the glass opaque when the light hit it.

It was at least big enough that we didn't stand out overmuch. Anything smaller and we would have drawn a lot more attention just for being strangers, and I didn't feel like being a part of anyone's drunken xenophobia.

The food was actually not that bad for bar food. It was too salty, and a lot of it clearly originated in a freezer before passing through a microwave. It was also true that the very best thing about any of it was the description in the menu, but it still wasn't bad. Or I'm less discerning after a few drinks, which is much more likely.

Clara picked at something that had been described as Tuscan pizza bites, but which were clearly English muffins with store-bought pizza sauce and old cheese. She had Iza on her shoulder, but a dark bar is one of those places where having a small naked woman on your shoulder isn't noticed, or is only noticed by people who are certain they're seeing things.

"She said he's sleeping in the rafters," Clara whispered, and we all resisted the urge to look up.

"He's still there?" I asked.

"Yeah, she's checked twice already."

"I could probably knock him down with a knife if I knew which rafter," Mirella said.

"I don't want to kill him," I said. I could picture her flinging knives at the ceiling, and that not going at all well.

"The knife handle, not the pointy end," she said, slapping my wrist. "And you should stop ordering beer. This is going to be a long night."

"I don't know, a few more beers and I'll be down with a plan to knock an iffrit from the ceiling in the middle of a crowded bar."

She huffed. "I could do it. Excuse me."

She got up and headed to the extremely tiny and unsanitary bathroom in the back while roughly every human male and half the women watched her go. She turned heads even when dressed down, although in fairness the hockey game on television was between periods.

"You know she likes you, right?" Clara asked.

"She's being paid to protect me," I said. "You make this sound like high school."

"Yeah, okay. It's just, every time you wince from that wound on your stomach she winces with you. And there's the hand-slapping-on-the-wrist thing, which is a dead giveaway."

"She does that when she's pissed at me."

"My god, Adam. Sixty thousand years, how'd you *ever* get laid?"

"Cheap shot."

Clara laughed and took a long sip of her beer. I couldn't fully grasp why, but it made perfect sense to be getting advice from her about women.

"She's not angry with you," she said. "I mean, when she acts huffy like she just did. She's angry with herself for liking you."

"Right."

"Fine, don't believe me."

I sighed, and decided I didn't want to know if she was correct at that particular moment. "All right, if we're playing at being honest with each other right now, tell me about the father."

"I'm not telling you anything about the father, I already told you that. I'm not even okay with you knowing about Paul."

"Does the father at least know his son has been kidnapped?"

"Yeah. Yeah, he knows, but he's letting us handle it."

"Did he have a choice?"

She groaned and looked at the ceiling. "No, he didn't have a choice, and he's not a part of his son's life so it doesn't matter. They've never met. And I don't want to talk about it."

"Okay, fine."

I stuck a fork into something that was described as a potato puff on the menu, but which looked suspiciously like a tater tot, as Mirella returned to the table. She put her hand on my shoulder when she passed behind my chair, which caused Clara to arch an eyebrow and give me a tiny *I told you so* grin.

But it was just a touch on a shoulder.

~

We were out of the bar and back in the SUV well before 2 a.m.

The SUV was parked four blocks away because any closer than that was inviting a criminal act, and none of us were in the mood to deal with that. The thing was so big there was plenty of room in back in case anybody was in the mood for a nap, which Clara was.

Mirella and I sat in the front and watched the digital readout on the clock change. Each minute took forever. It was like a microcosm of my entire existence.

"I can steal the thing myself," Mirella said after a while. She was in the driver's seat on the off-chance we needed to actually navigate the car somewhere on short notice.

"I'm sure you can," I said.

"Without being detected."

"You're insulted."

"I'm a little insulted, yes. Goblins are natural thieves, you know."

I never thought of them that way, but this wasn't the time to say that. "Well, you can't bring me with you, and there would be nobody to guard my body while you were gone."

"You're joking. You already tried to convince me you don't need a bodyguard once."

"Yes, I'm joking. But I'm not when I say this is best handled by an iffrit if we get a hold of one. If we can't, plan B is you breaking in and stealing it. But we're talking about something we're not even sure of the location of right now. We know it's in a building on Oxford Street in Cambridge, but that's like saying we know a book is in the library somewhere. What we need is someone who can get inside and wander around for a few days. But if it were a museum piece on display, a smash-and-grab would be fine."

"I understand. But these things sound foul. I don't know how you trust one to find you gold and still return to you."

"Iffrits only care about alcohol and having someone to drink it with. You'll see."

~

At 3 a.m. Mirella got out and scouted the bar, determining that both patrons and employees had left the building but that nothing else appeared to be going on inside either. We gave it another hour, then woke up Clara and left her groggy but conscious in the driver's seat while we headed back to the scene for a little breaking-and-entering.

"I still see nothing happening in there," Mirella said. "But it's very hard to tell."

She was trying to get a good look through the window. Even though the beer sign was turned off, the glass was so smoky it was really tough to see if anything inside was moving.

"If he's still asleep we can try your knife-throwing stunt," I said. "Might even make this easier."

It was ten minutes of lock picking before we made it inside, because there were a number of locks to get through. Quantity and quality of locks have an inverse relationship to the value of commercial real estate, I have learned. At least in cities.

It was dark inside, but thankfully we had a basic idea of the layout, even if it had been altered slightly by the repositioning of all the chairs to the tops of the tables. It was the bar counter we were looking for, and it hadn't gone anywhere.

Mirella pulled out a small flashlight, but I stopped her from turning it on with a gesture.

"Listen," I whispered. I could hear the sound of someone drinking something from a bottle, and after a second she could hear it, too. She nodded understanding.

I took the flashlight from her and went around to one end of the bar while she crept around the other end to cut off any potential escape route. On the count of three we both turned toward the liquor side of the counter, her with her hands outstretched to catch a small fleeing person and me with the flashlight flickering to life.

What we found was an empty space that had very recently been occupied by a tiny drinking person.

"Where did he go?" Mirella asked. I was about to respond when a cry came out from directly above me.

"Banzaiiiiiiiiii!" the iffrit shouted.

He had an empty beer bottle in his hand, upside down by the neck and intended for use as a weapon. And it might have been modestly effective—potentially even connecting with his target, which was my head—had he not shouted on his way down from the rafters. But hearing him coming, I took two steps back and watched him land face down on the edge of the bar. The bottle bounced harmlessly away.

I had him in my hands before he had a chance to move again, and was treated to a loud belch.

"Hello," I said.

"I'll fucking kill you! You and her both! Let go of me!"

I recognized the voice.

Of course I did.

Of all the iffrits I could have come across, it had to be the least trustworthy one alive.

"I don't believe it," I said.

He blinked as his pupils adjusted to the light in his face.

"Adam? Oh fuck, is that you?"

"Hi Jerry. You little shit."

~

*A*n hour later we were back in the hotel room dropping a sack of screaming iffrit on the nearest hard surface. Jerry screamed apologies for the entire trip under the assumption I was taking him someplace so that he could be tortured and killed. He held onto this belief up until he popped out of the sack and saw where he was.

"Heyyyy, this is some room!" he declared.

I would have been entirely justified in killing him. He had sold me out for next to nothing, despite having virtually no use for money beyond that which was used to purchase alcohol. And in particularly dark times I actually did consider hunting him down for just that reason. But the unfortunate truth was that Clara had done much the same thing—sold me out, albeit for very different reasons—so it was hard to justify murdering Jerry. I imagine there were a few bar owners in Philadelphia who wish I had.

"How's the arm?" I asked.

"It hurts when it rains. You got a fuckin' wet bar in here?"

Mirella drew her sword and held it against his chin. "He's disgusting. Can't I please kill him and we try something else?"

"Oh hey, honey, look at *you*. Damn, Adam." He spotted Clara on the bed, caught somewhere between fascination and disgust. "Heyyy, I remember you, babe. Loved the whole tied-up look you had."

"Oh god, Mirella just do it," Clara said. "Adam?"

I should mention that a portion of the disgust in the room had to do with Jerry's erection, which was on full display because of his lack of clothing. I've found that this is something you just have to accept if you're going to be around them for any real length of time.

"I'm thinking," I said.

"Aww, c'mon, Adam! You need me for a thing, right? What she said, you need my help? What can I do?"

I was actually thinking this was the best possible outcome because ironically, the one utterly untrustworthy iffrit I'd ever met was probably the most reliable one for this particular job. Jerry knew his way around museums, he was actually very smart for his species, and he was actively afraid of me. Better, I had just proven I could track him down if I wanted to. He certainly didn't need to know I hadn't been looking for him specifically.

"Put the sword away," I said. "The bar's over here, Jerry. Let's talk about what I need you to do for me. And how much she's going to kill you if you fuck it up."

CHAPTER 18

*"We could travel easier if we did not require an entire mule just to carry
our wine," Hsu complained one evening following a particularly
unpleasant excursion through rough terrain and rougher weather.
"We likely would," I agreed. "But until they devise a way to make wine
lighter, I don't see another solution."*

A real low point for all concerned was when Jerry noticed there was a tiny naked woman flying around the room, which nearly resulted in Clara murdering him with an olive fork. Iza was blissfully unaware of most of this because, so far as I have ever been able to tell, pixies have no idea what sex is.

This again raises the reproduction question and again I have no answer, but I will say that now I'm reasonably certain pixies and iffrits do not reproduce together. That's almost a foregone conclusion because iffrits are twice the size of pixies, but they were close enough that I was willing to consider possibilities, like maybe iffrits shrank during mating season, or pixies grew. It wouldn't be the weirdest theory I'd heard and it was better than the apparent asexual reproduction that was causing their respective existences. But given that Jerry had self-evidently never even seen a pixie before, and Iza was undisguised in her dislike of him, it just didn't seem like a good bet.

Notwithstanding Jerry's puerile interest in Iza, it was actually sort of nice to have someone around who liked drinking as much as I did. Granted this particular someone had indirectly gotten a couple of friends killed and tried to turn me in for a beer truck, but he loved alcohol in a way it was difficult to get anyone else in the room to fully appreciate.

Mirella had her moments, certainly, but it seemed like she usually drank mainly to prove that she could do it. Less pleasure and more dare. And Clara was almost a puritan nowadays. She'd never been a big drinker, and when we lived together she actually talked me into three years of near-total sobriety, only to discover I'm more difficult like that. She wasn't against alcohol, and she did move into the back end of a vineyard, but for her it was always something to sip.

For Jerry—and me when I have nothing better to do—drinking was like an endurance sport. And that was an attitude I kind of missed being around.

Either fortunately or unfortunately, there were other people in the room who knew we had to be up early and driving to the airport to get to Boston to steal an astrolabe to find a faery kingdom to show to a cabal of multimillionaires to buy back the son of Clara and someone I didn't know. This was no time for drunken benders and accidental fires and blackouts that lasted a few weeks.

It took Mirella tying Jerry back up in the sack and Clara physically removing bottles from my hand, locking the bar, and hiding the key before either of us agreed that it was maybe best if we just got some sleep, but we did it.

"I give up, I don't want to live anymore," I moaned as Clara attempted to get a jacket on me. I had succeeded in putting on pants by myself, and a T-shirt, but I required assistance for everything else. Shoes were next.

"Sixty thousand was long enough?" she asked.

"And not a second longer. Go ahead, have Mirella do it. She probably wants to right now."

"Don't test me," Mirella said. She was holding the sack of writhing iffrit as far away from her body as she could and looking like the other side of the window was a good place to put it.

"How you feeling, Jerry?" I asked. I don't imagine I said it loudly but it sure sounded loud.

"Fuck you, Adam," Jerry said.

"Good, that's normal."

Clara was shaking her head.

"What?" I asked her.

"I think I might owe you an apology."

"Really?" I could think of a dozen things she could apologize to me for, but basically none of them were things she would ever think were her fault. "What for?"

"All those years I gave you a hard time about drinking and you told me you *were* practicing moderation. I always thought you were just a bad liar."

"Apology accepted. Now before you find my shoes I think I need to go throw up again."

~

We didn't let Jerry out of his sack until we were in the air, and then he spent basically the entire flight being impressed by the plane and trying to figure out which locked cabinet hid the liquor. Happily, he never discovered Iza sleeping in her transparent box.

I spent the whole trip trying to make my head stop hurting, telling Jerry to shut the hell up, and figuring out which woman was more angry with me. Mirella seemed to be the best bet, which was a little surprising. Maybe Clara was right about her.

We did not land in Boston. We were very obvious about ourselves in Philadelphia, which was fine because there was no way anybody following us was going to grasp why we were there or what we found, because even if iffrits are known to the people Mr. Smith unquestionably had following us, the idea that one might be important was surely beyond their ken. And given how much more annoying Jerry was when he thought I wasn't about to kill him, I had to agree that usefulness was difficult to see.

But upon leaving Philly we were back on track to fetch the necessary artifact, and I preferred not to have anybody know it, so we flew in to Providence instead.

After landing we rented a car like normal people instead of buying one, and to rent it we used one of three spare IDs I had that came with a credit card. The identity was set up by Tchekhy and the card was funded through the financial machinations of Heintz, so as long as both of those people had kept that information to themselves we were not likely to be found in a credit search. Granted, the plane was not inobvious and we were pretty easy to pick out of a crowd, so if Smith had someone standing at the auto rental counter we were still marked. Hopefully Providence was the kind of destination that made a man on the ground unlikely.

From there we drove straight to Boston, a trip that took about twice as long as it probably should have because of the traffic between the two cities. By nightfall we were holed up in an inexpensive motel at the edge of Cambridge and I was ready for solid foods again.

"There's no bar," Jerry complained as soon as he reached fresh air. "This room sucks."

"We're on the down-low," I explained.

"On the what? I don't think you know how to be rich, Adam. Seriously."

"I bought a plane and an island."

"You bought an island?"

"Yeah."

"Is it floating in beer?"

"You're like a tiny frat party."

"Is that supposed to be an insult?"

~

It took a long shower, a shave, and a large meal at the Chinese buffet next to the motel before I felt enough like myself to proceed with the plan. Since that coincided with nightfall it worked out well for everyone, although maybe I was the only one who thought so.

"Can we at least buy him some underwear or something?" Mirella asked. Jerry was now stuffed in a backpack that I had on the ground next to the chair I was sitting in.

The chair was beside a table and part of a large collection of similar chairs and tables that made up an outdoor plaza that filled up the space between old Harvard Yard and some of the slightly more modern buildings that also belonged to the university. Beneath us was a tunnel that shuffled traffic from one edge of Harvard Square to all points beyond.

"He's really hard to shop for," I said. "We could maybe make him a loincloth out of a diaper, but he won't like it."

"I am incredibly unconcerned with his likes and dislikes."

We were facing the Oxford Street building that was soon going to be the target of a criminal act.

It took us a little while longer than it should have to locate it, only because it was not technically adjacent to any street, so there was some confusion. It was at the edge of the highly occupied public plaza in which we were sitting, and the plaza was very well-lit indeed.

The building was well-lit, too. It was the kind of modern

architectural glass-and-stone structure one might have expected from the MIT campus down the road, but not from a place as old as Harvard University. In fairness, it *was* their science center, and that's the sort of thing that screams for a modern touch.

It was open twenty-four hours a day, thanks mainly to the computer lab in the basement. I couldn't hope to understand why anyone needed a computer lab when basically every rectangular device on the planet was now a computer of some kind, but there it was.

"Are we waiting for something?" Mirella asked. "I could throw him through the front door if you're looking for a way to get him inside."

"No, we're waiting for some*one*. I called ahead. And there she is. I think."

A striking young woman in a dressy pantsuit and heels made her way across the cobblestones. She had her black hair pulled back and a pair of glasses on her face that I knew she would never need. One might mistake her for a busy executive were it not ten o'clock at night and the fact that she looked seventeen.

I stood up to greet her with a hug. "It's good to see you again, Brenda."

"You, too, Apollo," she said.

"This is Mirella."

Mirella stood and shook her hand, and shot me a worried look.

"She's a friend," I said, just in case that wasn't abundantly clear already.

Brenda was a vampire, and that was what had Mirella concerned, although I couldn't imagine it was *that* big a deal. Vampires aren't really terrible. They just tend to be moody, which I think is mainly due to an extreme version of seasonal affective disorder.

When I first met Brenda she was a hooker with terrible

fashion sense and a poor grasp of current events. She appeared to have stepped up.

"You look good," I said.

"I'm a little overdressed, I know. But I like the suit and I never get to wear it. And hey, I'm auditing a class here and my professor is super cute, so I really wore it for him, if you're getting all flustered or something. I think we might be the same age. The professor, not you."

I laughed. "I'm glad you're doing well. You know I can help you if you want."

"Nah, it's more fun this way. I'm gonna be the first vampire entrepreneur."

"Yes you are." I held up my expensive gourmet coffee as a toast.

There have actually been a lot of vampire inventors, a few vampire statesmen, and one or two business entrepreneurs that I know of. They aren't great with money, but they're good for big picture stuff as long as someone else handles the details.

"So what's in here that's got you two all excited?" Brenda asked. "Does it have to do with that smelly thing in the backpack?"

"Sort of," I said. "It's the end of a thousand-year quest, if you can believe it."

"Sure, why not? So this is the building you told me to check out, but, like, it's *open*, so I wasn't sure if I had it right."

"I'm trying not to let anybody know I am interested in something in there."

"Oh, okay, cuz you could just walk in but ... all right, so I think what you're after is on the third or fourth floor. That's where the science history stuff is kept. I didn't look around because that part's only open during the day, and you know I have a thing about daytime. There's a security desk that's got a guy at it most times. You don't really need a Harvard ID to get around, since the ground floor is open at both ends, but I have one you can use if there's a room that will take a keycard swipe."

"If an alarm is triggered," Mirella said, "who responds?"

"I'm assuming the guy at the guard desk, and after that, campus police. Their cars look just like regular cop cars, though, which was way confusing."

"You set off an alarm?" I asked.

"Not here. Campus police covers everything, and all the buildings have the same kinda alarm system. I cracked a window at the Fogg Museum last night to see what would happen. It took them about ten minutes to get to the window, and then all they did was close it again and drive off. I wasn't real impressed."

"Perhaps more alarms would have been triggered if you had gone inside," Mirella said.

"Yes. Perhaps," Brenda said, rolling the word over in her mouth like it was something she was going to start saying more often in the future. "Anyway, that's about all I got."

"That's plenty, thanks," I said.

"No problem. So are you gonna show me the thing in the backpack?"

"Only if you want to see him."

"Oh, it's a *him*. What happened to the pixie?"

"She's still around. She says hi."

I actually didn't tell Iza I'd be meeting with Brenda, but it seemed polite to say otherwise. Iza and Clara had stayed behind in the hotel room. Clara was supposed to be using the Internet to find out what she could about possible CIA black sites in Scotland, but she was probably fumigating the room instead, on the assumption that Jerry wouldn't be returning.

I checked around the plaza. There were a half-dozen other people there, in various states of motion, and one or two sitting on the other end of the place. It didn't look like anyone was paying attention to us. I opened the bag.

"Did you get all of that?" I asked Jerry.

"I got it. Hey lady, is there food in there?"

"Uhhhm, is he talking to me?" Brenda asked.

"Yeah, sweetheart, I'm talking to you."

"I don't eat food, little whatever-you-are, but there's a cafeteria and some candy machines."

"How about a bar? A liquor cabinet maybe."

Brenda looked at me, confused. "No, I don't think so?"

"Ahh, okay fine."

Jerry hopped out of the bag and scurried away. If anyone other than us saw him, they didn't react.

"Iffrit," I said in response to Brenda's bewildered look. "That's what they're called."

"Ew."

"Pretty much, yes."

"What's he going to do in there?"

"He'll run in through a side door and live in the walls for as long as it takes to find what I'm looking for. Probably set off every alarm in there once or twice, but at worst they'll think they have a vermin problem."

"They do," Mirella said.

~

Mirella and I returned to the plaza the following night to wait for Jerry to emerge. He didn't, but it was too soon to have expected him to, really. He also didn't turn up on the second night, or the third. By the fifth we were starting to get worried.

"I should go in and look for him," Mirella said.

"If the campus security can't find him you won't be able to either."

"They don't know what to look for. I can take your pixie for help. Or your vampire friend. I'm sure she can track him."

Brenda had returned twice to say hello, and Mirella was now

well aware of what her name was but had no evident intention of using it.

It was becoming difficult to pretend she wasn't acting jealous. In fairness, every time we turned around it probably seemed as if there was another woman from my past popping up. And I suppose both Clara and Brenda were difficult to compete with in the eyes of an immortal man, given neither of them will age. But Brenda?

I was inclined to explain that we'd never been romantic beyond letting her drink my blood that one time, but it seemed like it would be a better idea to leave Mirella's dissatisfaction unrecognized.

"He'll turn up," I said, regarding Jerry's continued absence. "He's signaled us."

"So you've said. I don't think a flickering light is a signal any more than I think a moved flowerpot is a signal. The building could be haunted."

"He's done a couple of hauntings, actually. He's really good at them."

She laughed. "That sounds fun. If he weren't such a disgusting thing I could learn to like him, I think."

"Don't let him hear you say that."

She flashed me a genuine smile, and it was adorable, because she almost never did that.

"So are you dealing with this any better?" I asked.

"How do you mean?"

"You had a little freak-out a while back. Can you live with the idea that I might not be crazy?"

"I'm coping all right. You do keep some odd company."

"For someone like me, sometimes the safest place is among other impossible things. We keep each other secret."

"Does that make you king of the impossible things?"

"I might be the *god* of impossible things."

"Hah! That's a dubious honor."

"Being a god always is."

She looked at her watch. "It's past the time he should have emerged. And it's been five days. We're running out of time. I don't suppose you have a contingency plan?"

"No. Do you?"

"Other than breaking in myself, which you refuse to let me do, I can't think of any. Unless you want to give up on this whole thing, let the woman's son die, and go visit someplace tropical."

"Ask me that again in a couple of days, I might consider it."

The truth was, we were cutting this much too close and we were relying on just about the most untrustworthy being I could name to deliver a solution. And, I had no real faith in that solution being effective. There was no other real choice, though. I didn't like the idea of Clara's son being killed, and I expected if I allowed it to happen I'd hate myself for at least a century, but I wasn't going to trade my life for his if it came down to it. I know that makes me a terrible person, but let's be honest, I'm kind of a terrible person sometimes. And maybe someday Clara would forgive me.

Iza buzzed past my ear. I was so used to this that it took me a minute to remember I'd left her with Clara and there wasn't any good reason for her not to still be with Clara unless something was wrong.

Mirella realized it, too. She was looking around the plaza.

There was nobody else there, but it was after midnight, and the weekend was over so I had thought nothing of it.

"Iza, what's wrong?" I asked under my breath.

"Trap," she said on her way by my ears. "Clara said trap. Clara said run."

"What happened to Clara?"

Mirella stood up, her hand on a hidden blade. "I'm sorry. I wasn't paying enough attention."

"To what?"

"I think we might be surrounded."

"Trap," Iza repeated.

I could hear someone walking up behind me. I didn't bother to turn because Mirella could see him just fine and I was pretty positive I knew who it was. And the drama of his dress shoes clacking on the cobblestones was kind of cool, actually. Very cinematic.

Without a word, Smith placed a small round object wrapped in a cloth on the table in front of me and sat down opposite us. This time he wasn't alone. There were two men next to him, both wearing the kind of gear you don't usually see in an American city, even after midnight.

At least the men were human.

"Do you want to tell me what it is?" he asked, without preamble.

I opened it up and took a look. "It's an astrolabe."

"It is indeed. A very old one, stolen from the building behind me by the tiny little man in the bag being held by my associate right now."

To illustrate, one of the men took a bag off his shoulder and dropped it on the ground. I heard a garbled exclamation of pain from inside the bag.

"What I would really like to know, Adam, is why this little man stole this very old astrolabe for you?"

"I like it," I said. "Used to own it, decided I wanted it back."

"Two weeks ago you and I came to an agreement," Smith said. He sounded really pissed. "You were given the freedom to find what you needed in order to do what *she* did."

"It hasn't been two weeks yet."

"Yes, because I'm *just that stupid*. I'm going to tell a killer to go off and find the thing that will allow him to appear and disappear and walk through walls and then I'm going to expect him to *give* it to me."

"When you put it that way it does sound sort of stupid." I don't really think of myself as a killer, because the notion is sort of a modern one. Historically, being a guy who was willing to take another guy's life if it meant living another day was just called "a guy."

"So two days ago when your little thief snuck out with that we intercepted him, took him to a nice dark room and interrogated him. But it turns out he's kind of an asshole and kind of an idiot, which is why you didn't tell him anything useful."

"Yeah, I don't really trust Jerry all that much."

"Very smart. Although to his credit he did keep what he *did* know to himself for longer than I expected."

"You should have given him beer. He would have opened right up."

"Meanwhile, that little tchotchke there went to the lab and do you know what the lab guys told me? They told me it's old, it's brass, and if you point it at the sky and spin a couple of dials it will tell you what time it is."

"Sounds about right."

"*What do* you *want it for?*"

"You said two weeks and it hasn't been two weeks," I said. I was repeating this because I thought it was important, yes, but also I didn't know what else to say just yet.

"And you spent one week and five days getting this when you could have just bought a fucking watch? Forget it, we're done. I tried being nice. Now I'm just gonna kill everyone and call it a wash."

I heard Iza's buzzing pick up an agitated tempo.

"Did you kill Clara?" I asked.

"What? No, why would I do that? No, I need her. We're going to re-create Grindel's immortality formula. That was pretty much always the plan, but I figured maybe we could get this other thing, too, before getting rid of you."

"You need me if you're ever going to do that."

"Nah, not really. I'm told Grindel's corpse wasn't all that useful because of the being dead thing, but Clara and the kid are plenty enough. *You* have a tendency to break everything you touch, so I'm not going to put you anywhere near that compound if I can help it. Best thing is to just take you out into the woods and kill you. You, too, honey. Don't think I've forgotten about you and all those pretty knives."

He stopped talking for a second and listened, and I realized he was looking for Iza.

"And her," he said. "I saw how useful she was in Istanbul. She moves too fast to show up on video cameras, did you know that?"

He looked over his shoulder and gave a nod to the other guy, the one who hadn't been carrying Jerry. This one had something else on his back ...

"Iza, fly away!" I shouted, but if she heard me she didn't react fast enough. Soon the entire plaza was blindingly bright with fire.

The man had a flamethrower.

I would love to say that I saw her get away, that she managed to get above the flames or something, and went off to live a nice long life somewhere. But I didn't see her at all, because the fire was too bright. I did hear her, though. And the sound of a pixie screaming is right near the top of the list of the most terrible things I've ever heard.

It was only a few seconds before the man with the flamethrower shut it down and we all blinked our vision clear. All except for Smith, who had evidently closed his eyes.

"I'm going to kill you for that," I told him.

"I wish I could say you'll have a chance to, I really do. But I'm not *that* stupid."

"You're going to gun us down right in the middle of Cambridge? The flames have probably already gotten someone's attention."

"No, we'll be taking you someplace more private for the formal execution. Don't worry, it's not far. And if you're thinking it's just three of us, I'm pretty sure your goblin has already alerted you to the fact that I have this place surrounded."

"Actually, no," Mirella said. "It's only the three of you now."

Smith laughed. "Fine, whatever you say honey."

He had a small microphone in his hand, which he spoke into. "Bring it in," he said.

Mirella looked at me. "Would you like the honor of killing him personally?"

Smith looked a little less happy. "Round 'em up, let's get out of here," he said into his mike.

"I think I really have to do it myself," I said. "It's a little cliché, but you understand."

"I do."

Something was flung from the darkness beyond the plaza. It was a little black piece of electronics, and it bounced along the cobblestones and came to a stop next to Smith's feet. He looked down at it for a second. "Hello," he said into his hand. He heard his own voice come out of the piece on the ground.

This got the attention of the men standing on each side of Smith. They didn't appear to need orders to understand that getting their guns out was a good idea. But guns can be surprisingly useless when someone has already thrown a knife at you and that knife has already penetrated your windpipe. It's remarkable how quickly one learns not to care about one's gun when one is suddenly deceased.

Mirella handed me her sword. I stood and pointed it at Smith.

"Tell me you're armed, so this at least feels fair," I said.

"You aren't going to kill me," he said. "I have Clara and the boy."

Brenda walked up. She had ten assault rifles slung over her shoulder. She looked really sharp in slacks and a silk blouse, and a pair of sensible two-inch heels. The weaponry was strikingly discordant.

"I can kill him," she said. "You want me to?"

"No, I can do it. Is everyone else dead?" I didn't hugely care because I was going to leave as soon as I was in a vehicle that could get me out of town, but I had a feeling three dead bodies in the middle of Harvard Square wasn't nearly as bad as thirteen.

"I'm not sure," she said. "I tried not to. They all had zip ties, so they're cuffed up if you're worried."

She really had grown. A few years back she was horrified to know I had taken someone's life, now she wasn't sure if she may have accidentally beaten someone to death.

To Smith I said, "I'm pretty sure I'm not going to drop everything to go save Clara. I made that mistake once before, remember? I try to learn from my mistakes when I can."

"If not her, then at least the boy," Smith said. "Or ... she didn't tell you, did she? Adam, you *do* know little Paul is your son, don't you?"

CHAPTER 19

"Don't gods have children?" Hsu asked once. We were talking about his own disappointment at not having carried on his family line, which would die with him.

"Gods have children," I said. "But I don't."

~

"That's a lie," I said.

My voice was firm but the tip of the sword betrayed a tremble, because while what he said was impossible it fit all of the evidence. It's just that I have not fathered a child—ever—so the idea that I was responsible for this one simply never occurred to me. But if I were Clara, I would know how many powerful people would want to get their hands on this child, and I would do what I could to keep him a secret. Even from his father. Especially from his father, actually.

"Adam, I'm gonna reach into my jacket here for a second, okay?" Smith said. He was sliding his hand past his lapel. "No weapon."

He pulled out a photograph and placed it on the table.

269

"Here's a picture of Paul. I know you haven't seen any because she cleared them all out of the house when she knew you were coming. I don't blame her, I mean look at him. Look at that face."

I did.

There was really no mistaking who the father of this child was.

"So ... congratulations?" Brenda said.

"Where are they?" I asked.

"Well, I'm not gonna tell you that. But I will tell you that if I don't return from tonight's escapade I can't guarantee their safety."

"You can't guarantee their safety now."

"That's true, but I'm the only one here who can try. Let me be honest with you, Adam. Little Paulie is going to grow up behind a fence. He'll have his mom there for at least as long as we need her, and maybe if she's really good she'll get to stay even after the lab folks are all done with her, but I can't promise that because I'm pretty sure she's planning on being a pain in the ass. What I *can* do is make sure Paul doesn't feel like a prisoner. Right now the only thing we don't know about him is what he's gonna turn into when he grows up, and there are a lot of people interested in the answer to that. But he can grow up in a cell just fine because science doesn't care if the test subject is happy. You understand what I'm saying?"

"I think you should kill him," Mirella said. "They won't kill Clara or Paul if he doesn't return. They're more important than he is."

"They can suffer a whole lot without being killed, sweetie. Ask your smelly little friend about that."

Jerry, it should be noted, could have released himself from the bag on the ground by now, but hadn't done so. I would have been concerned about this if I was concerned about Jerry.

"If I let you go, what happens?" I asked Smith.

"Well, first off, I clean up this mess here before it becomes a major news story."

"I don't care about that."

"You should. There's cameras everywhere now, Captain Caveman. At least one or two have your face on them. Nowadays that shit can go global in under a day, especially if this ends up looking like a terrorist thing. You think having a drawing of your mug in *The Boston Globe* is bad, wait'll you see how easy it is to get around when everybody with a smart phone is looking for you."

"Will *you* stop looking for me?"

"Nah, probably not. But you'll have a great head start. I don't really care if you live or die, Adam. I just don't want you fucking up what we've got going on. Maybe you can learn to deal with the idea that in a generation or two you're not going to be the only immortal man walking around."

"So I stay away, you leave me alone?"

"You stay away, I don't try very hard to find you."

I lowered the sword. "All right."

"Adam, you can't—"

"Let him go, Mirella," I said, handing her the sword. I shot a glance at Brenda, who shrugged. She had no idea what was going on anyway.

"You won't regret this, Adam," Smith said, taking out a phone.

"I already do." I grabbed the astrolabe, the picture of Paul, and the bag of Jerry. "Let's get out of here before his cleanup crew arrives."

~

*B*renda's new apartment was a huge improvement over the little space she used to have in Chinatown. It was a basement apartment in Brookline that had multiple rooms, carpeting, a working bathroom, overhead lighting, and electricity powering that lighting. It was even decorated somewhat tastefully.

After leaving Smith we fled to the rental car and debated where to go next for as long as it took Brenda to point out how close we were to her home. Since Smith was clearly unprepared for Brenda, he must not have known where she lived, which made it a safe place to be. Safer, at least, than the motel. The plane was also probably no longer safe, but it was not safe and in Rhode Island, so the option was moot.

"You can put him on the counter," Brenda said as soon as she got some lights on. She had a galley kitchen that looked entirely unused, because it was. I didn't open the refrigerator but I imagined if I did I'd see lots of blood and no beer.

I put the bag with Jerry still inside on her counter. It was a fifteen-minute drive from Harvard Square to Brookline, and Jerry hadn't moved or spoken in that time. I looked inside the bag on the way, just long enough to note that what was inside was bleeding a lot.

Mirella turned to Brenda.

"Do you have first aid?" she asked.

"I do. Hang on." Brenda put down her armload of semiautomatic weapons on the couch and disappeared into the bathroom.

I opened the bag. Jerry slid out onto the formerly pristine linoleum. He was a mess of dried and fresh blood, and it was difficult to tell where the wounds were and what had caused them.

He was still breathing, though.

"They flayed him," Mirella said, horrified. "He's missing patches of skin."

Let me reiterate that I had no love for Jerry the iffrit. There were many days when I wondered why I let him live after what he'd done to me. Smith called me a killer, and I guess that's true because only a killer would lament having *not* killed someone.

But I would never have done to Jerry what Smith did. I wouldn't have done this to *anything*.

Jerry shivered and shook, and fresh blood came from one of the cuts on his side.

"Towel," I said.

Brenda reappeared with a first aid kit, saw blood, and froze for a half second before disappearing again. She returned a few seconds later with a hand towel. I swaddled him in it like a baby.

"Jerry," I said.

"He's in shock," Mirella said.

"I know. Jerry, can you hear me? It's Adam."

Jerry's eyes fluttered, but didn't open.

"Asshole," he whispered.

"There you are."

"Kill those fuckers for me, would'ja?"

"Jerry, I need to know what happened to the astrolabe."

"Isn't that what this thing is?" Brenda asked, holding up the one Smith had given me.

"It's the wrong one," Mirella said.

Jerry laughed. It was a hoarse sound that betrayed the amount of liquid in his lungs. "Knew they were watching. Neat trick, huh?"

"Yes, that was very clever, Jerry. You're very clever. But now I need to know what you did with the real one."

"Hey, Adam ... you remember Hanratty's? What a place, huh? I wish ..."

He coughed up a load of blood and fell silent.

"Jerry?"

He wasn't breathing. I didn't know how to resuscitate an iffrit.

"He's gone," Mirella said.

"Awww," Brenda said. "He seemed like an okay guy."

"He kind of was," I said. "In his own way."

～

*B*renda actually did have some beer in the refrigerator. I briefly considered pouring some of it into Jerry's mouth to see if it revived him, and then because it didn't seem right for blood to be the last thing to pass over his lips. I decided just to drink it myself instead, while sitting on Brenda's living room couch next to a pile of guns, in the dark. It seemed like an appropriate tableau given the current circumstances.

After a little while Mirella came in and sat on the coffee table in front of me.

"Are you okay?" she asked.

"I think the cut has healed," I said. "We should probably take the stitches out when we have a chance."

"You know that isn't what I mean."

"Yes." I took a deep pull on the beer, and noted there were two empty bottles on the end table next to me. I had apparently been sitting on the couch for a little while.

"I don't know what it's like to have a child," I said. "Shouldn't I feel something?"

"I'm sure you do feel something."

"I guess, but I don't know what."

Familial bonding is essentially the only thing I have never experienced. Oh, I'm sure I had parents, and siblings, but it was so long ago I have almost no memory of it. Every now and then a smell or a sound will trigger something in me, a feeling—I guess —of being cared for. An ancient animal memory of my mother is how I think of it. But I don't remember her face or anything about her.

"You will know when you see him," Mirella said.

"Do you have children?"

"No," she laughed. "Not yet. Probably not ever. I have no plans for them."

"Me neither."

I've seen what parenthood can do to a person. When I had fewer scruples I used it to my advantage, especially in wars but also in business negotiations and the like. Finding a man's eldest son was like discovering an especially vulnerable nerve cluster. Hit it often enough and you'll have the man on his knees agreeing to whatever terms you need him to agree to. I imagine a part of me always wondered what it must feel like to be that involved in the life of another person.

Now that I had such a person, I didn't know what I was going to end up agreeing to, or if anybody was going to stop me from making that deal when the time came.

"We're going to have to find them," I said. "It's not the smart play. The smart play is to go to that tropical island you were talking about. I bet you look great in a bikini."

"I do," she said. "But he's your son."

"He's my son. So let's go do some incredibly stupid things."

～

Going right back to the plaza where we only just recently killed two people was an incredibly stupid thing, so of course we did it first. In my head it didn't seem all *that* stupid, because ultimately if Smith and his cohort were looking for us they wouldn't be checking there, but then we arrived at the scene and it just seemed like a bad idea altogether.

"I don't see anything unusual," Mirella said.

We were standing a safe distance away at the corner of a building on the far side of Oxford Street. She had the eyepiece of a rifle sight in her hand and was using it to check out the building. I was fighting the urge to pace.

To the naked eye it looked the way it was supposed to, with a large amount of foot traffic consisting mainly of Harvard students. There was no obvious police presence.

Mirella put away the lens.

275

"Two dead men, ten concussed men, and Smith amidst a five-second explosion of flames in the middle of the night, and there's no evidence any of it ever happened. You should find this disturbing."

"I do," I said. And I certainly did. It took a lot of juice to make a crime scene simply not happen. "But right now I find it very convenient. Let's go before I change my mind."

~

The Harvard Science Center was very much as Brenda described. There was a wide-open main floor that included an old IBM computer that was the size of a small truck, encased in plastic and probably no longer functional. Opposite that was a guard desk with a bored-looking Harvard security guard. Beside him was a set of elevators and a directory.

"The third and fourth floors," Mirella said, reading the directory and parroting Brenda. "That's where it would be."

"That's where it *used* to be," I said. "We're going to assume he got it out of there and put it somewhere else."

"Why are we going to do that?"

"Because otherwise we're back where we started and I don't like that conclusion."

"I greatly prefer the idea that our search might be confined to two partly secure floors rather than this entire building."

"We don't need to search the whole building. We only need to think like an iffrit."

Thinking like an iffrit brought us to the building's small cafeteria. It wasn't much more than a deli sandwich counter with a small grill and a soda machine, and definitely not the kind of place Jerry would appreciate.

"They don't have alcohol here," I noted.

"That's a good thing. If he'd set the building on fire it would have been counterproductive."

"I know, but when I decide to think like an iffrit that's the only thing I can come up with."

"He would have needed food, too. This is where the food is."

"Maybe."

I stood in the center of the mostly empty cafeteria and spun in a slow circle. There was a chain door at the entrance that would have closed off the space in the off-hours, but that wouldn't have stopped him any more than the vault holding the astrolabes had. He would have come in through a ceiling tile or a fault in a wall, or a vent, or something. I never really knew how he got into about half the places he managed to get into, actually.

I could only hope Jerry anticipated the possibility that he would not be the one returning to fetch the astrolabe and had made plans accordingly. If that were true I'd be looking for something only I was expected to notice.

But maybe that was giving him too much credit.

"Let's walk around some more."

~

Only about half the ground floor was publicly accessible, with the rest of the space taken up by closed-door lecture halls. We walked the floor twice without noting anything before trying the stairs that led down to a sub-level.

This was mostly a dead end as well, as it led to more lecture halls, public bathrooms, and the computer lab.

And two vending machines.

Both of the machines had *out of order* signs and yellow caution tape across the front of them. Mirella walked around one and peered at the back.

"It looks like mice got into the candy."

"It's supposed to," I said. "Okay, so I'm an iffrit. I think there might be someone outside waiting to snatch me up."

"Why do you think this?"

"I don't know, maybe he saw something unusual, but he knew. He said so. Whatever that was, it convinced him to take a dummy astrolabe."

"If he knew he was going to be taken, why did he risk leaving?"

"I don't know. But he couldn't stay in here forever."

I pulled one of the machines away from the wall and crouched down to Jerry's height. The machine's electrical cord had been chewed through.

"Do you have a flashlight?" I asked.

She had a penlight, which was close enough.

"People are staring," she said when she handed it over.

"Try and look like we're supposed to be here," I offered, as I checked out the wall.

"How am I supposed to do that?"

"I don't know," I said. "But in a few minutes you're going to have to pick the lock on this machine, so you'd better figure it out."

"What did you find?"

I leaned back and showed her what was written on the wall:

TRY A SNICKERS, ASSHOLE.

~

We decided against opening the machine right away, because in the few minutes we'd been there we had already attracted more attention than we wanted. So instead we slid the machine back against the wall, and went upstairs and took a seat in the cafeteria for what felt like probably the longest hour of my life. Then, with her lock-pick in hand, Mirella went back down to the broken vending machine and picked the lock.

"I don't think we needed to wait," she said when she came back. "The most interest I drew came from students who realized there was about to be free candy. I don't believe anyone discussed what I was doing with security. But still, we should leave."

"Was it there?"

"It was." She sat down and slid a cloth-wrapped disc across the table. "He jammed it near the back of the carrel. We're fortunate nobody came to fix the machine before we got to it."

I opened the cloth.

It had been a thousand years. From the moment it was handed to Hsu until he lost it and then found me in the Rhine valley, it had been a thousand years. I'd gone to Mangalore and fought my way out of the Talus compound and watched Hsu die, and this thing in my hands had meanwhile ended up somewhere in Persia, where it was discovered in the ground or in someone's attic, and sold or donated to a university in a country that didn't exist until a few hundred years ago. It was the impossible object that was supposed to open a door to an impossible place.

But it wasn't any of those things. It was a gold astrolabe. It felt cold and rough to the touch, like running a finger across the grooves of a vinyl record, but it didn't strike me as any more extraordinary than the brass one I'd seen twelve hours earlier.

I held it up in the light and turned it in my hand and fiddled with the still-functioning plates, and nothing happened except my heart beat faster in anticipation of *something* that just never came.

It was a gold astrolabe, and that was all it was.

"So?" Mirella asked.

I slid it into my pocket. "Let's get out of here."

~

The next stupid thing we did was return to the airplane. I had been thinking there was almost no way we'd make it all the way back there again without facing at least some token resistance, but at worst we were watched and our whereabouts reported. Nobody official or unofficial, armed or otherwise, turned up to impede us.

Possibly, Smith didn't want to create an international incident by holding a firefight on the runway of a national airport. Considering we brought the guns Brenda had taken—she hated parting with them but agreed they would probably be more useful for us than for her—it probably would have devolved into a firefight pretty quickly.

Brenda hated parting with us, too. She wanted to come along and help, and I nearly agreed, because she had turned out to be a whole lot more useful than the last time we'd encountered one another. But Smith bragged about sun lamps at this compound of his and I couldn't think of any reason why that might be a bluff. Besides, I'd already gotten Iza and Jerry killed, Tchekhy had *nearly* been killed, and Brenda was likely going to have to relocate and start over again before Smith found out who she was. Throw in Clara and Paul and probably Mirella and I was pretty sure I'd ruined enough lives in the past couple of months already. Brenda was better off far away from me.

We were in the air just before sunset with a full tank that would just get us over the Atlantic. I had to tell the pilot where we were going before we took off so he knew how much fuel to bring—the tanks were barely large enough to get us to Europe nonstop—and I told him Scotland without even knowing if that was the correct answer. That was where Smith said he'd be, and it was all I had to go on.

I hoped Tchekhy had better information.

"I did find this investment you spoke of," he said, after first explaining—again—that he couldn't figure out how to make me poor without crashing the world economy. I was on the super-secret phone with him, which was amazing given I couldn't get any of the other cell phones to work at thirty thousand feet. "It is a pool of venture capital funding loosely structured around speculative medical advances in the field of aging. I was able to track your funds to an account in Gibraltar."

"What the hell is in Gibraltar?"

"Goat farms and banks. It is not a place where there are things, it is a place where money is held. A fiscal haven. Governments go to this place and say, tell us where this money went, and they say, what money? We don't know what you are talking about. This is why rich companies and rich people use these places."

"All right, so the money went to Gibraltar. What then?"

"I have no idea."

"This is very unhelpful."

"I could try and assault the offshore holding company's computers to find out more, but it would take me many months and the money is not likely to be there any longer. You understand that if the persons running this account have any idea of what they are doing it will take years to find out where the money *actually* went? And without that access I cannot tell you how large this company is, or what percentage of the whole your investment represents."

"All right, I understand. What about the Scotland thing?"

"I have little useful news there either. Scotland is not large, but it is large enough to make identifying this compound you described very difficult. I have even borrowed some satellite feeds."

"The part about the sun lamps didn't help?"

"Many small facilities have nighttime lights, and it is not really possible to distinguish a sun lamp from a klieg light through a satellite image. And we are assuming the man who told you about Scotland was telling you the truth."

"I know, but it's all I have."

"Nearly all. You have actually invested in a holding company in Scotland. The investment was quite recent, and it looks as if funds movement with this holding company replaced the funds transfers you had been making previously to Gibraltar. It seems reasonable to assume they are interrelated."

"Maybe I'll look up that company, then. Is there an address?"

"It is the bank address. That will not help you."

"Fine, what's the name of the company, at least?"

"Leewan Sean Enterprises."

I nearly dropped the phone. "What did you say?"

CHAPTER 20

*H*eintz's apartment was unexpected. He was so fastidious in person that it only made sense for him to reside in one of those pristine places where the guys in shaving cream commercials live. I expected stainless steel and white walls and personal belongings that looked like they had just been bought and certainly never used. What we found instead was wood paneling matching brown leather furniture and an overall decorative style that wasn't a style at all.

In that sense we were at least in the right place. With Tchekhy's help we had identified the most likely current location of my private banker—Switzerland—and then had to narrow down his residence with Mirella tailing him to and from the banking building for three days. It would have taken less time if Heintz was a human being instead of a goblin, and even less if Iza was still alive.

Once we had the correct building we needed to figure out the apartment number. We were fortunate in that it was neither a large building nor a terribly private one, and with no concierge to have to get past, but it was still a pain. In the end we relied on the mailboxes to help us figure it out, and only by picking the locks on each box until we found one that had mail in it addressed to him.

"There's nothing here," Mirella said, having just completed a cursory search of the apartment. It could only be cursory since we were both avoiding the windows. "Although I don't know what to look for."

"I don't either. It's a modest place, don't you think? I imagined he made more than this."

"This is only where he lives. I doubt he brings dates here. Elves are not modest by nature."

"True. I remember—"

"Shh." Mirella held a hand up and pointed to the door. It was the third time she had done this because it was the end of the day and people were getting home, and there was no way to tell from the sound of someone walking down the hallway if they were coming to this door or a different one.

Then came a key in the lock, and Juergen Heintz let himself in.

I was sitting in his very comfortable leather chair in a corner and we'd left on no lights, which was as it had been left. Mirella melted away into a dark recess between the living room and the bedroom.

Heintz came in holding his mail, which he skimmed before placing it on the table next to the door.

The apartment wasn't large. The main living space had two areas identified mainly by furniture. I was in one such area, opposite which sat a very clean desk. Heintz walked to that desk and put his bag on it.

"I know you're here," he said without looking up from his desk. "I'm glad you have come."

"You were expecting me?" I asked.

"Of course I was. I'm going to draw the curtains so we can have some privacy, as I believe there is someone across the street with an unreasonable fascination in my windows, and then you and I can have a drink like proper gentlemen. And please inform Ms. Castille she will not be required to throw that knife in her hand."

~

few minutes later the curtains were drawn, a lamp was lit, and we all had drinks in our hands like civilized people.

"I'm glad you got my message," Heintz said.

"Leewan Sean Enterprises was a message?" I asked.

"Of course it was."

I've had more names than I can count, but a few of them stick out in my memory for the way they were used. Hsu, for instance, used to call me Li-Yuan, a name also associated with one of the immortals of Chinese myth. Li-Yuan was also Li-Yuan Iron-Crutch, and sometimes Li-Yuan Xian. This is the name most of the goblins—and elves, if we're going to call them that—have known me by, much in the same way Brenda and most of the vampires call me Apollo.

Most goblins of Asian descent stick with Li-Yuan Xian, but as one travels toward Europe the name gets Anglicized and bastardized until one is left with something that sounds more Irish than anything: Leewan Sean.

For a goblin or an elf, this is a name that represents a mythological immortal man. Outside that species it means almost nothing. And the last person I heard use the name was Juergen Heintz.

"How were you expecting me to get that message?"

"I expected that the man you have burrowing through my office's financial systems would tell you eventually. Incidentally, he's quite impressive."

"I'll tell him you said so."

"He is going to get detected soon, though. I've done about all I can to prevent that without it looking obvious that I'm doing so."

"Why would you ... no, never mind that. Tell me why you couldn't just call instead if you had something to tell me? Because you understand how this appears?"

Heintz didn't say anything at first. He took a sip of his drink—it was brandy, and it was above average—and pulled at his collar until his tie was loose. "Your requests put me in a quandary at times, sir. Some years ago you asked that I look into this group and further to do what was necessary to obtain details on where they were investing their funds. The only way to do that was to involve you in them financially. I did so. You asked that I report back what I had learned, and I did so there as well, up until I could no longer."

"Who stopped you?" Mirella asked.

She was sitting on the couch between us, with Heintz in his desk chair. He was looking less a banker than a harried businessman at the end of a long day. She still looked every inch an assassin.

"*He* did, in a way, when he told me who he really was." To me, he said, "The VC fund continued to invest in small medical projects over the past several years. None were as large-scale as the failed experiment about which I now believe you are *intimately* familiar, but they centered upon life-extending procedures and so on. I did, I think, share some of this with you. Nothing sounded particularly promising, and no large sums were committed."

"I remember," I said. "It sounded like a lot of mysticism and snake oil."

"So it was. But about two years ago the founders effectively rewrote their own prospectus. A promising lead had come up in the field of teleportation, of all things. It sounded preposterous, but there was documentation attached from various physicists and medical experts supporting the claim. I read these and found the arguments specious to a degree that bordered on fraud. Had you not instructed me to remain involved specifically in this venture I'd have pulled your money. And then by acclaim the decision to invest in this preposterousness was approved, and this had me curious enough to try and find out more."

"Why didn't you tell me about this?"

"I told you it was a potential military application before I knew we were discussing teleportation. Once I heard this I took it as such lunacy there was no way I was going to stop there. One does not tell one's largest client his money is going toward a tele-portation device without first obtaining much more information. Also, your demands were specific: report back on medical proce-dures. This was no medical procedure. I took that to mean I could satisfy my curiosity first and then alert you if anything came out of what I had learned. I know now that this was an error on my part, but such is life.

"Digging deeper meant investing more, which I was also free to do per your instructions. And when it came time to promise additional funds on the condition that I—speaking for you—be allowed to see the data supporting the claim, I learned the truth. The proof of principle was in the form of a human person, and this was the same person who had been at the center of their *last* major investment. It was unsurprising that this information had been held behind layers of confidentiality, because what was eventually going to be required was this person be taken into captivity and studied like a lab animal, and this is the sort of thing most would be morally opposed to.

"This immortal man was the key to both the teleportation concept and the eternal life project that was to be resuming."

He took another long drink and appeared to be in need of a smoke.

"I did not at that time associate *him* with you. It wasn't until after you told me who you were that I began to piece it all together. But by then you had left my office and we could not discuss this over the phone; I fear they have been listening. I needed to find a way to get you to come to *me*, preferably not in my office since I have had eyes upon me from the day I increased the investment. When I detected the cyber attack and saw that it had begun with someone clearly not you, signing in with your password, I did what I could. I opened the Leewan Sean Enterprises account. And I waited."

"And here we are."

"Here we are." He held up his glass as a long-distance toast, which I matched.

"That's quite a story," I said.

"It is the truth, sir. I have only ever acted in your best interests as I saw them."

"Tell me, Mr. Heintz," Mirella said. "Who are they?"

"Who are who?"

"The people behind the money."

"That is a foolish question."

"Why?"

"It presumes a singularity of vision that does not exist. *They* are not some group of people one can sit down at a table with. They are an unthinking market force, and the decisions they make are incremental ones arrived at by multiple parties along a chain of reasoning. No one or two or ten people met and decided they were going to imprison this man. That came about from a series of if-then statements. If it helps, think of these as the actions of a powerful but impersonal god."

"So I can't find them and convince them to leave me alone?" I asked.

"There is no *them*, that is what I'm telling you. The people who ultimately own the money backing this endeavor know very little about it, and the people beneath them know only money—is it stable or risky, what is the expected rate of return, and so on. Money knows no morality. The people making the immoral decisions are so far removed from the ones investing in those decisions as to make this an impossible thing to stop. The only way it will ever end is with their success or your death."

"Well then," I said, "I guess I had better die."

~

Heintz actually did bring home business from the office, it was just that he didn't leave any of it in the place. He had in his bag—in addition to blank forms that would become complex business contracts by the time he was done with them—the exact GPS coordinates of the compound I was looking for, along with a blueprint of the layout. He really had been expecting me.

We spent the rest of the evening hashing out the best way to distribute my funds following my demise, with a large portion of it going to the heir I had only recently discovered. This was provided said heir made it to the age of twenty-one, something I was soon to be directly involved in assuring.

Heintz was not so helpful when I asked if there was a way to simply destroy my wealth entirely. The list of reasons he gave for why that was impossible was long and tedious and used words I didn't completely understand, but he did promise to invest in a lot of risky things he expected to not pan out. In fairness, I think what I was asking him to do might have actually been illegal. Not in the *get me a fake passport* sort of way so much as the *he goes to jail for a long time and gets blamed for a government's collapse* sort of way. I didn't press the issue.

Besides, it didn't matter so much anymore if the money was gone as long as I never went near it again after I was dead.

~

"This is not going to be easy," I said to Mirella.

We were back on the plane again and I was looking at the blueprints. The compound took up a few acres on the Isle of Mull. It was impossible to tell much of anything from the layout other than that I would not be able to just walk in if I expected to walk back out again.

I asked Heintz about the possibility of him arranging a tour for me as a direct investor in the project, but he was quite adamant that this would not work. He had little doubt that the necessary people knew I was Francis Justinian, and besides it was so unusual for an investor to make a personal appearance that it would draw the wrong kind of attention.

"You'll figure something out," she said. She was sharpening a knife at the desk, and to be honest, it was incredibly sexy. I don't even know how it's possible to sharpen a knife sexily, but she was doing it. "You always do."

"How do you know that?" I asked. "You haven't been around me for that long."

"Long enough. And you've been alive for long enough for it to be true."

"Maybe." I put down the blueprints. "I'm wondering if I should just tell Heintz to kill me now so I can run off somewhere. This looks like a suicide run."

"Then do it. Run off."

"I can't."

"I know. It isn't who you are."

"It's sometimes who I am."

Mirella got up and walked to the edge of the couch. Leaning forward, she kissed me hard on the mouth, her hand on the back of my head to hold me still. It was sweet, passionate, fierce, and a lot briefer than I would have liked. She let go after a second or two and stood up again.

"What was that for?"

"You needed one."

"Could be I need more than just a kiss."

"You could, but that's all you're getting." She sat back down and resumed the knife sharpening as if nothing had happened. "So are we racing to Scotland now?"

We had not actually told the pilot where to take us yet, but that was where I intended to go.

"It's where the place is, so if I'm not running I guess that's where we're going."

"Do you want me to cut open the fence with my sword and take on a hundred armed men all alone?"

"No, I'll be there."

"Almost all alone. And what happens if we make it past that perimeter?"

"I'll think of something."

She sighed. "We can't just ride in there, shoot up the place, grab the girl and the child, and ride off again. Even if we survive, they'll find us."

"Do *you* have any ideas?"

"I have exactly as few ideas as you do, but I'm not going to dive into that headfirst, and you have no reason to. What was the name Hsu called you? Li-Yuan? And that was a god, right?"

"Kind of."

"Maybe you need to be more godlike."

"Vengeful?"

"Not vengeful. Gods don't have to rush anywhere because gods don't get any older. Gods are patient. Clara and your son aren't going to be dissected and destroyed this very minute. You know where they are, and you know a lot about who is running the place and even more about who's funding the place. Actually, from what I've heard, *you* are funding the place. So take your time. And when you're ready, burn it all to the ground like a proper god."

"Mirella, I think I may love you."

She flashed that brilliant smile again, and I wanted to get up and kiss her back, and thought maybe if I did it would make it okay not to go find Clara and Paul.

"I know," she said. "I hear that a lot."

PART III

THE EDGE OF THE WORLD

CHAPTER 21

We argued a lot about magic. Hsu claimed to have spent a part of his life in a kingdom governed by magic itself, whereas I had lived thousands upon thousands of years in this non-magical world and claimed there was no such thing. It was an assertion he couldn't abide.

"But surely there have been things you have seen that you cannot explain otherwise?" he said one night. This was a little bit after we'd seen what would now be called a shooting star. Hsu had muttered an oath to protect himself from the wrath of whatever god sent the streaking object across the sky, while I went on about how I once discovered that such things aren't much more than falling rocks.

"I have seen things I cannot explain, of course," I said. "And there have been many times I've attributed these things to magic of some sort. But without fail I've discovered a prosaic explanation eventually. It may take many lifetimes to settle the question, but the answers eventually manifest. The problem is that most men do not have the opportunity to wait a century or two for an explanation."

He shook his head.

"I do not have your perspective. But I see a world full of magic and I cannot understand how it is possible that you do not, unless you are being willfully blind to it."

"Perspective is important. Do you know that sometimes the sun disappears in the middle of the day? I have seen it happen. The first time I thought—as did all of us—the world was ending. But it reappeared and life continued, and the next time it happened I was less impressed. I have seen Greek fire burn ships at sea and been nearly convinced I was witnessing true magic, until the day I was shown how to make it myself. The recipe required no gods or incantations."

"You have no faith, then," he said.

At this time magic and religious miracles were essentially the same thing. There were people who called themselves witches, certainly, but these witches attributed their magic to a deity. Catholic priests also routinely used magic, claiming it was good magic coming from their God, even if it was a curse. To not believe in magic, for Hsu and probably anybody else at the time, was to not believe in gods. If nothing else, mine was an ironic stance for an occasional god.

"I have faith in many things," I said. "For instance, I have much greater faith in the ingenuity of mankind than I do in the gods mankind swears to. I have faith that if I see something impossible, an explanation will be found, one day, by someone."

"I have been to the faery kingdom and back, and I offer you an explanation now—magic."

"Magic is only the answer until a better one comes along."

~

It's not all that hard to rent a castle in Scotland if you know whom to ask.

Heintz was able to set up a second set of finances for me under a newly minted fake name, and funded it with monies from one of the very, very many do-nothing businesses I owned. It was something he did so quickly and efficiently I really had to wonder if anything he was doing for my sake was legal. And maybe if this was what he meant when it came to dealing with the people behind all of this—breaking laws in small ways was something they all did, and maybe nobody noticed when those little law-breaking moments added up to something big.

While I was busy establishing my new identity, we hired someone to play the role of Francis Justinian for long enough to take my jet from the UK to a hangar in Sri Lanka, and then to disappear. Meanwhile, various appointments were made for Mr. Justinian in different parts of the world that were either canceled at the last second or attended by someone who was tacitly not me. I was modestly certain that Smith and company were aware that I was deceiving them as to my current whereabouts, but also that they did not *know* my current whereabouts.

Those whereabouts were mostly in and about the lands surrounding the aforementioned Scottish castle.

I didn't need to rent a whole castle, but it was the nicest place in the area, and the most private by far. Everything else in the vicinity was full of people and livestock. Plus, coordinating assaults and sieges and military exercises in a castle was a pleasantly familiar thing for me.

The castle came with forty acres of unfarmable land. It was up on a rocky hill that overlooked the ocean to the west, with a simply spectacular view of the Isle of Mull. On some nights we could see the base with binoculars from the top of the castle. I liked the view.

We'd gotten a lot of much more up-close looks of the compound than just that. Mirella went on most of the sorties without me, just because I was slightly more recognizable, but I talked her into giving me two or three direct looks. I knew the place inside and out from photographs, but there was nothing like standing on the other side of the fence, even if it was from half a mile away, at night.

We had one room in the castle devoted to tactical maps and site photos that we'd been taking of different parts of the base for the past four months. One may well ask how we managed to get photos from *inside* the base, and the answer is, it turns out when I think like a god for a while I remember that more than a couple of people on this planet consider me one, and that one of those people has an army at her disposal.

Her name is Ariadne, and she's publicly employed as a technical advisor to the Greek government. Privately, she's the head of a secret religious sect that thinks I'm the god Dionysos. And while I'm not in possession of any real godlike powers, having a secret army of paramilitary satyrs at my disposal is pretty close. And having a castle to hide all of them in is, if not godlike, at least pretty cool.

All right, I'm exaggerating. It was only ten satyrs and not an army, but a satyr is worth ten or twenty men in a battle, so it was the equivalent of an army of a hundred and fifty. Which was great, because they only ate as much food as ten.

Speaking of food, Mirella and I decided early on that the best way to get at this base was through its stomach. It had a small army inside—a real one, not ten satyrs and a lot of hyperbole—and that army needed to eat. But the base was way out in the middle of nowhere, certainly too far for the island to support it without some help from the mainland. So food was shipped in.

The base had been there long enough for the food arrangements to have already been made, so I had to find the current supplier and buy them. This was less of a hassle than you might imagine, because I had no concern whatsoever with offering a competitive price or negotiating a reasonable deal. I just made the owners incredibly rich by suggesting an outrageous sum, and then I replaced the people doing the deliveries with my satyrs.

One of the things I learned in my time as a very rich man is that nobody really notices the help. Whether they're security guards, truck drivers, maintenance men, or the folks flying your private plane, if you don't need something from one of these people you're going to take them for granted. This is true even if you're in a high security location. The hard part is always making it past the security checkpoints, but once on the other side all anyone needs is a badge that says they belong and they're free to go all sorts of places. It helped that in this instance we were sneaking onto a base that was not located in the middle of a hostile region, and being run by a private conglomerate, so not only was there little suspicion of the locals, there was a lack of full-on military attitude.

This was not a formal government operation. Mr. Smith may have been CIA at one time, and it was very likely he was working with government monies, but this thing he had built on the Isle of Mull was an independent entity and the people manning the fences were private mercenaries. They made a show of looking military-official the closer they were to the gates, but inside the compound it was obvious this crew fell short of the kind of discipline expected from coordinated formal military training. Not to say some of them didn't have military backgrounds. Probably all of them did. But those backgrounds were all clearly different.

Unfortunately, there were still a lot of them and they had large guns, and nobody doubted that they all knew how to use those guns. Even if they were undisciplined enough to mow each other down in a firefight, they would also hit us, and that was no good.

Any plan had to begin with finding a way to neutralize the guards. When I was in this situation a few years back I had only one weapon at my disposal—an indiscriminate killing machine in the form of a very old and out-of-her-mind-hungry vampire. This worked, if you can call the deaths of fifty people a success. Since I couldn't use a vampire—I was still in touch with Eloise, but the sun lamps Smith bragged about were legit and they were attached to redundant power systems—I had to rely on something a little bit less scorched-earth. To that end I took advantage of the fact that we were supplying the food, and the single-source water supply being pumped into the base. I was told the food and water were tested for contaminants, but I was pretty sure what we were slipping into both wasn't going to be detected, only because nobody on the planet had ever tested for something like this. Because it wasn't technically from this planet.

~

I don't have a lot of history with the UK. I spent some time in England, and I've been to both Scotland and Ireland before, but not until after the Reformation. The first time I heard of the islands was back when they were Roman outposts and represented the westernmost reach of the Empire. Then the western half of the Empire fell apart and I lost track of what happened until after the entire region went through the chaos of kings and castles that resulted in the place I was renting being built.

I was standing outside that place and about a half mile down the hill, facing the water and thinking about what was going to be happening in another day.

Our plan was launching in sixteen hours, and it was about as complete as we could make it. I was expecting to be dead in seventeen or eighteen hours, because although complete, the plan was also legitimately insane. The smart thing to do was to call the whole thing off and run away. But I didn't feel like being smart and I couldn't think of anything better to do. And Mirella wasn't going to let me walk away.

So instead, I walked outside the castle and down the hill and cycled through the plan in my head for the thousandth time, and thought about how pretty the hills of Scotland were at night. Old maps showed this lovely place as a little blob on the edge of the Empire's longest arm. Just on the other side of where I was standing the legend HIC SVNT LEONES would have been written on those maps. It meant, *Here are lions,* which was cartographer shorthand for "We don't know what there is after this."

I was standing at the edge of the world.

I pulled the astrolabe from my pocket. I had done this a hundred times before, at first to fiddle, later just because it was something to have in my hands.

Walk toward the star that isn't there and step off the edge of the world.

That was what Hsu had told me. But the directions made no sense. I knew a dozen different uses for an astrolabe and none of them involved locating stars that weren't there. It didn't work that way.

Most of the features of an astrolabe involve identifying an object in the sky first and then using that to learn other things. It took advantage of the fact that the sun and stars rose and set, and the angles between the surface of the Earth and the celestial objects changed with the seasons. If you could identify a star, knew what the day was, and knew where that day was on the zodiac, you could figure out a lot of things.

I couldn't learn anything by pointing it at a star that wasn't there. Basically, that was the definition of the night sky: a black space occasionally broken up by a star here and there. Which part of that sky should I use to calibrate the rest of the astrolabe? The answer was not to pick a space and try it, as I had done that many times already, to no effect. I also tried it during the daytime when the sun was the only visible star.

There were a couple of things that kept me from giving up entirely. One was the way it felt. It was rough to the touch, as I'd first observed when I held it, but the weird thing was that it looked smooth. The wheels glided smoothly, too, and there was no visible indication that the surface was uneven or grooved. Yet that's how it felt. It was a little like looking at a three-dimensional picture while wearing 3-D glasses, then reaching out and finding the surface of the uneven object you were looking at was, in fact, a smooth surface.

Physically there *was* something different about it. I just couldn't understand what it was.

There was a full moon so visibility was pretty good, and a low ground fog actually improved the lighting a little since the fog glowed in the moonlight. I would have probably been in trouble if a predator was hiding under the fog, but there were hardly any predators left in the world. I held the astrolabe up again and rather than choosing a star that wasn't there I picked a familiar one, calibrated the astrolabe by pointing the rule at it and turning the plates to line up with my current latitude and zodiacal period. Then I lined all of those up with the dot on the top-most ring of the astrolabe—it was called a *rate*—that corresponded to the star I started with.

Having done all of that, I concluded that it was nearly midnight. Which was also what my watch said. Neither device summoned a faery.

"Walk toward the star that isn't there," I said aloud. My voice resonated with the countryside and also failed to summon a faery.

Hsu didn't actually say to point the astrolabe at this star-that-wasn't-there, he just said to walk toward it. And while keeping in mind that Hsu had never actually tried to use the astrolabe to accomplish this, it was a notable distinction.

I started spinning the plates around. Each plate corresponded to a latitude and a zodiac sign, and up to this point I had only been using it properly, as in, I stopped when I found the correct latitude and the appropriate zodiac symbol.

But there was something fundamentally impossible about these plates, which was another reason I hadn't given up on the astrolabe yet.

One of the first things I noticed on close examination was that it had too many latitude hash marks. My efforts a moment earlier in identifying the time could have instead been used to determine what my latitude was by turning the plate that matched up with the current time and seeing what that time with those star positions told me about my current latitude. But while it was true that latitudes could be broken up into as many small numbers as one cared to— most people stopped at 360—it was usually an even number, and there were an odd number of hashes on this wheel.

Much more obviously, there were thirteen zodiac symbols, with the thirteenth not represented by any symbol at all.

This was fundamentally impossible because the astrolabe should not have worked. Thirteen zodiac signs meant the plate was inaccurate for all of the other twelve signs, because it was supposed to be a circle divided equally into twelve spaces, not thirteen. The latitude plate's uneven hash marks would have also resulted in an inaccurate reading, but it would have only made it slightly less accurate—a circle divided by one hundred twenty is only marginally different than one divided by one hundred twenty-one.

But it was clear that the quarterly marks—for degrees 90, 180, 270 and 360—were correct. The extra mark was somewhere between 90 and 180, and after a little closer examination I had decided on the one that constituted the extra mark, as it was slightly longer than the others.

So I had a degree that shouldn't have been there and a zodiac sign that didn't exist on an astrolabe that shouldn't have worked but did.

I just didn't know what to do with this information.

Something about this particular evening, out in the rocky field among ground fog and the ghosts of long-dead Scots, made me take another look at the outer plate.

The last plate on most astrolabes was where the stars were located. In more modern renditions of the device, the plate contained a decent star chart and was transparent so one could see the other plate readings beneath it. Transparency wasn't really possible with an outer plate made out of metal, so the older astrolabes had ornate plates that looked decorative—sweeping curves of metal extending out from the center wheel in elegant S-shapes—but had a functional purpose.

Every dot corresponded to a prominent star. Some had dozens, but for basic functions there only needed to be ten or twenty. This one had fifteen.

A consequence of having so few stars was that it wasn't really possible to tell which star was being represented because there were no other stars next to it on the plate to fill out a constellation. A lot of astrolabes had the names of the stars written on them, but this did not. So the only way to determine which dots were for which stars was to reverse-calibrate it. That is, if you knew the common stars and you knew what the current time was, you could point the astrolabe at the sky and determine which of those stars gave you the correct time reading.

I hadn't done any of that calibrating because Abraham did, and he put it in the note to his son when he sent the astrolabe home. But he only identified fourteen of the stars.

I hadn't given it any thought before, because the obvious explanation was that it was calibrated for a star that hadn't been identified yet, and there were thousands to choose from. But maybe I had that wrong. Maybe this was *the star that isn't there.*

I calibrated the astrolabe, lining up the rule with the midpoint of the thirteenth sign and the 121st hash mark, and turning the rate to line up the fifteenth star. Since the rate wasn't pointing toward any particular actual star this left me with the problem of not knowing which direction I was supposed to be aiming the thing, so I just held it out in front of me and started walking.

And of course, nothing happened. The Scottish hillside looked no different than it had before. I was standing in the same field in the same fog.

But for the first time, the astrolabe felt smooth in my hands.

Something *had* changed after all, but it was hardly an Earth-shattering change. It was just that the odd grooved sensation in the gold had gone away, which was a long way from Hsu's promise of magic.

Down at the base of the hill I saw movement in the fog. Someone was coming toward me.

"Hello?" I shouted.

My voice sounded weirdly loud, like I was hearing it ricochet back through an amplifier. In response to my voice, the man—it looked like a man—moved more quickly and directly toward me, fast enough to suggest that he might be a threat.

"*BRESSSSSSS!*" the man shouted, followed by a series of words in a language I had never heard before.

It wasn't until I saw the shiny blade in his hand that I realized I was looking at no man.

I was looking at a faery.

"I'm not here to hurt you!" I shouted, and my voice echoed some more.

The faery seemed shorter than the last one I'd seen, but that was an illusion because the truth was I was taller. I could see my own footprints behind me and they looked like the prints of a child. I couldn't compare them to more recent prints because I was no longer leaving any.

The faery shouted *Bres* again—it was a name, and I knew the name but I couldn't recall where I'd heard it before—and continued to charge, looking very much like he wanted to kill me. I wasn't armed, and even if I had been I didn't think gunning down the first faery I met was a great way to make friends. Instead I put up my hands, which was the closest thing to a universal gesture of *no harm* I could think of, and hoped this allayed his concerns, whatever those might be.

There was a word I was supposed to speak, but I couldn't remember it, and he was almost on top of me. And then there was a second faery, only this one was a great deal closer. He put his hand on my shoulder and spun me around and shouted. "*BRESSSSS!*" and I still didn't know what this meant. But that was okay, since I was about to die. He raised his curved blade and meant to bring it down on my head, and just then the word came out of me all by itself: "*BYRGDDUN!*"

I raised my hands in self-defense, and in doing so dropped the astrolabe ...

... and then I was all alone on the hillside again. I fell backward and landed unkindly on the rocks, but my head had not been cleft in two so it was definitely not the worst outcome possible.

"Hello?" I called out, my heart pounding almost out of my chest.

There were no faeries materializing anywhere that I could see.

I got to my feet slowly and found the astrolabe. It was intact, fortunately. The settings had been altered on impact, so it no longer pointed to the star that wasn't there. I was intensely curious as to whether I would still be able to see and touch it if it hadn't been jostled, because I was pretty sure I had just traveled to Hsu's faery land and left only because I'd dropped his trinket. The astrolabe might have stayed behind if the settings hadn't been altered.

I decided I didn't want to know all that badly, though. For whatever reason, I was clearly not welcome there.

At least they didn't follow.

"Mirella's never going to believe me," I said aloud. It was good to hear my voice sound non-echoey.

I started heading back up the hill to the castle. On the way, I spotted one of the fourteen known stars from the astrolabe and decided to calibrate it to my watch again.

When I'd done this earlier the watch and the astrolabe were only a few minutes off, due more to user error than anything else. Accuracy relies on my being able to hold the astrolabe as straight up and down as possible. For truly accurate measurements, one is supposed to dangle it from a string tied to the top loop, something I didn't much bother with because I do, after all, own a watch for timekeeping. Also, even if I held it perfectly correct, I was still eyeballing my angle to the star.

It is not a terribly scientifically accurate tool is my point. However, I did expect it to be—for want of a better term—equally inaccurate from reading to reading. But while I'd gotten within a few minutes of my watch's time earlier, now there was a roughly forty-minute difference.

Either the watch was broken, or the astrolabe suddenly didn't work properly. Or—and this was my least favorite possibility despite being the most likely one—time passed at a different rate in faery land.

It was the most likely explanation because it also explained how Hsu could have been as old as he claimed while looking as young as he actually was.

~

"I don't believe it," Mirella said.

"I didn't think you would."

"No, I believe *you*. I can't believe you aren't happier about this."

"Because I solved an old mystery? It wouldn't be the first time."

"You have an object that allows you to actually *exit* this world in the same way your redhead does, and now we have a way to get in and out of there alive, and you look disappointed to have been proven wrong by a dead man."

"Maybe you didn't hear the part where they tried to kill me as soon as I showed up there."

"I could go with you. I'll fight the faeries—I'm sorry do I have to call them that?"

"That's what Hsu called them. You can call them something else if you want."

"No, it's all right. I can fight the faeries while you go and rescue Clara and Paul."

"Well, no, you can't."

"You don't think I can handle them?"

"I actually don't. I've seen one fight and you haven't, so you'll have to take my word for it. They're big and fast and scary. Besides, as soon as I let go of the astrolabe I dropped out of ... wherever the hell I was."

"If I have to call them faeries, you have to call it faery land."

What I was actually thinking about was what the physicist said when I asked him about branes. He would have called the place I went the *bulk*, I think. But that sounded even worse than faery land.

"I only stayed there as long as I had the astrolabe in my hand. I could maybe hold your hand but you can't fight a faery one-handed."

"You don't know that."

"I know that you think you can fight anything one-handed, and I know that the day you're wrong about that you'll end up dead. These things aren't going to congratulate you for giving them a good fight, they're just going to kill you."

"Fine," she said with a harrumph. "But that plan can't be any worse than the one we're actually trying."

"There I agree with you."

We looked at pieces of that plan together. It was scattered around the room, taped to walls and lying on tabletops. We were in one of the three dining spaces the castle had so there were plenty of tables from which to choose.

The plan hinged upon the efficacy of the hallucinogen we had introduced to the compound's food and water supply. If we'd worked out the dosage correctly and if enough of the people inside—or at least enough of the ones with guns—got dosed, this would be easy.

We weren't expecting easy, though, which was why we were going in with ten satyrs and lots of heavy guns. In the event we had to fight our way out we would at least be facing people—we'd only seen humans in the compound, which was good news —whose judgment was impaired by the drug.

"This is a very stupid plan," Mirella said.

One or both of us had said this daily since we began putting it together. Hopefully none of the satyrs heard us say it, because they were surprisingly gung-ho about the whole thing. Part of that might have been their youth, but most of it seemed to be because they were doing this for me, and I was kind of important to their religious beliefs. Amazingly, nobody questioned why an apparent god would need a force with machine guns to stand up for him.

"Do you want to back out?" I asked.

She looked at me with a little half smile on her face. She had been doing a lot of smiling these past few months. There had been no repeat of the kiss and I hadn't pressed the issue, but every now and then something like affection passed between us that I was eager to explore at my leisure, preferably when not planning a siege. I think at this point if she told me to abandon the plan and run away with her, I would. I think she knew it, too.

"I'm not going to go anywhere," she said. "You know that."

"I know. And we should probably get some sleep."

"Yes. But I need you to promise me something first."

"What?"

"You're a foolish man with delusions of heroism."

"Um, thank you?"

"I need you to promise you won't try and save me."

"I don't think I understand," I said.

"You understand perfectly. It's my job to protect you and I'm going to do that. You'll live through tomorrow. I *hope* to. But you don't get to risk your life for mine. That's not all right. Do you understand?"

"I'm sure it will never come to that."

"Tell me you understand."

"I understand." I had about a thousand things to say other than that, but I didn't think she was going to let me say any of it.

"Good. Now let's get some sleep."

CHAPTER 22

There was little in the way of protective ground coverage around the compound, which sat in the middle of a flat open field on an island full of such fields, so we had no way to get a scout ahead while it was still daylight to see how things looked on the inside. This made the last half mile of the trip the most terrifying portion, because by the time we were that close to the front gates we could be seen, and so by then there was no turning around. Yet we wouldn't be able to see what the inside looked like until we got closer.

The delivery had to be during the day because all deliveries were during the day. Negotiating an evening delivery would have required coming up with an explanation for one that made sense. Since the supplies in the trucks were loaded off a boat and we came on the same boat, that explanation would have had to make an otherwise unnecessary nighttime boat trip logical. And it wouldn't have been worth it because the compound was extraordinarily well lit, so we'd have gained almost nothing by traveling there at night.

Despite that, driving there in the sunlight was a little terrifying. I prefer darkness for this sort of thing.

"Can you see anything?" I asked for about the tenth time.

I was sitting in a space behind the driver in the lead truck. We were carrying enough food for a hundred and fifty people for four days, and that took up three box trucks when you added in the room required for ten satyrs. An eighteen- wheeler could probably have done the trick if we skimped a little on the food and the satyrs, but there were no eighteen-wheeler trucks for rent on the Isle of Mull.

The driver was a satyr named Lorgus. He was the eldest among them and the one most likely to be treated as a captain if this were a proper army. He also didn't get all weak-kneed when around me, which was something I look for in people who think I'm a god.

"I still see nothing, Philopaigmos," he said. *Philopaigmos* was my name to them. Long story.

"I can try with the lens," Mirella suggested.

She was crammed next to me. Neither of us were supposed to be there, for although we were dressed in the same coveralls as everyone else, we'd never been seen before inside, and as an ordinary-sized man and woman among a group of heavy-set six-foot-five bearded men, we were going to stand out. The coveralls would buy us an explanation that probably sufficed once inside, but until then there was no need to be seen.

"You can try," Lorgus said. "But I am telling you, we are not close enough."

We were speaking English for Mirella's benefit. Lorgus and a couple of the others were fluent, but for the most part the satyrs responded to Greek. The one in the passenger seat, for instance, had no idea what we were saying. So he looked a little alarmed when Mirella leaned forward and steadied her arm on his shoulder for long enough to hold the telescopic sight up.

"No, he's right. I'd say everything looks normal, but we're not close enough to see any abnormality. The gates are closed, as always."

She'd smuggled herself inside on two runs previously, never leaving the truck, to get an idea of what our formal incursion would be like. I had to think she didn't learn much while stuck riding like this. All I'd learned so far was that they needed better roads or the trucks needed better shock absorbers.

"It doesn't matter," Lorgus said. "We've been seen by now. If the situation on the ground is not to your liking we can just complete the delivery and leave. So long as nobody takes note of the Kalashnikovs we should be free to exit."

We arrived at the gate a few minutes later. Lorgus brought the truck to a stop and looked up at the camera pointing down from the top corner of the fence so that whoever was on the other side of the camera could get a good look at him.

The place was surrounded by a twelve-foot-tall chain-link fence with the usual daunting tangle of barbed wire above it. Inside the chain link was a second opaque white fence ten feet tall that was made of some sort of synthetic poly-blend that was usually used when people wanted something to look like wood but not rot like wood. The only purpose of the second fence was to keep people from seeing inside, and it worked just fine. It wasn't as impressive as a cement wall might have been, but the compound still had a temporary quality that was perhaps intentional.

Somebody was supposed to show up and open the gates, which slid aside electronically after a button was depressed. That button was in a circuit box attached to the white fence. The circuit box wasn't locked, but since it was on the compound side of the fence it didn't much matter.

After several minutes it became clear that nobody was coming to the fence to open it.

Lorgus waved more emphatically to the camera lens, which didn't do any good.

"Now we know," he said without turning. "At least one thing is different."

He got out of the truck and walked up to the fence.

"Hello?" he shouted, looking through the chain-link and acting more or less like any confused deliveryman would when confronted with an unexpected absence of people where there should be people. Nobody came running from the other side.

After waiting for another two minutes, Lorgus exhibited one of the qualities that make satyrs so useful. He jumped over the fence.

A few seconds later he had reached the circuit box and pushed the button. The gates slid open. He stepped back outside and waited to see if the opened gate caused anybody to come running. It didn't. He climbed back into the truck.

"We drive to the appointed location as if we had been let inside as normal," he said in Greek for the benefit of the second satyr, whose responsibility it was to radio the other trucks. *"Guns ready, but hidden."*

They all had the aforementioned Kalashnikovs—they were semiautomatic rifles whose brand I couldn't actually tell you, but we called them Kalashnikovs—on the inside of the jumpsuits they were wearing. The suits were extremely baggy, needless to say.

We drove slowly into the compound. Mirella and I peered through the side windows as well as we could, but it was too hard to identify anything going on out there, so we had to rely on Lorgus.

"Ordinarily," he said under his breath, "there would be people walking about. I have seen no persons. This is alarming. I am afraid to ask, but do you suppose we got the dosage wrong and poisoned them all?"

"I don't think it's possible to die from one large dose," I said. "Extended long-term use can drive you insane, but that's the worst of it."

"Hold on, there is someone."

He stopped the truck.

The man was leaning against the external wall of one of the barracks. He was dressed in a black sweater and olive green army fatigue pants, which was typical for the security force. Also typical, he had an M16 on a strap around his shoulders.

"Hello, friend," Lorgus called out. "How are you?" The man smiled, but didn't answer.

Lorgus was temporarily at a loss. "It's a lovely day, don't you think?"

"Yeah."

"Yes it is. We'll just be on our way, then."

"Right, hey. Bunnies, man," he said. "Bunnies. Right?"

"Right you are," Lorgus said happily. "Bunnies, indeed." To us he said, "I believe your plan is working."

"Either that or bunnies are the best thing ever," I said.

~

We stopped the trucks at the loading dock for the cafeteria.

Contractually, all the food that didn't come out of a vending machine was food we provided, and all of that food went into and came out of the cafeteria. Likewise, all the water used by the facility for drinking and bathing came from a large water tank that was replenished four times a month by a truck we also owned. So the people there had been drinking and eating high doses of hallucinogens for three or four days. We based this on expected consumption rates, numbers we'd spent two months collating. It was all very scientific, meaning I had nothing to do with the specific calculations.

According to those numbers, the peak impact of the drug would be roughly the same time we turned up with our delivery. It was on a curve, so there were likely a number of people there who were nearly lucid and a number who were far worse than the bunny fan we'd come across. If we were extremely lucky, that would be good enough.

Lorgus hopped out and opened the loading dock door, and then the satyrs went about unloading the cargo as they were supposed to. While they were doing this, Mirella and I climbed out and looked around.

The base was made up of a series of prefabricated buildings arranged in a grid. We were pretty clear about which of the buildings were living quarters, which were administrative, and where people went to eat. That left one building in the center of the place unaccounted for. It was the only building that was actively guarded every day, and it was where we assumed Clara and Paul were being held.

At the loading dock, Mirella and I weren't standing all that far away from the target location. It was just a quick straight-ahead between two administrative buildings and a dogleg right and we would be there. In my pocket was a cloned keycard to get us past the front entrance after the guards had been dispatched, and that card had taken me months and cost hundreds of thousands of dollars to obtain.

We had blueprints of the interior of the building that would hopefully narrow down our search once we were inside. And in the event of resistance we had a variety of coordinated responses to choose from, including one that had satyrs scaling the walls and providing suppressing fire from the rooftops.

In other words, we had a thorough plan, and it was going perfectly so far. All I had to do was start running for that building.

I couldn't bring myself to move. Something was wrong.

"It's way too quiet," I said to Mirella.

"You know where you are going?" Lorgus asked us.

"Yes," Mirella said, "it's not far."

I looked around. It was the kind of quiet I had learned to

distrust, largely because quiet like this was what usually preceded natural disasters like earthquakes and volcanic eruptions.

"I didn't realize how much of a canyon this place was," I said.

"How do you mean?" Mirella asked.

"On the Silk Road, there were stretches through the mountains that were basically designed for ambushes—low road, steep sides, good cover on the top of the pass. A few archers could take out a whole caravan if they planned it right."

"That may be true, but until we see evidence of this we should keep moving."

She was right. On the Road, the problem with sections like this was that they were the only way to get through certain areas. Once you started down that path you had no choice but to keep driving forward even if you thought you were in the middle of a trap.

"Let's go, then," I said. To Lorgus, I said, "We'll call for backup if it comes to it."

We didn't get more than twenty feet from the loading dock, though, before the trap was sprung. Later I decided the sense of unease I felt was attributable in part to the fact that all the windows on all the buildings around us were open, but it's likely I didn't notice this detail until there was a gun barrel extended out of every second one.

"That's far enough," said a familiar voice. It was Smith, talking through a loudspeaker.

Mirella went for the sword strapped to her back.

"Don't," I said. "It's a shooting gallery." I looked around and noted that more than one of the satyrs were reaching for their guns.

"Stand down, everyone!" I ordered.

"There won't be another opportunity," Mirella said. The look in her eyes was full of murder. "We can make the corner."

"I don't think we can."

Smith walked around that corner with two armed men next to him and a microphone in his hand.

"Good advice," he said, regarding the stand-down order. "Let's not turn this into a bloodbath. It's such a nice day."

He came to a stop in front of me. I was close enough to kill him if I didn't mind dying, too. I thought about it.

"So where'd I screw up?" I asked.

He turned to the man on his left.

"Tie them both up."

To me he said, "I think we can both agree the screwup was planning this thing in the first place, but I'll give you that. You probably couldn't keep away, huh?"

"Not really, no," I said as his man zip-tied my wrists behind my back.

"It was the drug," Smith said. "Clever idea, and I bet you thought our filters wouldn't detect it."

"I did."

"Except ever since your little excursion in the Pacific Northwest the government I sometimes work for has been trying to weaponize it. Soon as I saw what was coming in through the food I knew it was you."

I'd thought all the samples of the bacteria had died off before anyone had a chance to do much of anything with it. Then I remembered the huge vats of *kykeon* the cult left on the beach and realized the US government had all the samples it could ever need. It was a thought I probably should have had sooner.

This is what I get for coming up with a plan that doesn't involve killing everybody in sight.

"Anyway," Smith said, "glad you came. Come on, I'll take you to Clara. Say goodbye to your friends."

I turned to Mirella, already being pulled away to where the satyrs were being grouped together and disarmed. Nobody had bothered to take any of her blades away— they had just zip-tied her. And I knew she could get out of them with a wrist flick. I was pretty sure the reason they weren't worrying about that was that she wouldn't be given the opportunity. She knew it, too.

My eyes drifted up to the rooftops. There were snipers up there, too, one per roof. This was about as wrong as the plan could have gone, clearly.

There was someone else up there with them. He was on the rooftop directly behind Smith, on the corner several yards from the crouching sniper. It would have been easy for anybody to see him since he was standing up straight, but all eyes were on us so I was the only one who did. Probably, that was intentional.

He was a very old goblin, with wispy white hair balding on the top but long at the back and in a ponytail. He looked fit, and had a long sword in his hand. He was dressed in brown calf's leather that looked like it fit tighter than it did the last time I saw him. But overall, given the time and the place, Hsu looked pretty good.

I glanced away quickly, before anyone else noticed him. Provided anyone else could see him, of course. The possibility that I was hallucinating was real, and that was a much better explanation than that the man I saw die a thousand years ago was standing on a rooftop above me.

"Save my people first!" I shouted. I did it while staring at Smith, and I said it in an early pre-German dialect. One of the great things about this particular tongue, aside from the high likelihood that only Hsu would understand it, was that every word sounded unpleasant when shouted. This is still true of German, actually. I once got into a fight after calling a guy a pen.

"Cursing me out in dead languages won't help," Smith said.

"I know, but it makes me feel better," I said.

"Good for you. Come on, let's go."

I snuck another look at the rooftop.

Hsu was gone. If he was ever there.

CHAPTER 23

Smith walked me to the mystery building, alone, possibly thinking I was no threat with my hands bound. This was untrue, but I wasn't going to fight someone with only my legs and head if I didn't have to, and he was taking me to where I wanted to go anyway.

We went in through the unguarded front entrance, opened with Smith's keycard and not mine. I kind of wanted to know if all the money I spent on the skeleton key had been worth it but stopped short of volunteering to get the door for us.

Past the door, up a flight of stairs, and down a nondescript hallway and we were in a large office with a number of notable details: One wall had about ten flat screen televisions showing video surveillance footage of parts of the compound, and one chair had Clara in it.

Clara didn't look too bad. She was dressed like a hospital intern, she had on no makeup, her hair was a mess, and the bags under her eyes betrayed a lack of sleep, but it was apparent nobody had been actively torturing her. So that was good. She looked up and gave me a little smile.

"When are you going to stop walking into traps trying to

rescue me, Adam?" she asked.

"Can't help myself. And this time it looked like you actually needed a rescue."

"It was still a trap."

"I'm getting that."

Smith sat me down in a chair next to her. My hands were still behind my back, so this was super uncomfortable. Clara was not bound, but I had a feeling that was less of a concern in her case. I didn't see Paul anywhere but I was sure the idea of him was keeping her in check.

"Turns out I'm the father," I said to her.

"Yeah, sorry. I didn't want you to know, but if you were to find out I think I could have come up with a better way to tell you. That was probably unpleasant."

"Any idea how it's possible?"

"I dunno. You're the one who thinks you're infertile."

Smith sat down at the desk we were both facing.

"It's because you're both immortal," he said. "Oh, sorry to interrupt, I just thought we'd skip ahead if that's okay. We have a lot of ground to cover."

"How about you tell me why I'm not dead?" I asked. "You said yourself you don't need me if you have her and Paul."

"Right, that's a good starting point. We do need you. The kid's yours, but he doesn't have what we need."

"He caught the flu," Clara said.

"He was sick?"

"A couple of times when he was younger, and they gave him the flu here because they didn't believe me. He's better now."

"It doesn't look like he's immortal," Smith said, "and he doesn't have your immunity, so we're going to need you after all. But like I was saying, you needed another immortal in order to make a kid, which is why you haven't made one in so long. Your offspring end up with a better-than-average immunity, but as far as we can tell a normal lifespan."

"I haven't made one in so long? I've never made one." To Clara I said, "Can I come to birthday parties and stuff? This is all new to me."

Smith sighed. He was fiddling with the television monitor feeds, tapping through images of the compound, the majority of which had nothing going on in them.

"C'mon, where are they?" he said to himself, confirming that he was looking for something particular and not displaying a nervous tic of some kind.

"Who are you looking for?"

"Your friends. Ah, there they are."

The satyrs and Mirella showed up in the center of one monitor. It looked like they had been led to the basketball court, which was a few yards from the indoor gym. Overall the compound was actually not a bad place, with decent food and recreational facilities, and the Isle of Mull was really pleasant, weather-wise, a lot of the time. These were the things I thought of as my friends were put into a rather obvious shooting gallery line.

"Now then," Smith began, "to answer your unasked question, I *know* you've made children before. Biologically, it's actually possible to trace the X-chromosome in all human males back to a single parent, and it turns out the owner of that ur-chromosome is you. We found this out when studying little Paul's genetic markers, which are telling the scientists that he should be about fifty-nine thousand years old. It turns out that a really, really, tremendously long time ago you and some immortal hottie made kids, and those kids had a better immune system than the local stock, which gave them a slight advantage, and boom. So congratulations. You're not only a father, you're *the* father. *Mazel tov.*"

"That's impossible," I said, because I couldn't think of what else to say.

It wasn't impossible, it was just really hard to believe. I didn't remember having children, but I didn't remember much from the first few thousand years other than lots of blood and violence, so it was fair to think I could have had kids, and even could have had mates with long lifespans. No, it was *all* possible. Maybe I just wished I had gotten the information from a source I didn't hate.

"Plenty of time for a dialogue on this later, Adam. I want to get to the important part here." He tapped a button and one of the screens went from an outdoor shot to an indoor shot of a child's playroom.

Sitting at a little plastic table and working on what looked like a coloring book was my son. He looked like he was very intensely concerned about coloring inside the lines.

"Here's Paul. As I explained to his mother already, the room he's in can be flooded with cyanide gas any time I feel like it with the push of a button. This is your incentive to play nice while you're here."

"How nice?"

"I am never going to be so stupid as to allow you free run of the place, but maybe in a year or two you can have a day without your hands behind your back. That's probably the best I can offer right now. But the kid gets to live."

"Doesn't sound like a great bargain."

"Yeah, well, I'm not Bob Grindel either. And I think we both know without a pixie flying around to pick locks for you, there isn't going to be much you can do about it."

Clara looked like she had been slapped. "What happened to Iza?"

"She'd dead," I said. "I'm sorry."

She turned to Smith. "You did this?"

"Yeah, flamethrower. It really had to be done."

For a second or two it looked like leaving Clara's hands untied was a miscalculation. Had she leapt across the desk at that moment I wouldn't have bet against her.

"I'm going to kill you for that," she said.

"I'm sure, honey," Smith said. "Your boyfriend already *made* that threat, but okay. Can we continue? Super." He turned back to me. "So Adam, there's your incentive to play nice. And for proof that none of this is a bluff, please take a look at the screen with all of your friends on it. In a second I'm going to give the order and all of them will be shot where they're standing."

"Why?" I asked. "You have me, what's the point?"

"There's your hot little goblin girl, for one. I don't think letting her go is even a little bit safe. And I don't know about you but I don't want to deal with an angry satyr ever. By the way, a squad of satyrs armed with semiautomatic guns is a fantastic idea. I'm gonna steal it. Just not with any of these guys."

"You know you don't have to kill them."

"You're right, I don't. But I want to, so I'm going to. This is the thing you're not getting, Adam. I'm trying to point out to you that you're not in charge and you aren't going to get to be in charge, ever. You're done, you lost, and you're going to spend however much of the life you have left in this place, until we're sure we've learned everything we need to learn about you. Then we're going to kill you and we're going to kill her. If you're both super cooperative, we won't kill Paul. This is not a negotiation, it is a display of power."

Something was happening on the screen. In the foreground, one of the soldiers with a gun had gone from facing Mirella and the satyrs to facing the camera. He wasn't looking *at* the camera, which was above him and to one side but at something that was out of view of the lens, in the foreground somewhere. It was clear from his expression he didn't like what he was seeing.

"I don't think you're quite as in charge as you think you are, Mr. Smith," I said.

Smith looked at the screen.

"Don't know what you mean," he said, but then it was sort of obvious because the soldier wasn't just looking off- camera he was shouting at what he was seeing. "Huh."

Smith used one of the free screens to try and get an angle on who or what the guy was barking at, but before he could, the man started firing his gun.

"Jesus Christ, what?" Smith said as he fumbled for his microphone. He opened the channel and immediately the room was filled with the sounds of screaming and rapid gunfire. Obviously the soldier we saw using his gun wasn't the only one.

On the video screen the satyrs had fallen to their knees and crouched over to stay out of any stray gunfire. Mirella wasn't crouching, and her hands were no longer bound. Assuming nobody got in her way she could probably reach me in a couple of minutes.

"What's going on out there?" Smith shouted into his radio.

We heard no coherent response to the question, only more shouting. It sounded like a war movie audio reel.

The smaller screens had all come to life under Smith's direction, flipping rapidly from a number of benign indoor shots to rampant chaos and more than a little blood. If Smith had kept the entire military force on the base for our arrival it would have been about a hundred people, and from the look of it someone was killing every one of them.

On the main feed at the basketball court, a striking, tall, pale white figure appeared on camera.

Clara gasped. "What the hell is that?" she asked, more or less to herself.

As tall as the satyrs but thin and muscular, the faery was just as alarming as he had been a day earlier. In his hand was a silvery curved axe that was dripping blood.

Turning to his left and away from the camera, his movements became a blur when he spun his weapon around the empty air. It seemed like he was attacking nothing, except every second or two a flash came off the axe. He was deflecting bullets.

Smith looked nearly as pale as the faery. "What the fuck is that thing, Adam?" he asked. "What did you invite into my camp?"

"That's a faery," I said. "And I didn't invite him."

"You're serious?"

"Yep. Pretty scary, huh?"

"Yeah, he's fucking terrifying. Now tell him to stop killing my men or I'm going to gas the kid."

"I can't do that."

"Adam!" Clara gasped.

"No, I mean I can't because I don't know how. I'm not in charge of them. I don't even know how to speak their language. They're here on their own."

"They?"

"I'm sure there's more than one, listen to the audio."

"Dammit, Adam, I am serious. Paul dies if you don't—"

"I'm telling you, *I can't.*"

On the main screen the faery had moved off-camera, but the other cameras were still picking up plenty of evidence of a great battle that didn't appear to be going in a positive direction for the humans. Mirella, meanwhile, was back on camera and cutting the zip ties off all the satyrs. She appeared to be giving them orders.

"You people need to learn to recognize a bluff, and I am not bluffing here," Smith said.

He must have seen something in Clara because he pulled a gun from his pocket and put it on the desk. "Don't even think about it, sweetie. I was doing you a courtesy by leaving your hands free. You wouldn't stand a chance. Now tell him to stop the attack or I'll gas Paul, and if you come at me I'll blow your knees off before you make it over the desk. Clear?"

"She's clear, but you're talking to the wrong person," I said.

"I already tried talking to you. I figured maybe a mother's love would get through."

I laughed. "It might, I don't really know. The faeries aren't under my orders, though. And I didn't mean me. I meant her."

I nodded at the screens without elaboration, because none was needed.

The red hair is always the first thing anyone notices, even among a bank of monitors showing rampant bloodshed. The owner of the red hair— sometimes we call her Eve—was standing in the room with Paul and talking to him quietly. He looked like he was happy to see her. I wondered if it was the first time they had met.

Smith basically forgot everything else that was happening in his world at that moment and fumbled for a cell phone, and then a speed dial option.

"She's here, initiate the protocol. Initiate the protocol!"

Whoever was supposed to answer this call wasn't answering, though, even after he progressed to shouting. It didn't much matter because regardless of what the protocol was, Eve was already gone, and Paul with her. About the only consolation was now Smith had new video footage of her vanishing act to look at.

"*Dammit,*" he said, smashing his phone against the wall.

At that moment the door to his office was kicked in. Mirella burst through, her sword out and looking like it had seen some action in the past few minutes. Smith lunged forward for the gun on his desk ... and came up empty.

It was in Clara's hands.

Smith stepped back against the wall, as far away from both women as he could manage to get, and turned to the biggest immediate threat.

"Think about this, Clara," he said as calmly as he could.

It's possible he had more than that to say. Maybe something vaguely persuasive about how useful he would be alive, or something about how killing a man changes you, and maybe a line or two about little Paul growing up with a killer for a mother. I'm sure it was going to sound logical. But Clara didn't give him the time.

She fired, and it was a good shot, right in the center of the forehead. Mr. Smith stopped talking, and all the parts of him that didn't end up on the wall fell to the floor under the desk.

"Fuck you," Clara said under her breath.

~

 Mirella cut me free of the cuffs, and a few minutes later we were all heading for the exit, with her in the lead and Clara trailing behind, still holding Smith's gun. I felt like I should be talking to her about what she had just done, but I wasn't sure this was a good time, with Paul still missing and her still being armed.

"What's it like outside?" I asked Mirella as we ran.

"It's very violent," she said. "But those things don't appear to want to hurt any of us, so mostly the violence is directed elsewhere. They're faeries, aren't they?"

"They are. Do you still think you can take one?"

She hit the exit door ahead of me. "No. But it would be fun to try."

The carnage was just about over. There were parts of bodies all over the place, and a lot of blood, and I could hear someone crying for help somewhere, and something crunchy happening somewhere else. There was no gunfire.

There's something especially unpleasant about standing in the midst of a fresh battle, especially when that battle primarily involves swords and axes.

A war zone in a conflict settled with guns has a fresh gunpowder smell that overpowers a lot of the other odors, but while there was certainly a lot of that in the air, what was overwhelming was not that smell. It was odor of blood and the taste of iron.

There was also the sickening warmth. Bodies that had been holding a temperature warmer than the air had been opened up, and now they were letting out steam and heating up the open compound.

It was horrible and exhausting—exhausting because of how

tired I was of standing in the blood of other people. Pragmatically, I understood that this was a consequence of living this long, but emotionally every time I found myself alive at the end of one of these things I asked myself why any of it had to happen.

It was thoughts like these that caused me to abandon mankind and go off on my own in the wilderness somewhere for a century or two, but I couldn't do that anymore because there was no wilderness left.

Hsu was standing a few yards distant, talking to one of his faery men, when he spotted me and came running. Mirella dropped into a defensive stance.

"Relax, he's a friend," I said to her. To my left Clara had raised the gun, so I put my hand on the barrel and lowered it. "Everybody calm down, we're okay."

"My God," Mirella said. "It's Hsu, isn't it? Your dead partner."

"He got better."

"But how?"

"You get used to this sort of thing around Adam," Clara said.

"*The battle is won!*" Hsu shouted, sticking to the same dialect I'd used before. He put away his sword and then we embraced for several seconds while the women stood around looking awkward.

"*My friend, how are you still alive?*" I asked.

"*I have lived in their world. Time is different. The further you travel from this land and into theirs the greater the difference. I am an old man now, but not near as old as I should be by your reckoning.*"

"*I saw you fall to a Talus blade.*"

"*That you did. But, though near death, I did not pass. I was saved by my love. He and three of his brothers are who saved you and yours on this day.*"

I had no particular urge to ask him for an introduction, as my last close-up encounter with the faery folk was plenty terrifying enough. I was also alarmed to learn that only four faeries had just wiped out a hundred armed men all by themselves. I didn't think I really wanted anything to do with them if I could help it.

Not that I wasn't grateful.

"How did you know to come for me?" I asked. *"Was it because of the astrolabe?"*

"You used the star map and you spoke the word. This was enough. And well you did. They have another name for you, and it is not a name of someone they like. When you crossed into their world it set off different alarms, for different reasons. You know the name Bres."

I did. It was the name being shouted at me when I had stepped into the faery world. I couldn't place it then, but with Hsu standing before me I was able to connect it to where I had heard it before. I'd heard it from him. *"I am Bres to them?"*

"You did not know? I assumed you were being coy."

"Adam."

I turned. Clara had been standing by impatiently, waiting for me to get through this conversation.

"Does he know where she took him?" she asked.

"No but I'm sure now that the danger is over—"

"Ask him."

"The red-haired one is with you, I am sure," I said. *"Do you know where she took the child?"*

He looked confused. *"I don't understand."*

Clara understood not a word of what we were speaking, but she could read body language just fine.

"Oh, Jesus," she said.

"You know this woman," I said. *"She stepped out of the faery land, just as you did. She is pale of skin and with bright red hair. Earlier she appeared and took a young boy out of danger. We need to find her to get the boy back."*

Hsu looked afraid. No, more like awed.

"I have never *seen her, but I know of whom you speak. They have a great number of names for her, and many claimed to have met her but she is not with us. She is more legend than truth. Much like you."*

"Can you not simply return to your faery land and find her? She disappeared from a locked room with the child. She had to have gone through that world to do it. She must be there now if she is not here."

"It is not so easy to do, nor to explain to one who has never walked the shadow realm. Time there is a physical space. It would be as if searching an ocean without knowing the proper depth of what you seek. If she does not wish us to find her then I have no more chance of doing so than you."

"Goddammit, Adam, what is he saying?" Clara asked.

"Eve didn't come here with him," I said.

"But she ... why would she take Paul?"

"She saved him," I pointed out. "That was good, right?"

"Not if she doesn't bring him *back*, no."

"Excuse me, are we talking about the woman with the red hair?" Mirella asked.

"Yes," I said. "From the video."

"She has Paul."

"Yes."

"I'm not asking, I'm telling you," Mirella said. "She's standing over there."

We all turned around, and there she was.

She was dressed in a long flowing gown of a style I associated with Greece, although I'm sure it had a modern equivalent. She was barefoot. Her bright blue eyes almost glowed with a wildness I took for passion most times, but which could easily be taken for rage.

She had Paul in her arms. He was unconscious, which I hoped meant only that he was sleeping.

Clara saw her son and started forward. "Paul!" she shouted.

"Stop where you are, Clara," Eve said levelly. She put her hand on the back of Paul's neck.

"Hello, Urr," Eve said to me, using the oldest name I had. "I see you have a son. I'm going to break his neck in front of you."

CHAPTER 24

"*W*hat did she say?" Clara screamed.

Mirella had already disarmed Clara, which was good thinking, but now she was having quite a time holding her back without also hurting her.

Hsu had turned as pale as I'd ever seen him. He fell to one knee. The faeries that had just recently finished chopping down everyone that wasn't a satyr or goblin materialized behind him and also took a knee before her.

"*She is a god to their kind,*" Hsu whispered out of the side of his mouth.

"*I don't suppose I'm a god, too? That would be helpful.*"

"*You are, but not the good kind of god.*"

Eve hadn't moved an inch since making the threat. She looked at me with those amazing eyes and dared me to make the next move.

"All right," I said. "Everyone, let's calm down and ... have a seat. Let's sit down. And talk. Would that be okay?"

Eve nodded.

Slowly, I lowered myself to the ground and sat cross-legged in the dirt. The ground was a little muddy, and it would have been nice to imagine that was due to rain but I was pretty sure it was more because somebody had been killed on the spot I was sitting.

Eve matched my actions by lowering herself to the ground as well. She still held Paul firmly.

"He's only sleeping, right?" I asked.

"Yes, just sleeping," she said. "I haven't harmed him yet." Clara let out an unpleasant noise.

"Can we have some privacy?" I asked everyone behind me.

"Adam?" Clara shouted.

"Mirella, please get her out of here. It'll be okay."

Mirella looked at me and at Eve, and then back at me again. "You're sure?"

"I'm sure."

She nodded, and whistled to Lorgus.

The satyrs were some distance off, having kept mostly together and not taken up a weapon, which was probably a good idea since there was really no way to know for certain how the faeries distinguished between the ones they should kill and the ones they shouldn't. *Anything holding a gun* seemed like a good bet. And since the faeries were now standing next to me, the satyrs didn't look interested in coming any closer. But when it became clear that Mirella had to get Clara away, and that Mirella had no clean way of doing that without also damaging Clara, Lorgus ran over and helped by throwing the screaming mother over his shoulder and running with her as if fleeing from a fire.

I was kind of glad Paul wasn't awake.

"*Hsu, leave us,*" I said. "*She and I have much to discuss. Tell your faeries the gods have to convene in private. Maybe they'll buy that.*"

He smiled. "*A soldier needs no explanation to follow an order.*"

Standing, he gave a silent hand signal, and they all melted away, which was a really creepy thing to witness, I'll be honest.

"Now we're alone," I said to Eve.

"Yes, now we are," she agreed.

"Would you like to tell me why you're going to snap the neck of a seven-year-old?"

She smiled, and eased her hold on Paul, lowering him until he was cradled in her lap. It was a maternal gesture that made me think we were okay for at least a little while. I still took the threat seriously, though, because when it came down to it I knew next to nothing about the woman in front of me, even after ten thousand years.

We sat in silence for a long while. I was waiting for her to begin and it seemed as if she couldn't quite figure out the best way to do that.

"For the longest time," she said finally, "this was about you remembering. That was what I kept waiting to happen. One day you would look into my eyes from afar and I would see something different from all the other times. Not hope, or excitement, or lust or any of the other emotions you displayed when you saw my face. I wanted to see your expression after you remembered what had happened. But after we spoke last I realized that I was never going to be having that moment, because you were never going to remember."

"You wanted to see shame," I said.

"*Nearly* that, yes."

I'm ashamed of a lot of the things I've done in my very long life. I get that everyone has done things they feel bad about in hindsight, but I'm not talking about the time I pulled a girl's hair and made her cry in second grade, I'm talking about murder and pillage and rape. It had been a tumultuous sixty thousand years, let's say. And the fact that I was still alive meant only I was very good at these things.

I have mostly sworn off that degree of violence—there's not much room for it in the modern world, and I really don't have the stomach anymore. But I know how to do bad things, and I know what to say to get other people to do bad things. I may not look like much, but I'm Darwin's fittest.

I'd known for a little while that Eve had a problem with some act I performed in the distant past, but she never gave me much of a hint and there's just too much history to go through. After a few years of thinking on the problem I decided there was no way I would ever recall the exact event she was holding against me. Then I drank a lot and passed out, which is how I seal most of my major decisions.

"It's been a pretty weird couple of days already," I said. "I learned there was such a thing as a faery kingdom yesterday, and then an actual faery tried to kill me. Today, four of them, along with a friend who should have been dead for the past thousand years, came to my rescue. An hour or so ago I learned that while Paul is my son, he is *not* my first child, and that I was just about as wrong about not being a father as it is possible to be. And now you're here, after a ten-thousand-year chase, to punish me for a crime I don't recall committing. Kafka appears to be scripting my life right now. So why don't you tell me what I did to you and I can add it to the long list of things I feel bad about, maybe without any kids dying today?"

"You should watch your tone, Urr. I still have your son."

"I don't doubt your sincerity. I'm just tired. Once again I'm sitting in the blood and viscera of a stranger who died because I'm still a part of this world, and I don't want to do this anymore. It's been too many years. So if you want to let him go and take my life instead, go ahead."

Eve took all of that in, nodding slowly.

"It has indeed been too many years," she said. "But if your life was what I wanted, I could have had it a long time ago. Death is peace, and I don't want you to experience that."

She brushed the hair off Paul's face and thought for a while about what she wanted to say next, while I wondered exactly how many times she had resisted the urge to murder me in my sleep.

"There used to be more of us," she said finally. "More like you, more like me."

"Immortals."

"Ordinary people with long lifespans. People who didn't know what aging was. Not many of us, but some. We lived together for many, many years."

"I don't remember this."

"No, you weren't a part of it. This was before you came to be. We had our own little tribe. For how long, I don't know. Our children, though ... our children knew old age, and disease. The first any of us experienced death was with a child's death—from a sickness, or from an accident, or just growing old and infirm. And we didn't understand. Aging was a curse visited upon our families, not a normal thing at all. In some ways I still think this is true. And we begged ... we begged to our gods for an explanation. They didn't answer, or they were not there."

"How many were you?"

"I don't know. Not many. Enough to produce one or two children a year. Enough to make their suffering—and aging was suffering—unbearable to us. And when it was clear the curse would not be lifted by our silent gods, we settled on exile instead. If a child came of age without falling to sickness or predation we held a celebration for them, something like a funeral but where the deceased was invited to participate in the mourning of their own demise. And then we would banish them into the world, to go and start a tribe of their own, or join a tribe that already was.

"We knew of many other tribes around us, of course. Mankind was still rare and unusual and competing for the future with other things that eventually lost that competition. And because of this competition we also knew violence. But mostly we were left alone, because while we prayed to our gods for an understanding of sickness and aging and death, the other tribes prayed to us. And we were better gods, for when asked, we answered.

"Our children spread out across the land, teaching what we knew to the people they came to lead. We knew much by then, for we had been living off of the land for so very long. We knew hunting, and planting, and the order of the seasons. We knew the stars. We had words but no written language because we never died, so we had no need to preserve our wisdom for others to recover.

"We knew peace. The savage tribes of mankind seemingly knew only war and bloodshed and covetousness and lust, but we and our children's tribes knew brotherhood and culture and *polis*, and how to mollify the savages without violence."

She took a breath and then met my eyes again with a look that was unmistakably hateful. "And then you came along."

"Was I one of you?" I asked.

"Did you come from us, you mean? Were you one of our children? No. And at first we thought that you were only one more savage, another tribal Caesar destined to consolidate your forces and have it fall apart when those forces became too large and disparate for you to control. Or for age, infirmity, or disease to strike you down, as it had for all the others that came before. But none of those things happened, because even though you did not come from our stock you *were* like us. And like us you had some around who were also long-lived. You also whelped children. Those children were no more immortal than were ours, but the lessons you imparted to them were very different. You learned your ways of living from the savages, and you treated peace like a weakness.

"We were unprepared for the likes of you. Never before had we seen such a combination of animal ferocity and human intelligence. You could not be reasoned with, for you did not speak in our words and you seemed only interested in death and spreading your seed. You could not be outsmarted, for you had tactics and weapons we had never imagined. And you would not die.

"Your kind swept across our lands. It may have been ten years, or a hundred, or five hundred, but eventually your children came to fill the niches we had held as ours for a thousand years or more.

"Then came the great battle."

She stopped for a time, still playing with Paul's hair gently, not looking much like someone about to harm him. It was like I wasn't even there anymore.

I was trying to remember the battle she was talking about, but it was too long ago. I recalled war on many scales, but not in a real coherent sense. It was all mostly just a lot of brutality and blood and things nobody really ever wants to see. I didn't remember being in charge of a vast army at any time, but vastness has a different meaning depending on the period. Fifty people could be an army under the right circumstances.

Mostly, I was having trouble with the idea that I once shared the Earth with people who were like me and also didn't age. That seemed like something I shouldn't have forgotten.

"I have told the story of the great battle many, many times before," she said. "What did the faery call you? When you appeared before him yesterday in the shadow realm, did he have a name for you?"

"He called me Bres," I said.

She smiled. "That is one of your names. To his folk you are Bres of the children of Domnu, and I am Brigid, mother-god of the children of Danu. You and your kin were the offspring of darkness and evil, and mine of light and goodness. You slew Nuada in a great battle before your army fell to their greatest god-warrior, Lugh. Bres returned to lead the children of Mil and drive the children of Danu from the earthly plane to where they now reside. So you see, you are a part of their creation story. And in that same sense you are also Seth, and Loki, and Yala. You are the Jester, the wild card. You are also Cain."

"The man who invented murder," I said.

"It's an exaggeration, I know, but all mythology is. Dionysos would know this better than any man. The truth is there *was* a battle, and it may not have been a great one but it was a final one, for when it was over all of my people were slain, including the real man who is named by the faeries Nuada. He was my love and my mate, and he had been that to me for a millennium. You, a half man with a grunt for a name, sliced his belly open before my eyes. And it was these eyes that spared my life, for you liked the look of them. It did not appear to matter to you that they were filled with hatred."

There was a lengthy silence, a moment of respect for the vast thing that was not being said. But the truth was in that time and place I would not have just kept her around because I liked her eyes. I may not remember what I did to her, but I knew what happened to women after wars.

"I would likely have died then as well," she said, "but one of the folk from the realm of the faery took kindly to me, and spirited me away. It was he who taught me how to walk the shadow realm alone. I thought it was the world of the dead for a long time, and spent many years looking for my love there. And when I wasn't doing that I was watching you.

"It was a while before I realized time passed differently in their world than it does in ours. By the time I understood this and decided to return to this world, many thousands of Earth years had passed. I had taken on the pallor of my faery friends— as would you if you lived there for long enough—and my hair had become red. I used to claim it was red from the blood of my tribe, but I think I just willed it, in the same way we alter our skin. By the time you laid eyes upon me once more after many thousands of years had gone—for you—I am sure I was unrecognizable."

"What are they?" I asked. "The faery folk."

"They are a people, like us, but from a different kind of world. Despite their own mythology, I do not believe they ever lived on

Earth. But they can visit, and they can watch. It's an easy thing, watching. If you travel to the edge of this world you can see without being seen, and you are nearly in time with all that is here. When you traversed the veil yesterday you encountered it. Travel deeper and this world fades and theirs comes into focus. It is a good place, but in many ways they covet the richness of this realm more than their own. The things they eat, the places they build, are all taken from here or copied from here. In some ways their creation myth, and the notion that they were banished, is all that keeps them out. That, and their fear of you."

"They're afraid of *me*? They're terrifying."

"That they are. But their legends also call for a time when Bres will raise another army and cross the veil into their world and drive them away once more. Your encounter yesterday was with a scout who was there specifically to protect their world from you. They would do the same regardless of who crossed over on the assumption that he who did so alone was the legendary Bres. That it happened to actually *be* you who made that journey is enough to make one rethink the inaccuracy of predictive mythology.

"But then you spoke the word, and the word was relayed to he whom the word belonged to, and then to your friend, and he knew of only one man who could have known the word. This is how you were rescued by a people who believe you are their destroyer-god."

"What do they think of you?"

"They are afraid of me as well. I did not stay longer with the one who rescued me than it took for me to learn how to travel unassisted, so we have little association. To them I am another sort of god, in the same way I am also Artemis, and Eve, and Danu, and Ganga, and Isis. And sometimes I am Kali, and Hel. You are not the only death-bringer here.

"I do not live with the faery folk. I do not live anywhere. The place I belonged ceased to exist some sixty thousand years ago.

You and your kin killed it and replaced it with this world, and I do not like this world half as much as you do."

"I'm not really all that fond of it myself."

"So you often say. But you've lived every second of your life here in this sluggish plane, and you keep going even when you've seemingly run out of a reason to. This is your place, and I'm envious of you for having it, as much as I'm angry for the loss of what could have been if you had not come along.

"And I suppose I could have simply ended it all. It was a consideration, many times. When we last spoke it was after I had allowed myself to be a captive, and I had done so partly because I no longer cared if I lived. I only lacked the courage to die by my own hand. When you risked your life to save me it's true I was in no real danger, but that doesn't mean I would not have died without your intervention.

"There were other times when I felt the only appropriate way for me to die was *at* your hands, but I couldn't bring myself to allow that either. So I am stuck. The only thing I know for sure is that I needed you to feel the pain you gave me, in some small way, for at least a little while. And once that was finished, maybe you would feel strongly enough about what I had done to end my life for me."

Her remarkable eyes lifted from the sleeping child in her lap and back to me. "But that isn't going to happen, is it? I know that now."

"You mean am I going to kill you? No, of course not."

"What if I gave you no choice?"

"Honestly, I don't know."

I didn't, either. I couldn't see myself hurting her, but if it was between her and Paul, I wasn't really sure what I'd decide. I had no real emotional connection to him, and if fatherhood came with some kind of overriding brood-protection instinct, I either didn't have it or that sort of thing only kicked in for people who had met their children sometime before they were required to protect their lives. On the other hand, an adult was threatening the life of a child, and as a member of the human race—so far as I knew—I did feel like I should be doing whatever I could to save his life.

If I had to, I could probably signal Mirella and she could kill Eve for me. It would be just about the same thing, provided one allows for the idea that Mirella is akin to a weapon I can control. That was sort of true. Eve would take it that way, certainly. The actions of my tribe were the actions of me in her eyes. And since my tribe had supplanted hers, the actions of every man and woman on Earth were *de facto* my fault. That was a crazy way to look at the world, but it was how she saw it, and I guess if I had had the capacity to check out of this reality like she did, for centuries at a time, I might see a more straight line cause and effect.

She was right about a lot of things, though. She would never get the satisfaction of seeing me remember and be ashamed of what I'd done. I, of course, felt awful about what happened to her, and I don't doubt that I was both directly and indirectly responsible for it, but I was having a lot of trouble imagining a world with a dominant humankind that was also run the way she described her own tribe. If I hadn't come along when I did, someone else would have eventually, and they probably wouldn't have needed to be immortal.

That was how history worked. The new always destroyed the old eventually, whether it was Eve's idealist tribe or the Roman Empire. And it wasn't anybody's fault. The old systems just stopped making sense eventually. They were either too large to sustain or relied on things being true that were no longer true.

What happened to her tribe was what I saw happen to Athens, and Constantinople, and Alexandria, and countless other places that used to be brilliant and beautiful. History was by definition one long chaotic, violent mess sometimes interrupted by magnificent eras of peace that reminded everybody life occasionally wasn't awful.

"But you aren't going to kill him," I said. "That isn't who you are."

"No, it's not. It's who *you* are."

"It's who I once was. I've grown a little."

She grinned a tiny bit. "Maybe a little."

She pulled Paul to her breast and stood slowly. I did the same, and remained still while walked him over to me.

"He's starting to wake up," she said, as she gently handed him over.

He was heavy in my arms. It had been a long time since I'd held a child for any reason other than the child had just picked my pocket and I wanted my wallet back. I was inclined to ask how she'd kept him sleeping so soundly through what had to be a scary time, but decided to leave it alone.

"Tell me something else, then, Urr, since you are neither going to kill me nor give me the satisfaction of dying. What is it that has kept you going? For while I am older than you, I have lived many of those years in the accelerated time of the faeries. I don't see what there is here worth staying alive for."

"I think before you can judge the merits of this tribe you need to join it," I said.

Paul was indeed waking up. Very obviously being in Eve's arms had been a factor in his sleeping.

"Get to know some people," I said. "See some art, take a crappy job somewhere, and rent an apartment."

"Drink too much, like you do?"

"Sure, why not? Drinking can be a participatory act if you do it right. Just take part for a little while, and then come find me again and we can talk without threatening children."

It was easily the most inspirational thing I'd ever said while standing in someone else's blood.

Eve looked around the corpse-strewn compound, perhaps

appreciating the irony as much as I was. "When I look at this world, this is all I ever seem to see."

"Look harder, then. Or stop running away from it so much."

She nodded. "Maybe you're right. Goodbye, Urr. I will find you again sometime. Unless, I suppose, you figure out how to find me."

"I might, if I can do it without upsetting the faeries."

She smiled, brushed Paul's hair, and then turned and walked off into nothing.

Paul was wriggling in my arms, so I put him down, making sure he could stand first. I could already hear his mother running for us from what sounded like clear on the other side of the camp.

I took a good look at him, as he rubbed the sleep from his eyes and looked around. He was confused, clearly, and scared, but otherwise was a lot like a tiny version of me, or maybe a version of me after I woke up not knowing where I was. This was something that actually happened to me a lot.

"Hello, Paul," I said.

I knelt down to his eye level because something in my past reminded me kids were less threatened if you did this. Although I may have been thinking of bobcats.

"H'lo," he said. "Who are you?"

"My name's Adam." I extended my hand and we shook. He had a firm grip for a seven-year-old. "I'm a friend of your mommy."

"Okay."

"She's coming right now for you."

"Okay. I made her a picture." He looked around again, and I realized we were still standing among corpses. "I don't know where it is."

"Look at me, Paul," I said, which I thought was important because I was not a dismembered body. "What was it a picture of?"

He looked at me. He had Clara's eyes. "It was a horse. Mommy likes horses. The man said if I drew a good one he'd let me see Mommy, so I need to find my picture. Do you know where it is?"

At that moment I kind of wished I remembered what it was like to be seven, just to know how to stand on a street surrounded by death and worry about a crayon drawing of a horse. "I think it must have been a very good drawing."

"It was. It was my best one."

"Well, the man must have thought so, too, because here comes your mother."

As soon as Clara was reunited with Paul we set about destroying all the video footage we could find in the compound, and then we exited as quickly and calmly as possible. It was a little bit of a challenge given everything we'd seen—the satyrs, being disposed to believe in gods walking the Earth already, were particularly shaken by the faeries—but we had to look like everything was perfectly okay for as long as it took to reach our boat and get off the island.

I don't know who ended up finding the mess we'd left behind. Smith had evacuated all the scientists prior to our arrival, so it was probably one of them. Whoever it was, they didn't keep the information to themselves, because before long the secret CIA black site where "at least twenty" people died was international news. That it was not a CIA-sanctioned site nor was it only twenty-odd people was a detail best taken up with the newspapers, which I wasn't about to do. Although I may have been responsible for a certain exclusive that showed up a few weeks later in the London papers connecting the Scotland massacre with a similar incident a decade earlier in the southwestern United States.

I'm not sure what happened to the consortium of rich people who had invested so much time and money in finding me and farming my biology, if anything happened at all. Francis Justinian pulled all his funds from the investment shortly after the Isle of Mull base became public, and it was probably safe to say he wasn't the only one.

That was actually the last official financial act of Mr. Justinian before he died tragically in a skiing accident in Vail. The accident didn't make much of a splash at all, newswise, because nobody had actually ever heard of Mr. Justinian, despite his being one of the richest men in the world.

Entirely unreported was the recent discovery of one Paul Justinian, a fake name for a real heir.

Per the decedent's last will and testament, the entire estate was liquidated, with half the money going to charity and the other half into a trust in his son's name, to be received once the boy turned twenty-one. Mr. Heintz, while sad about having to bury me, was actually excited by the estate sale and the prospect of getting to advise Paul and his mother in the years to come. It was the sort of thing that excited Mr. Heintz, just in general. He was probably also happy to work with someone whose requests were slightly more sane, and who grasped finance as well as Clara did.

A few months after that, the Harvard University Science Museum received a piece of mail anonymously. To the amazement and confusion of the curator, the package contained a rare astrolabe that had disappeared from the collection several months earlier. "It's a really extraordinary piece," the curator was reported as saying. "The only one of its kind."

*A*fter I got Clara and Paul to safety, she made it clear that she didn't want me to be involved in their lives. I would be upset about this if it was the least bit surprising, but considering knowing me had put them both in a huge amount of danger, it made sense. It was probably better that way. I could never find and destroy the consortium that had come after us, but as long as Clara and I were not together we were probably both safer, since they needed each of us to work out the science. Well, or Eve, but she had a get-out-of-this-reality-free card. Paul, being mortal, would not be of use to anyone.

I don't know what happened to Eve. It was safe to assume she went back to lurking in the faery realm, but there was a chance that she took my advice and decided to become a waitress in Hoboken or something. Anything would have to be better than just watching the world go by.

Hsu couldn't answer regarding her whereabouts. He was still in awe for having seen her, as were his faery friends, but they had no way to locate her even in their own realm.

What he could do was try and convince me to go there with him, and I actually thought about it if only because it was something new and it had been a really long time since I'd had something new. But ultimately I decided to pass. Their world went by too quickly, and I have enough trouble with people growing old and dying before my eyes when time is going by at the usual pace. And one day maybe I'd get to meet my son as an adult, even if it was only for a little while. I didn't want to miss that.

~

*T*he last thing Francis Justinian officially did before he ceased to exist was fire his only employee. Mirella took this pretty well, considering she expected to not survive protecting me. We parted ways at the Seattle airport, which was the nearest international hub to my former residence.

I had a new fake identity in my pocket and a credit card with enough of a credit line to get me a flight just about anywhere in the world and about a week or two of food and drink, after which I was going to be left to my own devices.

This was how I expected things to turn out eventually, not because I'm a poor manager of money—although I am—but because it was the only way to break from my old identity completely. If anyone thought I was still alive and wanted to find me they wouldn't be able to do it by following a money trail.

I was eyeing a flight to India. It was as good a place as any to disappear for a while, I knew the place, and if I thought I could get away with it maybe I'd find some time to get into China and look around, since that was one of the only places on my mental map that was mostly blank.

"Excuse me." I turned around to find Mirella standing there, looking exactly as I'd left her an hour earlier, which is to say looking fantastic. "I'm looking to hire a bodyguard. I wonder if you know someone?"

"A bodyguard? What do you need a bodyguard for?"

"Well." She pirouetted slowly. She had on three-inch-heeled leather boots with jeans and a tight white blouse with a great deal of cleavage showing. Given she was about to get on a flight I was nearly positive she had no knives hidden on her this time, which I found inexplicably arousing. "Don't you think this body needs some guarding?"

"I do, yes. I think it could use a lot of guarding, actually. I'd like to guard it myself."

"Would you? That's good. You look like a capable guard. And as it turns out, I am a very rich woman."

"Is that so?"

"My last employer was unusually generous. I think he was sweet on me."

"I don't blame him."

"Yes, he was very nice. Unfortunately, he died. No fault of mine, of course."

"No, of course not."

She stepped up to me. With the heels on she was nearly eye level, which made it easier to tilt her chin and give her one of my better kisses. Not my absolute best, since we were still in public and we had on clothes, but a pretty good one.

"You know this is a terrible idea," I said. "Someone may find me by connecting you to your former employer."

"They might. But you see, on the one hand we have the millions of dollars sitting in my private bank account, the bungalow and beach I just purchased with a tiny percentage of that money, and the great likelihood that I will find the string bikini in my luggage unnecessary when sunbathing on my private beach. On the other hand, we have the possibility that someone will connect me, a rich heiress, with a bodyguard who let her last client die on a mountain, and this someone will in some way present to us a risk that neither I nor my new body-guard can handle. It seems this is a fair exchange of risks."

"You've thought this through."

"I am very thorough."

"Then I agree with your reasoning."

"I'm glad. I will hire you conditionally, and once we are alone, you can show me your résumé and I'll consider your application at length. I hope you aren't the sort of bodyguard who is uncom-fortable with sleeping with your boss."

"Oh no, that's exactly the kind of bodyguard I am. Now where is this island? Is it a place that gets hurricanes? I'm not very fond of hurricanes."

ABOUT THE AUTHOR

Gene Doucette is a hybrid author, albeit in a somewhat round-about way. From 2010 through 2014, Gene published four full-length novels (*Immortal, Hellenic Immortal, Fixer,* and *Immortal at the Edge of the World*) with a small indie publisher. Then, in 2014, Gene started self-publishing novellas that were set in the same universe as the *Immortal* series, at which point he was a hybrid.

When the novellas proved more lucrative than the novels, Gene tried self-publishing a full novel, *The Spaceship Next Door*, in 2015. This went well. So well, that in 2016, Gene reacquired the rights to the earlier four novels from the publisher, and re-released them, at which point he wasn't a hybrid any longer.

Additional self-published novels followed: *Immortal and the Island of Impossible Things* (2016); *Unfiction* (2017); and *The Frequency of Aliens* (2017).

In 2018, John Joseph Adams Books (an imprint of Houghton Mifflin Harcourt) acquired the rights to *The Spaceship Next Door*. The reprint was published in September of that year, at which point Gene was once again a hybrid author.

Since then, a number of things have happened. Gene published three more novels—*Immortal From Hell* (2018), *Fixer Redux* (2019), and *Immortal: Last Call* (2020)—and wrote a new novel called *The Apocalypse Seven* that he did not self-publish; it was acquired by JJA/HMH in September of 2019. Publication date is May 25, 2021.

Gene lives in Cambridge, MA.

For the latest on Gene Doucette, follow him online

genedoucette.me
genedoucette@me.com

the planet. She just doesn't know it.

The Frequency of Aliens

Annie Collins is back!

Becoming an overnight celebrity at age sixteen should have been a lot more fun. Yes, there were times when it was extremely cool, but when the newness of it all wore off, Annie Collins was left with a permanent security detail and the kind of constant scrutiny that makes the college experience especially awkward.

Not helping matters: she's the only kid in school with her own pet spaceship.

She would love it if things found some kind of normal, but as long as she has control of the most lethal—and only—interstellar vehicle in existence, that isn't going to happen. Worse, things appear to be going in the other direction. Instead of everyone getting used to the idea of the ship, the complaints are getting louder. Public opinion is turning, and the demands that Annie turn over the ship are becoming more frequent. It doesn't help that everyone seems to think Annie is giving them nightmares.

Nightmares aren't the only weird things going on lately. A government telescope in California has been abandoned, and nobody seems to know why.

The man called on to investigate—Edgar Somerville—has become the go-to guy whenever there's something odd going on, which has been pretty common lately. So far, nothing has panned out: no aliens or zombies or anything else that might be deemed legitimately peculiar… but now may be different, and not just because Ed can't find an easy explanation. This isn't the only telescope where people have gone missing, and the clues left behind lead back to Annie.

It all adds up to a new threat that the world may just need saving from, requiring the help of all the Sorrow Falls survivors. The question is: are they saving the world with Annie Collins, or are they saving it from her?

The Frequency of Aliens is the exciting sequel to *The Spaceship Next Door*.

Unfiction

When Oliver Naughton joins the Tenth Avenue Writers Underground, headed by literary wunderkind Wilson Knight, Oliver figures he'll finally get some of the wild imaginings out of his head and onto paper.

But when Wilson takes an intense interest in Oliver's writing and his genre stories of dragons, aliens, and spies, things get weird. Oliver's stories don't just need to be finished: they insist on it.

With the help of Minerva, Wilson's girlfriend, Oliver has to find the connection between reality, fiction, the mythical Cydonian Kingdom, and the non-mythical nightclub called M Pallas. That is, if he can survive the alien invasion, the ghosts, and the fact that he thinks he might be in love with Minerva.

Unfiction is a wild ride through the collision of science fiction, fantasy, thriller, horror and romance. It's what happens when one writer's fiction interferes with everyone's reality.

Fixer

What would you do if you could see into the future?

As a child, he dreamed of being a superhero. Most people never get to realize their childhood dreams, but Corrigan Bain has come close. He is a fixer. His job is to prevent accidents—to see the future and "fix" things before people get hurt. But the ability to see into the future, however limited, isn't always so simple. Sometimes not everyone can be saved.

"Don't let them know you can see them."

Graduate students from a local university are dying, and former lover and FBI agent Maggie Trent is the only person who believes their deaths aren't as accidental as they appear. But the truth can only be found in something from Corrigan Bain's past, and he's not interested in sharing that past, not even with Maggie.

To stop the deaths, Corrigan will have to face up to some old horrors, confront the possibility that he may be going mad, and find a way to stop a killer no one can see.

Corrigan Bain is going insane ... or is he?

Because there's something in the future that doesn't want to be seen. It isn't human. It's got a taste for mayhem. And it is very, very angry.

Fixer Redux

Someone's altering the future, and it isn't Corrigan Bain

Corrigan Bain was retired.

It wasn't something he ever thought he'd be able to do. The problem was that the *job* he wanted to retire from wasn't actually a job at all: nobody paid him to do it, and nobody else did it. With very few exceptions, nobody even knew he was doing it.

Corrigan called himself a fixer, because he fixed accidents that were about to happen. It was complicated and unrewarding, and even though doing it right meant saving someone, he didn't enjoy it. He couldn't stop —he thought—because there would always be accidents, and he would never find someone to take over as fixer. Anyone trying would have to be capable of seeing the future, like he did, and that kind of person was hard to find.

Still, he did it. He's never been happier.

His girlfriend, Maggie Trent of the FBI, has not retired. Her task force just shut down the most dangerous domestic terrorist cell in the country, and she's up for an award, and a big promotion.

Everything's going their way now, and the future looks even brighter.

Unfortunately, that future is about to blow up in their faces…literally. And somehow, Corrigan Bain, fixer, the man who can see the future, is taken completely by surprise.

Fixer Redux is the long-awaited sequel to ***Fixer***. Catch up with Corrigan, as he tries to understand a future that no longer makes sense.

<u>**FANTASY**</u>

The Immortal Novel Series

Immortal

"I don't know how old I am. My earliest memory is something along the lines of fire good, ice bad, so I think I predate written history, but I don't know by how much. I like to brag that I've been there from the beginning, and while this may very well be true, I generally just say it to pick up girls."

Surviving sixty thousand years takes cunning and more than a little luck. But in the twenty-first century, Adam confronts new dangers—someone has found out what he is, a demon is after him, and he has run out of places to hide. Worst of all, he has had entirely too much to drink.

Immortal is a first person confessional penned by a man who is immortal, but not invincible. In an artful blending of sci-fi, adventure, fantasy, and humor, IMMORTAL introduces us to a world with vampires, demons and other "magical" creatures, yet a world without actual magic.

At the center of the book is Adam.

Adam is a sixty thousand year old man. (Approximately.) He doesn't age or get sick, but is otherwise entirely capable of being killed. His survival has hinged on an innate ability to adapt, his wits, and a fairly large dollop of luck. He makes for an excellent guide through history ... when he's sober.

Immortal is a contemporary fantasy for non-fantasy readers and fantasy enthusiasts alike.

Hellenic Immortal

"Very occasionally, I will pop up in the historical record. Most of the time I'm not at all easy to spot, because most of the time I'm just a guy who does a thing and then disappears again into the background behind someone-or-other who's busy doing something much more important. But there are a couple of rare occasions when I get a starring role."

An oracle has predicted the sojourner's end, which is a problem for Adam insofar as he has never encountered an oracular prediction that didn't come true ... and he is the sojourner. To survive, he's going to have to figure out what a beautiful ex-government analyst, an eco-terrorist, a rogue FBI agent, and the world's oldest religious cult all want with him, and fast.

And all he wanted when he came to Vegas was to forget about a girl. And maybe have a drink or two.

The second book in the Immortal series, Hellenic Immortal follows the continuing adventures of Adam, a sixty-thousand-year-old man with a wry sense of humor, a flair for storytelling, and a knack for staying alive. Hellenic Immortal is a clever blend of history, mythology, sci-fi, fantasy, adventure, mystery and romance. A little something, in other words, for every reader.

Immortal at the Edge of the World

"What I was currently doing with my time and money ... didn't really deserve anyone else's attention. If I was feeling romantic about it, I'd call it a quest, but all I was really doing was trying to answer a question I'd been ignoring for a thousand years."

In his very long life, Adam had encountered only one person who appeared to share his longevity: the mysterious red-haired woman. She appeared throughout history, usually from a distance, nearly always vanishing before he could speak to her.

In his last encounter, she actually did vanish—into thin air, right in front of him. The question was how did she do it? To answer, Adam will have to complete a quest he gave up on a thousand years earlier, for an object that may no longer exist.

If he can find it, he might be able to do what the red-haired woman did, and if he can do that, maybe he can find her again and ask her who she is … and why she seems to hate him.

But Adam isn't the only one who wants the red-haired woman. There are other forces at work, and after a warning from one of the few men he trusts, Adam realizes how much danger everyone is in. To save his friends and finish his quest he may be forced to bankrupt himself, call in every favor he can, and ultimately trade the one thing he'd never been able to give up before: his life.

Immortal and the island of Impossible Things

"I thought I'd miss the world."

Adam is on vacation in an island paradise, with nothing to do and plenty of time to do nothing.

It's exactly what he needed: beautiful weather, beautiful girlfriend, plenty of books to read, and alcohol to drink. Most importantly, either nobody on the island knows who he is, or, nobody cares.

"This probably sounds boring, and maybe it is. It's possible I have no compass to help determine boring, or maybe I have a different threshold than most people. From my perspective, though, the vast majority of human history has been boring, by which I mean nothing happened, and sure, that can be dull. On the other hand, nothing happening includes nobody trying to kill anybody, and specifically, nobody trying to kill me. That's the kind of boring a guy can get behind."

Nothing last forever, though, and that includes the opportunity to *do* nothing. One day, unwelcome visitors arrive in secret, with impossible knowledge of impossible events, and then the impossible things arrive: a new species.

It's *all* impossible, especially to the immortal man who thought he'd seen all there was to see in the world. Now, Adam is going to have to figure out what's happening and make things right before he and everyone he loves ends up dead in the hot sun of this island paradise.

Immortal From Hell

Not all of Adam's stories have happy endings

"Paris is romantic and quests are cool. But the threat of a global pandemic kind of sours the whole thing. The good news was, if all life on Earth were felled by a plague, it looked like this one could take me out too. It'd be pretty lonely otherwise."

--Adam the immortal

When Adam decides to leave the safety of the island, it's for a good reason: Eve, the only other immortal on the planet, appears to be dying, and nobody seems to understand why. But when Adam—with his extremely capable girlfriend Mirella—tries to retrace Eve's steps, he discovers a world that's a whole lot deadlier than he remembered.

Adam is supposed to be dead. He went through a lot of trouble to fake that death, but now that he's back it's clear someone remains unconvinced. That wouldn't be so terrible, except that whoever it is, they have a great deal of influence, and an abiding interest in ensuring that his death sticks this time around.

Adam and Mirella will have to figure out how to travel halfway across the world in secret, with almost no resources or friends. The good news is, Adam solved the travel problem a thousand years earlier. The bad news is, one of his oldest assumptions will turn out to be untrue.

Immortal From Hell is the darkest entry in the Immortal series.

Immortal: Last Call

"I'm something like sixty-thousand years old, and I've probably thought more

about my own death than any living being has thought about any subject, ever. I used to be unduly preoccupied with what might constitute a "good death", although interestingly, this has always been an after-the-fact analysis. What I mean is, following a near-death experience, I'll generally perform a quiet review of the circumstances and judge whether that death would have been objectively good, by whatever metric one uses for that kind of thing. I'm not nearly that self-reflective while in the midst of said near-death experience. Facing death, the predominant thought is always not like this."

A disease threatening the lives of everyone—human and non-human—has been loosed upon the world, by an arch-enemy Adam didn't even know he had.

That's just the first of his problems. Adam's also in jail, facing multiple counts of murder, at least a few of which are accurate. He may never see the inside of a courtroom, because there remains a bounty on his head—put there by the aforementioned arch-enemy—that someone is bound to try to collect while he's stuck behind bars.

Meanwhile, Adam's sitting on some tantalizing evidence that there might be a cure, but to find it, he's going to have to get out of jail, get out of the country, and track down the man responsible. He can't do any of that alone, but he also can't rely on any of his non-human friends for help, not when they're all getting sick.

What he needs is a particularly gifted human, who can do things no other human is capable of. He knows one such person. He calls himself a fixer, and he's Adam's—and possibly the world's—last hope. That's provided he believes any of it.

Immortal: Last Call is the sixth book in the *Immortal Novel Series*, and also the end of a long journey for one immortal man.

∾

Immortal Stories

∾

Eve

"...if your next question is, what could that possibly make me, if I'm not an angel or a god? The answer is the same as what I said before: many have considered me a god, and probably a few have thought of me as an angel. I'm neither, if those positions are defined by any kind of supernormal magical power. True magic of that kind doesn't exist, but I can do things that may appear magic to someone slightly more tethered to their mortality. I'm a woman, and that's all. What may make me different from the next woman is that it's possible I'm the very first one..."

For most of humankind, the woman calling herself Eve has been nothing more than a shock of red hair glimpsed out of the corner of the eye, in a crowd, or from a great distance. She's been worshipped, feared, and hunted, but perhaps never understood. Now, she's trying to reconnect with the world, and finding that more challenging than anticipated.

Can the oldest human on Earth rediscover her own humanity? Or will she decide the world isn't worth it?

The Immortal Chronicles

Immortal at Sea (volume 1)

Adam's adventures on the high seas have taken him from the Mediterranean to the Barbary Coast, and if there's one thing he learned, it's that maybe the sea is trying to tell him to stay on dry land.

Hard-Boiled Immortal (volume 2)

The year was 1942, there was a war on, and Adam was having a lot of trouble avoiding the attention of some important people. The kind of people with guns, and ways to make a fella disappear. He was caught somewhere between the mob and the government, and the only way out involved a red-haired dame he was pretty sure he couldn't trust.

Immortal and the Madman (volume 3)

On a nice quiet trip to the English countryside to cope with the likelihood that he has gone a little insane, Adam meets a man who definitely has. The madman's name is John Corrigan, and he is convinced he's going to die soon.

He could be right. Because there's trouble coming, and unless Adam can get his own head together in time, they may die together.

Yuletide Immortal (volume 4)

When he's in a funk, Adam the immortal man mostly just wants a place to drink and the occasional drinking buddy. When that buddy turns out to be Santa Claus, Adam is forced to face one of the biggest challenges of extremely long life: Christmas cheer. Will Santa break him out of his bad mood? Or will he be responsible for depressing the most positive man on the planet?

Regency Immortal (volume 5)

Adam has accidentally stumbled upon an important period in history: Vienna in 1814. Mostly, he'd just like to continue to enjoy the local pubs, but that becomes impossible when he meets Anna, an intriguing woman with an unreasonable number of secrets and sharp objects.

Anna is hunting down a man who isn't exactly a man, and if Adam doesn't help her, all of Europe will suffer. If Adam *does* help, the cost may be his own life. It's not a fantastic set of options. Also, he's probably fallen in love with her, which just complicates everything.

www.ingramcontent.com/pod-product-compliance
Lightning Source LLC
Chambersburg PA
CBHW070740190726
48292CB00002B/354